THE VIRUS

 A BLACK SPRING **CRIME & THRILLER** BOOK

First published in 2020
by Black Spring Press
Suite 333, 19-21 Crawford Street
Marylebone, London W1H 1PJ
United Kingdom

Cover design and *typeset by* Edwin Smet
Author photograph Jennifer Johnson
Printed in England by TJ International Ltd, Padstow, Cornwall

ISBN 978-1-913606-30-5

This book is a work of fiction. The characters, incidents, and dialogue
are drawn from the author's imagination and are not to be construed
as real. Any resemblance to actual events or persons, living or dead,
is entirely coincidental. This book was previously published by
Heinemann in 1982, under the title *The Marburg Virus*.

2020 Edition proofread by Todd Swift

PREFACE BY THE AUTHOR

For most of the seventies I lived in Brussels where I worked for the European Commission. Though I was a civil servant dealing with European environmental issues, one of those 'faceless bureaucrats', out of office I was a writer of topical thrillers. Having already had four such books published, by the beginning of 1979 I was casting around for a new theme which, I hoped, might be both entertaining and instructive.

It was Frans Froschmaier, one of my German friends, who – over a long liquid lunch – came up with what seemed like a promising idea.

'Why don't you write about what happened in Marburg a few years back?' Frans said. 'That's a good subject for a thriller. There was a mysterious outbreak of a deadly disease in the town. They still don't know what caused it.'

The next weekend I drove from Brussels to Marburg, an ancient university town, situated on the river Lahn, north of Frankfurt.

I nosed around the cobbled streets till I came to the medical school. I talked to both the students and the professors. Quite soon I came up with a theory. Twenty-three persons had been infected by the mystery Marburg virus, and twenty-three persons had died. One hundred per cent mortality! One of the first to be infected was a medical student, a member of the *Schagende Verbindung*, one of the university's famous duelling fraternities. Some of the other fatalities had also been medical students.

That was enough for me to put two and two together. What do medical students need, I asked myself, apart from beer and sex? Research facilities, obviously. And that meant mainly rats and mice but also whatever primates were still permitted to be used for research purposes. One of the professors assured me that a decade or so earlier when the outbreak happened in Marburg, they were still using monkeys caught in the wild in Africa and imported into Germany.

By the time I returned to Brussels, I had sketched out a plot. Student infected by monkey in lab is a member of famous German duelling fraternity. Blood spilled in a duel infects a fellow student. The proximate cause of the infection is contact with a green monkey imported for research purposes from central Africa. When a new outbreak of the deadly Marburg virus occurs in real time, threatening to become a pandemic, these historical insights will prove crucial.

I flew to Atlanta, Georgia to visit the United States' famous Center for Disease Control (CDC). I went to Burundi to find green monkeys that could have been the source of the infection. My book's hero, Dr Lowell Kaplan, a brilliant epidemiologist working for the CDC, has an advantage over those engaged in the current race to find an antidote to the coronavirus. He knows, or thinks he knows, the original source of the infection. If he can track down and capture a live green monkey from the very tribe of monkeys which supplied the Marburg Medical School at the time of the first outbreak, maybe the boffins will be able to develop and manufacture an antidote and rush it out to stem the growing pandemic so that, in the nick of time, humanity can be saved.

Of course, there is a deal of skulduggery involved in the race to find an antidote, or a vaccine, for use against the deadly Marburg virus. In my novel I finger both the CIA and the KGB specifically. In those days biological warfare was a hot topic. Maybe it still is.

When my book appeared in 1982 under the title *The Marburg Virus*, it garnered some good reviews. I remember one in the *Daily Telegraph*, by Stephen Glover. 'There are some novelists' wrote Glover 'who, by instinct or study, understand perfectly the indispensable components of a thriller. Stanley Johnson is one of them. *The Marburg Virus* contains exactly the right ingredients of suspense, violence and sex; all of them against well-chosen, exotic backdrops.'

Will the fight against Covid-19 be as successful as my fictional hero was in fighting the Marburg virus? Is there another Dr Lowell Kaplan out there, some brilliant scientist, able to come up with an antidote or vaccine in the nick of time? We must hope so.

Thinking back to my own book, I can't help feeling that governments around the world, our own included, need to be ruthlessly focussed on the search for an antidote or a vaccine. Without in any way diminishing the importance of precautionary measures of containment or mitigation, mass immunization would surely prove a crucial factor in stopping the spread of Covid-19 or in preventing further outbreaks, e.g. the 'second wave' we are hearing about.

Following the Marburg experience (fictional though it may be), some of that research, it seems to me, should be aimed at tracking down the original pathways of the infection, including possible animal to human pathways. There has been much speculation, for example, that the possible source of Covid-19 could be some wild animal – bats, or pangolins, perhaps – purchased in one of Wuhan's local markets where the trade in wild animals to be used for food or medicine is commonplace.

We need to work with the Chinese authorities to pursue this and other avenues. Perhaps there is a still a chance of finding, as Dr Lowell Kaplan eventually did, some special 'reservoir group' of carriers whose blood cells or genetic material may help find the vaccine or the antidote to Covid-19. Was wildlife implicated? Where could that wildlife have come from? What trading patterns could have been involved? Was there movement of people too, as possible carriers? Questions must be asked. And answers must be found. Finding a vaccine or an antidote is not as easy as picking up a pebble from a beach. There will need to be strong international cooperation, between East and West, North and South.

In the final chapter of my book, the President of the United States, newly immunized as a result of a vaccine developed from the bio-cells of green monkeys discovered by Kaplan in Burundi, visits stricken patients in isolation units to show that the tide has turned in the fight against the disease. Drums roll. Trumpets sound. And of course, the President gets re-elected.

Well, that's what happens in the book. Will the story of Covid-19 have a similar 'happy ending'? We can only hope so.

Stanley Johnson May 7, 2020

CHAPTER ONE

DOCTOR LOWELL KAPLAN, Head of the Bureau of Epidemiology at the National Center for Disease Control in Atlanta, Georgia, was on the telephone to Japan. He sounded worried. He was worried. He pushed back a lock of thick greying hair which had fallen over his forehead and hunched forward as he spoke, the suppressed energy visible in every line of his body.

'Okay,' he shouted into the phone. 'It differs from A-Brazil, but does it have *pandemic* potential? That's the question.'

Clearly dissatisfied with whatever was being said to him from the other side of the world, he slammed down the instrument and turned to his assistant, a fair-haired woman about thirty years old, who throughout the conversation had been seated patiently across the desk.

'They don't know, Susan. They just don't know. Or if they do, they're not saying.'

'We'd better call a conference on this one, Lowell, hadn't we? This is a pretty sensitive area.'

Lowell Kaplan swore out loud. 'Sure,' he said bitterly. 'We can call a conference. That's what we always do. Then, if we make the right decision all the guys who were there on the day remember it and never stop patting themselves on the back because they got it right. And if we make the *wrong* decision, then who do you think carries the can? I do, as Head of Epidemiology. It's *my* neck that's on the line, not theirs.'

Susan Wainwright looked at him fondly. She had been working with Kaplan for over six years, in fact ever since he had been with the Center. She had, over the years, grown to admire the integrity of this man. She had seen how he handled himself during the course of a painful divorce. She had watched, without really meaning to, how he had dealt with his two children just coming into their teens at the time of the break-up of the marriage. He had shown an infinite amount of patience and tenderness. On the busiest days, he was always ready to take a call from Jimmy or Lorna. Even so, she sometimes felt a sneaking sympathy for Martha Kaplan, whom she knew as an occasional visitor to the office. It was true that Lowell Kaplan was a 'workaholic'. Sometimes she had wondered, ruefully, whether Lowell was interested in anything except work – and, of course, his kids. Many other men would not have hesitated to make a pass at her if they had spent as much time in her company as Kaplan had. Susan Wainwright knew that she was not 'Miss World'. Heads didn't turn when she walked into a restaurant. But in her heart she knew she had a great deal to offer.

Involuntarily she sighed. 'I still think we ought to have a conference. Set out the facts. Examine the financial implications. Get some kind of reading on the probabilities.'

Lowell Kaplan sighed. 'Okay. Go ahead and set it up. And this time, I'm going to want a record. Tape it, if you like. That's the safest way. I want there to be a clear statement of each person's position on this issue. That way we can nail 'em if we have to.'

*

Later that day, Lowell Kaplan took the chair at the hastily convened conference. He had deliberately kept the meeting small, with no outside invitees. The Center's long-standing policy was to take as many decisions as they could on an in-house basis. Long experience had taught them that the further up the line you went, the more complicated any particular item became. It was amazing how quickly an issue could become political. Vested interests always seemed to lurk round the nearest corner. In fact, Kaplan often wondered if there were such a thing as a wholly scientific, wholly rational, wholly objective basis for action. He tried to operate as if there were, but he knew only too well that he frequently didn't succeed.

He hung his coat behind his chair, loosened his tie and looked around the room at the half dozen men and women who were gathered there. He had been at the Center for Disease Control in Atlanta for the last six years and he could honestly say that it had been the most fascinating and rewarding period of his life. He had never before felt himself so challenged. That cluster of unpretentious buildings in an Atlanta suburb where he was privileged to work was the strategic command post in the world-wide fight against disease. Military men could count the missiles ranged against them. His job, and that of his team, was to work with unseen enemies whose presence was often unsuspected.

Of course, much of the game, sometimes the most difficult part, lay in anticipation and prevention. Again the military metaphor applied. Deterrence was always the best defence. But sometimes something would slip through the net. The alarm bells would ring. When that happened, reflected Kaplan, he could count on his colleagues to rise to the emergency. They were, he thought, like some highly trained, highly mobile fire-fighting unit. Their job was to get to the scene of the blaze and to extinguish or contain the flames before the conflagration engulfed the world. Up till now they had succeeded. Somehow, thanks to skill and professionalism and a fair measure of good luck, they had managed to stay ahead. But Kaplan occasionally wondered how long the winning streak would last. He was one of the few who knew how close the world sometimes came to disaster. Already, the defences were stretched taut almost to breaking-point. And all the time, thanks to mass-travel and the continued force of urbanization, the dangers became more acute. It wasn't plague which Kaplan feared. They knew how to deal with plague. It wasn't cholera or typhus or any of the known diseases. What he feared was the unknown. Some sickness which would spread like wildfire among the population and against which all known remedies would prove to be of no avail.

Thank God they didn't have that kind of problem this morning. What they were dealing with today was tricky in the extreme but not tragic. Or at least not yet. That was an important distinction.

'Okay,' he began. 'Let me set out the facts, as I see them. The Japanese reckon they have found a new flu virus. They're calling it A-Fukushima. They've had half a dozen cases in Fukushima already and a couple in Osaka.'

There was a map of Asia on the wall at one side of the conference room and Kaplan gestured in its general direction while Susan Wainwright pushed coloured pins into the offending cities.

'I was on the phone to the Japanese health authorities this morning and I think I should tell you they're taking the problem seriously.'

Lowell Kaplan paused. He lowered his spectacles and looked over them. The thick greying hair on his head seemed to bristle with energy. A dark shadow covered the lower part of his face, indicating that here was a man who had shaved early in the morning and who had put in a long day's work already.

'The question is,' he continued: 'Do we have a drift, or do we have a real shift? Dr McKinney, what's your view of this one?'

Kaplan had addressed the question to a tall, good-looking man of around thirty-five who was Head of the Center's Virology Division. Heads now turned in his direction.

James McKinney took his time and when he spoke there was still the trace of a Scottish burr which denoted his lowland ancestry. McKinney had come over from Edinburgh to do post-graduate work at the Center and had decided to stay on. The Center had been only too glad to have him. His painstaking methodical approach was precisely what was needed.

'As far as we know – and we haven't had a chance to look at all the evidence ourselves, since we haven't had a sample set of cultures from our Japanese friends yet – there is a very fair likelihood that we are indeed dealing with an antigenic shift. The Fukushima virus *appears*' – he made the vowel-sound stretch out until it seemed almost as long as the Firth of Forth bridge itself – 'to differ in its surface proteins from the influenza virus at present circulating in the human population.'

He continued for some minutes.

'Thank you, James.' Lowell Kaplan interrupted him at last and brought the conversation round to the essential political point.

'Our present vaccine,' he said, 'is a multi-purpose unit, directed to A-Brazil, A-Texas and B-Hongkong. The first thing we have to decide is: do we simply add A-Fukushima to the existing unit or do we replace, say, A-Brazil with A-Fukushima? If we do decide to do one or other of these things, how soon and how completely can the manufacturers respond? We also have to bear in mind the liability question. Our current vaccine is well-proven and has a high degree of acceptability. If we modify it and embark on a mass campaign aimed at thirty or forty million people, or even a more modest effort aimed at twenty to twenty-five million people, we may run into a side-effects problem. In that case, the program could grind to a halt, and we could find ourselves going into the winter flu season without any protection at all.'

There was a long silence after Kaplan had finished speaking. Most of them remembered the swine flu fiasco of the mid 1970s, when the mass-vaccination campaign personally approved by President Ford got torpedoed by a host of malpractice lawsuits following the appearance of the Guillain-Barré syndrome in a small but measurable number of vaccinees. None of them wanted a repetition of that affair. This time they would move cautiously if they moved at all.

Lowell Kaplan turned to Susan Wainwright.

'What's the word from the manufacturers on this one, Susan? How much time do we have?'

Susan Wainwright ran a hand over her hair, pushing a straying lock back into place. 'If we're going to change the vaccine, the manufacturers are going to have to rebatch. That means they have got to get the eggs together, say, twenty million eggs, and you can't do that overnight. I'd say we have to make up our minds within the next ten days if we are to get cooperation from the manufacturers.'

'What about price?'

Susan Wainwright was hesitant. 'That's not really my province,' she said. 'But I'd say if we request a new vaccine less than six months before the start of the new flu season, the manufacturers will really screw us on price.'

'You're probably right,' said Kaplan. 'So, do we adapt and pay the price, or just go along with our current vaccine? Do we just assume that A-Fukushima is a flash in the pan? Do we run *that* risk?'

Before Lowell Kaplan had a chance to elicit answers to his question, the bleeper in his top pocket started its urgent signalling.

'Dammit!'

He picked up the nearest phone.

The voice at the other end said: 'Dr Kaplan? We have a RED ALERT here. You're needed at once in the Data Center.'

'Gentlemen, ladies, will you excuse me?'

With quick strides, Lowell Kaplan left the room.

An hour later, the problem of next season's influenza campaign – important though that was – had been pushed out of Kaplan's mind. His thoughts were wholly concentrated on the call that had come in from New York. Over the past several years, he had had to deal with numerous epidemiological emergencies; that was the nature of the job. But from the brief conversation he had had with New York he knew that this particular summons was special. Deepdown, he felt supremely confident; equal to any challenge. The famous phrase came back to him: 'Thou art weighed in the balance.' Well, if he was going to be weighed in the balance, he would not be found wanting.

Lowell Kaplan was met at Kennedy Airport by Dr Charles Graham, an old friend. Where Kaplan had ended up at the Center for Disease Control in Atlanta, Graham – who was a New Yorker, anyway – had gone to the Division of Tropical Medicine at Columbia University.

As they rode into the city together, Graham filled in the details. 'I don't know how much they told you,' he began, 'but I'll begin from the beginning and try and give you the whole picture.'

'Go ahead. All I've had so far is a brief talk on the telephone with New York City's Chief Medical Officer. And he sounded worried as hell. Then I left at once for the airport. Delta had to hold the plane, even then.'

As they joined the stream of traffic coming into the city in the early evening, Graham reviewed the history of the case so far.

'What we've got is a young female student – around nineteen years old – who's been spending the summer in Europe. She returned from Brussels a few days ago, came straight to her apartment in the city and went to bed. One morning, six days later, she had a pain in her throat and could barely swallow. She consulted her doctor, who examined her and found several blisters on her neck and yellowish ulcers in the back of her throat and inside each cheek. She had a fever and seemed unusually nervous.

'During the next three days her temperature soared; she

began bleeding under the skin, there was swelling in her neck, she appeared unusually weak and drowsy, her speech grew slurred, her mouth was dry, she had great difficulty in swallowing and her face alternately flushed and turned pale. By then her doctor was extremely alarmed. He called us up and we had her brought in to Columbia-Presbyterian Hospital. That was four days ago. Since then we've had her in an isolation ward.'

The traffic thickened as they crossed the Triborough Bridge and waited impatiently for the line of cars to pass the toll booth.

At last their driver threw his handful of coins at the basket and the light went green for them.

'And how is she now?' asked Kaplan.

'Bad. In fact, I don't think she's going to make it. She's lost twenty pounds in two days and most of her hair. I could weep. She must have been a real looker before this happened.'

'I know. That's the worst part of this job. You're dealing with people, not just patients.'

As they passed through Harlem on their way to the hospital, Kaplan looked out at the crumbling red-brick tenement blocks, the garbage piled high on the street-corners, the tattered store-fronts. If ever there was a place ripe for the spread of disease, this was it. He shivered.

They parked in the hospital forecourt, walked down the long main corridor to the bank of elevators at the end and rode up to the isolation ward. Outside the ward they donned gowns, masks and gloves. They entered the room and stood beside the bed. For a long minute, neither of them spoke.

At last Dr Graham said: 'I don't think there's much else we can do. We've tried to keep her hydrated but she loses it as fast as we put it in. She's quiet now, but before you came she was literally writhing in agony. She was sweating so much you could have driven a steam engine.'

Kaplan looked at the wasted, shrivelled figure on the bed. It was hard to recognize what a beautiful girl she must once have been. Her blonde hair had come out in handfuls, her skin had dried out and cracked, her face was contorted.

'Heart?' Kaplan asked.

'Not good. She's been under terrific strain. Personally, I don't think she's going to last the night.'

'Is she sleeping now, or is she in a coma?'

'I'm not sure. She moves in and out.'

As they spoke the girl stirred on the bed. She tossed her head from side to side and mumbled a few words.

Kaplan tried to make out what she was saying.

'Mon... mon... monkeys,' the girl said, suddenly audible. 'Green monkeys.' She rolled back her head and appeared once more to drop into a trance.

Kaplan looked at Graham with amazement. 'What do you make of that?'

Graham shrugged. 'She babbles quite a lot. Often about animals. I haven't heard her talk about green monkeys before.'

After they had scrubbed up, they went to Dr Graham's room. 'We've run all the tests we can do here,' Graham said. 'And there's nothing we can pin-point as the specific cause of the disease. We don't know what we are dealing with. We think it could be something tropical in origin, but we're not sure.'

'Had she been to Africa before coming back to the States?'

'Not as far as we know. But maybe she was in contact with someone. We are trying to track down her family at the moment to see if we can learn anything about her movements.'

Kaplan stood up and walked over to the window. Far below, the cars were streaming northwards and out of the city. The last rays of the sun glinted on the Hudson River.

He turned back to his colleague.

'We should expect to have other reports, here or around the world, if this is a known disease. We've contacted the World Health Organization – WHO – in Geneva. So far, nothing.'

'What did she say to her doctor?'

'Not much, apparently. She was pretty sick by then.'

'I might go and talk to him. Do you know where he lives?'

'His office is in Washington Square, down in the Village. And we have the keys to her apartment if you wanted to visit that.'

Kaplan was in a sombre mood as he caught a cab downtown. There was something in what he had just seen that had moved him deeply. A head on a pillow; a form on a bed. Pipes and tubes. Masks. Temperature charts. All the paraphernalia of sickness. Yet once there had been an identifiable personality there, a face to be known and loved.

He went to the apartment first. Detective work was part of his job – often a large part – but he always felt awkward moving around among someone else's possessions. The place was larger than he had imagined. Diane Verusio, as he had learned the girl was called, lived in a rather graceful house on Bank Street, a couple of blocks from the river. Her apartment was on the first floor.

The first room he entered was a spacious sitting-room, giving out onto the street. It was prettily decorated and lined with books and pictures. The dominant theme was wildlife of every kind. Over the mantelpiece was a huge photograph of Nrongoro crater at sunset, with a cheetah's head in the foreground poking out above the grass. There was also a photograph of treetops with a group of elephants at the waterhole. Next to it stood a smaller picture of a girl in a safari outfit. A young, attractive face with a wide smile and honest eyes. It was hard for Kaplan to link the face in the photograph with the wasted form he had seen on the bed in Columbia-Presbyterian.

On the table in the middle of the room was a stack of papers and reports. Kaplan glanced through them quickly. One in particular caught his attention. It was entitled: 'PRELIMINARY DRAFT OF REPORT BY THE INTERNATIONAL CAMPAIGN AGAINST VIVISECTION – The Use of Monkeys in Medical Research.'

Monkeys! He remembered the words Diane Verusio had gasped out during his visit to the hospital. There must be a clue here, he thought. He put the report in his pocket. He would find time to read it later.

Still with an uneasy sense of being an intruder in another person's life, Kaplan moved from the sitting-room into the adjoining bedroom. The bed was unmade and clothes were strewn about the room.

His eyes fell on an airplane ticket lying on the floor. He picked it up and examined the remains of a return coupon: Brussels – New York. The outward flight had been May 5th and the return was dated June 6th. That was twelve days ago. He made a note of the flight numbers and dates and put the ticket in his wallet.

He stood there for a moment beside the bed, thinking. In his experience, most exotic tropical diseases had relatively short incubation periods. The girl had entered hospital four days ago. She had, according to Dr Graham, experienced the onset of her illness two days before that when she complained of a sore throat and a headache. With an incubation period of, say, six days, Diane Verusio could have become infected on the very day she travelled. Well, thought Kaplan, that figured. Airports, particularly in the summer months of mass travel, were the breeding grounds of diseases. A great tide of humanity flowed through them. With the new standby system, people often packed the terminals waiting for places on overcrowded planes. In the most literal sense, they breathed in each other's germs.

He lingered for a few minutes in the bedroom, suddenly overwhelmed by the sadness of it all. The girl was going to die. He was sure of that. Who was going to come and clear up, pack up the clothes, fold away the sheets? Who was next of kin?

On a small table next to the bed was a framed colour photograph. Two smiling girls stood side by side, their arms about each other. One of them was clearly Diane Verusio. Who was the other? Kaplan wondered.

He picked up the photograph and studied it carefully. There was a strong family resemblance between the two faces. The other girl was younger and darker than Diane, brunette rather than blonde. A younger sister, perhaps? A cousin? Kaplan looked at the picture for a full ten seconds; looked especially at the younger girl. He had a strange, almost psychic feeling that the soft brown eyes were saying something to him, pleading with him almost.

Later that evening, after he had left the apartment on Bank Street, Kaplan called on Diane Verusio's medical practitioner.

Isaac Reuben was an elderly gentleman, well into his sixties. When Kaplan entered the surgery on Washington Square, the doctor took his time in rising to his feet behind a cluttered desk. He walked round to greet his visitor and Kaplan warmed instinctively to what he saw. Isaac Reuben was of short but solid build; he had a pepperpot mixture of black and silver short curly hair. A grey cardigan was buttoned across a generous paunch. The fingers of his hands were short and stubby. Reuben wore a wedding ring, Kaplan noted, but from the general disarray of the doctor's appearance and surroundings, Kaplan suspected that he was a widower.

It was the kindliness of Reuben's expression that struck Kaplan immediately. His eyes, small and dark, peered out from beneath black bushy eyebrows.

Kaplan's glance fell on a framed and faded photograph on the mantelpiece. Reuben, noticing, explained.

'My parents. Isaac and Miriam Rabinowitz, arriving at Ellis Island in 1897. We changed our name to Reuben during the First World War.'

It was typical of the man that he should put his visitor at ease in this way. There was something so natural and unforced in the doctor's manner, that Kaplan had no difficulty in explaining who he was and why he had come.

It turned out that Reuben knew the Verusio family well.

'Our families were immigrants together. The Verusios came from Southern Italy. *We* came from Russia. But when we all reached New York, it didn't make a damn bit of difference where we came from. We all had to pitch in together.' He returned to his seat behind the desk. 'I knew the whole family well. It had its share of bad luck, I can tell you. The parents were tragically killed in a plane crash a year or so ago. Now there's this business with Diane.'

He sat back to listen while Kaplan elucidated the various hypotheses regarding the source of Diane's illness.

'Yes, she did tell me where she had been,' he volunteered, 'but it wasn't Africa or Asia or the Middle East. She only went as far as Belgium.'

Kaplan nodded in agreement. The air ticket which he had seen gave no indication of an itinerary extending beyond Europe.

Reuben continued: 'I believe in looking first for causes nearer home. We can consider the exotic explanations later.'

'Did she have any cuts or lesions?'

'Not as far as I could see.'

'Did she mention any physical contact?'

The old doctor leaned forward across his desk.

'You're talking about venereal transmission? Frankly, I don't think she was that kind of girl.'

Kaplan felt suddenly ashamed. He remembered the homely nature of the apartment he had just visited, full of books and pictures of wildlife.

'No, of course not,' he said quickly. He changed the subject. 'One last question, doctor. We are going to have to try and trace her contacts. All her contacts. We'll get onto the airline, though I'm not sure that will do us much good. You can't rely much on the passenger manifest nowadays, particularly with these standby flights. In any case, with most exotic diseases, the infectious stage is linked to the first appearance of the symptoms. My guess is that she wasn't in a position to transmit the infection, whatever it is, to anyone else until after she got back to her apartment. Do you know if she saw anyone there?'

'I asked her. I think the answer is probably no. There's no doorman in her building. She told me she went straight to bed when she reached home. When she called me, I went round to her.'

Kaplan smiled. 'You must be one of the last doctors to make house-calls.'

The old man smiled. 'I know I'm a bit old-fashioned. But when someone says they're ill, I don't believe in making them drag themselves through the streets.'

Kaplan stood up to go. He had made a decision.

'Dr Reuben, I hope you won't think I'm making a lot of unnecessary fuss, but I think you should come into the hospital yourself. As a precaution.'

The old man looked surprised. 'Whatever for?'

Kaplan explained. 'Look at it this way. On present showing, it looks as though Diane Verusio – somewhere, somehow – has contacted a dangerous exotic disease. The girl is very sick. Very sick indeed. She's probably going to die. We don't know, or at least we don't know yet, what the disease is. And we don't know how to treat it. We know it's infectious because Diane Verusio caught it from someone or something. She wasn't born with it. The likelihood is that you were the only unprotected person with whom she was in contact during the infectious phase.'

'What do you mean?'

'I mean that when you had her moved from here five days ago, she was taken by ambulance under sterile conditions to the Columbia-Presbyterian Hospital. At the hospital, she has been in the maximum isolation ward.'

The old doctor took it well. 'Young man. One way or the other I've been exposed to almost every disease you can think of in my life. And they haven't got me yet. I'm pretty tough, you know. I've probably got enough antibodies in my blood to sink a battleship.'

Kaplan looked at him with admiration. This was a man who had probably seen the worst that life had to offer. You didn't maintain a general practice in Greenwich Village without developing a certain immunity.

'I don't doubt that you're tough, doctor. That's not my worry. My worry is that we may be dealing with something new. Entirely new. Being tough may not be enough.'

The old doctor scratched his chin. 'I'll come on in to hospital, if you like, but you'll have to give me time to transfer my appointments.'

'Thank you, doctor. I'll have an ambulance pick you up. Meanwhile, no contacts of any kind.'

As they walked to the door, Kaplan had a last thought. 'Was Diane Verusio an only child – or did she have brothers or sisters?'

Reuben stopped in mid-stride. 'Didn't I tell you about Stephanie, Diane's younger sister?'

When Kaplan shook his head, the doctor went on: 'Stephanie Verusio is one of the most remarkable people I have ever met. If I was a younger man, I would have fallen in love with her myself.' A wistful look crossed Reuben's face. 'I almost did fall in love with her when she was growing up in New York. She had such fire and verve. And she was a real beauty too. I don't think I've ever seen such a beautiful young woman.'

'Where is she now? We ought to let her know about her sister. Do you know where she lives?' Kaplan was aware that his interest in Stephanie Verusio was more than merely professional. He had a brief mental image of a pair of soft brown eyes smiling at him out of a framed coloured photograph.

Reuben answered his question in the negative. 'I heard that Stephanie had gone to live abroad. But I don't know where. Even the best general practitioner doesn't know everything.'

The dreamy moment had passed.

Kaplan reverted to his normal, brisk matter-of-fact self. 'Don't worry, doctor. We'll track the family down somewhere. We're used to that kind of thing.'

They stood in the hall together, talking for a minute or two. Kaplan's glance fell on a framed photograph of the President of the United States. It was inscribed: 'To Isaac Reuben, with best wishes and warm thanks for all your help.'

Kaplan was intrigued – what had Reuben done that had elicited such a glowing testimonial?

'That's nice.' Kaplan nodded in the direction of the photograph.

Reuben was not to be drawn. 'Good luck to you,' he said.

Kaplan's last glimpse was of a pair of old black brogues,

which looked as though they had seen at least thirty winters, shuffling back into the room, as Reuben closed the door.

CHAPTER TWO

KAPLAN CALLED HIS OFFICE before he left New York later that evening.

'Susan, I'm coming down with some specimens. Can you warn them that I shall need the Hot Lab. And I could use some help. We're probably in for an all-night session.'

There was a car to meet him at the airport. He made it to the Center in twenty-five minutes which, thought Kaplan, was probably a record. Susan Wainwright was already waiting for him. There was concern in her voice.

'Christ, Lowell, you look tired.'

'I *am* tired.' Commuting to New York from Atlanta, Georgia, was a far cry from commuting from, say, Westport, Connecticut.

'The Lab's clear,' Susan said. 'I've warned them that we may be working late.'

Kaplan grunted. For the moment he felt too exhausted to speak.

The Hot Lab at the Center for Disease Control in Atlanta, Georgia, is, in a literal sense, a world within a world. Its correct title is Maximum Containment Laboratory, though 'Hot Lab' is the more customary usage. It was built during the 'seventies to satisfy two major requirements. The first was the protection of the outside world from diseases which were being investigated in the Hot Lab. The second had to do with the safety of personnel working inside the Lab with lethal materials of one kind or another. To achieve these two objectives, the Hot Lab was constructed as a box within a box. An outer building housing the air purification plants, waste disposal units and other necessities was erected over the inner shell. Kaplan had once explained the principle to Susan Wainwright when she had first joined him as his assistant.

'All the air is airconditioned and cleaned. We retain inside the building itself 99.99% of all particles larger than 0.3 microns. All solid waste is steam-pressured in autoclaves before being removed. All liquid waste is sterilized at ultra-high temperatures.'

They reached the Hot Lab over some covered metal catwalks which connected it to the main complex of buildings. Kaplan waited while Susan Wainwright went ahead and used the chemical shower.

When his own turn came, he stood there naked for two or three minutes, letting the water beat the tiredness out of him.

Susan who had already gone on through the air-lock called to him on the intercom.

'Lowell, are you okay?'

'Yeah, I'm just coming.'

They got into their lab garments. Each of them wore a positive pressure suit made of one-piece flexible urethane plastic with zipper. Each suit was fitted with an air filter and a device which cooled air for breathing; it also carried three minutes' supply of air in case of emergency. When they were ready they moved on through into the maximum containment area itself. The doors clicked shut behind them and, as they did so, the inflatable rubber gaskets expanded, producing an hermetically sealed airtight fit.

Their first act, once inside, was to clip themselves onto the airline, their sole umbilical connection with the outside world. The airline was fed by compressed air piped in from cylinders outside the building. Similarly, the air they exhaled through their face-masks was piped away to the service area where it was filtered and sterilized before being released.

Without this umbilical access to an outside source of air, scientific use of the Hot Lab's facilities would have been greatly hampered. With it, they had almost complete freedom of movement and could stay in the Lab as long as the outside air supply lasted.

The Hot Lab itself was divided into two sections. The first was filled with glass cabinets. A line of them ran down the center of the room, and others were ranged along the walls. The air inside the room was under negative pressure in relation to the air outside the Hot Lab. In the same way, the air inside the cabinets was under negative pressure in relation to the air circulating within the lab.

'We work with the specimens inside the cabinets,' Kaplan had explained during that first guided tour, 'using the automatic handling devices. If we make a mistake and there's a leak from the cabinet, that leak – because of the negative pressure – doesn't contaminate the room outside. Similarly, if there is a spill in the maximum containment area, that spill should never go beyond the Hot Lab itself. It should automatically be limited to where it occurs, again through negative pressure.'

A major advantage of the pressurized suit was that the researcher was no longer limited to working on material within the cabinets. Since he had built-in protection, he could move into the second area – again through an airtight door – where material could be removed from the cabinets and handled in a much more direct way. This was both safer and more convenient. There was always a risk, when handling items with rubber gloves and through armports, of the researcher sticking a needle into his own finger instead of the cell he was seeking to inoculate. Being able to work in the open was an important step forward in toxicological research.

Lowell Kaplan and Susan Wainwright moved straight on to the 'open' area. Their first task was to receive the specimens they had brought down from New York through the double-door autoclave which connected the containment area with the outside.

Lowell Kaplan carefully removed the watertight metal container from the outer container he had brought on the plane from New York. Inside the sealed watertight container were test-tube specimens wrapped in cotton. Susan

Wainwright stood beside him, like a nurse assisting at an operation. She took the outer and the inner wrappings from him and disposed of them; she passed him the tools of his trade; she assisted him with advice and encouragement.

For an hour they worked in silence, the clear plastic face-plates of their pressure suits making possible the use of instruments requiring accurate vision.

Through an electron microscope capable of magnification up to a million times, Kaplan examined blood samples taken from the patient. Hunched over the eye-piece, he saw the strange shapes almost immediately. Susan Wainwright noted down his remarks as he spoke.

'Unusual morphology.' Kaplan was always laconic when he had his eye to the microscope. 'We've got pleomorphic filaments here of exceptional length. Straight rod particles. Some are bent into horseshoes or b's, as well as hooks and loops. The ends are rounded. In some cases one pole is dilated. We have occasional branching.'

'What's the present magnification?'

'One hundred thousand. I'll take it up to two and then three hundred thousand.'

At the higher magnifications, the shapes were more clearly apparent. 'I think we're dealing with a virus all right,' Kaplan exclaimed. 'But I've never seen one quite like it. There seem to be three basic forms. First, there's the naked helix; then we have coiled structures enclosed by a membrane; finally, there's a circular form or torus. I think this last must be the mature virus.'

'Can I have a look?' Susan Wainwright was anxious to see for herself. Over the years she had graduated from being a fledgling assistant into a fully-trusted collaborator.

For several minutes she observed the peculiar structures in silence. Kaplan stood next to her, watching intently behind his perspex face-plate and breathing steadily from the supply of pure air being piped into the Hot Lab.

'What about size?' he asked. 'It struck me that the mean length is fairly high.'

Susan Wainwright agreed. She looked at the scale etched at the side of the plate. 'Some of the particles are over 900μ. I'd say the mean length is around 700μ with a cross-sectional diameter of between 70 and 80μ.'

Kaplan nodded. 'That means for the safe elimination of the infectious agent by filtration we'd need a pore size of 100μ or less.' He took over the microscope once more.

Speaking slowly and clearly so that Susan could note precisely what he was saying, he completed his observations.

'The ends of ring-shaped particles apparently do not merge, even if they touch. The nucleo-capsid usually consists of a single strand. Breaks in the nucleo-capsid are generally found in the coiled portion; they are probably artifacts. Each ring usually contains four helix fragments.'

He turned off the power and straightened up. 'What the hell is it, I wonder?'

Susan looked at him. 'Your guess is as good as mine.'

Lowell Kaplan moved towards the door. 'I think we're going to have to feed this one into the computer.'

They exited from the Hot Lab, following in reverse order the procedure they had used to enter. They unclipped themselves from the airlines, crossed the double door airlock, again made use of the chemical shower and finally emerged into the outside world. Telefacsimiles of Susan Wainwright's notes were already waiting for them on the other side. The originals had been consigned to the maximum containment facility's waste disposal system without ever leaving the inner sanctum.

The computer facility to which Kaplan had referred was in its way as unique as the Hot Lab itself. Over the last fifteen years the Center for Disease Control had been building up an unrivalled store of information on diseases. Collectors from all over the world had availed themselves of the Center's special mailing facilities to convey bits of dead or dying people, of every shape and form, size and colour. The airtight containers used were capable, supposedly, of surviving a plane crash or terrorist attack. Special instructions, including a telephone number to call in an emergency, were printed on the boxes in a half-dozen languages. There had been one or two mishaps, but nothing had gone seriously wrong. By the end of the 'seventies, Atlanta, Georgia, was the proud possessor of the world's largest collection of deep-frozen diseases. If a sperm-bank could be called a life-bank, this was the opposite; it was a death-bank.

Apart from information contained in jars and bottles,

the Center for Disease Control possessed an unmatched collection of computerized records stored under a binary coding system. Even where the Center did not itself possess tissues or cultures relating to a particular disease, it had taken steps to acquire the maximum possible data from available sources and to store that data on tape at the Computer Center.

The Computer Center was located on the fourth floor of the building. Access was limited to those in possession of a special pass. This restriction was in force not so much because of the sensitivity of the data, but because of the damage that untrained or ham-fisted utilizers could inadvertently cause.

A young man called Vincent Peters was on duty in the computer terminal that night. He had been warned to stand by, and to clear the lines for some high-priority work. Clearly gratified to be in on the action, he was doubly pleased when Kaplan appealed to him.

'Give us a hand, Vincent, will you? I've an urgent trace request here on what could be a dangerous pathogen, and I don't want to be stalled behind some routine enquiry from Peoria.'

Vincent Peters pushed back a dark lock of hair which had flopped forward over his forehead.

'She's all yours, Dr Kaplan. I've already told Peoria to wait till the morning.'

In practical terms, the Disease Control Computer Center in Atlanta, Georgia, was not much different from hundreds of other such centers up and down the country. A data bank is a data bank, whichever way you look at it – the repository of millions of pieces of information stored on magnetic tape. It is the system of retrieval whereby specific information may be hunted down and recovered that makes a unit more or less effective for its purposes. In this respect, through the development of sophisticated enquiry techniques, the Disease Control computer facility was exceptional. In particular, the PRS – Pathogen Record System – had proved invaluable on account both of the extent and depth of the material incorporated in its magnetic files and, as important, of the particular system of pathogen classification used.

Kaplan had been closely involved in the design of the pathogen classification system, notably in establishing that all viruses be cross-classified under seven main categories:

A – Morphology: shape, size and ultra-structure

B – Physicochemical structure

C – Antigenic properties, such as immunofluorescence, neutralization, complement fixation, etc...

D – Resistance to physical and chemical treatment

E – Experimental hosts, which could range from monkeys to man, and cultivation

F – Pathogenesis: how harmful to humans/animals

G – Immunity

To obtain a quick and accurate answer from PRS, it was necessary to have reliable data concerning at least five of the seven categories. PRS could, in that event, take a cross-bearing on the given materials and, through a process of logical deduction, zero in on, or at least somewhere near, the identity of the target.

'I'm not sure we've really got enough to go on, Vincent,' Susan Wainwright smiled as she handed over the data sheets, 'but I think you could make a start.'

The young man took a quick look at the papers, noting the extent of the information. He nodded. 'Let's give it a whirl.'

Mentally, Kaplan had prepared himself for a long wait. The more obscure the information, the longer the search-time, for the millions of 'bits' of information in the data 'core' were automatically loaded in order of frequency. After fifteen minutes the printer had still not begun to chatter. The pale blue light on the control panel indicated that the programme was running. Apart from that, there was no sign of activity.

'Jesus!' exclaimed the young technician. 'When you reckon that machine is searching at the rate of 200,000 bits a second, and it still hasn't come up with anything, either the information isn't there or else it's really digging back into history.'

'How far back can you go?' asked Susan Wainwright tensely. Like Kaplan she was beginning to show the strain of a long day.

'To the late 'fifties if we have to,' replied Vincent Peters, 'though some of the data from that period is in pretty bad shape. Hey, wait a minute! I think we're getting something.'

A different light, red this time and labelled 'PRINT-OUT', came up on the console. Simultaneously, the printer started clacking, and a long wide sheet of paper began to emerge from the machine.

Kaplan, unable to suppress his impatience, ripped it off, took one look and went pale.

This was that he read:

DATA SUPPLIED CONFIRMS PRESENCE OF VIRAL AGENT. STRUCTURAL PATTERNS EXHIBIT MANY FEATURES SIMILAR TO THAT OF VESICULAR STOMATITIS AND RABIES VIRUSES OF RHABDOVIRUS GROUP. HOWEVER DIFFERENCES WITH RESPECT TO SIZE, FORM, BEHAVIOUR IN CELL CULTURES AND PHOTODYNAMIC SENSITIVITY TO METHYLENE BLUE SHOULD BE TAKEN INTO ACCOUNT IN DETERMINING THE DEFINITIVE CLASSIFICATION. PRS ESTIMATES WITH PROBABILITY AT 95 PER CENT LEVEL THAT AGENT IN SAMPLES ANALYZED IS IDENTICAL TO THE SO-CALLED MARBURG VIRUS.

Then there was a gap on the printout, after which followed the words:

WARNING WARNING WARNING

WARNING WARNING WARNING

MATERIAL UNDER EXAMINATION CONTAINS DEADLY PATHOGENS. RESEARCHERS AND TECHNICIANS SHOULD TAKE ALL NECESSARY PRECAUTIONS IN ACCORDANCE WITH LABORATORY SAFETY MANUAL HEW PUBLICATION

NO CDC 77-8118. NO FURTHER WARNING WILL BE ISSUED.

'Oh, my God!' Kaplan was aghast. 'We've got an outbreak of Marburg! Jesus Christ!'

He passed the sheet to Susan Wainwright.

'What does it mean?' she asked. 'What do we do?'

'We hit the panic button.'

At that moment the telephone in the Computer Center rang, Kaplan picked it up. He listened for thirty seconds. Then, as he put the receiver down, he swore out loud.

'Damn it to hell!'

'What's the matter?'

'She's dead.'

'Who's dead?'

'The girl. Verusio. And the doctor, Reuben, has come down with the same symptoms. You know what that means? It means that unless we move fast half the population of the United States could be wiped out overnight. The Black Death would have nothing on Marburg.'

Taking back the printout from her outstretched hand, he made for the door.

CHAPTER THREE

LOWELL KAPLAN MISSED his week-end with the children.

He called his ex-wife from the airport as he left Atlanta for New York for the second time in less than thirty-six hours.

'Martha, I'm really sorry about this. We've got a crisis on our hands and I've got to get back to New York.'

'For God's sake, Lowell! The kids will be desperately disappointed. You promised to take them camping.'

'I can't, Martha. I'll make it up to them.'

'The trouble with you is that work always comes first.'

Kaplan replaced the receiver with some irritation. Martha, he thought, had never understood the nature of his work. You didn't go camping when the lid was about to blow. But as he walked to the plane he couldn't help feeling that there might after all be something in what his ex-wife had said. Perhaps he did always put work first. Perhaps he should have more time for himself. Having more time for himself might be a way of having more time for other people. Without meaning to, he found himself thinking about Stephanie Verusio.

Before the plane landed in New York, he went to the toilet to freshen up. He stared long and hard at his face in the mirror. The eyes were clear and grey; the eyebrows thick and matted. His nose and chin were strong and determined. There was no mistaking the energy and vigour in every line of his features. 'Fuck you, Kaplan,' he said to himself. 'You can't get it right, can you?'

There was a police escort at Kennedy to take him into the city. Less than an hour after touch-down, Kaplan stood on the dais in the lecture theatre on the ground floor of the Columbia-Presbyterian Hospital. If the hospital, as seemed likely, was to be the nerve-center of operations, he wanted to be sure, right from the start, that all personnel were fully informed. Doctors and nurses had been notified of the urgent meeting, while he was still on the plane.

The group of men and women who confronted him looked tense and anxious. Kaplan was tense and anxious himself. None of them really knew what they were dealing with. The situation was unprecedented. There had never been an outbreak of Marburg disease in the United States before. Indeed, apart from that first occurrence in Marburg, Germany, back in 1967, there had been no other recorded incident anywhere in the world. Kaplan began by giving them the facts as he knew them.

'Ladies and Gentlemen.' His voice was controlled, but the inner stress was evident. 'Today, for the first time in our medical history, the United States is in a Red Alert situation. We are not threatened by enemy bombers or missiles. We are threatened by disease. According to electron-microscope examinations which we have conducted at the Center for Disease Control in Atlanta, Georgia, at the request of the local health authorities' – he gave a brief nod in the direction of the New York State Epidemiologist, a tall bearded man who sat on the platform behind him – 'two patients in this hospital have been infected with the Marburg virus. One of them, Diane Verusio, has died. The other, Dr Isaac Reuben, is dangerously ill.'

He paused and looked around the room. He saw that he had their complete attention.

'You should all know that you will, each and every one of you, be at considerable risk. On past form, your chances of survival if you should happen to contract the disease are very small. There were twenty-three confirmed cases in Marburg in 1967. All twenty-three died.'

His audience gasped audibly as he spoke and murmurs broke out along the benches. Kaplan held up his hand for silence.

'What is more, there is no known antidote. No vaccine has been developed, in spite of efforts made after the 1967 outbreak.' He noted a hand raised at the front. 'Do you have a question?'

Joel Price was one of the younger physicians on the staff of the isolation wing of the hospital. An intelligent and articulate man, he usually went straight to the heart of any question.

'What is the nature of the transmission?'

'We don't know. In the two cases so far identified, there could have been actual physical contact, through blood or sputum or whatever. But we cannot rule out airborne or aerosol transmission with all that that implies. From what we know of the 1967 episode, the Germans were never able to rule it out either.'

Once more there was a gasp of concern. Every public health man knew there could be no more serious danger than airborne transmission of a highly infectious and lethal disease against which there was no known remedy. One person sneezing in a crowded subway could infect a hundred others. Each one could in turn pass on the disease to a hundred more.

'As you can imagine,' Kaplan continued, 'the possibility of airborne transmission in a case like this will impose the greatest strain on our resources. Since we have no vaccine, we have to rely on total containment of the outbreak. That means we have to begin here. And it means we have to begin now.'

He paused and glanced in the direction of the doors leading into the auditorium. As planned, uniformed guards were on duty. Kaplan gave a brief nod in their direction, acknowledging their presence. When the moment came, those doors would be locked. No one would enter and no one would leave. He was not ready yet to give the word. One or two late arrivals were still trickling in. He had to be sure that all potential contacts were in the net before he pulled the cord tight. Playing for time, he was deliberately more long-winded than he might otherwise have been.

'The first thing we must do,' he continued, 'is to inventory the type C facilities which we have available both here in New York and indeed throughout the United States. Does everyone here understand what I mean by type C facilities?'

There were blank looks on many of the faces which confronted him.

Kaplan explained: 'A type C facility is a maximum isolation facility which meets the following conditions: One – it must have a separate structure with its own air conditioning, heating and ventilating system. I can't stress how important this is when the possibility exists, as it does in this case, that a virus may be disseminated by air. Two – it must have adequate water, electricity, heating, cooking and ventilation. Three – within the separate structure, there must be a separate isolation room with a toilet, a bath or shower, and a sink for the patient. This room should be operated under measurably negative air pressure, and all exhaust air should be passed through a filter with an efficiency of at least 95% based on the DOP – dioctyophthalate-test method. Four – the facility must possess an anteroom in which medical personnel can change into and out of protective clothing. The anteroom must have a shower and a sink for use by everyone leaving the isolation room. It should be operated at a pressure intermediate between the isolation room and the outside, and thus form an air barrier. Five – there should be an office-communication area outside the anteroom with dependable telephone service to the outside. Six – there should be adequate communication, preferably by 'intercom' units, between each of the rooms of the facility.' After this recital, Kaplan turned to the New York State Epidemiologist.

'Dr Jones, can you tell me how many type C facilities of the kind I have just described there would be in New York.'

'One.' Dr Marvin Jones replied without hesitation. 'And that's not available.'

'Why not?'

'It's right here in the hospital and it's being occupied by Dr Reuben at this time.'

Kaplan managed a smile. 'I suppose we should be thankful for small favors.' He turned serious. 'You're positive there are no other type C facilities?'

'Yes, sir. None in New York City; none in New York State. Frankly, once smallpox was licked the maximum isolation concept tended to fall out of favour. There just didn't seem to be a need for it. We never did build the units we planned to build. You know how it is. Shortage of funds, mainly. Each unit costs upwards of two million dollars. On a one unit per patient basis, that's two million dollars a patient.

'My guess is that, if you took the United States as a whole, you wouldn't find more than half-a-dozen type C facilities, and even those are likely to be at Federal centers of one kind or another.'

'How do you mean?'

'I'm talking about CW and BW centers. Like Fort Mahon in Texas. Or Fort Sumter in Virginia. When you are working with chemical warfare agents or bacteriological warfare agents, of course you have to have maximum isolation facilities. But then you are dealing with a totally controlled situation. I mean, they're putting that stuff into people deliberately.'

Marvin Jones couldn't help feeling vaguely resentful. Atlanta people always had the glamour role. They jetted in and out, poked their noses into this corner and that rather like the FBI being called in to help out the local sheriff. And yet, when something went wrong, it was easy to blame the locals. If something went wrong now – and he had a horrible feeling that it might – it would be only too easy to blame the State and City Health Departments for not building the type C facilities which all the experts had assured them would never again be needed.

'I'm not blaming you.' Kaplan interrupted his thoughts. 'I'm not blaming anyone. I just wanted to know the extent of our reserves.'

He turned once more to the audience. 'Some of you may remember the story of the battle of Balaclava. The British troops were stretched out in what was known as the Thin Red Line. Our thin red line, the line that separates the United States and possibly the world from disaster, is half-a-dozen type C facilities scattered around the United States.'

Again Kaplan paused. As a scientist, he was conscious that words like disaster were to be eschewed wherever possible. He had always had a healthy scorn for the reaction – or, as he saw it, the overreaction – of most people to news of sickness or disease. A morbid fascination with the minutiae of ill-health had no part in his make-up. Yet it was difficult to find a more appropriate word. Disaster had not struck – not yet. But it was certainly around the corner.

He took them through the problem step by step.

'We have reason to believe that Dr Reuben was Diane Verusio's only contact in the infectious stage. From the Marburg case-histories,' he added parenthetically, 'it appears that the infectious stage coincides with the onset of the first clinical symptoms and ends about six days later, if death has not already intervened. If it is true,' he continued, 'that Diane Verusio infected no one else except Isaac Reuben, then we have been unbelievably lucky. It means we can concentrate on identifying and then isolating all contacts Dr Reuben might have had, particularly during what we suppose is the infectious phase. If we can do that today, or at the latest tomorrow, before these contacts themselves have had the time to develop clinical symptoms, we stand a real chance of getting this thing under control by placing all possible contacts in isolation.'

There was another question from the back of the room, this time an unidentified voice: 'What if there are more names than places?'

Kaplan took it in his stride. He gave it to them straight from the shoulder.

'Then we're in trouble. Big trouble.'

He had almost finished. 'When I have stopped speaking, a team from Atlanta, assisted by officials from the Health Department, will be interviewing each and every one of you so as to establish a profile of your movements in regard to both patients. If you are suspected of having been in contact, you will be isolated forthwith. I want you to know that, since I was myself in contact with Dr Reuben, I shall this evening be taken to Fort Sumter in Virginia, to a maximum isolation facility there. I hope to come out of it alive.'

There was a nervous laugh from the audience as Kaplan stepped down from the dais. At the same moment the guards locked the doors to the lecture theatre, and a team of white-coated men began to move along the seated rows.

*

The old man had never felt sicker in his life. He was sure he was going to die. To him, Kaplan was just a disembodied voice talking a million miles away across the ether. He replied mechanically to the questions, fighting for breath and racked with pain. His liver ached fiercely, his hair, what was left of it, was coming out in handfuls; rashes had broken out on his trunk and extremities.

'Jesus, can't you leave me alone,' he groaned. 'I told you, I saw nobody that day after you left. Remember, I came straight into the hospital in the ambulance.'

Kaplan remembered, but he wanted to be sure. His training had been very precise on this point. Check and double-check. Don't take the patient's word for it. Ask specific questions.

'Who did you have lunch with that day?' He spoke into the intercom, addressing the blanketed figure which lay in the bed on the other side of the glass partition.

'I didn't have lunch. I ate at my desk!'

'Who did you see before lunch?'

Reuben groaned. His throat felt dry; his whole body felt dry, but still the sweat poured off him.

'Nobody. Ask my assistant. She'll know.'

'We've asked her. She's in isolation herself now. Who else did you see?'

Reuben lifted himself half off the bed and stared through the partition at Kaplan.

'Nobody. Now, for God's sake, leave me alone.'

But Kaplan couldn't afford to leave him alone. He had to squeeze out every last bit of information.

'Your assistant says you made a house-call that morning. Can you tell us where?'

'No.'

'No, you didn't make a house-call? Or no, you won't tell us where?'

The old man collapsed back on the bed. In a low voice, he gave a name and an address.

'Look after her, won't you, when I've gone?' He continued. 'My sister. She lives alone. I'm all she's got left.'

'We'll look after her.' Kaplan's voice was gentle. He leaned forward to speak softly into the intercom. 'You're going to make it, Isaac. I know you're going to make it. You're going to beat the book.' Kaplan moved away. He had one more duty to perform, an unpleasant one.

At death, Diane Verusio's body had been double-wrapped

in large, impervious plastic bags in the isolation room. The bags had each been sealed with tape after the removal from them of as much air as possible. The bagged body had then been moved to the anteroom and similarly sealed in a third large, impervious plastic bag for subsequent transfer to the autopsy room in the basement of the hospital. Like the isolation room, the autopsy room could be operated under measurably negative air pressure with respect to the adjacent rooms.

Kaplan had given the most careful instructions.

'All doors and windows of the autopsy room are to be kept closed during the autopsy,' he had ordered. 'Air exhausted to make the room pressure negative must be passed through a filter of at least 95% based on the DOP test method. All articles from the autopsy room must be sterilized before removal, and the room must be decontaminated after the autopsy.'

He had gone on to specify the details of the decontamination process, and had further instructed that all clothing worn by autopsy personnel should be removed within the autopsy room, double-bagged and incinerated or autoclaved. Autopsy personnel were to shower with soap and shampoo immediately after removing their contaminated clothing. After decontamination of the autopsy room, the filters in the exhaust air system of the room were to be carefully double-bagged in impervious plastic and autoclaved or incinerated. Maintenance personnel involved were to wear gowns, gloves, masks, caps and booties. Such protective clothing was to be double-bagged and autoclaved or incinerated. Maintenance personnel were to shower with soap and shampoo immediately after removing their contaminated clothing.

He arrived in the hospital basement, expecting to find the autopsy in progress. Instead, the body still lay double-wrapped in the plastic bags on the autopsy table. The room remained at normal pressure and there was no sign of any activity.

'What gives?' Kaplan addressed the Chief Technician with some annoyance.

The man shrugged his shoulders. 'They won't touch her, I'm afraid. The unions have passed the word.'

Kaplan's irritation increased. 'They have a job to do, haven't they?'

The man turned away. 'Find your own people, doctor. My men aren't performing any autopsy in this instance.'

'Why?'

'Look!' the man pushed his face close up to Kaplan's. 'Let's not kid each other. You and I know what we're dealing with. Marburg, isn't it? Yes, some of us heard your little lecture. It wasn't just the doctors and nurses.' He turned on his heel. 'I'm not putting my men at risk and that's final.'

Kaplan knew when he was defeated. 'Well,' he said, 'can you persuade your people to fill the plastic bags with formalin embalming fluid and, when they've done that, to place the body in an airtight coffin and seal the coffin?'

'I'll do what I can. What do we do with the coffin?'

'The army will pick it up. They won't cremate it. They'll incinerate it in a special furnace that kills viruses, O.K.?'

The man shrugged. 'You know best.'

Kaplan had been allocated the room next to that of Dr Charles Graham on the top floor of the hospital. Dr Marvin Jones, the New York State epidemiologist, had an office nearby. The three men were sitting around Kaplan's desk at the end of one of the longest days he could ever recall. There had been a constant stream of instructions to give and information to receive. The telephone had not stopped ringing. For the moment, Kaplan believed they were on top of the problem.

He looked at his watch. It was already six p.m. He had spent the whole day at the hospital, supervising operations and looking after other people. Now it was time to look after himself. If he had contracted the disease from Isaac Reuben, he reckoned he had several days before the symptoms would begin to develop and the onset of the infectious phase; but he didn't want to take any risks.

He looked at his colleagues. 'Marvin, Charles. You'll have to be in charge this end. James McKinney will be in charge back in Atlanta. I'll try to stay in touch from Virginia, but if I go down with Marburg...' He spoke lightly, but the three of them knew the very real risks.

Kaplan got up from his chair, held out his hand, then drew it back. Handshakes were best avoided. The other two men understood the gesture and appreciated it.

He called down to the transport unit. 'Is the ambulance ready?'

'Ready and waiting,' came the reply.

To be on the safe side, Kaplan had decided to leave New York under full isolation conditions. Wrapped up to the neck in a sheet of impervious plastic, his mouth and nose covered with a high efficiency surgical mask, he entered the ambulance. The driver and attendant wore protective clothing, and the vehicle was equipped with two-way radio. The route was worked out in advance; police escorts organized at critical intersections.

Towards midnight, they arrived at their destination. Without leaving the ambulance, the driver and attendant, wearing plastic gloves, removed the mask from the patient, double-bagged it and replaced it with a clean mask. Kaplan was then wrapped to the neck in a second covering of plastic. The driver and attendant removed and double-bagged their own clothing except coveralls, and put on clean gowns, gloves, masks, caps, and booties passed to them through a window of the ambulance.

As soon as Kaplan had been taken into the isolation facility, the ambulance personnel set about the decontamination of the vehicle, using paraformaldehyde. This procedure took twelve hours; not until it had been completed were the men able to report on their two-way radio that their mission had been successfully accomplished.

For the next four days, from his room inside the maximum isolation facility at Fort Sumter, Virginia, Lowell Kaplan continued to mastermind the emergency operation. Around four o'clock in the morning on the fifth day of his incarceration, with just the first hint of dawn in the June sky, he woke with a burning sensation in his throat. His eyeballs ached, and he felt as though he was going to vomit. He had a fever and his nose had begun to bleed.

Clinically, Kaplan's illness followed much the same progression as the cases recorded in the 1967 outbreak. In fact, the medical circumstances of the three recurrences of the disease – namely Verusio, Reuben and Kaplan himself – only served to confirm the accuracy of the computer's original diagnosis. By midday of the first day Kaplan's fever had increased to 39°C without rigors. The nausea continued and he experienced frequent, occasionally uncontrollable, vomiting. He also suffered from watery diarrhoea, sometimes with admixtures of blood or mucous.

The characteristic, non-itching, maculopapulous rash started on his face the following day. It progressed to the trunk and extremities. At first, it consisted of tiny, sharply defined spots, located around the hair follicles; then it developed into a rash of middle-sized maculae, which merged to form a diffuse, dark-red erythema. The rash affected nearly the whole integument; it was specially marked on the scrotum. At the same stage, Kaplan developed an enanthema on the soft and hard palates, consisting partly of tapioca-like blisters. He also developed conjunctivitis and photophobia.

On the sixth day of his illness, while he had inwardly given up hope, Kaplan was dimly aware of a conversation taking place near his bedside. A plastic-suited figure, breathing in oxygen through a face-mask like some under-sea diver, was in the room and talking on the telephone. The words reached Kaplan across the waves of his sickness. Almost against his will, for by then he hoped for death, a quick merciful death, as much as he hoped for anything, he caught the note of hope in what was being said:

'Don't worry about transport,' the voice in the room was saying, 'we'll handle that. The military have a plane stand-ing by, and we can be with you by lunch-time. Just make sure you have the stuff ready. We're going to need a pint. More, if possible... Yes, of course I realize there are others. I'm not trying to deprive them. But dammit, Kaplan has to have priority, doesn't he? We need him. The whole country needs him if we're going to lick this thing.'

Kaplan heard the phone being put down and then the sound of two people talking quietly together.

'It's incredible,' one voice was saying, 'it looks as though Reuben is pulling through.'

'But that's a statistical impossibility.'

'Well, it's happened. They've just told me on the phone. There is a good chance of serum, and we'll be able to use that to help Kaplan in his fight for life.'

'And the others?'

'Yes, the others, too. But Kaplan above all.'

The voice faded as a fresh bout of delirium intervened. When, twenty-four hours later, Kaplan once again recov-ered his mental equilibrium, he was conscious of an over-whelming sense of relief. Much of the pain had gone, and though a general sense of weakness remained, he could feel that his strength was beginning to return. It was as though a cloud had passed from the land. He knew that, thanks to Dr Reuben's life-giving serum, he was going to survive.

The antibodies which the old doctor had developed in his fight for life had in turn helped Kaplan; and they would help others too.

Feeble though he was, Kaplan realized that – amazingly, incredibly – a line of defence against the Marburg virus had been created. It wasn't the whole answer because, in the nature of things, one man's serum could only give a limited measure of protection. But at least the suspected cases could be treated, and those who had had immediate contact with the disease could be inoculated. That evening, when the telephone rang beside his bed, he was already well enough to answer it himself. It was Susan Wainwright. He could hear the tears in her voice.

'Lowell, can you hear me?'

'Sure, I can hear you. I've been down a long way, Susan, but I'm coming back up.'

'Oh, Lowell, I'm so glad.'

'So am I. What about the others? There were others, weren't there? I wasn't the only one?'

'That's for later, Lowell, when you're really better.'

'It's bad?'

'It's not good.' She wouldn't say any more. 'Reuben sends his regards. He says to remind you he told you he was tough.'

'Susan,' the effort of speaking was beginning to tell on Kaplan, 'how is Reuben's sister?'

'She's dead.'

Kaplan groaned. 'Didn't they give her the serum?'

'There wasn't enough, Lowell. They gave it to you.'

Kaplan groaned again. 'Did Reuben know?'

'Reuben knew. He insisted that you should have it.'

'Oh my God.' Kaplan put down the phone and turned his face to the wall.

CHAPTER FOUR

FOR THOSE WHO had not been intimately involved, the incidence of disease which occurred in New York in the summer of 1982 passed rapidly into history. The *New York Times* noted the recovery of one of the victims, Dr Isaac Reuben – 'a medical practitioner of long standing in this city' – and the death of several others. It mentioned that serum had become available during the course of the outbreak which had aided the survival of at least one of the victims. Making a comparison with the Legionnaire's disease which had laid waste a veterans' convention in Philadelphia in 1976, the *New York Times* commented: 'We may never know the ultimate, or even the proximate, cause of this recent threat. What we do know is that it was successfully contained, and that is something for which the City of New York, the United States and perhaps even the civilized world itself, should be duly grateful.'

For Lowell Kaplan, now fully recovered from his illness after a three-week period of convalescence, things weren't quite as simple as they seemed to be to the *New York Times.* He knew just how close they had been to disaster. Marburg, after fifteen years, had come out of the closet with a vengeance, and Kaplan did not intend to ignore that fact. The personal response combined with the professional one. He knew the effect the disease had had on himself and on others, and was determined that it should not strike again. One morning, when he was back at his desk at the Center for Disease Control in Atlanta, he put a call through to New York and spoke to Isaac Reuben.

'I just wanted to thank you,' Kaplan had said simply. 'You saved my life.'

The old man answered: 'God has given you time. Use it, son.'

Kaplan wanted to say something about Reuben's sister, but somehow the words would not come. Perhaps some debts were better left unacknowledged, he thought, as he put down the receiver.

'You know,' he turned to Susan Wainwright, once again his constant companion at work, 'that man Reuben is a saint.' For a few moments they talked about Reuben and about the events of the past weeks.

'What are you going to do now?' Susan asked. There was an anxious note in her voice.

'Aw, hell!' Lowell smiled. 'I think I'll take a vacation for a few days. I might go to Europe. I haven't been there for a couple of years.'

Susan Wainwright relaxed. A broad smile crossed her pretty face.

'That's wonderful, Lowell. That's just what you need. Whereabouts in Europe?'

She caught the mischievous expression in Kaplan's eyes.

'Ever heard of a town called Marburg on the Lahn?' Kaplan replied laughing.

'Honestly, Lowell!' She remonstrated. 'You never give up, do you?'

*

Kaplan flew overnight to Frankfurt. The plane was half-empty and he was able to stretch out for most of the flight. He awoke with the sun to see the flat countryside beneath him criss-crossed by autobahns and other high-speed roads. Even at this early hour, Germany was a nation on the move.

Frankfurt airport itself was a gleaming antiseptic place. A smiling freckled girl rented him a car at the Hertz counter. Less than half-an-hour after landing, Kaplan was on his way.

He left the autobahn twenty minutes out of Frankfurt to drive up through the vast forests of the Lahn region. He twisted through sleepy villages and crossed bridges over clear sparkling streams. He could not help contrasting the magic of the scenery with the nature of his errand. Somehow it seemed so far-fetched, so implausible. Here he was, looking into something that had happened over fifteen years earlier in a small town in Germany, an incident that was unique in medical history. Twenty-three persons infected; twenty-three persons dead. No other disease had such a fatality rate. Not Lassa. Not Ebola. Not even the bubonic plague itself. Yet the extraordinary thing was that so little was known about the Marburg virus. Somehow a wall of silence had grown up around the episode and its aftermath. Why? That was the question.

He checked in at the Waldeckerhof, a modest hotel near the station. In the afternoon, tired from the long flight and the drive, he slept for a couple of hours. Then, towards evening, with the bells of the famous church of St Elizabeth – Elizabethkirche – ringing out for Evensong, he set out on foot.

He had been given a map at the desk of the hotel, but he didn't need to use it. The Landgraf Schloss, once the seat of the ruling princes of Hesse, towered 900 feet above the town. Kaplan made his way towards it, through narrow streets with overarching houses and up mediaeval staircases which connected one level to another. As he climbed, Kaplan had the distinct feeling that he was walking back through history and that he would eventually find himself in another century. Ducking under archways, twisting round corners as he followed the cobbled path upwards, he had a vivid sense of what towns like Marburg must have been like six hundred years earlier. He could smell the stench of closely packed humanity, the halt and the blind populating the streets, the insanitary conditions and, above all else, the fear of disease. The mediaeval towns of Europe were no strangers to the cry 'Bring out your dead'. They had been ravaged by the Black Death, and they had been ravaged again by the Plague. Marburg, unlike other cities of similar antiquity, had had a third visitation. Looking at the passers-by in the street – some clearly visitors like himself, but others equally clearly locals – Kaplan wondered how many of them recalled the 1967 incident or realized what a close call it had been.

Where the road began to skirt the ramparts of the castle, he saw a sign saying *Alte Universitet*, and realized that he was nearing his destination.

Professor Franz Schmidtt's residence was a solid affair, suitably professorial in character, set in a large, leafy garden just outside the edge of the campus. From the stag's antlers mounted, Bavarian fashion, above the front door to the heavy shutters which guarded the Schmidtt family's privacy, the house bore all the marks of bourgeois success. The manicured lawns with their picturesque gnomes, the neatly gravelled drive, the sweeping view over the roofs of the old town to the river meandering in the distance, all testified to Professor Schmidtt's status.

In fact, Franz Schmidtt was a heavyweight in more senses than one. When Kaplan first met him, they had been students together at Yale Medical School. Schmidtt, Kaplan recalled, had had a reputation as an athlete and as a dab hand with the sabre. Kaplan doubted that the Professor would be lithe enough to perform such feats now. He had thickened considerably about the waist and his complexion was markedly florid. But there was no mistaking the genuine warmth in his welcome.

He came out onto the doorstep followed by his wife,

a tall, rather beautiful but strained-looking woman with straight grey hair swept back from her forehead.

'Lowell! Wonderful to see you. Come on in. Such a surprise! I couldn't believe it when I got your cable.'

'Franz, Heidi! It's fantastic to see you both. How marvellous you look! You haven't changed in years!'

Kaplan shook the Professor's hand warmly and gave Frau Schmidtt a kiss on both cheeks before following them inside.

They sat with drinks in the living-room. Kaplan realized that the Schmidtt family was incomplete.

'Isn't Paula joining us?' Lowell asked.

'So you remember my little Paula?' Schmidtt sounded pleased. 'How could I forget her? Remember, you brought her with you last time you came to Washington on an N.I.H. Conference. We had a great time. I guess she was around sixteen then.'

'I guess she was. Well she's Head of Medical Records at the Clinic now. She takes her work seriously.'

'But I imagine she has time for some fun?'

It was Frau Schmidtt's turn to answer. She looked faintly disapproving.

'Marburg's a difficult place to be young in. There are so many...' – she searched for the right word – 'so many different influences. A girl can be swept this way and that. Remember, Paula grew up during the great radical movement of the late 'sixties. That was when the young people thought they were going to change the world. I'm not sure she's ever recovered.'

Heidi Schmidtt had no time to say more. The front door banged shut and a slim, dark-haired girl in her early thirties entered the room somewhat breathlessly.

'I got held up,' she said in German. Then she noticed Kaplan, and her face lit up with pleasure. She rushed over and threw herself into his arms.

'Lowell!' she cried, switching to English. 'How tremendous to see you!'

Kaplan blushed. It was a long time since an attractive young girl had given him such a welcome. Fleetingly, he wondered whether Paula's gesture was not just a little over-exuberant, a little false, but the thought passed almost as soon as it occurred.

'What are you doing here?' Paula asked, disentangling herself from Kaplan's arms.

'Didn't your father tell you?'

Franz Schmidtt interrupted. 'I didn't see her this morning. Paula was in Berlin for the week-end and she went straight to work when she got back.'

'In Berlin? What were you doing there?' Kaplan asked with interest.

'Oh, just staying with friends,' the girl replied vaguely.

She sat down and had a drink with them. Later, when she had left for a 'meeting' in the town, Kaplan said: 'I hope I'll have a chance to talk to Paula properly. I have always thought there's a lot to her.'

'There certainly is.' Frau Schmidtt spoke with feeling,

indicating that she had tangled with her strong-willed daughter more than once in the past and had come off second-best.

She went off to prepare the supper.

Over the meal, Kaplan came to the point. 'Franz, you were here throughout the late 'sixties, weren't you? I'm right in thinking that you came straight back to Marburg after Yale?'

'Yeah.' Franz dug deep into the large pile of boiled potatoes which took up half his plate.

'And you were at the University Clinic, weren't you?'

'Sure, all the time. I'd just begun in toxicology. I was working out the first protocols for the animal-testing of new drugs. Bonn took it over later, and now they've written it into the rules. Why do you ask?'

Kaplan looked at his hosts, two earnest, kindly Germans, the one a respected pillar of his profession, the other his house-proud wife.

'Franz, Heidi,' he said. 'Not long ago, I was desperately ill. In fact, I almost died. If I am here today, it's thanks to the grace of God together with a little bit of the devil's own luck.'

'But what happened to you?' There was real concern in Franz Schmidtt's voice.

'Yes, tell us,' echoed Heidi. 'This is bad news. Are you still ill?'

'No, I'm fully recovered. But it was a close-run thing.'

Kaplan began at the beginning with Diane Verusio's

death in New York, followed rapidly by Reuben's sickness and the other fatalities. He described the symptoms in some detail.

Professor Schmidtt and his wife listened to him with obvious fascination.

'And did you discover the cause?' the Professor asked when Kaplan stopped speaking. 'Do you think it was an outbreak of Lassa fever in New York? Some of the symptoms seem similar.'

Kaplan lowered his voice. 'No, it wasn't Lassa. It wasn't Ebola. We're sure of that. We ran an EM on serum and tissue culture from the first case and from all subsequent cases. They all pointed to the same thing. An outbreak of...' he paused '... Marburg virus. We kept it as quiet as possible. We didn't want to start a panic. But it was Marburg all right.'

He watched his old friends closely as he spoke and was quick to catch the cautionary look which Heidi flashed her husband. Franz, who was about to speak, pulled himself up. After an awkward pause, he said in a deadpan, give-nothing-away voice:

'Marburg virus? I'm not sure what you mean, Lowell. This Marburg? Marburg on the Lahn? We have no virus here.'

His wife pushed her chair back in such haste that it almost fell over. 'Coffee, gentlemen,' she interrupted. 'I think we'll take it into the sitting-room.'

For the time being, Kaplan decided not to press the point.

Somehow, he would get Schmidtt on his own later. He followed his hosts into the hot, overfurnished sitting-room, where they sat together over coffee and liqueurs. Their talk was strained. An awkwardness had descended on them, as though the mere mention of the Marburg disease could itself create a blight on the surroundings. At last, Franz Schmidtt suggested that they might take a walk round the old town.

'The Schloss looks superb when it's floodlit, and there's nothing like a walk to clear the head. It's too hot in here anyway.' He laughed heartily and turned to his wife. 'Heidi, are you coming?'

Frau Schmidtt seemed in two minds. It was clear to Kaplan that she was anxious not to let her husband too far out of sight, but a look of resignation suddenly passed over her face.

'No, you two go. It's been a long day, and I'm tired. Try not to be late.'

Schmidtt and Kaplan walked together through the town. Even though it was past eleven o'clock, the steep narrow streets were still crowded, and from the bars and wine cellars came the noise of students.

'The university is still in session,' said Professor Schmidtt. 'They'll be breaking up for the summer in a couple of weeks. In the meantime, they're getting in some drinking before they go.' He laughed again. 'We may join them eh, Lowell, old friend?'

The sound of singing blared up from one of the cellars.

Kaplan recognized the tune. 'Isn't that the old Horstwessel song? I thought it had been banned in Germany since the fall of the Third Reich.'

Schmidtt looked a bit embarrassed. 'These things tend to creep back, you know. In any case, the Horstwessel song was never officially banned. It just wasn't sung. We in Germany prefer not to be remembered of the Nazi era.'

Schmidtt's English – or rather American – was normally so perfect that Kaplan was surprised at the grammatical mistake: 'remembered' for 'reminded'. He hoped his host had not been too rattled by his reference earlier that evening to the Marburg virus.

He put his hand on the other man's arm as they walked. 'Franz, I hope you didn't mind what I said. I didn't mean to upset Heidi. You know me well enough to know that.'

'Of course, I realize that.' Franz half-turned as he walked to look his friend in the face. 'But you must be aware, Lowell, that even though some things have crept back, like the song you just heard, there are other things we still prefer not to talk about. What happened here in Marburg in 1967 is one of those things.'

'Can you tell me about it now?'

'Later. I want to show you something first. I think it will help you to understand.'

They ducked under an archway and climbed down half-a-dozen steps. The street was so narrow that three people could not have walked along it abreast.

'This is the oldest part of the old city. It dates back to the earliest part of the Middle Ages. The university's clubs have always met here. Remember that the university is almost as old as the town itself. They have grown up together. Each one needs the other. Ah, I think we have arrived.'

Franz Schmidtt gave three short knocks, followed by three long knocks.

'Is that a code?'

'Yes, of a sort.'

The door opened. A young bearded man confronted them, and Schmidtt said something to him in German. The man laughed.

'What's he saying?' Kaplan asked.

'He's saying you're never too old. Once a Hessenkraut, always a Hessenkraut.'

'And who or what is a Hessenkraut?'

'Literally, a cabbage from Hesse. Actually, it's the oldest fraternity in Marburg. And the most famous. The Chancellor himself is a member, and so is half the German cabinet. They've all been at Marburg University at one time or another. They were all Hessenkrauts.'

'As you know, we have Phi Beta Kappa in the States. Is it the same kind of thing?'

Franz Schmidtt smiled. 'I have several friends who are Phi Beta Kappa, but I'm not sure how they would make out as Hessenkrauts.'

'Why do you say that?'

'Wait and see.'

They went inside. A wave of sound hit them. Wreaths

of smoke obscured the interior, and visibility was poor. Groups of students were sitting at tables, drinking and talking. There was a great deal of laughter.

They sat down at one of the tables and ordered beer. While they were waiting for their drinks to arrive, Schmidtt explained: 'We will all be going upstairs in a few minutes. Drinking is downstairs; upstairs is...' he paused '... er, the other thing.'

'What other thing?'

Before the Professor had time to reply, there was a general movement to the stairs. One or two of the students greeted Schmidtt as they elbowed their way up.

'Good evening, Herr Doktor. It is not often we have the pleasure of seeing you here.'

'I like to keep in touch.'

The room which they entered at the top of the stairs reminded Kaplan of a mediaeval refectory. Long oak tables were ranged along each wall. At the far end was a dais, raised about two feet above floor level. From the high roof whose rafters had been blackened by centuries of smoke hung a variety of shields, spears and other weaponry. Students were packed into every corner. Some were drinking and talking; others were clustered about a green baize card-table where an official of the club, whose rank was denoted by the golden cabbage which dangled from a chain around his neck, was clearly taking bets.

Schmidtt thrust forward through the crowd to the edge of the dais and Kaplan followed him. They found chairs and sat down.

A few seconds later a uniformed figure stepped smartly through the door onto the dais. Kaplan took in the clear features and flaxen hair of a youth who could not have been more than eighteen years old. In addition to a gold-embroidered pillbox hat which sat askew on his head, he wore a frogged jacket with high tasselled epaulettes.

The youth raised a trumpet to his lips. A short spatter of notes produced a sudden silence in the room. At the same instant, from either side of what Kaplan now saw was effectively a stage, other uniformed officials entered the room. Each of them carried a razor-sharp sword which, with a well-rehearsed gesture, they proceeded to hold out to the crowd.

A roar of approval went up. Glasses clinked as more beer was downed. Some of the gathering banged impatiently on the heavy tables calling for the show to begin.

The point of it all dawned on Kaplan at last.

'Good God!' he exclaimed. 'Are they going to duel? I thought duelling disappeared from German universities years ago.'

'It didn't disappear,' Schmidtt answered. 'It just went underground. You can't wipe out a tradition like duelling overnight. It's in the blood. There have been duelling fraternities at Marburg Univerisity for four hundred years, and I think the tradition will continue as long as the university itself continues. The object is to wound, of course, to scar the face, not to kill. The bout will be over as soon as that has been achieved. One of the contestants will be marked for life. Perhaps both will be. But they will carry their scars proudly.'

Before Kaplan had time to comment, the youth who had first appeared on the dais blew another blast on the trumpet. At this signal, two other uniformed young men sprang from the wings to join their seconds on the dais. Each was presented with his sword and with a pair of metal goggles.

'To protect the eyes.' Schmidtt's voice had dropped to a whisper because by now a hush had descended on the room.

'Of course.' Kaplan understood the purpose of the goggles but he couldn't help feeling that they added an incongruous touch to the ensemble.

The club official who had been sitting at the green baize table now rose to his feet and walked over to the stage to inspect the contestants and their equipment. He handed a blue sash to one and a green sash to the other.

'Blue and Green are the traditional colours of the Hessenkraut *Verbindung* – student fraternity. This is also a *Schlagende Verbindung* – a Fighting fraternity – because its members are obliged to fight with swords.'

Schmidtt would have gone on to explain the finer points of the fraternity system when he was interrupted by the umpire who had begun a solemn address to the participants.

'He's telling them that there is a maximum of thirty rounds in the fight with five blows each per round,' Schmidtt explained. He gripped Kaplan's arm, communicating his own excitement to the American.

'Seconds, stand back!' the umpire called. 'On your guard, gentlemen! Fight!'

The first hit came within seconds, as Green aimed a slashing blow at Blue's face. The point of the sword neatly caught the top of Blue's left cheekbone and sliced it three clear inches in a diagonal line towards the corner of the mouth.

The whole room exploded with a roar of enthusiasm at one of the best and earliest strikes seen for years in a student duel.

'First hit to Green,' the umpire shouted. 'Stand back!' The contestants sprang apart, swords at the carry.

As the audience cheered, Blue's seconds came forward to dab the flesh where it was cut and bleeding. The contestants returned to the on-guard position.

'Ready, gentlemen. Fight!'

The two students once again began to hack away at each other. This time Blue was handicapped by the blood which continued to pour down his face. The students roared their support indiscriminately. What they wanted was action. Who won, who lost was of less concern.

'Another strike to Green! Stand back, gentlemen.'

It was a nasty slicing blow, which had carved the flesh from hair to jawline. There was loud booing from the audience.

'That one's going to need stitches later,' Schmidt commented, his professional interest evident. 'That's why the crowd is booing. The cuts are meant to be clean, and they are meant to heal without needing stiches. Stitches spoil the effect.'

'By God, they're purists, aren't they? Is Blue going to continue? Surely he'll give up now, won't he?'

Schmidtt looked at the man in the blue shirt, by now a hideous sight. The blood had run down and spattered his clothes.

'No, he won't give up. He's collected two scars, but he needs a third before being admitted into the cabal.'

'What's the cabal?'

'That's the inner circle of the Hessenkraut fraternity, the cream of the cream, if you like.'

'What about Green? Doesn't he want to collect some scars too?'

'Oh, Green's already a member of the cabal. He will have earned his scars some years back. He's simply volunteered to fight the novice, for whom tonight is a kind of initiation test.' His tone changed. 'Come, I think we've seen enough.'

They pushed through the crowd and back down the stairs the way they had come. After the noise of the fraternity house, the streets seemed very quiet and empty. They walked in silence, each one wrapped in his thoughts.

When they reached the Professor's house once more, it was evident that Frau Schmidtt had already gone to bed.

'Let's have a nightcap,' said Schmidtt, pouring two large balloons of brandy.

The two men settled into deep armchairs facing each

other.

The Professor was the first to speak.

'Lowell, my old friend.' Schmidtt looked fondly at the American. 'Why do you think I took you to the Hessenk-rauts' this evening?' When Kaplan did not reply, Schmidtt continued: 'I took you there because I wanted you to under-stand some things about us.'

'To tell the truth, Franz, I'm surprised the authorities al-low that kind of thing to go on at all.'

'They don't. Duelling is illegal today, just as it was in the 'sixties. In fact, in the 'sixties, it was even more anachro-nistic, as you would see it. Remember what it was like in Germany then. Remember the student movements and the power of some of the student leaders. Danny the Red, Rudy Dutshcke. In France, they toppled de Gaulle and brought Paris to a standstill. Here, in Germany, it was touch-and-go. There were riots in the streets, all right, but by a miracle there was no spark to light the powder-keg. But there could have been, by God, there could have been!'

'What do you mean?'

'I mean that what happened here in Marburg in 1967 could have provided the spark, could have rocked Germany to its foundations. Remember, this is a very tense country. We live in the shadow of the Soviet Union on the one hand and of the United States on the other. Materially, we might look good, but we have still not recovered as a nation from the trauma of the Second World War. Always, there are forces at work in our midst ready to exploit the divisions and tensions that exist.'

'Tell me about 1967.'

Schmidtt took a large sip of brandy and lit a cigar.

'Yes, I was here, all right,' he said. 'It was not long after I returned from the States that the trouble began. The Head of the Virology Department at the University was a remarkable woman called Irma Matthofer. She was about fifty years old, an extraordinarily able and forceful personality. She ruled her department with a rod of iron, drove herself and her colleagues hard, sometimes to the point of exhaustion. Her speciality was vaccines. She believed passionately that vaccination as a medical technique was the key – and a cost-effective one – to mankind's fight against viral diseases. Many would say, and not merely in Germany, that the development of polio vaccine, for example, owed as much to Frau or, I should say, Professor Matthofer's work as to that of Salk and Sabin; but she never received the credit, least of all from the Nobel Committee. She was bitter that her contribution had not been recognized, and I think she was probably right to feel bitter. It was a clear case of injustice.

'But what she felt personally was one thing; her professional life was another. Far from letting her disappointment deflect her from the central path of her research, she threw herself into her work with increased vigour, almost as a form of compensation, and drove her people harder than ever...'

'What was the line of her research?' Kaplan interrupted.

'Cholera. As you know, existing cholera vaccines have begun to lose their effect and in any case are difficult to mass-produce. She thought she was on the track of a totally new concept when the tragedy occurred.'

Professor Schmidtt rose to refill his glass before continuing. 'Back in the 'sixties,' Franz Schmidtt resumed his tale, 'medical research was a large consumer of imported animals. In Germany, the Marburg Clinic was one of the main culprits. I use the word deliberately. Over the last few years we have all come to realize that many animals needed for medical research can be custom-bred in Europe or America for the purpose. We don't have to raid nature for them.'

'I wish everyone felt the way you do,' Kaplan interjected. 'I know of centres in the United States today still importing wildlife in large quantities. And I'm talking about medical centres, not zoos.'

Schmidtt took the interruption in his stride. 'Fifteen or twenty years ago,' he continued, 'the Marburg Clinic, particularly the Virology Department under Frau Professor Matthofer, was importing large numbers of animals, mainly from Central Africa, where the export trade was well-organized. Monkeys especially were imported, of every shape or size. Some of them were used in toxicological research, much as they are today – although, of course, we have our home-grown varieties nowadays. But others were being used specifically in the Virology Department. What Irma Matthofer had in fact discovered – and the discovery was extremely important to medical science – was that the kidney cells of monkeys were invaluable as media for the culture of viral-based vaccines. They would thrive there as they would nowhere else.'

'Go on.' Kaplan was listening with rapt attention.

'Irma Matthofer grew increasingly excited as her research progressed. You have to understand something of our national psychology to realize just what her achievement meant. Germany as a nation, and the Germans as a race, have made notable contributions to scientific research, but these have not always been for the good of humanity. I need not elaborate. Frau Matthofer's monkey research was a different business. Here, perhaps for the first time, a German and, what is more, a German woman, would be responsible for a major medical breakthrough. Something that could do more to restore Germany's standing in the eyes of the world than almost anything else you can think of.'

'You are modest about your country's achievements.'

'Perhaps. But let me go on. Professor Matthofer was in full cry. It was in her nature to put maximum pressure upon her people. Inevitably, there was a slip-up. The monkeys were caged in the lab. One of Irma Matthofer's research assistants, a young chap called Peter Ringelmann, made some elementary error while handling an animal and got himself bitten. Shortly after, he fell ill. We believe that the source of his illness was the monkey bite. Five days later he died, exhibiting the symptoms which you, Lowell, have described and which you know only too well.'

'What happened after that?'

'Twenty-two other people died, every single one of them infected by Ringelmann. There was a positive contact in each case.'

'Good God! How can you be so sure?'

'Ringelmann had scars on his cheeks, freshly made scars. It was perfectly clear how they had been acquired; he was a member of a duelling fraternity. What only became clear later was that each and every one of the twenty-two other casualties had been present on the occasion of Ringelmann's initiation. Three of them had actually been his seconds. The rest must have been involved in one way or another. Perhaps they had handled the blood-stained clothes, or had been contaminated by sputum. There might even have been airborne transmission – we don't know.'

'Ah!' exclaimed Kaplan. 'So you didn't rule that out?'

'No, we couldn't. Anyway, the long and the short of it was that we had a potential scandal of the first magnitude on our hands. It wasn't just the deaths themselves that mattered, although, God knows, twenty-three out of twenty-three was – and is – pretty horrific...'

'To the best of my knowledge, an unprecedented medical phenomenon,' Kaplan commented.

'Exactly. But the extraordinary circumstances which surrounded the deaths were in a way more alarming. For, you see,' (he leaned forward in his chair), 'on the particular night that Peter Ringelmann fought his duel, the Chancellor of the Republic himself and two members of his cabinet were among the audience. Once a Hessenkraut, as I told you, always a Hessenkraut. If that had come out, think what the student revolutionaries would have made of it. The government would have been brought to its knees overnight. God knows what would have ensued.'

The Professor leaned back in his chair and was silent for a time.

Then he continued: 'That was why, when you mentioned the Marburg virus this evening, I pretended not to know. As far as Germany is concerned, we have buried the Marburg story and the Marburg virus. It didn't happen.'

'You didn't wholly succeed. I told you we had Marburg data on our computer file in Atlanta.'

Schmidtt shrugged the objection aside. 'I agree there were one or two references in the medical literature of the time. But these were purely concerned with the pathology of the incident. There was never any mention in the press of duelling or of the fact that the Chancellor was present on the fatal evening. We've kept the lid on the story for fifteen years.'

'Does it really matter if the story comes out now?'

A frightened look passed across Franz Schmidtt's face.

'I've already said more than I should. I had better keep quiet. But I beg you, Lowell, now that you know what happened, to keep it to yourself. Of course the story must not come out. In Germany, old politicians never die; they don't fade away either, they stick around. I said the Chancellor and two of his colleagues were there that night. That's not strictly true. Half the cabinet, and I mean today's cabinet, were there. It was a Gala occasion, the 400th anniversary of the Hessenkraut fraternity. They had all come down from Bonn for the occasion.'

'How the hell did you limit the outbreak?'

'We were lucky to be dealing with a controlled situation. We knew the names of everyone who had been in the fraternity house that evening. We took them all into preventive isolation. It stretched our facilities to the utmost, I can tell you.'

'Even the Chancellor?'

'Yes, even the Chancellor. We had him under observation for a fortnight. We gave out the story that he was indisposed with 'flu of a particularly severe kind.'

A thought suddenly occurred to Kaplan. 'How do you know all this, Franz?'

'My dear Lowell, I was there.'

'You mean you were a spectator at the duel.'

'No, I wasn't a spectator. I was a protagonist.' The words seemed to cost him an immense effort. 'I was the other man involved. I was the maestro that evening; Ringelmann, the novice. Do you remember when we were at Yale together that I represented the University at the sabre? I...'

Schmidtt seemed to have difficulty in completing his sentence. Kaplan got up and went to stand beside the other man's chair.

For the first time, he noted the scars which were

three-quarters hidden by the bushy sideburns.

'I'm so sorry, Franz,' he said quietly. 'So very sorry. If our computer hadn't thrown up the trace, I would never have come here to remind you of all this. And Heidi. It must have been terrible for her.'

'It was. For years we have lived under a cloud. Of course, in the most practical sense I didn't suffer, professionally speaking.'

'What do you mean?'

'I mean that when Professor Irma Matthofer was dismissed from the University, I received my promotion to be Head of the Toxicology Unit at the Clinic. That was the lucky break – for me, anyway. I felt sorry for Irma. It was yet another injustice coming on top of the first one. She didn't deserve it. She was just the sacrificial lamb. They cooked up some story about the unreasonable requests she had imposed upon her staff, leading to a breakdown in laboratory discipline.'

'Didn't anyone follow up the monkey lead? Wasn't any attempt made to find out which of the monkeys infected Peter Ringelmann and where it came from?'

'I told you 'no'. We had instructions from the highest political authorities that any follow-up of whatever sort would be regarded as treason.'

'Treason!' Kaplan was incredulous.

'Not just treason, but high treason!'

Kaplan lapsed into silence, trying to absorb what he had just heard. That the politicians had played the game with a heavy hand didn't surprise him, though the efforts at concealment struck him as somewhat exaggerated. He wondered fleetingly if there were some person or persons in high places with a reason, apart from the Hessenkraut affair, for keeping a tight lid on the Marburg incident. 'And that's where matters have rested for over fifteen years?' he asked at last.

'Until you came along, the file has been dead. I beg you, Lowell,' (he leaned forward), 'leave it that way. I fear I have been dangerously indiscreet. If you start stirring things up, no good will come of it.'

Lowell Kaplan's voice was gentle. 'Franz, you know I can't leave things the way they are. There was one outbreak of Marburg virus back in 1967. You were lucky and got it under control. There was a second outbreak this year in the United States. This time *we* were lucky; we got it under control. But one thing I promise you, Franz, if there's another outbreak, we will not be lucky again.'

'Third time unlucky?'

'You said it.'

Schmidtt saw Kaplan to the door. On the step, Kaplan paused for a moment.

'By the way, what happened to Irma Matthofer after she was dismissed?'

Schmidtt hesitated for a fraction of a second. 'I just don't know. It was a great mystery. She just disappeared from one day to another.'

'And the cholera vaccine programme?'

'We dropped it like a hot potato. From the moment that monkey bit Ringelmann, the vaccine programme was doomed. We leave cholera to the World Health Organization.'

Kaplan walked back to his hotel through the sleepy streets. The floodlights on the Schloss had been turned out. The roistering students had gone home. The river Lahn ran quietly beneath the bridges of the old town. It all seemed so peaceful. And yet how much had gone on beneath the surface.

Tomorrow, he would begin digging.

★

He arrived at the Clinic early the next morning. Thinking about the problem overnight, Kaplan had decided that it was worth, even after such a lapse of time, trying to discover more about the source of Ringelmann's infection. Had a monkey really been responsible? If so, where did it come from? Was there any surviving documentation on shipments of monkeys brought to Marburg from Africa in the late 'sixties? Another reason for heading in the direction of the University was the fact that the Schmidtts' strange but attractive daughter, Paula, was now Head of Medical Records at the Clinic. It seemed too good an opportunity to be missed.

Paula Schmidtt, when he finally located her office, seemed surprised to see him.

'I wasn't expecting to see you up bright and early this morning. I hear you and father had rather a late night.'

'Yes. It was late. We were talking.'

'And drinking!' She smiled. 'I saw the glasses when I came down this morning.'

As they sat together in the cramped but well-ordered room, Kaplan looked at his old friend's daughter appraisingly. As he had already had cause to observe, young Paula had grown up into a handsome woman. Her dark hair, like her mother's, was pulled back from her forehead and tied neatly behind. Her brown eyes looked at him steadily. Her expression was composed; almost, Kaplan thought, too controlled. It was as though she had learned to discipline herself to the exclusion of all frivolity. He could sense that she was a woman of strong convictions, though he was not so sure that they were convictions of a kind he would wish to share.

'Tell me,' she said. 'How can I help? My father told me at breakfast today that he tried to dissuade you from looking into the question of the Marburg virus, but that you are not inclined to be discouraged.' She looked at him frankly.

'My father is frightened, Lowell. He truly believes it is better to let sleeping dogs lie.'

'And do you believe that?'

She was silent for a while. The expression on her face indicated that she was pondering a particularly difficult question.

'No,' she finally replied. 'The past is the past, and the

present is the present. After fifteen years, you are trying to track down the source of the original Marburg outbreak. You think it may help to understand what happened in this recent outbreak. I'm prepared to help you, Lowell, because I believe in the truth.'

Lowell Kaplan did not doubt the conviction with which the young woman spoke. He wondered, nevertheless, whether Paula Schmidtt, a product of West Germany's radical 'sixties, would ever truly take sides with someone like himself, whose bags and baggage were so clearly marked with the stamp of the U.S. Government.

Brushing these reflections aside, he expressed his gratitude for her cooperation and came straight to the point: 'Franz told me that the student Ringelmann was bitten by one of the laboratory animals – a monkey – during an experiment. Apparently there was a lapse in the handling precautions. From what Franz told me the presumption has always been that the monkey was the original vector of the Marburg virus. My question is: were any tests done on the animal and do you have records of those tests?'

She shook her head. 'I've talked to my father about this in the past. Yes, we think a monkey was responsible. Ringelmann, before he lapsed into insanity, said he thought he might have been bitten, though we were never able to find any skin punctures.'

'Did you do an autopsy?'

'No. We ruled that out straightaway as being too dangerous. Ringelmann's body was incinerated without autopsy.'

Kaplan nodded. 'We had a similar problem in New York. Mind you, I couldn't get the people to do the autopsy anyway. They just refused point blank.'

Paula Schmidtt smiled in sympathy. 'In Germany, workers never refuse to work!'

She resumed her story. 'So we never knew if Ringelmann had indeed been bitten by a monkey. And, if he had, we certainly never knew which monkey. In view of the nature of Ringelmann's illness, we thought it best to take no chances at all. It was decided to gas every single monkey being held for research purposes at the Clinic at that time. They were gassed without being moved, in their cages or wherever they were to be found. Their bodies were disposed of under safe and sterile conditions.'

'How?'

'All the research animals together with any materials associated with them were incinerated at temperatures of over 1000°F. A whole wing of the Clinic was closed down, and it didn't reopen for six months.'

Kaplan sensed that this enquiry was leading nowhere. He could see that Paula Schmidtt was trying to be helpful, but they weren't moving in the right direction.

'So you have no records of any tests performed on the monkeys themselves.'

'No.'

'Do you know where the monkeys came from?'

Once more she shook her head. 'I thought my father told you that the whole issue was shoved under the mat.

There were no enquiries. We came through in 1967 by the skin of our teeth. Nobody was going to start rocking the boat by instituting enquiries which had been expressly forbidden on the highest authority.'

He pressed her. 'But say you had wished to make enquiries? Would you have been able to? Back in 1967, were proper records kept of the movement of animals, of the arrival and departure of monkeys, and so on?'

Paula Schmidt drew herself up proudly. It was almost as though he had issued a challenge. 'In Germany, we always keep records.' She gave a wave of her hand. 'In this building, we have records going back for the last ten years. Every single patient who has passed through this clinic, every single experiment which has been conducted, has been fully documented, and you will find the details here on microfilm.'

'What about fifteen years ago and more? Do you still have those records?'

She shook her head. 'Not here. Not at the Clinic.' Then she appeared to remember something. 'There's just a chance that there are some old records at the Schloss. We used to store them there before the new Clinic was built. In the old days, most of the medical department was up by the Landgraf Schloss. They may still have some files there, although I believe they've begun a programme to clear most of the old stuff away because they need the space for a tourist cafeteria.'

Kaplan leaped to his feet, as though every moment

counted. 'Do you know your way around up there, Paula? Do you think we might go and take a look?'

She appeared to hesitate. 'Well, I've got a lot of work to finish off here...' Then she paused, seeing how important it was for him. 'All right, I'll come, but I don't hold out much hope.'

She had her car at the Clinic, and she took him with her. They parked in the forecourt of the Schloss and walked up to the entrance. There was a souvenir shop-cum-ticket-office in the gate-house. Paula Schmidtt showed her university card to the guard.

'Are all those old records still stored in the basement?'

'Basement? What basement?' The old man laughed. 'We have dungeons here, not basements.'

The cold hit them when they went below. The staircase led deep into the bowels of the castle. Mediaeval suits of armour, with slit-eyed visors, jumped out at them around corners. Ancient instruments of torture hung from the walls.

They came eventually to a large storage area filled with filing cabinets, boxes of various dimensions and piles of loose dossiers. 'Good God!' Paula sounded despondent. 'I don't see how we can find anything here.'

'Let's give it a try anyway.'

It was Lowell Kaplan who found it. For half an hour they had poked through the junk. More than once, Paula had seemed to suggest that it would be a fruitless search and that they might as well give up. But the American was not easily deterred. The 1967 records were the only lead he had. If he couldn't find them, he was really back at the beginning.

Paula Schmidtt was watching him as he opened the last drawer of the last filing cabinet. He pulled out a large, dog-eared, floppy-covered book.

'Paula, come over here.'

She was beside him in a moment, and took the book from him. 'I think you've found something.'

The legend on the cover of the book had faded somewhat, but it was still clear enough to read. She read the German words first and then translated. 'It says: 'Marburg University Clinic – Records of animals imported for research purposes – 1960 to 1969'. Perhaps this is what we are looking for.'

She turned over the pages quickly until she came to the entries for February and March, 1967. Each entry recorded the arrival of a crate of monkeys for use in Professor Irma Matthofer's cholera vaccine research program. The records showed the date and approximate location of the animals' capture.

They looked at the sheet together.

'They seem to come from all different parts of Africa,' said Kaplan. 'Zaire, Uganda, Tanzania, Chad, Upper Volta – it's hard to know where to begin. I don't see how we could pin anything down with this kind of variety to choose from.'

Kaplan studied the sheet. 'Do you think I could take this

book away?'

Paula Schmidtt looked doubtful. 'Better not.' She laughed nervously. 'I know it may sound funny seeing the state they're in, but I'm meant to be responsible for these records, too. As Head of Records, I couldn't let you or anyone else remove one of the books.'

Kaplan was about to protest that if he hadn't found the book, no one would have known it was there anyway. But he thought better of it. He didn't want to push his luck.

'Can I copy some of these entries down then? There may be something there which we don't see at the moment.'

'Go ahead. I'll read them out if you like. I'm sorry we don't have a photocopy machine down here. There didn't seem to be a need for one.'

Kaplan laughed. 'It won't take us long.'

He began to write as she read out the details.

'Feb 24, 1967. 20 forest guenons, caught central Congo basin, location approx. longitude...; latitude...; 15 talapoins, caught Senegal, location approx. longitude...; latitude...; 6 patas monkeys, caught savannah area of northern Uganda, location approx. longitude...; latitude...'

She had reached the seventh item on the list when her tone, which had begun to register boredom, changed.

'Hello! Here's a consignment which has been delivered to Peter Ringelmann himself. Look, he's signed in the margin.'

Kaplan looked. There, sure enough, was the name of the dead man. He read the details.

'March 10, 1967. 20 green monkeys, caught Kugumba region eastern Zaire, location approx. longitude...; latitude... For use of Professor Matthofer. Transit via Kinshasha and Brussels.'

Brussels! Kaplan felt suddenly excited. Diane Verusio had contracted the Marburg virus a few days after passing through Brussels airport. Fifteen years earlier, a shipment of monkeys destined to be used by a man who later died of Marburg fever had passed in transit through Brussels. Surely there was a connection there somewhere, however remote.

He looked at Paula. 'What do you think? Do you think that was the bunch we're looking for? Do you think Ringelmann was signing his own death warrant?'

She shook her head. 'It doesn't mean anything. Look.' She pointed to several entries further down the page. 'Ringelmann has signed for those, too.'

He saw that she was right.

'Oh.' There was no concealing his disappointment. 'I thought we might have had something there.'

She shrugged, strangely offhand. 'You may have something or again you may not. It's impossible to tell.' When they had finished their work, they climbed up the stairs again, handed the keys back to the guard and went to the car.

'Can I drop you somewhere?'

'The Waldeckerhof, if it's not out of your way. My car's there.'

At the hotel, instead of embracing as they had when they first met, they shook hands rather formally.

'You've been very kind, Paula.'

'Don't mention it. I hope you find what you're looking for. By the way...' – she asked the question with studied casualness – 'will we see you at home this evening, or are you on your way somewhere?'

Kaplan made up his mind. For the time being he had learned all he could in Marburg.

'I'm going to Brussels.'

The woman raised her eyebrows. 'Brussels?'

Kaplan was more specific. 'Brussels airport, to be precise.'

She nodded, dead-pan, and drove off, leaving him standing there. Kaplan felt puzzled. There was something about this handsome young woman which he did not fully understand.

CHAPTER FIVE

KAPLAN HAD A QUICK LUNCH at the hotel and was *en route* by half-past one. He decided to stick to the autobahn all the way to Brussels. In other circumstances, he would have been inclined to take in cities like Cologne and Aachen on his way; but today was different. He felt compelled by an increasing sense of urgency. Thank God the Germans had refused to introduce speed limits on their autobahns. He put his foot down hard on the accelerator pedal of the large black Mercedes which he had hired at Frankfurt, and moved into the fast lane.

After the Belgian frontier, he slowed down. The Belgians took a different view of speeding. But with the needle hovering around the 140 k.p.h. mark, it still took little more than an hour on the relatively empty E5 to reach the outskirts of Brussels.

He looked at his watch, and saw that it was already six o'clock in the evening. He hesitated. He could go on to the airport in the hope of finding a responsible Belgian official still at his desk, unlikely at that hour, or he could postpone the task until the following day and drive straight to the château.

It had been a long, gruelling day and he decided he had

earned a break. At the next intersection, he cut across from the E5 to the E10 and swung south on the road to Namur. The Mercedes clipped a corner of the Forêt de Soignes as he turned down a country road signposted 'CHATEAU D'HUART: 10 kilomètres. Privé.'

The guard on the gate was ready for him. 'Monsieur Kaplan?'

'Oui, merci.'

With an unctuous smile, the guard waved him through.

Kaplan drove over broad undulating land. The harvest was beginning to ripen. Two or three times, pheasants whirred away from under the wheels of his car. Count Philippe Vincennes was reputed to have one of the best private shoots in Belgium, some said in Europe. Kaplan passed through forests, where the trees stretched upwards to form a seemingly endless canopy. He forded two streams whose water sparkled white in the early evening sun. The Belgians certainly knew how to enjoy their wealth, he thought as he cruised – now at a much easier pace – towards his destination. A strange people, *les Belges!* An idiosyncratic nation, torn apart by linguistic rivalries, yet amid all the tension there remained these astonishing oases of wealth, privilege and power. Men like Philippe Vincennes might stay out of sight, protected by 6000 hectares of their own land and guarded night and day by a score of faithful retainers, but out of sight was by no means out of mind. The king would not dream of asking Monsieur X or Monsieur Y to form a new administration without first soliciting the advice of men like Vincennes. He might not always follow their counsel, but when he didn't he usually regretted it

The château came into sight round a long bend; it was breathtaking in its magnificence. It had a long low front of soft grey-yellow stone. The shuttered windows gave out onto a cobbled courtyard on one side; on the other they took in the great sweep of the Forêt de Soignes. At either end, slender slate-roofed turrets had been built which added grace to the château's evident solidity. Kaplan pulled the car off the road at the entrance to a carttrack which ran off to the right, and for a few moments allowed his eye to absorb the scene. It was usual, he reflected, for tourists to Europe to enthuse about the famous châteaux of the Loire valley. Few people realized that, within 50 kilometres of Brussels, some of the finest château architecture in the whole of Europe was to be found. If these gems were little known, it was because they remained largely in private hands, hands of men like Philippe Vincennes who had been astute enough and rich enough to buy at a time when the original owners were begging to be relieved of their crushing burden.

His eye ranged past the château towards the east. In the far distance, he could see the line of the motorway leading to Brussels. Nearer at hand, some workmen were engaged on tree-felling operations. As he sat there, taking it all in, a herd of cattle numbering two or three hundred head moved slowly across the frame from left to right. The magical, almost film-world quality of the place hadn't changed.

It was five years, thought Kaplan, since he had visited Count and Countess Vincennes at home, and then by invitation of their eldest son, Louis, whom, like Franz Schmidtt, he had met at Graduate School in the States. Louis had encouraged him to visit the family whenever he happened to be in the vicinity.

Kaplan had telephoned before leaving Marburg, and had been agreeably surprised at the warmth with which his call was received. Covering the last few yards of the drive, he remembered the conversation. He was hoping, he told the Count, to see the whole family.

'Ah, but Louis is away,' the Count had apologized. 'He is in Zaire on business.'

Kaplan's attention had been altered by the reference to Zaire. Of course, the Vincennes family, with a finger in most pies, would certainly have dealings with the former Belgian Congo, but Kaplan was struck by the coincidence of one reference to Zaire as the provenance of a shipload of monkeys being so quickly followed by another.

In spite of Louis' absence, the Count had pressed Kaplan to pay them a visit. 'Hélèna and I are always glad to see our friends, particularly from the United States. You know, we are becoming quite reclusive in our old age.'

'I can hardly believe that, Count,' Kaplan answered. The hospitality of the Vincennes was legendary.

'And what brings you to Brussels, Lowell?' the Count asked. 'Pleasure, I hope?'

'Not entirely.' Kaplan was evasive. 'I'm on the track of something.'

'What, some strange disease in Belgium?'

'Well, I have to make some enquiries. To do with the transit of wildlife through the airport.'

The Count had exclaimed: 'Wildlife at Brussels airport! How extremely interesting!' And he had repeated his invitation in unexpectedly forceful terms.

Unable to shake off the feeling that he was really an actor on a movie-set, Kaplan swung round in a wide arc and berthed the Mercedes in front of the main door. The wheels scrunched on the gravel and there was a rich and satisfying clunk as he shut the car door behind him.

The Count himself came out to meet him. Philippe Vincennes was a well-preserved sixty-five. Immaculately dressed in a blue blazer and fawn slacks, deeply tanned, with brilliantly white teeth and a fine head of silver hair, he had that totally relaxed air which only great riches can provide.

'Lowell, how good to see you!' His command of English was perfect.

A couple of servants hurried forward, competing to carry Kaplan's case inside.

'Perhaps you would like to see your room and then join me for a drink on the terrace? We will dine around eight. I have asked one or two friends whom I thought you might like to meet to join us.'

Kaplan raised a mental eyebrow. It seemed as though Count Philippe Vincennes had already arranged something for his benefit. He wondered what it was.

Forty minutes later, when he had washed and changed, Kaplan came out to find his host on the terrace. They looked out onto a magnificent avenue of trees.

'The longest beech drive in Europe,' the Count explained. 'Planted shortly after the battle of Waterloo.' He surveyed his domain with a practised eye. 'You see that forest in the middle-distance there? That's where Blücher's army was resting when the word came that the battle of Waterloo had already been engaged. If Blücher had not force-marched his men across country, Napoleon would have won and the course of history would have been changed. What was it that the Duke of Wellington said after the battle of Waterloo?'

'A damned close-run thing.' Kaplan was prepared to show that he too had studied history.

A servant came out onto the terrace and refilled their tall-stemmed champagne glasses. When he had withdrawn, the Count addressed Kaplan smoothly: 'You must be used to 'close-run things' in your work, Lowell, but surely not in connection with Brussels airport? I was interested in what you said on the telephone about the transit of wildlife.' The Count paused. When he spoke again, his rich-brown face gleamed with fervour. 'I can assure you that there is absolutely no export of live animals through Belgium. I have spoken with my friend, Willy van Broyck, who is the Minister for Trade and in charge of such things, and he has given me his categorical assurance that there has been no such traffic for the past several years. He will be here tonight, and you may speak to him yourself.'

Kaplan was astonished at the trouble which Count Philippe Vincennes had gone to on his behalf. He had just begun to thank his host when other guests were shown out on to the terrace, and the Count rose to greet them. Some twenty persons altogether had been invited. They included the British Ambassador to Belgium and his wife, a Turk who was NATO's Deputy Secretary General and a small dapper man with sharp mobile eyes who turned out to be Willy van Broyck, the Minister for Trade. Kaplan found himself trying to make conversation with van Broyck's wife, an ugly Flemish woman who spoke little French and less English. He was relieved when the signal was given for the party to go into dinner, a sumptuous affair which Hélèna, the Count's wife, insisted on referring to as a 'modest family supper.' There was a flunkey behind every chair. Wine flowed in abundance. Course followed course with bewildering variety, each more exquisite than the last.

'Woodcock shot on the estate.' The Count beamed down the length of the long table. Kaplan, from the other end, where he sat on the Countess' right, saw the old man's reflection upside down on the polished surface. There was something faintly sinister about it. He was not sure he would care to be a woodcock on the Count's estate.

After the cheese and the dessert, the Count called for port and liqueurs, and Hélèna Vincennes led the ladies out of the room. The men moved towards the Count's end of the table and reseated themselves.

Kaplan found himself next to Willy van Broyck. Evidently not concerned with pleasantries, the little man came straight to the point.

'The Count tells me, Mr Kaplan, that you propose to investigate our airport for the traffic of wildlife. You are wasting your time, you know. My country rigorously enforces the Washington Convention on the Protection of Endangered Species.'

'I'm sure, Mr van Broyck. I'm more interested in what has happened in the past. I understand there was quite active trade through Brussels...'

'I do not think that is so, Mr Kaplan.'

'Forgive me, but...'

'The past is the past,' the Minister interrupted sharply, and turned to his neighbour.

Kaplan was left with the distinct impression that the Minister was posting a KEEP OUT sign on this particular stretch of territory. He suspected that the message came as much from Count Vincennes as it did from van Broyck.

This impression was confirmed when, later in the evening, after they had joined the ladies, Kaplan noticed van Broyck engaged in earnest, muttered conversation with the Count. More than once, he saw them glance in his direction. After a while, the Count excused himself from van Broyck and left the room. When he returned, Kaplan observed that his splendid white hair was slightly damp, as if he had been caught in a shower.

By eleven o'clock the other guests had gone home.

Kaplan told his hosts that he proposed to take a quick turn on the terrace before himself retiring for the night. Outside, he bent down and touched the grass. It was wet; it had indeed rained during the evening. He went back into the house, reflecting on the events of the day. Beneath the surface glitter of the company and the lavishness of the arrangements, he could detect an ominous undercurrent: there was something rotten, something dangerous in the air. He wanted to find out what it was. He felt sure that there was more to Count Philippe Vincennes than met the eye. On previous occasions when he had visited the château in the company of Louis Vincennes, the Count's son, he had had the same impression. Tonight it had been confirmed. He felt sure that the Count and van Broyck had been talking about him. And why had the Count disappeared outside like that in the middle of the evening?

Kaplan's room was on the first floor of the château, above the courtyard. The bed was turned down and he noted that his pyjamas had been taken from his suitcase and laid on the pillow. He wondered which of the Count's servants had been responsible for that little gesture. Had the man, or woman, who unpacked his pyjamas also been through his things in a systematic way?

He put his hand to the bottom of the case. The report was where he had left it, under a pile of shirts. Kaplan didn't believe it had been disturbed but he could not tell for sure. He took the document out of the case and sat down on the bed to reread for the second time Diane Verusio's report on vivisection and the use of monkeys in medical research. As he picked it up he could not help visualizing the scene as it had confronted him that fraught afternoon in Greenwich Village. He could see the unmade bed, the clothes on the floor, the photograph on the mantelpiece. Diane Verusio would never go back to Greenwich Village but Kaplan knew the moment he first read her report that she had not died in vain.

He flipped through the passages, reminding himself of the key passages. Instinctively he felt sure that there was a connection between the trade in endangered species, as investigated by Diane Verusio, and the incidence of Marburg disease. He had learned from Franz Schmidtt that monkeys from Africa had been suspected as the cause of the original outbreak. Diane Verusio had been investigating the trade in monkeys and then had gone down with the disease. Surely there was a connection between the two! There just had to be.

'Almost all major medical research centers in Western Europe and indeed in the Soviet Union are involved,' he read:

'The trade in live animals, often animals belonging to rare and endangered species, is probably worth over US $3,000 million annually. Africa is at the heart of this trade, being the source and origin of many of the animals, especially monkeys and other primates, used for research purposes. One of the key questions the author of this report has attempted to answer is: Just how do the animals enter Europe? In theory, all European governments have undertaken obligations in the context of various international conventions which would make importation impossible. In practice, it is clear that these obligations are being breached, and breached in the most blatant manner.'

Later in the report, Diane Verusio examined the various ways in which live animals were entering into trade. Kaplan could not help admiring, as he had done the first time he had read the report, the thoroughness with which the author had done her work.

He came to another underlined passage:

'Apart from the entry into Europe of certain Asian species, e.g. rare parrots via Hong Kong and London (a loophole which the British authorities are determined to close), the most probable route for major illegal importation is Belgium. With its close links to Zaire, which as the Belgian Congo was a former Belgian colony of major importance, Belgium – and in particular Zaventem airport at Brussels – is the ideal 'entrepôt' or staging-post for the illegal trade in wild animals. High Belgian officials, politicians and other prominent men are thought to be involved...'

Kaplan put the report away, burying it once more at the bottom of his suitcase. With men like Philippe Vincennes around, it was hardly sensible to have thirty pages of dynamite lying on one's coffee table. He turned the light out and drifted into sleep.

The Count was up to see him off at eight o'clock. He looked remarkably fit and spry for a man of sixty-five or so.

This morning he was wearing a navy-blue blazer with gold buttons, a pale blue silk shirt with a cravat, cream trousers and a pair of white canvas shoes. He smiled at his guest benignly.

'Ah! my dear Lowell! Did they give you breakfast? Did you try the 'jambon d'Ardennes'? I've always thought it goes down very well at breakfast. Particularly with figs.'

'A marvellous breakfast,' he replied. 'And thank you so much for your hospitality. Give my best regards to Louis when he gets back from Africa.'

The Count, standing on the steps in front of his château, waved him off and watched the long black car accelerate away.

Kaplan came to the bend in the drive. He remembered it was here, where woodmen had been working in the forest at the roadside, that he had stopped the previous afternoon on the château side to admire the view. Travelling in the opposite direction, he turned the steering wheel of the car to the left and saw the château slide out of view in his rear-vision mirror.

It was just as he was preparing to accelerate into the bend that he saw the tree across the road. He made a split-second decision. The tree had not been there the previous evening. There had been no storm in the night which might have brought it down. If the tree was where it was now it had been put there for a purpose. He had a fleeting mental image of the Count coming back into the room with damp hair, and he made up his mind. He jammed his foot on the brake and flung the Mercedes into reverse. He was already round the bend and out of sight of the tree, reversing at some 25 k.p.h. and gaining pace, when he heard the sound of machine-gun fire. Simultaneously, a tattoo of bullets ripped along the coachwork of the roof of the car. Kaplan kept going. Once over the bridge, he backed the car into a clearing and roared forward once more, back in the direction of the château. He reckoned time was on his side. Whoever had laid the ambush was now on the wrong side of the tree for easy pursuit.

As he swung off the drive down the cart-track where he had pulled in the previous day, he caught a glimpse of the château. There was no tall figure standing on the front steps; the Count had obviously gone inside. The motorway ran to the east. Kaplan did not stand on ceremony. He crushed the first two gates he came across. There was something gratifying about the sound of splintering wood.

He made ground rapidly and paused at the top of a rise to see if he could detect any sign of pursuit. The countryside seemed peaceful. In the distance, the turrets of Count Philippe Vincennes' château were shedding the last traces of morning mist. Whoever it was who had fired at him, Kaplan concluded, had now given up.

However, he had no wish to linger on enemy territory. He could see the Namur–Brussels motorway across a field of wheat. He hoped it was the Count's wheat. He put the car at the standing crop as a hunt follower might put his horse at a hedge, and smashed diagonally across the field. He hit the hard shoulder of the motorway at around 50 k.p.h. and pulled neatly into the stream of morning traffic.

As he drove he found he was trembling. In his work for the Atlanta Center for Disease Control Kaplan had from time to time been exposed to considerable danger. Anyone who worked with lethal pathogens took risks. But this was the first time to his knowledge that someone had taken a pot shot at him and he found the experience unnerving. He kept an eye on the rear-vision mirror. He doubted if he was being followed. Not by the Count's men at least. No one else had taken the cornfield route to the office that morning. But still it paid to take precautions.

He didn't go right on into the city. Instead he took the ring road to Zaventem. In the parking-lot at the airport he sat for some time in the car, trying to work things out. He had a feeling that he had been on his own long enough and that quite soon now he was going to need assistance.

He left his car in the parking-lot. Apart from a line of bulletholes in the coachwork and corn in the front bumper, the rented Mercedes was not much the worse for wear.

When he entered the terminal, Lowell Kaplan had no very clear idea of what his next step ought to be. Of one thing, however, he was quite certain: he needed a large cup of hot coffee.

There was a restaurant on the upper level and he made directly for it, picking up an *International Herald Tribune* on the way. He stopped in mid-stride when he saw his old friend Franz Schmidtt's photograph on the front page and the caption: GERMAN TOXICOLOGY EXPERT FOUND SHOT.

'Jesus Christ.' Kaplan could hardly believe it.

Shocked, he fetched his coffee and sat down with the paper. The story didn't go into details. Apparently the Professor had been surprised in his study at home the previous afternoon. There was no indication as to who the intruder was, nor why the Professor should have been attacked. There followed a brief résumé of Schmidtt's career.

As he sat there, Kaplan wondered whether Schmidtt's sudden death might in some way be linked to his own visit to Marburg and to the conversations which they had had. Had the bluff and genial Franz Schmidtt been talking out of turn? Could his house have been bugged? Would the German authorities have gone to such lengths as to actually murder the man to ensure that a story which they had first suppressed over fifteen years earlier stayed buried? It was sheer speculation, of course; but in the light of the attempt on his own life that morning it did not seem to be wholly improbable. Kaplan realized that he was getting into murky waters.

Arming himself with a fistful of five-franc pieces, he went to a phone and looked up the international code for Germany. Frau Schmidtt herself answered.

'Heidi! It's me, Lowell Kaplan. I just heard the news. This is dreadful.'

'God damn you, Lowell.' The hatred in her voice was unmistakable. 'You should never have come. You should never have got him to talk…'

'Heidi! I never realized…' Kaplan was talking to himself because the line had gone dead.

He went back to the restaurant and ordered another coffee. Shocked by the conversation he had just had with Schmidtt's widow, he needed time to recover. He sat at the table and stared bleakly at the runway where the morning traffic was already building up.

'Excusez-moi, est-ce que la place est libre?'

Kaplan looked round to see a man of about forty, with thinning red hair and a ginger moustache standing by the table. He wore a blue SABENA uniform with a perspex ID card stuck to his breast pocket.

'Help yourself.'

The man took a seat and ordered breakfast. While waiting for his coffee and croissants to arrive, he asked Kaplan:

'Are you English?'

'American.' Kaplan's response was gruff. He didn't want to engage in small talk.

'Ah, where are you going?'

'I'm not going anywhere, actually. I'm just visiting the airport today.' Kaplan looked at the SABENA ID on the man's lapel and an idea occurred to him. Perhaps it would be worth making conversation after all.

'I guess you work here.'

'Yes. I just came off the night-shift. I like to have breakfast before heading home.'

'You guys speak English pretty well.'

'We have to. Even if I didn't work for SABENA, I'd probably still speak English. With the Walloons fighting the Flamands and vice-versa, English is a kind of neutral language.' He laughed.

'What kind of work do you do here?'

'I'm on the cargo side. I'd say half the business of this airport is cargo.' The Belgian looked out of the window towards the tarmac apron. 'See that Air Zaire 747. That makes four flights a week to Kinshasha. Exclusively cargo.'

Kaplan felt his interest quicken. 'What kind of cargo?'

There was a momentary hesitation in the man's reply.

'Oh, any number of things. Anything you can think of. Don't forget the links between Belgium and Zaire are very close. The Zairian President still comes to Brussels every two months or so to pick up his instructions. He even keeps a house here, more of a palace really, in Uccle, which is one of the French-speaking quarters.'

Lowell Kaplan decided to play a hunch. He took out his card. 'Look, I wonder if you can help me. I'm from the U.S. Government. I'm with the Center for Disease Control in Atlanta, Georgia. My job is to track down exotic diseases at home and abroad, wherever such diseases can threaten the health of the people of the United States.'

The man seemed impressed. 'I've heard of the Atlanta Center. You do a good job.' He offered Kaplan his hand. 'By the way, my name is Jean Delgrave.'

Kaplan gave the man the necessary background. It took some time and Delgrave listened throughout with close attention.

'So you see,' Kaplan concluded, 'we believe that the girl may have contracted the disease right here at Zaventem, and that the vector may have been an animal, probably a monkey imported for medical research purposes. Does any of this sound possible? Is there still trade in live animals through Zaventem? I know that under the Washington Convention, states undertake to prohibit the import into, or transit through, their territories of animals belonging to rare and endangered species. But I wondered...'

Delgrave laughed out loud, interrupting him. 'My dear sir, you don't really believe all that, do you?' He looked quickly around the bar and lowered his voice. 'Don't you know that this is a multi-million dollar business? You can't stamp out the trade in wild animals just by signing a paper. I'll tell you something.' He lowered his voice still further. 'I see cargo transiting every day through Zaventem in flagrant breach of the Washington Convention. Some of the biggest names in Belgium are involved. Of course, I turn a blind eye. We all do.'

'Why don't you protest?'

'I have a job. I don't want to lose that job. If my superiors in the SABENA hierarchy don't mind, why should I mind? Look at that plane,' he pointed out of the window to the Air Zaire aircraft. 'She came in this morning. She hasn't been unloaded yet. They park it on the apron there, off to one side and they wait till dark before they take the stuff off.'

'What stuff?'

'The livestock, the animals. There was a time when

half of them would be dead. The conditions were terrible. Cooped up in cages for forty-eight hours and more with no food or water. And God knows how long they'd been held before that at the collecting camps in Zaire or other parts of Africa.'

'Are conditions better now?'

'Yes, they are. The people who run this trade realize it's bad business letting the animals die. They lose money and they don't like losing money.'

Jean Delgrave stood up abruptly. 'I've said too much. It's too dangerous. I shouldn't be seen here talking to you.'

Kaplan took the point. He remembered the ambush he had nearly fallen into a couple of hours earlier. He wanted live witnesses, not dead ones.

'Look, Mr Delgrave. You've got to understand one thing. I am an epidemiologist. I'm only interested in the trade in live animals in so far as this trade proves to be the cause of infection that could have consequences for health in the United States. Enforcement of international treaties to which Belgium is a signatory is your concern, not mine.'

'The big men behind the trade won't see it like that. If you pursue your enquiries, whatever your motive, they'll see you as a threat. And then – watch out.'

Kaplan pressed him: 'Can you meet me later? Tonight? Somewhere we won't be observed.'

'Why? What more can I tell you?'

'I want details of cargo movements in Zaventem at the beginning of June this year, especially June 5. I want to know, for example, if live monkeys from Africa were transiting through here at that time.'

Delgrave was incredulous. 'There are no records of this trade.'

'Of course there are records.' Kaplan coaxed the man to his point of view. 'There are always records. There will be false records for the international inspectors who exist only to be duped, and there will be true records for the men who run the business.'

A shifty look crossed the Belgian's face.

'It may be expensive. I may have to bribe certain people.'

As soon as the man mentioned money, Kaplan knew that he had him where he wanted him.

'Funds will not be a problem. Believe me, when the United States wants some information, we are prepared to pay for it. And pay well.'

Jean Delgrave smiled. The scraggy ginger moustache turned up at the corners.

'I'll do my best.'

Kaplan had one last request. 'Delgrave, can you spare me your ID till this evening? You won't need it until you come back on duty, will you? I'd like to have a look around.'

Jean Delgrave's initial reluctance was overcome when Kaplan pressed ten thousand Belgian francs into his hand.

'That's on account. For expenses. There will be more later.'

Kaplan pinned Delgrave's plastic ID to his lapel. The faces weren't very similar. Delgrave's – at least in the photo – had a narrow pinched look which Kaplan didn't much fancy. But no one ever looked at the photos – not in his experience anyway. Having the badge was what counted.

When Delgrave had left, Kaplan sat for a few minutes finishing his coffee. Then, looking quite plausibly like a SABENA official going home after night duty, he walked out of the building. Instead of making for the carpark, Kaplan turned left and made his way round to the perimeter gate. There was a guard on duty who showed absolutely no interest as Kaplan, wearing the badge and looking purposeful, strode on through.

There was no one standing near the Air Zaire plane, as Kaplan walked straight up the steps. Fifteen minutes later, he came down them again. He had never felt so shaken in his life.

Shortly after one p.m., Lowell Kaplan drove his rented Mercedes with the corn still stuck in the bumper and the bullet-holes still in the roof, inside the tall security gates of the U.S. embassy on Brussels' Boulevard de la Régence. Seconds after that, he was checked through the security grill by the marines and escorted up to Tim Boswell's office.

Boswell, number two in the U.S. mission, was a tall lanky man who was occasionally mistaken for John Kenneth Galbraith. His and Kaplan's paths had crossed in Washington once or twice when Kaplan had been at N.I.H. and Boswell, who was a career diplomat, had one of his periodical domestic assignments at the State Department.

'Lowell, good to see ya' – the tall Bostonian drawled. 'You seem to be in a bit of a scrape.'

Kaplan sat on a leather sofa facing the U.S. flag. Behind the desk, the gilded bald-eagle crest and signed portrait of the President indicated that Boswell was a ranking foreign service officer. The diplomat stretched out his long legs across the rug and lit his pipe.

'The cablegrams announcing your Marburg visit were copied to us,' he said. 'But that was routine distribution within Europe. You had better bring us up to date.'

Kaplan did so. It took him some time. When he came to describe the duelling scene which he had witnessed in the fraternity house in Marburg, Boswell let out a long whistle.

'I knew that kind of thing still went on. I hadn't realized it was the way you say.'

'Yeah, it was really incredible.'

'And Schmidtt was really the guy who was involved back in '67?'

'So he said.'

Boswell shook his head. 'That must have been kinda hard to live with.'

Kaplan pulled that morning's edition of the *Herald Tribune* out of his pocket.

'Did you see this?' He pointed to the picture of Professor Schmidtt.

Boswell gave another whistle.

'I can't believe our German friends would do that. Not to cover up an event that took place almost fifteen years ago. That's going too far. Even for them.'

'Schmidtt was frightened. He didn't want to talk. Who else could have got to him?'

Boswell was not convinced: 'We may make some enquiries of our own.'

They left it there. There was nothing to be gained from speculation. If it really was a cover-up, then they could be sure that any police investigation into Professor Schmidtt's death would come up with precisely nothing.

Kaplan turned to the events of the morning, giving a blow-by-blow account of his visit to Count Philippe Vincennes' château, including his narrow escape from the ambush that had been prepared for him.

Once again, Boswell was shocked. 'Now that's really going too far. Vincennes gets away with a lot. But he really can't go around trying to eliminate honoured guests from the U.S. Do you want to bring charges?'

Kaplan shook his head. 'We couldn't prove anything. He's too clever for that. But I think you could make the wildlife thing stick.'

'What do you mean?' Boswell removed his pipe from his mouth and looked at the other man with interest.

'What wildlife thing?'

Kaplan fished in his briefcase and produced Diane Verusio's report. He described the damning indictment the report contained of Belgium's role in the illegal trade in wildlife and his own suspicions of the activities of men like Philippe Vincennes.

'What's more,' he concluded. 'I'm sure the Minister for Trade is in this too.'

'Willy van Broyck?'

'Yes. There has to be collusion by the authorities.'

'Can you prove it?'

'I think I can.'

Taking a deep breath, Kaplan told Boswell what he had seen when, a few hours earlier, he had gone aboard the Air Zaire 747 parked on the runway at Zaventem.

'Tim, you simply have to understand; it was horrendous. There were leopards and cheetahs in there, two giraffes who couldn't even stand upright, half-a-dozen antelope of one kind or another and I'd say two hundred monkeys. I don't know the details of the Washington Convention but I'm damn sure those monkeys were all protected.'

Kaplan gave the other man a full account and Boswell took it all in. From time to time he made notes. When Kaplan had finished, the diplomat rose to his feet and paced the rug in front of his desk.

'Lowell, I can't tell how grateful I am that you've been able to file this report. We are all grateful. We've suspected for some time that Belgium was allowing the convention to be breached. I can tell you that the U.S., as a major signatory, is going to lean very hard indeed. I'll have a word with the Ambassador and cable Washington straightaway.'

'What about Vincennes? Are you prepared to put him out of business?'

Boswell was emphatic. 'We'll certainly try to nail him.

It may be difficult. We need hard evidence. As you know he has many friends in the Government. Besides, this animal trade is only a side-line for him. He's got plenty of other irons in the fire. He doesn't need this to survive; it's gravy to him.' He looked at his watch. 'Talking of gravy, it's lunchtime. I'll take you down to the Quai Sainte Catherine.'

'Quai? I didn't know Brussels was on a river.'

'It isn't any longer. They bricked it over.'

Even though the river had disappeared, the little fish restaurants along the Quai Sainte Catherine were still very much in business.

'The speciality is lobster or *moules* – mussels. The Bruxellois are very keen on mussels,' Boswell explained. 'With chips of course. *Moules et frites.*'

'I'll stick to lobster.'

Two hours later they were still at table and half way through their second bottle of wine.

'You know, Tim,' Kaplan wiped away some crumbs of fish from his mouth, 'I rather fancy living in Europe for a time. I think I work too hard. People over here know how to relax.'

Boswell looked around the fashionable little restaurant. It was after three p.m., but the place was still half-full.

'I'd say the Belgians certainly know how to eat. So do the French. You ought to make a quick trip to Paris before you go back.'

'I'd like to.' Kaplan had a quick mental image of the photograph he had seen of Stephanie Verusio. Hadn't Dr

Reuben mentioned that she lived in France? Perhaps they'd tracked her down by now.

Boswell folded his napkin and pushed back his chair.

'I've got to get back to the office. We'll put Washington in the picture, Lowell. There are a whole number of angles to this thing. We have to have the right people looking at it.'

As they left the restaurant and entered the long black bulletproof limousine waiting for them at the curb, Boswell added: 'What about your meeting this evening with Delgrave? Can we help on that? This Marburg business is now a priority of the U.S. Government and that means it's my priority too.'

Kaplan shook his head. 'I think I'll go alone. I don't want to scare him off.'

'We'll keep you covered anyway. You won't necessarily see us. But we'll be there.'

Kaplan felt reassured. He was not a hero, and had no wish to become one.

Later that day, Kaplan was once more to be found in a Brussels restaurant. It was a small dimly lit place in one of the little streets near the Grand Place they'd agreed on.

Jean Delgrave was out of breath when he finally arrived ten minutes late for the appointment.

'I came the long way round. Through all the back streets. I wanted to be sure that I wasn't followed.'

Kaplan handed back the ID. 'Thanks. It was most useful. Did you have any luck?'

Delgrave was cautious. He patted his inside vest pocket

to indicate that the papers were there.

Kaplan understood the gesture at once. He took out a brown envelope and laid it on the table.

'There's fifty thousand francs.' He had drawn it at lunchtime at the Embassy.

Delgrave smiled. 'That is most generous.'

With a quick movement, they exchanged envelopes.

Kaplan glanced at the information on the sheet. It was, as he had hoped it would be, a list of animals which had passed through Brussels Airport in the first days of June. Details were given of the number and type of animal contained in the cargo; of the places the animals had been caught and of their intermediate or final destinations.

'Good! This is just what I was looking for.' With increasing excitement, Kaplan examined the material. He looked for any references to monkeys. There were several but one in particular caught his eye.

'June 5. One green monkey. Caught Kugumba Region of Eastern Zaire, location approximately... latitude... longitude...'

The information fairly leapt at him from the page. Kaplan wanted to shout. At last he had the cross-bearing he was looking for. For both the list he had seen in Marburg and now the list which he held in his hand had a reference to *green monkeys caught in the Kugumba region of Eastern Zaire.* Both lists gave the approximate location where the animals had been caught. *In each case the latitude and the longitude were virtually identical!* Here at last was the precise fix not just on the vector – the green monkey – but on its geographical origin!

He finished reading the entry... 'Longitude approximately... Found sick on arrival; gassed in cage and incinerated.' He said to Delgrave, making his voice sound as casual as he could in the circumstances:

'This entry here. It speaks of a green monkey coming from Zaire. Apparently the animal was found to be sick on arrival. Is that very unusual?'

'It's not unusual for an animal to be sick on arrival. We often have to destroy them.' He looked at the list. 'What's unusual is to have a *green* monkey. I've never heard or seen of one myself. That must be something very rare indeed. It was probably destined for a zoo. Antwerp zoo perhaps. But don't talk to me about animals. Talk to someone who knows. I'm just a cargo official.' Delgrave looked at his watch. 'Nom de Dieu! I must get to work. I'm still on the night shift.' With a smile and a wave he was gone, patting his pocket to reassure himself that his reward for a day's work was properly stowed.

After Delgrave had departed, Kaplan was left there at the table with half a bottle of wine still to drink, wondering just how Diane Verusio had had contact with one sick green monkey at Brussels airport. Had she gone into the cargo shed, once the animals had been off-loaded? Had she, like him, bluffed it out and boarded the Air Zaire plane itself? Or had something else happened? How he wished he knew the answer.

Beyond that, there was the question: what to do next? Just assume that a green monkey from the Kugumba region of Eastern Zaire was indeed, as he now supposed, the vector of the Marburg virus. What were the next steps to take?

After finishing the wine and paying the bill, he took a taxi to Tim Boswell's house in Kraainem where they had a quiet bachelor dinner together. (Tim's wife, Lucilla, had already gone back to the States for the summer.) Kaplan brought Boswell up to date on the story.

'Delgrave came through all right,' he said. 'I don't know where he got the information from but he found it somewhere.'

Boswell puffed on his pipe. 'We might take a look at Delgrave, anyway. I'd like to know exactly what kind of a job he does for SABENA.'

The two men talked about different aspects of the case. Boswell had used the afternoon to good effect in spite of the amount of wine he had consumed at lunch.

'You know, there's something that puzzles me. Remember you told me this morning about the original duelling incident in Marburg, back in 1967, where the students were infected by, er, Ringelmann? Wasn't that his name?'

Kaplan nodded. 'It's a fact. Twenty-three out of twenty-three victims in the 1967 episode *were* Marburg University students.'

'I'm not disputing that,' Boswell intervened quickly. 'It's something else. Didn't Professor Schmidtt say that the Chancellor himself had been present?'

'Certainly. That was one of the reasons for the cover-up. If that fact had come out, it could have brought down the government.'

Boswell tapped out his pipe into the fire-place.

'Well, here's something curious,' he said. 'I got on to our people in Bonn and they got on to the Chancellor's office. The U.S. has pretty good cooperation with the authorities in the Federal Republic as you can imagine. They dug through the files and came up with the log of the Chancellor's movements for the period in question. The official diary is negative, they say. There's no mention of any visit to Marburg in April 1967.'

Kaplan was not put out. 'But you wouldn't expect to find that kind of visit recorded in the official diary. This was a man having a night out at his old school.'

Boswell smiled, a sardonic smile that illuminated his Bostonian features.

'I'd agree with you, but for one thing.'

'What's that?'

'The diary also shows that the Chancellor was on a tour of Latin America at the time. And that is a matter of record. There are press clippings and newsreel pictures to prove it.'

Kaplan was bewildered. 'I don't understand. Why would Franz invent something like that?'

'I'm not sure,' Boswell replied slowly. 'But we ought to find out.'

CHAPTER SIX

PAULA SCHMIDTT DELAYED her journey to Berlin because of her father's death. She was three days later than she had originally planned.

Her mother, distraught with grief, pleaded with her not to go. 'You've just been to Berlin. You've seen your friends. Why go again? Don't leave me alone here. Not now.'

The tension showed in the girl's face but she was implacable. 'It's not for pleasure that I go, mother. It's business. I have to consult some medical experts.'

'But the investigating officers may wish to talk to you again. They may have some news about Franz's murder.'

'They must wait till I return.'

Dressed in black, Paula caught a British Airways plane to Berlin from Frankfurt. (It was one of the anomalies of Berlin's status that Lufthansa still had no flights to Berlin.) She took the bus into the city from the airport. The driver called out the stops over the public address system: 'Templehof, Spandau, Potsdamer Platz...'

She got out at the Potsdamer Platz and looked around. She was too young to remember the place as it had been before the Second World War. But her father had described it for her.

'When I was a boy,' Franz had told her, 'I saw the Zeppelin airship, the R3, making one of its last flights over the Potsdamer Platz. I remember the trams stopped in the square and all the people stood around looking up at the sky. That was in 1933.'

She blinked back tears when she thought of her father. He had been a good man. He should never have talked so much to the American! 'They' would have left him alone if he hadn't talked. Sometimes she hated 'them'. But it was too late. There was no turning back.

Today, the Potsdamer Platz which had seen so much life and movement before the war was a bleak, forbidding place. It had been destroyed by allied bombardment and then, in August 1961, the infamous Berlin Wall was built across the square. The bleak grey concrete slab stretched away into the middle distance, dividing house from house and block from block. Someone had scrawled on the wall at one point the words HIER IST FREIHEIT GEENDET – Here Freedom Ends. Paula's lips curled into a half-sneer as she took her place in the queue which had formed at the foot of the wooden platform. Freedom! They talked of freedom! What did they know of it? Had the men who wrote those words visited the Berlin ghetto where thousands of immigrant Turks – so-called *Gastarbeiters* or 'guestworkers' – were crushed together under slum conditions? She shuffled forward a foot or two as the queue moved towards the base of the ladder.

As she passed the tacky souvenir shops which sold sepia-tinted postcards of Berlin in the good old days, Paula

Schmidtt recalled the time when, in her early 'teens, she had joined the vast crowd in the Potsdamer Platz to listen to President Kennedy telling the crowd: 'Ich bin ein Berliner'. Her father had still been in the States but they had sent her back to visit relations in Berlin. She remembered that Chancellor Adenauer had been there with Kennedy on that cold day in January 1963. So had Willy Brandt, then Mayor of West Berlin. After the speeches, men had mounted the platform as she was about to do now, to look out sternly onto a different world. Sixteen years later, President Carter had done the same thing. By then Paula's political preferences were inalterably set.

She climbed up the steps with some Australians in front of her and some Japanese behind. At the top, she spent some minutes looking into East Berlin across the cleared area covered with barbed wire and concrete traps. There were mines there, too, she knew; and sensors of every kind. Down here, men had met their deaths trying to escape. Some of them had been shot down in cold blood and left to die where they fell. There was a time when she might have sympathized. Not now.

She stood pressed up against the wooden railing and checked her watch. It was exactly one p.m. She opened her handbag and took out a packet of Marlboroughs. Then she rummaged again in the bag and produced a lighter. She let the flame flare for three full seconds before lighting the cigarette.

Two hundred yards away, in the top left window of one of the grey forbidding blocks of houses that bounded the eastern edge of the cleared zone, a 'Vopo' – an East German frontier guard – was watching through powerful binoculars. He noted the time the black-clad woman arrived on the wooden platform, the brand-name on the cigarette package and the play with the lighter.

'Fritz,' he called out to his companion (the Vopos were never trusted by their superiors to stand guard duty alone; they always performed in pairs), 'she just showed up. You had better ring through and tell them.'

By then, Paula Schmidtt had climbed back down the platform and was walking along the wall towards the centre of the city. She walked briskly, concentrating on her business.

When she reached the Kurfürstendamm, West Berlin's main shopping street, she turned east. Her pace slowed to that of an afternoon shopper. From time to time she looked at the window displays in the big stores. She didn't wish to appear conspicuous.

Almost at the end of the Kurfürstendamm were the blackened remains of Berlin's Memorial Church. The building had never been repaired. It stood as mute testimony to the destructiveness of war. But part of it was still in use today as a place of prayer. There was a roof of sorts over the south transept and the pews were still in position.

Paula entered the church and went to the seventh pew from the front on the left hand side. For a few minutes she knelt in prayer. Before she left, she pinned a small white envelope containing a full report on Lowell Kaplan's visit to Marburg to the underside of the ledge in front of her. Later that day, an old woman, also dressed in black, entered the Memorial Church and knelt in prayer precisely where Paula Schmidtt had knelt. The old woman was remembering, no doubt, a husband or a son killed in the war. When she departed, the small white envelope had disappeared.

CHAPTER SEVEN

JOSÉ RODRIGUEZ, the fat and swarthy Brazilian who had served as the Director-General of the World Health Organization for the past three years, was in his most expansive mood.

'Have a cigar, my dear Lowell,' he said, welcoming the American to his light and airy office on the top floor of the WHO's new gleaming glass-fronted building overlooking Lake Geneva.

Kaplan declined. 'I see you have not yet launched your personal anti-smoking campaign, José,' he joked, 'in spite of WHO's worldwide efforts in that area.'

Rodriguez laughed. He leaned back in his armchair, clutching the eight-inch Havana in one hand and waving the other as he talked. Smoke wreathed upwards.

'I never believe in practising what I preach. I can't see what one thing has to do with the other. Besides, we never got very far with that anti-smoking campaign. We put it on because we thought we might keep you Americans interested in the work of the organization. But then you had the change of administration in Washington and nobody on your side seemed very much interested in the tobacco problem any longer. So we've more or less dropped it.' He looked wistful. 'The trouble is this organization has been too damned successful on the whole. We had the anti-malaria campaign and got rid of the mosquitos. Then we had the anti-smallpox campaign. 'WHO licks mankind's oldest enemy: smallpox!' That's what the headlines said in 1977 and the funds poured into our coffers. But now we're running a bit low on enemies and the organization's finances are suffering.' He took another puff on the cigar.

The trend of José Rodriguez' remarks encouraged Kaplan. He had wondered, as he flew into Geneva that morning from Brussels on the eleven o'clock plane, about the best way to inform Rodriguez about the Marburg virus. Rodriguez' complaints of the lack of 'sex-appeal' in WHO's routine everyday work provided the opportunity.

'In my view, José,' he said, 'and please don't take this as a criticism, you spend too much time in this organization thinking about the classic diseases – polio, typhus, tetanus, smallpox, malaria, cholera and so on. The third world majority has been getting at you. The Africans and the Asians and even the Latin Americans are trying to turn the WHO into just another development agency. You won't keep the organization going that way, José, because you won't keep your major donors interested. And it's the major donors who count, and the people in those countries who make up the aid lobby.

'No,' Kaplan continued, 'what you've got to give them is drama, excitement, intellectual challenge. Take the Marburg virus, for example. Is there a greater single threat to mankind than Marburg?'

When Rodriguez looked blank, Kaplan answered his own question.

'No, there is no greater threat. Yet WHO has done nothing. Absolutely nothing about it. If the Marburg virus passes into general circulation, half the population of the world could be obliterated overnight! When you've got a lethal airborne viral agent against which there are no known vaccines, you're in big trouble indeed. Well?' He looked at the other man challengingly.

The Brazilian was clearly nervous.

'What Marburg virus? I know there was an outbreak of infection at Marburg. But that was way back at the end of the 'sixties, soon after I joined WHO. We tried to look into it but we could never get any cooperation from the West German authorities. They just shut up tight. Since we heard nothing more of it, I've always assumed that it was a case of misclassification. Perhaps they had a particularly virulent strain of 'flu in Marburg that year. Some of these 'flu viruses can seem pretty exotic.'

Kaplan stood up and walked over to the window. He looked out over Lake Geneva. The fountain was steadily sending its jet of water two hundred feet into the air. The plumes of spray drifted away on the afternoon wind, occasionally reaching the late eaters who sat over their coffee and liqueurs at the lakeside restaurants.

He turned to face his host. 'José, I've come to you today because I need your help and that of WHO. I wasn't exaggerating when I said a moment ago that the Marburg virus was possibly the greatest single threat to mankind...'

'Lowell,' the Brazilian interrupted him. 'Perhaps you had better begin at the beginning.'

Two hours later, when the late afternoon sun was slanting over the lake, José Rodriguez asked two other members of his staff to join the meeting. The first was WHO's Deputy Director-General, the Russian Ivan Leontiev – a tall raffish-looking character who from time to time sported a monocle and who had clearly enjoyed his time sampling the fleshpots of the West. The other man was a bearded Englishman called John Cartwright who had thick horn-rimmed glasses and a serious professional manner. Rodriguez introduced him to Kaplan as WHO's resident ecologist.

'What Cartwright doesn't know about animal vectors isn't worth knowing.'

Kaplan greeted the two men warmly. Though he was taken aback by the fact that Rodriguez' deputy was a Russian, he quickly decided that this was irrelevant. After all, the WHO was an international organization and the Russians had just as much right to occupy high positions there as they did in, say, the U.N. itself. What counted was the calibre of the man, not the nationality.

Rodriguez, who had recovered from his initial scare (no Director-General of the World Health Organization likes to be told that there's a lethal disease threatening mankind which he and his people haven't even heard of), quickly took charge of the meeting. He spoke with emphasis and enthusiasm. Long before Kaplan had concluded his story, the Brazilian had realized that if WHO could add a victory over the Marburg virus to those it had already won in the malaria and smallpox campaigns, his own stock would rise enormously. Since he was up for reelection the following year, that was a factor of considerable importance quite apart from any benefits there might be for mankind as a whole.

By the time the jet of spray in the fountain on Lake Geneva had been turned off for the evening, José Rodriguez had identified the essential options:

'As I see it,' he said, 'from what Kaplan has told us, it is possible, even probable, that the green monkey is the vector of the Marburg virus. It is also possible, even probable, that one particular tribe of green monkey, namely a tribe which lives in the...'

'Kugumba,' Kaplan prompted him.

'Kugumba region of Eastern Zaire is the vector in this particular case.'

He looked at the other three men and saw that they agreed with his summing-up so far.

'As far as we know,' (José Rodriguez tapped the ash from his long-dead cigar), 'there is no other reservoir of the Marburg virus. We cannot, of course, be one hundred per cent sure. But since there have been only two outbreaks of the disease in over fifteen years and both have been linked with green monkeys, I would say that there is a very strong presumption that this is indeed the case. I repeat: as far as we know there are no other vectors and no current cases of infection among human populations. Is this correct, Lowell?'

Kaplan nodded.

'As I see it therefore,' Rodriguez continued, 'we can do one of two things. The first option is that we can forget about the Marburg virus. We can hope that it stays where it is, well and truly buried in the jungles of Central Africa. Fifteen years or more elapsed between the first outbreak of Marburg and the second. We can sit back and hope that five hundred years or more will elapse between the second outbreak of Marburg and the third. What are the pro's and the con's of this first course of action? The pro's are that by doing nothing, that is to say by not trying to track down the source of the disease, we will not be exposing anyone needlessly with all the risk that this entails. The con's are that there may be another release of the virus into civilization. This may occur by the same route as the first two outbreaks, that is to say the capture of a wild animal and its transport to some centre of population. Or it may occur in any even simpler manner. The forests of Eastern Zaire are no longer inviolate, any more than – in my country – are the forests of the Amazon. If there is another release, as Kaplan has so well put it this afternoon, we have effectively no defence beyond first-stage isolation and very limited possibilities of serum-immunization.'

The three other men present nodded, agreeing with Rodriguez' presentation of the problem.

'What is the second possible course of action, gentlemen?' Rodriguez continued. 'It is that we go in there and ELIMINATE THE VECTOR, that is to say THE GREEN MONKEYS THEMSELVES!'

He paused dramatically, waiting for the full effect of his words to sink in.

It was Ivan Leontiev who spoke first. He removed his monocle and looked around the room. Speaking impeccable English he said:

'I entirely agree with you, my dear Director-General, I think the second course of action is correct. We must surely eliminate the vector, if by eliminating the vector we can eliminate the disease itself. I believe that this organization should mount an expedition to Zaire to find the green monkeys in the Kugumba region and that you, José, should lead this operation. It will surely turn into one of WHO's greatest triumphs.'

José Rodriguez acknowledged the compliments of his deputy with a wide smile which set his fat olive-hued jowls quivering.

'Does anyone disagree?'

Instinctively Lowell Kaplan wanted to say that *he* disagreed with Ivan Leontiev. He thought the Russian had been altogether too glib in his support of Rodriguez. It was almost as though he had prepared the speech in advance.

Logically, of course, Kaplan couldn't fault Leontiev's argument. If there was only one vector for the disease and no other potential sources of infection, e.g. laboratories where a virus was stored for medical or research purposes, then of course by eliminating the vector, you could eliminate the disease itself. What's more, the green monkey wasn't like the ubiquitous mosquito. Only one tribe was involved and thanks to his own detective work they now had a pretty shrewd idea of precisely where it lived.

Before Kaplan could comment on what Leontiev had said, Cartwright intervened. He pulled at his beard nervously, clearly concerned at the direction the discussion had taken.

'Director-General,' he coughed apologetically to signal his reservations, 'I agree that it will be a major health and public relations triumph if WHO can announce to the world that Marburg disease has been eliminated once and for all. But we also have to think of the practical politics of this operation. Isn't there going to be an outcry from the conservationists if we move against the green monkeys, destroying them ruthlessly in their natural habitat?' Cartwright's voice trailed off as he saw Rodriguez looking at him scornfully.

'My dear Cartwright.' There was a cutting edge to the Brazilian's voice. 'Just how naive can you be? You don't suppose WHO is going to announce this operation *in advance*, do you? No Sir! We announce it when it is over; when we have succeeded; when the last green monkey has been eliminated, and when Marburg disease is no longer a threat to mankind. That is the moment we go public; and that is the moment the world will applaud. The lives of a few diseased animals will at that point appear a small price to pay compared to the inestimable benefits our actions will have brought.'

Whatever further objections he might have felt, Cartwright decided to leave them unvoiced. José Rodriguez had clearly made up his mind. Kaplan too left the meeting convinced that the decision to eliminate the green monkeys was correct. In many ways, he could see the force of the conservationists' argument, as presented by Cartwright. There was something horrible about the deliberate destruction of a species. But, for the life of him, he couldn't see the alternative.

He walked back up the hill from the WHO to the Intercontinental at Petit Saconnex. There was a message waiting for him at the desk. It was from Susan Wainwright in Atlanta, Georgia.

'HAVE TRACED STEPHANIE VERUSIO,' he read. 'ADDRESS 16 RUE DU FAUBOURG ST. HONORE PARIS XVIe TELEPHONE 767-1814 STOP STEPHANIE HAS BEEN IN AFRICA LAST SEVERAL MONTHS STOP HAVE ADVISED HER OF SISTERS DEATH STOP STEPHANIE WISHED TO RETURN IMMEDIATELY TO UNITED STATES STOP HAVE ASKED HER TO WAIT TILL YOU MAKE CONTACT BEST SUSAN.'

Before going upstairs to his room, Kaplan asked the hotel to book him on a plane to Paris the following morning.

Whatever other urgent business he might have, the need to visit – and to console – the sister of the dead girl must come first.

CHAPTER EIGHT

KAPLAN DIDN'T IN THE END get away from Geneva until after lunch on the following day. Within the World Health Organization, planning for the Zaire expedition went immediately into top gear and Kaplan found himself drawn into the discussions. It was obvious from an early stage that U.S. logistical support would be of paramount importance. Twice that morning Kaplan was on the phone to Tim Boswell in the U.S. Embassy in Brussels and Boswell in turn was in touch with his Nato counterpart.

One small thing which arose in the course of Kaplan's second conversation with Tim Boswell puzzled him.

'By the way, Lowell,' Tim had said. 'We made some discreet enquiries with SABENA about that fellow you met. They've no record of a Jean Delgrave working at Zaventem. Half a dozen other Delgraves and three Degraefs. Are you sure you got the name right?'

Kaplan had been indignant. 'Of course I'm sure. I used the man's ID.'

'Well, we're still checking,' Boswell had told him. 'The airport puts a lot of work out to contract. He could be one of the contract staff.'

They had left it at that. Kaplan had thrust the matter out

of his mind. No doubt some light would be shed on it in due course. For the moment he had other preoccupations. He still had misgivings about the Zaire option. It seemed so brutal, so unsubtle – just to go into the jungle and blast the monkeys to death. Yet he found it hard to fault Rodriguez' logic, nor that of Leontiev, his deputy. (Christ, what a sinister type that Leontiev was, with his monocle and upper-class English accent!) And there was no doubt that the U.S. Health Authorities were backing the Rodriguez approach to the hilt. The U.S. Ambassador to the United Nations in Geneva had called on Rodriguez in person with a message of support. He would never have delivered that message if the State Department and the Department of Health and Human Services (which included the Atlanta Center itself in its responsibilities) had not agreed.

All these thoughts were very much in Kaplan's mind during the course of the brief flight from Geneva to Paris. And they stayed with him as he rode into the city in a taxi from Orly airport. So engrossed was he indeed in his own concerns that he arrived at Stephanie's address in the little street behind the old church of St Sulpice without quite re-alizing how he had got there.

He was immediately struck by the charm of the place. A heavy oak door opened off the street on to a wide stone staircase. This in turn led up to another heavy door on the first floor of the building. There was an iron bell-pull very much in keeping with the mediaeval atmosphere. Kaplan announced his presence by giving it a long firm tug.

She came to the door at once; she had been expecting him since six that evening and her face was a mixture of anxiety and interest.

'Dr Kaplan, come in. I'm so glad to see you.'

She was exactly like her photograph. Slim of build, with soft brown hair, clear eyes which looked straight at yours. Her skin was deeply suntanned as though much of her life had been spent out of doors. There were shadows under her eyes. The news of her sister's death was still very recent.

She offered him a drink and poured one for herself. They sat together in a light spacious room which looked out onto the churchyard. The window was open and the noise of the traffic came up from the street. But it wasn't a harsh aggressive sound; more of a gentle reminder of the world beyond the oak doors and the stone walls.

'How long have you lived here?' Kaplan asked.

'Five years. Ever since I moved to Europe. Of course I travel a lot, so I'm often away.'

'I understand you've been travelling recently. That's how you missed hearing about...' Kaplan wasn't sure how to phrase it, so he concluded: 'missed hearing the news about your sister'.

An expression of intense pain passed across Stephanie's face. Kaplan said gently: 'Would you like to tell me about Diane? Perhaps it would help.'

'Yes, I think it would. You're the first person I've been able to talk to since I heard about it.'

Kaplan thought for a moment that she was going to cry,

but she pulled herself together, took a gulp of her drink and began.

'You know, Lowell' – somehow she had switched almost without thinking from the formal Dr Kaplan to Christian names – 'Diane was an amazing person. That's just something you have to understand. She was really committed to her work, wholly committed. We were both involved in the campaign against vivisection and in the protection of wild animals more generally. She concentrated on North America. I moved to Paris and looked after the European end. But that was only part of it. Essentially, anything that concerned animals concerned us. We both of us had money. We inherited when our parents were killed in a plane crash in Africa, flying over the Nrongoro Crater in Tanzania.'

'I knew that. Dr Reuben told me.'

'So you met Isaac? He's a wonderful man. I sometimes think he's much more than just a family doctor. Diane was very close to him. She often sought his advice. I had the feeling sometimes that she was almost...' she paused 'professionally involved with Reuben – as though she shared some secret project.' Stephanie laughed. 'That's nonsense, of course.'

'They were close, I know,' said Kaplan. 'Diane went to Reuben when she came back to New York. He sent her to hospital.'

Kaplan remembered the day he had visited the hospital in New York, remembered the young woman lying on the bed and the blonde hair falling out in handfuls.

In some uncanny way, Stephanie must have been following his thoughts.

'We may not have looked alike. She had blonde hair. Mine's brown. But we thought alike. We worked well together.'

'From what I've read you were highly professional. I saw the report Diane made on the trade in live animals. I found a copy of it in her place in Greenwich Village.'

Stephanie seemed surprised. 'So you went there, did you? You get around.'

'We have to. We can't afford to miss a trick.'

'You have the authority?'

'I can flash a badge if I have to.'

Stephanie digested that information. Then she said: 'Diane was updating that report when she became ill.'

'Did she say anything to you before she left Europe about feeling sick?'

'No. As a matter of fact, I never heard from her again. The day she flew back to the States from Brussels, I went down to Somalia, to look at the ivory trade. A lot of poaching of elephants is going on in the Horn of Africa. The government down there is probably involved in the illegal export of ivory. We wanted to pin it down. I was pretty much out of touch.'

Stephanie pressed Kaplan about her sister's death and its possible or probable cause. For a moment he wondered whether it was wise to tell her everything. Then he decided that, whether or not it was wise, he was going to do it anyway. Her sister had died for the cause, so to speak, and Stephanie deserved to know the details.

He pulled out the list which the man who called himself Jean Delgrave had given him two days earlier and carefully explained his current hypothesis.

Stephanie took the list from him and studied it carefully.

'So you think Diane may have had contact with a sick monkey in the cargo shed or somewhere at Brussels airport. That's not absolutely impossible, but I must say I find it rather odd. Diane wasn't the kind to go around sticking her finger inside monkey cages and waiting for it to be bitten. She knew the dangers. Did she tell her doctor she'd been bitten by a monkey?'

'No, she never mentioned anything of the sort to Reuben. But once, when I saw her in hospital – she was delirious at the time – I heard her babble about monkeys, green monkeys, actually.'

'Did they autopsy her? Did they find anything there?'

'No, there never was an autopsy. They wouldn't touch her in the hospital morgue. There wouldn't necessarily have been a bite anyway. We have evidence of aerosol transmission.'

'Poor Diane!' There were tears in Stephanie's eyes. 'What a way to go.'

They went out to dinner in a little restaurant on the Rue Dauphin. Somewhere in the background came the strains of The Magic Flute. The waiters shimmered among the candlelit tables, napkins draped over forearms and wine-bottles at the ready. After three days of almost constant travel and activity, Kaplan began to relax.

'What kind of life do you lead here, Stephanie? Paris is a glamorous place, isn't it? I know a lot of Americans who wouldn't mind a few years in Paris.'

Stephanie considered his question seriously. 'I'm not sure if Paris is such a glamorous place. Most Parisians live in pretty cramped apartments. You won't find many town-houses, like you have in New York. And the traffic's terrible. Besides, even when I'm in Paris, I'm working most of the time.'

As they ate, she described her work and her conviction that, unless the wildlife of the world could be saved, the world itself was probably not worth saving. The intensity with which she spoke had the effect of transforming her face. Stephanie Verusio passed from being arrestingly pretty to being exceptionally beautiful. Kaplan wanted to stretch out and take her hand across the table.

He did not do so. Somehow he felt too shy. He was out of practice. Too much time spent chasing strange diseases, and not enough time devoted to the pursuit of women. It was Stephanie who touched his hand lightly across the table, not the other way round.

'Tell me about *your* life, Lowell. I've said enough about mine.'

Suddenly, Lowell Kaplan found himself talking about his own life with a frankness which he would not have believed possible.

Normally, he was a reticent man. He shrank from the direct answer to the direct question. When pressed to say something about himself, he tended to mumble and change the subject as though he found a hundred other topics far more interesting. But tonight was different. He felt happier than he had felt for a long time.

'I was married for twelve years, you know.' Kaplan paused to select a variety of cheese from an incredibly well-supplied cheese-board. 'Some of it was good. Most of the time we were at each other's throats.'

Stephanie said nothing, so Kaplan continued searching for the right words. 'The problem with marriage is that people grind away at each other for too long. It's not one fight that matters. It's the cumulative effect of a hundred, a thousand incidents. It's too exhausting, too debilitating. I miss not having the kids though. That's hard.'

Stephanie said gently: 'I understand.'

'I wonder if you do. Have you ever been married?'

Stephanie smiled. 'I've never been brave enough. And, somehow, the animals seem to have taken up all my time.'

They crossed the Boulevard St Germain and walked back towards St Sulpice. It had rained while they were in the restaurant. The lights of the street lamps and shop windows were reflected in the damp pavements. They stopped outside the door of her apartment.

'Come on in,' Stephanie said. 'I'll make you some more coffee.'

Kaplan did not refuse. He had enjoyed his evening more

than he could possibly have imagined. And he wanted it to continue.

Upstairs, she clung to him, sobbing.

'Don't you understand, Lowell? I loved her. I don't know what to do now she's gone.' The tears streamed down her cheeks. 'First my parents. Now Diane. It's too much.'

He held her to him. There was so much he understood and so much he could never understand.

Later, when she had calmed down and he was making ready to leave for his hotel, she pleaded with him.

'Lowell, don't go. Not now. I need you tonight.'

They made love in a brass four-poster bed which Stephanie had bought in an antique shop off Les Halles when she first came to Paris. Kaplan stayed the night.

They had breakfast in bed. Then, pushing the tray aside, they made love again. There was none of the urgency there had been the previous evening. It was as though a dam had burst on a river. Now, after a temporary turbulence, the water was flowing smoothly again.

Stephanie leaned back on the pillow. Her auburn hair fell down onto her shoulder. The shadows had gone from beneath her eyes. There was no sign of the desperate sorrow of the previous evening. This was a young woman very much in control of herself and her surroundings.

'What are you going to do now, Lowell?' she asked.

'I'm not really sure.' Kaplan wondered whether in the intimacy of the previous day he might not already have told Stephanie too much.

She grabbed his arm. 'Lowell, monkeys are my field. They are the most wonderful creatures on earth. They are intelligent; they are beautiful.' There was an urgent pleading note in her voice. 'Diane was trying to save the monkeys, not to get them destroyed. Why not leave them alone?'

'Stephanie.' Kaplan's voice was gentle. He put his arm round her. 'It's not as simple as you think. Even if you stamp out the trade in animals – and, believe me, I'd like to see that happen – anyone can go into the jungle and get infected. It's not just a question of transporting the animals on planes.'

'Then, let them stay out of the jungle. Do human beings have to be everywhere, messing everything up? Have the animals nowhere to call their own? My father's life work was trying to protect the fauna of the forests and the savannah. Not to protect it for tourism. Or for some other commercial purpose. But just because the animals – and the trees and the plants – have a right to live too. We live the way we want to. Why shouldn't they?'

Kaplan sighed. 'I wish I could help, Stephanie. I really wish I could.'

He felt her stiffen and pull away.

'You're not levelling with me, are you?'

Suddenly angry, she leapt from the bed and stood facing him across the room. Her hair was flung back from her shoulders and fire flashed from her eyes.

Kaplan couldn't bring himself to lie. He sat upright in the bed. 'I shouldn't tell you this... because it's a breach of security. But I'm going to because I can't deceive you. Certainly not after last night and this morning.' He spoke gently now, trying to get her to understand. 'We have to destroy the green monkeys, Stephanie. You must understand that. There's no other way.'

She looked at him for a long second and then picked up her clothes and went into the bathroom.

'You had better go,' she said.

★

After Kaplan had gone, Stephanie sat alone in her apartment. For a time, she thought about him. The man attracted her, more than anyone she had met in a long time. Otherwise, whatever the circumstances, she would never have gone to bed with him.

But she thought he suffered, like so many other scientists, from tunnel-vision. He simply couldn't see the wider picture.

After several minutes' reflection, interrupted only by the bells of the church opposite, she rose to her feet, went to a drawer and pulled out a map of Central Africa. She found the Kugumba region of Eastern Zaire and the area indicated by the coordinates on the piece of paper which Kaplan had showed her. She was sure Kaplan had not realized that she had memorized the map references when he passed her the list the previous evening. He had been too absorbed in the story he was telling.

As she looked at the map, an idea began to form in her mind. She looked at her watch. New York was six hours behind Paris; so it was four o'clock in the morning there. It was too early to call at the moment. She would wait till after lunch.

Dr Isaac Reuben's assistant took the call, shortly after the surgery had opened for the day.

'This is Stephanie Verusio calling from Paris, France. Can I speak to Dr Reuben, please?'

She had to wait three minutes before being put through; the doctor had a patient with him. Ten minutes later when she put down the telephone, there were tears of gratitude in her eyes. For if Reuben had been surprised by her request, he had given no sign of it. Stephanie had pleaded with him.

'Kaplan told me what you did for him. Can you do it for me too? I need your help.'

Reuben had interrupted her as she began to go into the reasons. 'Stephanie,' the slow kind voice brought back the image of the man across the distance that separated them, 'I don't need to know all the details. You're your father's daughter. That's enough for me. And you're your sister's sister. That's another reason. And there's a third reason too. Do you know what it is?'

'No, what?'

'You're someone very special yourself. You've never asked me for anything before. Now you're asking and you must have a very good reason.'

After she had finished talking with Reuben, Stephanie

set about organizing her departure. Reuben had said it would probably take twenty-four hours for the serum to arrive. She might need another twenty-four hours after that to make the necessary preparations. Today was Wednesday. If all went to plan, she could be on her way by the end of the week.

As she was getting ready for bed that evening, the telephone rang. It was Lowell Kaplan. For once, the American sounded unsure of himself.

'Stephanie, I'm sorry I had to go like that.'

There was a coolness in her reply. 'It's not really your fault, Lowell. You have your world. I have mine.'

He hesitated. 'But the other thing – it was wonderful, wasn't it?'

Her voice softened. 'Of course, it was.' She replaced the receiver.

Stephanie sat up in bed, reading. She wanted to refresh her memory about the green monkey and its place in the scheme of things. Her textbook was a primitive one. Most of her library had remained in America when she moved to Europe. But it served the purpose:

'New World monkeys include the spider, woolly, capuchin, howler, vakiri, saki, douroucouli, squirrel, titi and marmoset monkeys. Some species have a prehensile tail and all have round nostrils separated by a broad septum. Old World monkeys include the proboscis, langur, colobus, macaque, mandrill, mangabey and guenon monkeys. They are to be found in Africa and Asia, including Malaysia and Japan. They range from mountain forests to open plains. Some have tails and some do not, but all have downward pointed nostrils and a narrow septum.'

She couldn't find much about the green monkey itself beyond the following statement:

'One very rare species of guenon is the green monkey, occasionally reported by travellers in Central Africa. Some theorize that the greenness of the green monkey is caused by the presence of a special fungus in the fur, peculiar to this species of monkey. The green monkey is noted also for its beauty and great agility. It is to be distinguished from the cognate species, the grey-green monkey – also found in Central Africa – which does not have the distinctive fur fungus.'

She put the book down and turned out the light. Her mind was full of monkeys of every type and description. Some swung by their tails through the canopy of the forest, screeching warnings as intruders entered their domain; others groomed each other contentedly, at one with their surroundings. In her dream, she saw herself living with a tribe of green monkeys, their fur a brilliant green and their eyes like emeralds. And some of them, just a few of them, say five out of twenty, had even brighter green fur than the rest and eyes that blazed with an even deeper emerald colour. These monkeys she dreamed – they were both male and female – were those that carried the virus. And in some strange way their very beauty was linked to the disease which they bore in their blood.

CHAPTER NINE

STEPHANIE VERUSIO had visited Africa half a dozen times with her parents, and once they had spent a season camping out in the Serengeti. They had criss-crossed the park, following the huge herds of migrating animals: wildebeest, hartebeest, antelope, gazelle, impala, giraffe, elephant and lion – the plains seemed to overflow with an abundance of game. For a young impressionable woman it was an unforgettable time. The tropical sun sinking swiftly to the horizon; the sudden noise of the African night; the cries of the hunter and the hunted became part of her. She lived Africa; she breathed it; she dreamed about it. It was in her blood. She could not suppress her excitement as she prepared for her departure.

The serum arrived as planned towards the end of the week. Stephanie had a friend at the Institut Pasteur who asked no questions and expected no answers but was content to inoculate her as she requested. On the Friday night she flew from Paris to Nairobi. Less experienced travellers might have supposed that the best way to get to the Kugumba region of Eastern Zaire was to go to Kinshasha, the capital of Zaire and then to travel across country. Stephanie made enquiries of people she knew had first-hand knowledge of the area. She found out that, actually, the best way to the Kugumba region of the Eastern Congo was to cross Lake Tanganyika from Burundi, the tiny state which lies at the very heart of Africa, like a bull's eye in a dart-board.

It was a long flight down from Paris to Nairobi and she didn't sleep much. Her mind was full of the task which lay ahead of her. She had to find the tribe of green monkeys and then, however impossible it might seem, she had somehow to move them to safety before the armies of the night descended on them. How far should she try to move them? Fifty miles? A hundred? More? Was there a danger that they would return to their original haunts in the Kugumba region where they would run the risk of extermination? If so, how could she keep them guarded and for how long? And who would help her in all this?

There was also the risk of infection. Reuben had come through with the serum. Half a pint of his blood was now mingled with her own and the antibodies should already be racing in her blood stream. And he had promised, as an old friend, to tell nobody. But how long would the protection last? Two months? Six months? A year? Or for ever? She believed she had taken the most effective measures possible to protect herself against the Marburg virus. But she would have liked to have known for sure.

There was another reason why she did not sleep much on the flight down. The sun came up on the port wing of the plane around 5 a.m. when they were still over Southern Sudan. The day was cloudless and she soon shifted to a window seat so as to watch the continent unfold beneath her. For her, there was always something magical about this. First the desert, then the savannah, then the jungle, then once more the bush and finally the more populated landscape of village and field as the big jet came in over the Game Park to land at Nairobi airport.

She had checked her luggage through, so all she had to do was to change planes. Air Burundi ran a D.C.3 from Nairobi to Bujumbura – ran it, that was, whenever they had enough petrol for it to fly and enough maintenance staff to keep the sparking plugs clean. Today was one of the lucky days.

The last leg of Stephanie's journey was a relatively short one. Shortly before noon, the old plane, which had probably been kicking about different parts of Africa since the Second World War, started its descent towards Bujumbura. She had her first glimpse of the massive geological feature called the Nile-Zaire ridge, running north to south through the country. She saw the stands of primeval forests on the very summit of the ridge, the great trees which seemed to reach up towards the undercarriage of the plane. Then, suddenly, they were over flatter ground. Beneath the starboard wing the Ruzizi river flowed through the plain into Lake Tanganyika. They were near enough to the surface of the water for her to see a couple of hippopotamuses wallowing in the mud. And across the lake, towering now above the plane as it came in to land, loomed the mountains of Eastern Zaire. Somewhere in those mountains she knew she would find what she was looking for.

Quite apart from the facts of geography, which made it preferable to approach the Eastern Congo via Burundi rather than making the long trek eastwards from Kinshasha, Stephanie had another compelling reason for making Bujumbura the launching pad for her African expedition. That reason was a tall, graceful member of the Tutsi tribe called Michel Ngenzi. Ngenzi was a long standing friend of her father's and so of hers. He was also a one-time Professor of African Geography at the Université Libre de Bruxelles and a prince of the former royal house of Burundi. For Stephanie, contacting Ngenzi was a matter of supreme importance. With his assistance, she believed she had a chance of succeeding in her objective. Without it, she was not even sure she knew where to begin.

Bujumbura possessed a modest airport – and that was probably an understatement. Whereas in neighbouring Kenya the British had left an enduring legacy in the form of a police force which paraded in neatly pressed khaki shorts, the sole occupant of the custom post at Bujumbura airport had a French képi cocked to one side of his head, a pair of rumpled jeans and a shirt whose once colourful pattern had been bleached by several years' exposure to the tropical sun.

He flipped through the pages of her passport in a desultory way.

'Vous êtes Américaine, hein?'

'Oui.' Stephanie thought it safer to stick to monosyllabic replies. The passport could speak for itself.

'Qu'est-ce que vous allez faire en Burundi?'

'Du tourisme.' Stephanie gave the classic response.

Safely through customs and immigration, Stephanie took a taxi from the airport into town. A twenty-minute drive along a hot bustling road brought her to Bujumbura's one and only international hotel, known as the Source du Nil. (Burundi, along with half a dozen other countries, laid claim to the headwaters of the Nile and had demonstrated the seriousness of this claim by naming its hotel in an appropriate fashion.) The Source du Nil, at least partially, lived up to its name. It was a large modern place, reputedly built with airline money, set on the shores of Lake Tanganyika. Guests could look north towards the Ruzizi or due west to the mountains opposite. The hotel had a swimming pool, a couple of bars and a nightclub – in fact all the modern conveniences which tended to be lacking elsewhere.

Stephanie checked in at the desk, filled in the registration card and surrendered her passport for inspection. One of the numerous youths who hung around the desk helped her to her room with her luggage.

When the boy had gone, she shut the door and went to the phone. It was a year since she had last spoken to Michel Ngenzi. She had called him on that occasion to tell him about her father's death in the plane crash. The news had shaken him because Ngenzi had been Roger Verusio's closest African associate. They had worked together, for over fifteen years, cataloguing the fauna and flora of Central and

Southern Africa. The classic work, *Birds of Burundi*, had appeared only two years earlier under both their names.

After a couple of attempts, she heard the number ringing. A voice answered in French: 'Allo, oui.'

'Est-ce que c'est bien le Professeur Ngenzi? Ici c'est Stephanie Verusio à l'appareil.'

She heard a shout of joy at the other end. 'Stephanie! Tu es ici à Bujumbura?'

'Bien sûr.'

'C'est incroyable!' Michel Ngenzi changed quickly to English, knowing Stephanie's linguistic limitations. Several years' residence in Paris had not yet produced, Stephanie was ashamed to admit it, total linguistic proficiency.

'This is incredible,' Ngenzi continued. 'When can we meet? I have so much to tell you about the new book. I am carrying on your father's work where he left off.'

'And I have much to tell you.'

'I shall send the car for you at 6 p.m.'

Stephanie replaced the instrument and went out onto the balcony of her room. Thank God she had been able to get hold of Michel. She had tried to contact him before leaving Paris; but it was almost impossible to get through to Burundi on the international lines. The one time she had succeeded in raising Michel Ngenzi's house, she had been informed that the Professor was away and was not expected back for a few days.

She stood there gazing out. Down below, and slightly to the right, a string of race-horses grazed on the lush well-watered lawns of the Bujumbura Yacht Club, and there was someone waterskiing on the lake in front of the hotel.

What a strange country it was! On the one hand, desperate poverty; a *per capita* income as low as any in Africa. Yet, on the other, extreme concentrations of wealth in just a few hands. For those race-horses, she knew, were not owned by white expatriates, but mainly by members of the governing classes. And it was not a tourist waterskiing on the lake, but a young black man.

Out of interest, she went back into the room to unpack her binoculars from her luggage. Then she returned to the balcony again to focus on the scene below. The speedboat – with the name VICTOR painted on its bow – roared across the calm surface of the water, while the young man who followed in its wake performed all kinds of stunts. He slalomed from side to side, clearly enjoying himself hugely. Then, still careering along at well over twenty knots, he bent down and removed one ski. This he held under his arm while with his other arm he hung onto the tow. She watched fascinated. There was so much grace and power there; the muscles rippled beneath the skin. The young African had thrown his head back and was laughing through the spray.

Suddenly, she saw him bend down again to take off the second ski as well. Good God, Stephanie thought, you can't water-ski without skis. You'll fall on your face! But she was wrong, because the skier flattened his body backwards and raised the balls of his feet so that they took the shock of the water.

Stephanie watched with the binoculars until, about a mile out from shore, the boat slowed and the man on the rope splashed down into the lake. The boat curled round to pick him up.

A land of contrasts indeed; she picked up her interrupted train of thoughts. Great wealth, great poverty. A land where the tall, graceful Tutsis still reigned supreme, as they had for hundreds of years. And yet their hold on power was really paper-thin. Forming less than 10 per cent of the population, the Tutsis were, she knew, constantly threatened by the majority race of the Hutus.

At the beginning of the 1970s, the Hutus had risen up against their masters and had been ruthlessly crushed. At that time, hundreds of thousands had died on both sides in an outbreak of mass-savagery. Now, Stephanie had heard, the tension was once more building up. The Hutus had begun to recover from the beating they had taken and were looking for revenge.

Later that evening Michel Ngenzi had explained the situation to her.

They were on the veranda of the Professor's house, a large brick-and-stucco building set back on a hill overlooking the lake. The gardens stretched half-way down the hill and as Michel Ngenzi and his guest sat with their drinks, looking to the distant hills, the Professor's servants were busy watering the bougainvillaeas and the hibiscus. At the bottom of the garden, a pair of peacocks stretched their wings, and a donkey, ears laid back, munched contentedly in the shade of a flame-tree.

'The government is trying to keep the lid on, Stephanie,' Ngenzi said. 'It's sitting on the pot as hard as it can, but I tell you the cauldron is beginning to boil over.'

'Where do you stand in all this, Michel?' Stephanie was curious about Ngenzi's personal position. 'If the cauldron boils over, won't you get scalded as well?'

Michel Ngenzi's smile was a work of art in itself. It illuminated the characteristic aristocratic features of the Tutsi – narrow septum, and delicate bone structure – and flooded her with warmth.

'Stephanie, believe me I understand the situation here. Better than you think. I think the present government of President Mtaza is headed for trouble. They won't be able to keep the lid on just by sitting on it. There must be reforms, genuine reforms. The Hutus must be given a greater share in power otherwise there will be an explosion.'

'You're part of the élite. Why don't you tell the President that?'

He smiled sadly. 'President Mtaza used to be my best friend. We grew up together. We came from the same village. As boys we went to the famous missionary school – you've probably seen it set high up on the hill above the town – run by the White Fathers from Belgium. We were very close. I can remember the time when Albert Mtaza and I started work on the very first ever catalogue of the wildlife of Burundi, after I came back from Brussels. We used to go every weekend out to where the Ruzizi river flows into

Lake Tanganyika and watch the hippopotamuses and the crocodiles. And the birds. My God, you should have seen the birds. I used many of the notes I made then in the book which your father and I eventually produced.'

'What happened?'

'To President Mtaza?'

'Yes.'

'Power went to his head. He couldn't understand that if this nation is to survive, one tribe cannot rule another as the Tutsis today rule the Hutu. Nor will it survive if one day the situation is reversed and the Hutu rule the Tutsis. Burundi will only survive, Africa will only survive, if we can put an end to tribalism, if we can work together. I tried to tell Mtaza this, but he won't listen. And now he doesn't want to hear from me at all. He lets me get on with my work, but that is probably because of our old friendship. But I'm not really *persona grata* with the government.'

'And if there is another explosion, what will happen? The Hutus will take over?'

'Not just the Hutus. Today in Burundi we have the classic situation. The Communists are helping to foment tension. Look at the map of Africa today. Burundi is a tiny country, a pinprick on the map. Yet, think how crucial it is geopolitically. It straddles the main transport links. If you want to go north-south in Africa, you cannot avoid Lake Tanganyika. Burundi controls all traffic on the lake. More than that, Burundi straddles the east-west route as well. The Communists have both wings now, in Angola and Mozambique. They have great influence in Tanzania and Uganda. The only thing that stops the Communist-financed east-west highway being pushed through from Dar-Es-Salaam to Beira is the fact that we won't let it through Burundi. But if we have a revolution here, if some spark ignites the conflagration, then God knows what will happen. If Burundi goes Communist the whole of Southern Africa will be encircled. By then of course it may already be too late for Zimbabwe. But South Africa will be doomed as well. And think what that would mean for all of us. We don't need a Communist regime, any more than we want to be exploited by the Western powers. Here in Burundi we must be our own masters, and work things out our own way.' He paused, and then said with all the emphasis he could muster. 'And President Mtaza's way is not the right way. That I know. It will only lead to violence and bloodshed and a take-over by one faction or the other.'

Stephanie looked with great fondness at her old friend. She knew that Ngenzi was being amazingly frank with her. Burundi was a country, like many others in Africa, where you thought twice before criticizing the regime.

But Ngenzi's position was clearly ambivalent. He was a Tutsi himself and a high-born one at that. He was a friend of the President. And besides he was a gentle good man, who abhorred violence. He would not force the pace of change himself.

She pressed him. 'Michel, who is the leader of the opposition? I don't mean the moderate opposition, people who think like you do. I mean the radical opposition.'

A nervous look passed across the Professor's face.

'Look, Stephanie. It's not a good idea to talk too freely about these things. If I've done so tonight, it's because I wanted to put you in the picture.' He leaned forward. 'But I'll tell you what I've heard. I've heard that Mtaza's own son, Victor, may be planning some kind of coup.'

Stephanie was amazed.

'But isn't he a Tutsi like his father?'

'He is and he isn't.'

'What do you mean?'

'I'll explain. Victor Mtaza's mother was the third of President Mtaza's wives and she was a Hutu. There is inter-marriage between Hutus and Tutsis and President Mtaza at the time was trying to set an example.'

'Did it work?'

'Not really. Victor Mtaza's mother died not long af-ter Victor's birth – in mysterious circumstances. I've even heard the story that President Mtaza himself killed her in a fit of anger. So you see,' Ngenzi concluded, 'Victor Mtaza is half-Hutu. Apart from that, he may feel he has his mother's death to avenge. He may succeed in his political ambitions. He's a very charismatic young man.'

'Does he go waterskiing?' Stephanie suddenly remem-bered the name VICTOR painted on the side of the boat.

'I don't doubt it. He'll want to keep up his image as part of the ruling classes, so as to avoid exciting suspicion.'

Stephanie thought of the bravura performance which

she had witnessed on the water that afternoon.

'He certainly manages to do that. How did you hear about him?'

Michel Ngenzi nodded with his head in the direction of the servants who were still watering the flowers at the bottom of the garden.

'Those are Hutus,' he said. 'They hear these things.'

'Before the President himself?'

'Mtaza would be the last to hear. I can promise you that.'

Stephanie shivered. The night was drawing quickly in. The cicadas had begun their evening chorus. And the moon had begun to rise, blood red, across the lake.

'I hadn't realized it would all be so complicated when I decided to come down here.'

'Why did you decide to come?' the Professor asked quietly. 'Isn't it about time you told me?'

By the time Stephanie had finished it was quite late. Ngenzi's servants had brought dinner out to them as they talked. They had coffee afterwards and still Stephanie had not completed her tale. When at last she had said all that she wished to say, Michel Ngenzi drew himself up to his full impressive height and paced about the terrace, thinking.

Finally, he turned to her.

'What makes you sure these really *are* the green monkeys you are looking for?'

'Because we have two independent references.'

'More than fifteen years separate the first reference from the second.'

'But tribes of monkeys will often stay in the same place for much longer periods, won't they?'

'Provided nothing disturbs their habitat.'

'Nothing has.'

'Except, according to your story, trappers on at least two occasions. Has anyone talked to those trappers? Verified the locations?'

'Michel, you know how it is, just as well as I do. The trade in wildlife is very much an under-the-counter business. We don't know who originally caught the monkeys. People don't leave their calling cards on a nice plastic tag attached to a collar round the monkeys' necks. We're lucky to have as neat a reference as we do about where the green monkeys were found.'

The Professor was thoughtful. 'I think it's odd that you have such precise information on this point. It's almost too precise.'

'What do you mean?'

'I mean it's almost as though someone wants those monkeys to be found.' He appeared to puzzle over the problem for a moment or two, then he moved on to something else.

'Frankly, Stephanie,' he resumed his seat on the terrace next to her. 'I don't think it can be done. You may find those monkeys. But what will you do when you have found them?'

'I thought we might move them on somewhere; somewhere they couldn't be found.'

He shook his head. 'You can drive them out if you know

what to do. But they'll come back, especially if – as you think – the tribe has been living in the same place for a very long time. And if they come back, then they'll be exposed to the same threat as before. If the WHO people don't exterminate them the first time, they'll try again and again. Until they do. And if they don't come back, but find some other habitat, they'll be hunted down elsewhere.'

She pleaded with him. 'Surely it's worth a try, Michel. You of all people must see that. You've made your life with animals. You knew my parents and my sister. You must see what it means.'

'Would you like me to help?' He smiled. That wonderful Tutsi smile. 'Would you like me to come with you? Get a team together. It's been some time since my last field trip and I've always had a fondness for monkeys.'

She could hardly believe her ears. She had never dreamed that she might be able to persuade Michel Ngenzi to come with her. She had wanted his advice and encouragement. That would have been enough. But to have him on the expedition itself was almost too good to be true. She stood up and kissed him on both cheeks, standing on tiptoe to do so.

'Are you sure you can spare the time?'

'If I can't spare the time for this kind of thing, what do I have time for?' He raised his glass. 'Let's drink to it? To the green monkeys!'

'To the green monkeys!' Their glasses clinked.

Stephanie came back to Ngenzi's house around lunchtime the following day. She was fretful with impatience.

'When can we leave, Michel?' she asked. 'The WHO team isn't going to be hanging around. We are probably only a few days ahead of them.'

Ngenzi explained the problem to her:

'I've already spoken to my people,' he told her. 'I can get the guides and porters we need. They know the area. There's a lot of movement between Burundi and Eastern Zaire. Frontiers don't mean so much in this part of Africa. But there's one man I'm waiting for and he's upcountry at the moment visiting his village. His name is Kodjo and he's lived his life in the jungle with monkeys. I may know about them from a professional and scientific view-point – I know the difference between the genus and the species. I can tell a marmoset from a macaque. But Kodjo knows them right to the tips of his fingers. If we are going to move those monkeys we are going to have to go about it the right way.'

'Which way is that?'

But Ngenzi would say no more. 'Wait till Kodjo joins us.'

Kodjo finally reappeared early on Sunday morning. He seemed to know that his presence was eagerly awaited. He was a young man, about twenty-two years old, with an engaging smile.

'I'm sorry, I'm late, boss. My wife had a baby. We had to have the 'mwemba'.'

Ngenzi explained to Stephanie that the 'mwemba' was a special ceremony to celebrate the birth of a child.

'It's basically an excuse to drink. It probably took Kodjo three days to recover.'

When he learned of the task that lay ahead, Kodjo looked doubtful. 'I'll try,' he said.

Later, Stephanie saw him at the bottom of Professor Ngenzi's garden squatting on all fours, prancing in and out of the hibiscus and uttering weird howls and growls.

'What's he doing, Michel?' Stephanie asked.

'He's practising,' Ngenzi replied. He wouldn't say any more.

They decided to leave that evening as soon as the moon came up.

Stephanie went back to the hotel to pack up her things and check out of her room. She told them to hold most of her luggage.

'Ah, so you're coming back?' The prospect seemed to please the hotel manager. He liked guests who tipped well. If his staff was happy, he was happy since there was just a chance that they would show up for work in the morning.

'How long will you be gone?'

'I'm not sure.'

Stephanie turned to go. As she did so, a tall handsome African, who had been standing near the desk, addressed her.

'Vous allez en safari, mademoiselle?'

She immediately recognized the man she had seen water-skiing that first afternoon and at the same time recalled the conversation she had had with Professor Ngenzi on the subject of Victor Mtaza. 'Pas exactement...' Stephanie didn't quite know what to say but knew instinctively that it would be a mistake to say too much.

The big white teeth flashed.

'Oho? Not exactly?' Victor Mtaza's eyes roved over the pile of baggage which she was taking with her. He saw the cameras and the guncases and the other equipment which she had gathered.

Then he appeared to lose interest. 'En tout cas, bon voyage.'

As he stepped out of the lobby, Stephanie saw him exchange some words with one of Professor Ngenzi's African servants who had been sent over to help her with her things.

In the car she asked the driver casually:

'Who was that man who came out of the hotel ahead of me, Charles?'

'That was Victor Mtaza, Madame. He's the President's son.'

'Do you know him, Charles?'

'Oh no! Victor Mtaza is a big fish. He swims in Lake Tanganyika. Charles Obonjo is just a little fish who swims in the puddles of the road when the afternoon rains have gone.'

Stephanie left it at that. There were far too many things she didn't understand about Africa for her to begin chasing every stray straw in the wind. But she wondered idly why Charles Obonjo didn't want to admit to an exchange which she knew he had had.

That night the moon rose at around 10 p.m. Half-an-hour later, two cars pulled out of the drive of Professor Michel Ngenzi's private residence and headed south along the road which bordered the lake. Ten miles further on, they pulled off the road into a clearing.

'This is the place.' Michel Ngenzi got out of the leading car.

'What's that?' asked Stephanie. She pointed to a large perpendicular stone which stood in the clearing, clearly visible in the moonlight.

'Go and see.'

Stephanie was able to read the inscription. 'At this point on the shores of Lake Tanganyika Stanley met Livingstone 25 XI 1871.'

'What a place to begin!' she exclaimed.

'Let's hope we all return safely,' Professor Ngenzi replied softly. He touched the stone with his hand and then brought his hand to his forehead.

'Come.' He beckoned to his party. 'It is time to go.'

The boats were waiting for them by the shore. The porters shuffled forward with the food and equipment for the journey. Ten minutes later, they were off.

'Oars first,' ordered Ngenzi.

Now that they were on their way, the Professor was even more evidently in charge than he had been during the preparations. He had shed his city clothes and wore only the umbana, the characteristic loincloth of the high-caste Tutsis. He sat in the prow of the boat, the moonlight glancing on his bare shoulder. Stephanie could not help being struck by the dignity and inner peace of this man whom she had known for so long.

At last, when the lights of the city of Bujumbura were no more than a distant glow, Ngenzi gave permission for the outboard to be started. From the shore only the keenest listener would have detected the sound of the engine above the night wind.

Stephanie Verusio leaned back in the stern of the boat. Ahead of her the mountains of Zaire loomed larger and more ominous with each passing minute. Somewhere among those mountains was a tribe of monkeys. She was going to find those monkeys and save them. That was what her father would have tried to do. That was what her sister would have tried to do. She thought about her parents and her sister.

From the other end of the boat, Ngenzi saw the tears in her eyes, large drops of water glistening in the brightness of the tropical night.

'Don't cry, Stephanie.' His voice was gentle.

Stephanie put her hand to her face and brushed the tears away. 'I'm sorry. Sometimes I feel overwhelmed.'

CHAPTER TEN

BUKAVU! HAD HE BEEN ASKED six months earlier if he expected during the first week of July to fly, via the Zairian capital Kinshasha, to a half-baked town at the southern end of Lake Kivu in the Eastern Congo, Lowell Kaplan would certainly have said that the odds were against it.

His life as a top epidemiologist working for the U.S. Government was a full and interesting one. Even so, he would not normally have anticipated spending his summer vacation in a dilapidated barracks left behind by the Congolese army when they cleaned out the Mulelist rebels back in 1964. Nor would he have anticipated sharing those same barracks with a fat and perspiring Brazilian, namely José Rodriguez the Director-General of the World Health Organization; with Rodriguez' Russian Deputy, the tall and sinister Ivan Leontiev, and with an earnest bespectacled British scientist called John Cartwright.

But Kaplan was determined to make the best of the situation. He decided that his priority task was to lick the WHO team into shape. Each morning before the sun grew too hot, he encouraged his colleagues to exercise on the weed-infested concrete square in front of the barracks.

'One, two, three, four,' Kaplan would shout, setting the pace for the others. Leontiev declined to participate, pleading a gamey leg. But Rodriguez and Cartwright turned out, the former with an offended look as though he found it beneath his dignity, as head of a body concerned with global health, to demonstrate a personal concern with physical fitness.

The Congolese part of the operation was in another hut across the square. Protocol required that the Zairian government should be nominally in charge, with the WHO team in an 'advisory' role (in much the same way, Kaplan reflected, as the Americans had had an 'advisory' role in Vietnam). So a short thickset Zairian soldier called Colonel Albert Mugambu had been assigned to liaise with them.

Mugambu had taken his task seriously. He had produced a squad of some forty men who were now encamped at the Bukavu base, along with the normal complement of wives, grandmothers, chickens, sheep and goats. It was a scruffy lot but, for the time being, they had nothing much to do but wait.

They had been in Bukavu about three days when the equipment arrived on board a Hercules Transport aircraft belonging to the United States Air Force. Mugambu roused his men and they proceeded to unload. When it was all piled on the tarmac, and Kaplan was able to make a thorough inspection of what Uncle Sam had been able to provide given a day or two's notice, his heart swelled with a measure of patriotic pride. What other nation, he thought, could produce fifty brand new breathing apparatuses and a similar number of plastic pressure suits between breakfast and tea? What other nation could produce at the drop of a hat a similar number of recoilless rifles capable of firing high-velocity darts tipped with curare on roving targets? What other nation for that matter would have sufficient stocks of curare in the first place?

As they stood there looking the equipment over, Kaplan had explained to Mugambu the tactics to be followed:

'We can't fire ordinary weapons at the animals. That's too dangerous. The impact of a bullet on bone and flesh will cause a spatter effect. Even if your men are protected with the pressure suits and the breathing apparatus, the contamination could remain. Since we don't know how long the virus can survive after the death of the vector, we can't afford to take that chance. We need a clean kill. That means we've got to be able to hit the monkeys without wounding; the animals have to fall where they are hit and we have to be able to pick up the bodies intact.'

Mugambu didn't completely understand the talk about vectors and viruses.

'Can't we burn the jungle?' he had asked cheerfully. 'My men would enjoy that. Then we wouldn't even have to use the darts.'

'Are you prepared to control a forest fire?' Kaplan had replied sharply. 'Remember, we're talking about several hundred thousand square miles of jungle out here in the Eastern Congo. Once you get started, you may not be able to stop. Besides, we're not running some punitive expedition. We're not operating a scorched-earth policy. As I understand, there are a lot of animals in there besides the green monkeys. They've got a right to live.'

Mugambu didn't seem to be much interested in the question of animals' rights. He shrugged and turned on his heel. Later that day Kaplan saw him roaring drunk surrounded by half a dozen of his men. 'I'd trust that guy to start a fire,' he thought. 'But I'd never trust him to put one out.'

But he knew that he would have to live with Mugambu. There was no way they could carry out their assignment without the logistical support of the Zairian army.

The problem of path-finding, which Kaplan had felt might prove to be extremely difficult, was solved for them in a surprisingly simple way.

Hot and tired after a long day's sorting and organizing the equipment which had just arrived in Bukavu, the WHO team sat huddled in their hut over a large-scale map of the area.

'Frankly,' said Kaplan, 'we have a set of map references and I can see the numbers on the map. I can see where we've got to go. But I'm not sure I see how to get there. Are there paths through this jungle? I'd ask Mugambu, but we won't get any sense out of him.'

Rodriguez had looked at Leontiev and Leontiev had looked at Cartwright. None of them knew the answer.

They were still discussing the problem when there was a

commotion at the door and Mugambu entered with a lot of banging and clattering, followed by two or three of his men and a frightened-looking native.

'This fellow has been hanging around the camp,' said Mugambu, who reeked of beer. 'He says he understands we are interested in monkeys.' The Congolese Colonel spat on the floor of the hut. It was clear that he did not regard a troop of monkeys as a suitable subject of conversation.

'Ask him what he wants to tell us.' Kaplan didn't have much time for Mugambu's posturings.

Mugambu spoke to the man in his own language. He turned back to the party.

'He says he knows where the monkeys are. He can take us to them.'

There was a noticeable stir of interest in the hut.

'Is he talking about green monkeys?' Kaplan asked.

The man nodded enthusiastically and rattled off something in a local dialect.

Mugambu translated for them. 'Yes, he means *green* monkeys.'

'Ask him how he knows where the monkeys are.'

Once more Mugambu spoke to the man. When he saw that he had their interest, the native visibly gained confidence. His answers were more rounded and filled with circumstantial detail.

Even Mugambu seemed to be interested in the man's next answer.

'He's a trapper,' he relayed the information. 'He has a

depot near here where he keeps the animals. He waits till he gets a sufficient number and then he ships them out. Sometimes they go via a dealer in Kinshasha. Sometimes via Bujumbura. He caught a green monkey earlier this year and he remembers where. He says there was a whole tribe of them.'

Kaplan had yet another question to ask. 'Does he think the green monkeys are still where he last saw them? Can he really take us there?'

The man nodded enthusiastically and then proceeded to speak for some time without pause.

Eventually Mugambu was able to explain.

'He says that thirty miles south of here the river Uzizi, which is a tributary of the Ruzizi, enters a defile, perhaps fifty yards wide with steep cliffs on either side. The defile lasts for about half a mile. After this, there comes a saucer-shaped crater partially forested. A kind of deep-sided valley. This is where the monkeys live. At the southern end of the valley, the river once more enters a defile, just as impassable as the first. As far as he knows, the monkeys have never left the valley. He first discovered the place fifteen years ago.'

'Fifteen years ago?' Kaplan's voice quickened with interest. It was fifteen years since the first outbreak of Marburg disease. 'How often does he go there?'

'Very rarely apparently. And when he does he is not always successful in catching the monkeys. He says he caught a green monkey when he first went to the valley but that he didn't catch one again till this year.'

Kaplan exchanged glances with the other members of the team. 'I think we have the confirmation we need, gentlemen, don't you?'

*

Michel Ngenzi and his small band had been marching for three days through the jungle. They had landed their boat on the Zairian side of Lake Tanganyika and had hidden it with care by the shore.

'I hope we can find it when we come back,' Stephanie had said. Tough as she was, she didn't relish the prospect of a forced march round the northern end of the lake.

'We'll find it all right,' Ngenzi had replied. He cast a practised eye along the shoreline taking in the distinctive landmarks, a broken branch here, a half-submerged tree there. To Stephanie one stretch might seem very like another. To Ngenzi, trained from birth to detect the subtle interplay of light and shadow, no ten yards were quite like the next.

Once the boat had been concealed, they had made camp by the water's edge. Stephanie had slept fitfully. It was her first night out in the open for quite some time. She had to re-accustom herself to the sound of animals snuffling around the camp and to other sudden noises of the night.

They breakfasted by the lake that first day and took the opportunity to consult the map which Ngenzi had brought with him.

The Professor sounded apologetic. 'I'm afraid it's more an explorer's chart than a proper map. In fact I rather doubt if it's been updated since Stanley himself passed this way. But it's all we've got. We'll have to do the best we can with it.'

Stephanie looked over his shoulder.

'It seems as though the particular place we're aiming for, going by the map reference I had from Kaplan, is somewhere on this tributary of the Ruzizi.' She peered closer. 'It seems to be called the Uzizi.'

Ngenzi examined the map closely. 'As far as I can tell from the contours, we ought to be looking for a valley somewhere around the 2000 foot level. The Uzizi appears to pass through a kind of defile on entering the valley. See here' – he pointed with his finger at the map – 'the contours are all bunched. The valley itself seems to spread out about half a mile on either side. It's hard to tell what's on the floor of the valley but my guess is that we'll find grass as well as tree cover. On leaving the valley, the Uzizi once more appears to pass through a steep defile before running on down to join the Ruzizi.'

As she listened to him speak, Stephanie did not find it difficult to visualize the abode of the monkeys. In her mind's eye, she saw a green mountain valley and a sparkling river running through it. A valley as remote as any on the face of the earth. A valley where in some incomprehensible way nature had achieved both the perfection of creation and its nemesis. She remembered her dream.

By the end of the third day Stephanie's legs were aching, but she was enjoying herself immensely. To walk by day through the primeval rain-forest, where the immense canopy of trees towered overhead almost shutting out the sun; to make camp by night and sit around the fire till it was time to turn in, surrounded by people, like Michel Ngenzi, whom she knew and trusted; to hear these men talk of the forest and of the ways of the forest and of Africa past and present – all this was for her a profoundly moving experience.

That night the conversation turned to the Mulelists. 'Who were they?' Stephanie asked.

'They were followers of Robert Mulele,' Ngenzi told her. 'He was a strange charismatic man who was one of the leaders of the rebels back in the 'sixties. His followers would go into battle in a half-drugged state. He tried to convince them that they were invincible, that they had only to point their fingers at the enemy and chant and shout and they would be victorious. Mulele's influence was particularly strong in this part of the Eastern Congo. Even today the Zairian army from time to time announces the capture and execution of Mulelists whom they will have rounded up in some drive through the jungle.'

'What happened to Mulele himself?'

'He was murdered one night in Elisabethville. They chopped up his body into about a thousand pieces.'

Stephanie shivered. It was a harsh country. Justice was the law of the strongest. Almost as though to make her point, a mountain lion roared nearby. Instinctively they gathered closer to the camp fire.

By the end of the next day's march, they were about ten miles short of their destination. Ngenzi decided to send out a scouting party. He turned to two of his men and addressed them in their native language.

'You two, Thomas and Edouard, I want you to find the best path to the Uzizi. If you locate the valley, try to discover the way down. Get back here by nightfall tomorrow. We'll wait for you.'

The two men left that night, slipping quietly off into the forest with no more luggage than loin-cloth and panga.

Stephanie welcomed the break while they waited for the two men to return. She washed her hair in a stream and felt better. While she waited for it to dry she talked, in French, to Kodjo whom she now thought of as the 'monkey man'.

'How come you know so much about monkeys and apes, Kodjo?'

Kodjo smiled at her. He had a warm trusting face and he was delighted that the white woman, Stephanie, wanted to converse with him. At home in his village he might have a wife and child, but at heart he was still a boy. His movements, his gestures were lithe like a boy's.

'I grew up near the ridge, miss. There was a tribe of monkeys there. They were my friends.' He spoke the last words simply, a matter-of-fact statement.

'You mean the Nile-Zaire ridge in Burundi?' Stephanie remembered the great forest-clad crests she had seen from the air the day she flew in to Bujumbura.

'Yes, miss. My village is two hundred miles north of Bujumbura. It lies at the foot of the highest summit of the Nile-Zaire ridge. Our fields have crept part of the way up the side of the mountain. We have burned the trees, cultivated the land. But the monkeys are still there at the top of Lwungi.'

'Lwungi?'

'That is the name of the mountain above my village,' Kodjo explained. 'It is one of the sacred places. The kings of Burundi are buried up there on the summit among the trees. Our kings are always buried in the sacred groves. That is why we will never go further up the mountain. To do so would be to violate the spirit, the 'mwami' of our royal ancestors.'

Stephanie nodded. She had heard much about the traditions of kingship.

'I hope I have a chance to visit your village one day.'

Kodjo was honoured. 'I will take you to my village, miss. We make 'mwemba' for you!'

'I thought 'mwemba' was for when someone had had a baby.' 'Oh, there are different kinds of 'mwemba'!'

'I'm not surprised.' She laughed.

Later that afternoon, Stephanie saw that Michel Ngenzi was looking worried. A frown creased the tall gentle face.

'My men should be back by now,' he told her. 'I can't understand what's kept them.'

At dawn the next day, when the two scouts still hadn't returned, Ngenzi's concern had deepened into real anxiety.

'We're going to go on. But we're going to move very cautiously. I have a feeling that something's gone wrong.'

★

Colonel Albert Mugambu had established his base of operations on the rim of the saucer. From where he sat he could look onto the valley floor. Two-thirds drunk though he was, he could nevertheless detect that the scene held a certain appeal. The expanses below contained a fair number of trees, but they were by no means totally forested. The long grasses probably concealed lion, or even cheetah. Mugambu hoped that when this monkey-business was over he would be able to have a go at some 'real' game. He rather fancied slinging a cheetah skin across his shoulder or, better still, having one made into a forage cap as President Mobutu himself had done.

He was reflecting on the various sartorial possibilities, when a squad of soldiers emerged into his view.

'What is it, Staff-sergeant?'

Staff-sergeant Mlanga, who was in charge of the party, did a passable imitation of a salute.

'Prisoners, sir!' The squad parted to reveal two frightened-looking Africans who, by the look of them, had been handled none too gently.

'We were patrolling the rim of the crater when we found these two men,' Staff-sergeant Mlanga explained. 'They were looking down into the valley.' And he added: 'We think they may be Mulelists. But we haven't interrogated them. We brought them straight in. We thought you would like to see them.'

Mugambu's interest was aroused.

'Mulelists, eh?' He turned to Mlanga. 'Thank you, Staff-sergeant. I think I'll interrogate them myself.' He belched evilly, a drunken man scenting pleasure. 'Take them out of earshot,' he ordered. 'I'll be along in a minute.'

★

It was Ngenzi himself who found the bodies of his men. They had been thrown unceremoniously onto the track where it led to the rim of the crater. Already the flies had gathered and the stench of death was noticeable.

'Mon Dieu!' Michel Ngenzi stopped in mid-stride. 'Who the hell did that?' He turned to Stephanie. 'Don't look.'

But Stephanie had already seen the broken bodies and the mangled limbs, and the sight appalled her.

Ngenzi knelt down to examine the bodies more closely.

'They were tortured,' he said in a voice choked with emotion. He was a man who flinched from violence, any kind of violence. Besides, the two men had been with him a long time. 'But I think there was something else, besides torture.' Ngenzi continued. 'Look at the expression on their faces.'

Stephanie saw what he meant. There was a contorted agonized expression on each of the faces. She would not have believed such anguish possible.

The bodies had been lying face up in the long grass. Ngenzi now gently turned them over and, as he did so, he gave a sharp exclamation. 'Look, darts! Darts in the back. Poisoned darts. That's what killed them.'

Gingerly he pulled out a dart from one of the bodies. He examined it carefully. 'No blood! No blood at all. The point of the dart is so fine that it can enter the tissue and flesh without breaking them.'

'Don't touch it,' Stephanie cried. She had a sudden terrifying vision of the Professor collapsing in front of her.

'I'm not going to.'

Ngenzi pointed to the brown stain on the tip of the dart. 'It could be curare. The deadliest nerve-poison known to man. The South American Indians have been using it for centuries.'

'Is it used in Africa too?'

'Not to my knowledge.'

Ngenzi examined the dart carefully.

'This isn't a native product, anyway. It's a manufactured item.'

'What do you think that means?'

'I think it means someone has got there ahead of us,' Ngenzi replied slowly. 'If you wanted to kill the green monkeys without creating conditions for further contamination, that's what you'd use. High-powered darts, tipped with curare.'

'Does that mean we're too late?'

'Maybe. Maybe they've already killed the monkeys.'

'Do you think your men talked?' Stephanie asked. 'Do you think we could be walking into an ambush?'

Ngenzi regarded the remains of his scouts. He seemed quite certain of his reply.

'No, I'm sure they didn't talk.'

Stephanie looked at the large man whom she had come to love and trust as she had loved and trusted her father.

'I think we should go on.' She spoke softly but there was determination in her voice. 'What do the others think?'

Ngenzi turned to his men. 'Kodjo? Charles?'

'We want whatever you want, boss. Only take care.'

'We'll bury the bodies first and then we'll go on.'

It took them two hours to bury the bodies. When they had finished, Ngenzi fashioned two rough crosses and placed them at the head of the graves.

'Were they Catholic?' Stephanie asked.

'Part Catholic, part animistic. In this part of Africa we have a tendency to mix up the different traditions.'

He knelt in prayer and the others knelt with him. At last they moved on, still in single file.

'We'll make camp at the rim of the crater,' Ngenzi said. 'Out of sight. We'll wait. And we'll watch. No fires. No noise.'

They found a cave used by animals about one hundred feet below the rim of the crater. The entrance was about four feet across and two feet high but the cavity inside was large. Once they were installed within, they pulled grasses and fronds and branches into position to disguise the entrance.

That evening, just before dusk, Ngenzi slipped out with a pair of binoculars.

'I'm going to get down to the floor of the crater. I want to see if the monkeys are there.'

'Be careful,' Stephanie urged him. 'Think what happened to the others.'

'I'll be careful. Come with me, Kodjo.'

Stephanie saw the forms of the two men slither into the long grass of the hillside below and, an instant later, disappear from view.

Stephanie waited with increasing anxiety as one hour passed and then another. She used the binoculars but still could see no sign of the two men. Wherever they were, they were completely concealed by the natural cover.

By her watch, two hours and ten minutes had elapsed before the men returned. Both were winded but Ngenzi, after the gloom which had seized him earlier with the murder of his scouts, was now in a visibly elated mood.

'They're beautiful.' He pulled himself inside the cave. 'I've never seen anything so beautiful.'

Later, when he had rested from the steep climb back up to the rim of the crater, he told them about the monkeys.

'They're definitely guenons. But the most wonderful guenons I ever saw. Typical guenon markings. Agile. They were leaping from tree to tree as if they were flying colobuses.'

'Colour? What colour?' Stephanie was anxious to pin it down.

'Hard to say. Green or greenish, certainly. I didn't get close enough. Frankly, I didn't want to. I'm not protected with antibody-rich serum the way you are, Stephanie.'

'How many?'

'I'd say five hundred altogether. All in one place. In a clump of trees more or less in the middle of the crater.'

'How much time have we got?'

'Not much. We've got to move them soon, if we are going to move them at all.'

They spent the night in the cave, huddled together for warmth. They could not run the risk of lighting a fire since they had no idea how close the 'enemy' were. (Inevitably they thought of the other side as the enemy; now more than ever after what had happened to Ngenzi's two native men.) Stephanie found it hard to sleep. She was not naive by any means; in fact she had probably had a wider experience of life than most American women of her age. But she found it difficult to absorb the events of the afternoon and evening. She shuddered when she thought about poor Thomas and Edouard. Could it be, she wondered, that men like Lowell Kaplan were associated with such bestiality? Could he believe that the end, any end, justified those particular means? She thought back to the time she had spent with Kaplan in Paris. In so many ways, it had been good. But she felt a bitterness now towards the man, an anger which made her almost wish she had never met him.

At last she drifted off to sleep to be awakened when Kodjo slipped out of the cave before dawn.

'Where's he going, Michel?' Stephanie was instantly alert. Ngenzi was crouched just outside the mouth of the cave watching the rim of the rising sun break over the lip of the crater.

'He's going to try to drive the monkeys out of the valley.'

'All by himself?'

'That's all he needs.'

From below they heard the bark of a chimpanzee. 'There he goes,' said Ngenzi. 'Kodjo's on his way.'

When he saw her look of astonishment, he explained: 'The chimpanzee is the guenon's historic enemy. It's an old trick of the trappers. They imitate the bark of the chimpanzee to drive the monkeys in the way they want them to go. Monkeys will run from a chimpanzee when they won't move for a lion. Kodjo's an expert.'

Stephanie nodded. She remembered the story Kodjo had told her about growing up near the monkeys on the summit of Mount Lwungi, on the Nile-Zaire ridge. What a coincidence that he should now be involved with another tribe of monkeys, only a couple of hundred miles west of his home ground!

They heard the bark again, fainter this time. To the east, the sun rose red above the rim of the crater.

Stephanie was about to follow Ngenzi out of the cave when she was brought up short.

'Jesus!' The exclamation had escaped almost involuntarily from Ngenzi's lips. As the sun rose, he had seen at once what they all, following his gaze, now also perceived. Along the crater's rim, silhouetted against the rising sun, was a row of soldiers. They stood there motionless in the dawn light, the line of their helmets broken by crude attempts at camouflage.

'They're all around.' Ngenzi whispered, instinctively lowering his voice. 'They've got the crater surrounded. Back into the cave everyone!'

As he spoke, they heard a shouted order and the line of men began to move slowly down the hill.

They lay on their stomachs on the earth floor, peering out through the grasses which concealed the entrance to the cave.

'The monkeys are in the trees each side of the river which runs more or less through the middle of the valley.' Ngenzi kept his voice to a whisper. 'Kodjo's only hope is to drive them down river towards the defile at the bottom of the valley and to hope that they can escape that way.'

'And how will Kodjo escape?'

'Kodjo will find a way.' Ngenzi spoke with confidence.

The light grew quickly stronger. For Stephanie that was always one of the most noticeable features of tropical Africa. The day broke as quickly as it faded. They heard some soldiers passing quite close to the entrance of their hiding-place. Ngenzi clutched a long-handled hunting knife. The rest of the party raised their pangas.

Stephanie felt particularly defenceless. She had a sheath-knife from her Girl Scout days and this she now grasped in a firm fist. But she wasn't sure that she was ready to use it.

At a range of less than ten yards, they were able to see the equipment which was being carried by each and every Congolese soldier.

'My God,' Stephanie whispered as she saw the breathing apparatus, the pressure suits, the rifles. 'They're not taking any risks, are they!'

Ngenzi put a finger to his lips. 'Shh! There're more to come.'

Another party was passing the hide-out. They were equipped in the same way that the first party was, but this time there was a difference. The second squad consisted of two men only and both of them were white.

Stephanie Verusio gave a start of anger as she recognized Lowell Kaplan. She hated him at that moment more passionately than she had ever hated anyone in her life. And to think that she had been to bed with the man! She almost spat in disgust. Tunnel-vision wasn't the word for it. More like myopia. As he passed, she wanted to call out to him, to plead with him to stop the massacre which she knew was about to begin. Ngenzi laid a warning finger on her arm.

'Don't move. Don't say anything. It's too late for that.'

Kaplan was talking into the W/T. He stopped virtually in front of the mouth of their hide-out and she could clearly hear what he was saying.

'Cartwright? Can you hear me? We ought to be directly across the valley from you now. We'll take the southern hemicycle, and we'll move in down the slopes of the crater towards the river in the middle. The monkeys are in the trees alongside the river. Take it easy. Descend at the same rate as we do. That means you'll have to keep your eye on us. But I'll also come in on the W/T from time to time to give you an altitude reading. We're spread out along the 1500 foot contour right now. We're going to drop at the rate of about 500 feet every half hour till we reach the bottom; then we proceed at the pace of a slow walk. Mugambu will give the order to fire when we're all in position. Is that all clear? Over and out.'

She heard Cartwright's voice coming in loud and clear from a distance of less than two miles away.

'That's fine, Kaplan. We have you in view now. Just tell your men not to fire any of those darts by accident. We're right in your line of fire.'

'The same goes for you, friend. Keep your ammunition for the monkeys.'

Once again Stephanie felt her anger boiling over and once again Ngenzi had to restrain her.

The bark of the chimpanzee came from down below. Urgent. Insistent.

'That's Kodjo,' Ngenzi told her. 'He must be near the monkeys now.'

After that, there was nothing they could do except wait. Wait in the hope that Kodjo would succeed and that both he and the monkeys would escape.

By mid-morning they realized that it was too late. They

could see that the line of troops virtually surrounded the trees in the centre of the valley.

'They know what they're doing all right,' Ngenzi commented despairingly. 'The guenons will always stay in the trees rather than run in the grass.'

'And Kodjo?'

'God knows where Kodjo is!' There was a note of despair in Ngenzi's voice. He had already lost two of his best men. He did not wish to lose a third.

It had been a long time since they last heard the sound of the chimpanzee in the valley below. Looking down, they wondered where Kodjo could be. Was he somewhere inside that ring of death? And if he *was* still inside, how could he ever hope to escape? Stephanie found that she had begun to pray; to pray for the monkeys, for herself, for Kodjo, for Ngenzi, for the two men who had already died, for an end to the whole horror. 'Oh Lord,' she prayed. 'Spare us all.'

Ngenzi overheard her. 'The God of Africa has his own ways, Stephanie. He will not always seem to hear you when you pray.'

Involuntarily, she reached for his hand and held it for a long moment.

There was a sudden noise at the entrance of the cave. The grasses and fronds were pushed aside and Kodjo, gasping for breath, pulled himself inside.

Stephanie flung herself on him.

'Kodjo! I'm so glad you made it! Did you find the monkeys?' Kodjo shook his head, totally crestfallen.

'Too late, Miss Stephanie! I was too late. I only just escaped from the ring of soldiers myself. The long grass hid me.'

When he had recovered himself, he said:

'I'm not sure if the monkeys would have moved anyway. I didn't get close enough, I know; but when I barked from a distance, they didn't take much notice. Perhaps there aren't any chimpanzees down on the valley-floor.'

The whispered conversation was interrupted by the first volley of sound as the circle of soldiers closed in. They saw the men advancing steadily, ruthlessly. One step at a time.

'What chance do they have?' Stephanie was sobbing. 'What chance do they really have?'

The first monkeys fell from the branches of the trees. They were too far away to hear the death-screams of the animals; but they could imagine it all.

Stephanie watched through the field-glasses for five minutes. Then she put them down and turned her face to the wall of the cave. When it was all over, they watched a squad of soldiers gather the bodies of the animals where they had fallen. The men went about their work slowly. They were not used to moving in pressure suits with breathing apparatus on their back. They piled the animals, carcass upon carcass, in a clearing, handling them from a distance with six-foot long tongs. Even though all the men wore masks, all contact with the infected animals was to be kept to the barest minimum.

Ngenzi watched them. 'The fools!' he exclaimed. 'Do they think they can leave that pile of bodies there? Is that the way to destroy the virus?'

Now that the slaughter was over, Stephanie found herself once more able to watch.

'I think they're going to burn them,' she said. 'Isn't that a flame-thrower they're bringing up there?'

By late afternoon, the search parties had completed their work. Hour by hour the pile of bodies had grown larger. Now that it was over most of the soldiers had climbed back up the sides of the crater. The WHO team remained below.

As far as José Rodriguez was concerned, the operation had been a complete success. Once he had become acclimatized to the jungle, he had obviously thoroughly enjoyed himself. He could already see the headlines. 'Rodriguez leads WHO expedition to Zaire jungle to eliminate mankind's latest scourge!' He would see that the international press gave the story the right treatment and that adverse publicity was kept to a minimum. He had heard something about harsh punishment meted out to a couple of blacks while he and the rest of his team were having their afternoon siesta. Enthusiasm, he supposed, on the part of Mugambu, the silly ass! He'd have to make sure the press didn't pick up that kind of detail. And he didn't want any pictures of the monkeys either. With the curare-tipped darts sticking into them, it was altogether too strong meat. Time and time again in his professional career as a doctor and administrator, he had come up against the strength of the animal-lovers lobby. That was why he had given the order: Absolutely no photographs of the monkeys. No longshots; no close-ups, no nothing. Plenty of pictures of José

Rodriguez, mind you, on his mercy mission to save mankind. The fat Brazilian smiled.

Ivan Leontiev, like his boss, had absolutely no regrets over their mission or indeed over the manner in which it had been accomplished. Animals, large or small, meant nothing to him. If the sperm-whale carried a lethal virus, he would have helped to eliminate the sperm-whale with as much enthusiasm as he had just showed in helping to eliminate the tribe of green monkeys. (The fact that the whaling fleet of his own country, the Soviet Union, had already made a pretty good job of eliminating the sperm-whale was, in Leontiev's eyes, neither here nor there.) Animals aside, Leontiev had other good reasons for rejoicing over the day's events. His smile was not as full and fat as that of Rodriguez. After all, he was a Russian not a Brazilian. But it was still a smile.

Unlike Rodriguez and Leontiev, Cartwright, the bearded naturalist, was sickened and disgusted by the whole business. He had already determined to hand in his resignation as soon as he got back to Geneva. He blamed no one except himself. At the time of preparation he had thought that the operation was justified. Though he had had scruples on certain points, he had gone along with it. Now he knew that he was wrong. A naturalist was like a doctor. He took a hippocratic oath not to harm under any circumstances those whom he was sworn to protect. Once the bodies had been piled, Cartwright turned his head aside and walked away. He had seen enough. He had no wish to see more. A tribe of green monkeys – and perhaps it was the only tribe of green monkeys left in the world – had been destroyed. That was something his conscience would have to live with for the rest of his life.

For Lowell Kaplan, things were much more complicated. He couldn't help recalling the conversation he had had with Stephanie in Paris not long before. He remembered the fire and the passion with which she had spoken of the animals and of her mission in life. He would have given the world not to be standing where he was now standing. The day's carnage had left him feeling more exhausted than he had ever felt in his life. It was not the physical effort which had tired him, though that had been strenuous enough. It was not the grind of eight hours' march day after day through the equatorial forest. No, it was the emotional trauma of being party to a massacre. No more, no less. For as long as he lived Kaplan would be able to see the death-throes of the monkeys as they were, one after another, transfixed by the lethal darts; would be able to hear the quick thud as the bodies hit the ground beneath the trees. He found himself hoping that the monkeys had not suffered too much. By five o'clock that day, it was all over. There was nothing left except a patch of smouldering ashes on the river bank in the middle of the valley. By nightfall, the long grasses, which had been creased when they brought in the flame-throwers, were already re-asserting themselves. The African sparrows, callous as ever, quickly returned to the great over-arching trees which had served as shelter to the monkeys. The gazelle which had disappeared at the first hint of armed men came coquettishly back to the crater, tripping delicately round the edge of the circle of scorched earth.

A cheetah flickered quickly in and out of the grass.

Michel Ngenzi and his party slept for the second night in the cave, taking it in turns to keep watch. When day broke and they looked out once again into the valley, the last smouldering fumes had disappeared.

Ngenzi himself went out to reconnoitre. He was not prepared to risk any more of his men. When he came back, he said: 'It's clear they've all gone. Pulled back to Bukavu, I should think. There's not a sign of them. I think we should leave now. There's nothing more we can do.'

Stephanie looked at him. 'I want to go down there. There may be something still alive down there.'

'What's the point?' Ngenzi tried to dissuade her. 'You saw what we all saw. Nothing could have survived that holocaust.'

'I'm going down.'

'In that case, I'm coming with you.'

'You're not protected. I've got the serum. You haven't.'

'I'll stay back.'

Four hundred yards from the river and the trees, Ngenzi stopped to let her go on ahead. He sat down on a fallen tree and took out his binoculars so as to be able to keep her under close observation.

For half-an-hour he watched her poking in and out of

the trees; then she began to quarter the area systematically. From time to time he saw her stop, as though she was examining the ground. Once she looked in his direction and signalled with her fingers that she wanted another twenty minutes. He waved his agreement but at the same time pointed towards the sun as though to say: 'Don't be too long!' They had a long way to go that day and he wanted to get started.

When the twenty minutes were almost up, he saw her bend down and reach to pick up something from the ground. He focused on her with his binoculars. She had an animal of some kind in her hand.

She was waving now and running towards him in her excitement.

'Stop!' he shouted. 'Don't come any closer. What have you got there?' He cupped his hands to make his words carry.

'I've got a monkey. A baby monkey,' she called back. 'I'd say about six weeks old. Somehow it must have managed to escape.'

'Hold it up. Let me take a close look at it through the glasses. Don't let it bite you or scratch you.'

'It's not going to. It thinks I'm its mother.'

At a range of two hundred yards, Ngenzi examined the animal through the glasses as she held it up for him. Something puzzled him. The colour of the animal wasn't right. He was an expert. He knew about these things. There was too much grey in the fur of the animal. Perhaps it was the distance. In spite of the powerful degree of magnification which his binoculars afforded, two hundred yards was hardly an ideal range from which to conduct a scientific examination.

'Come closer,' he shouted.

She came closer, cradling the animal in her arms. He could get a clear view now of the markings. They were guenon markings all right. The tiara of fur about the head; the beard and the moustache; the stripe on the rump. But the colour was definitely not right. It wasn't green. It was grey-green.

Ngenzi knew that there was one infallible test if one wished to distinguish the true green monkey from the cognate species, the grey-green monkey. The difference between *Cercopithecus viridens* and *Cercopithecus quasiviridens*, which was the scientific name for the grey-green monkey, was a question of fungus in the fur.

'Have a look at the fur,' he shouted. 'Run your fingers through the fur. Does it leave a stain?'

Stephanie knew what he was talking about. She remembered what she read in the text book that night in Paris, the day Kaplan left – she felt a sudden stab of anger as she thought of the American – anger, yes, but was there a trace of regret as well?

She did as he asked. She ran her hands through the animal's fur. There was no trace of any fungus.

'Nothing,' she shouted.

'Do it again. Rub the animal behind the ears.'

The little monkey was visibly reassured to be tickled behind the ears. It simpered with pleasure.

'Still nothing.'

Negenzi stood up and walked towards her. If there was ever a time when he had staked his life on his scientific competence, this was that time.

'I want to take a closer look,' he called.

'Are you sure?'

'I'll take the risk.'

She walked part-way to meet him.

Still, he took care. He circled her twice examining the animal from all sides. He asked her to hold it up by the front paws so that he could look at its underside. Finally he was sufficiently convinced by what he had seen to touch the animal itself.

He spoke to it as he worked; talking to it in a low voice; speaking in the dialect of his childhood, a kind of ki-swa-hili which was what he always used when working with animals.

'Now, then, don't worry! I'm not going to hurt you. Nobody's going to hurt you. Okay, so they killed your mother and your father and your brothers and sisters. But those were mad men, dangerous men. We're not like that. We want to help.'

He unscrewed one of the lenses from his binoculars. He wanted to be able to examine the animal's fur with the aid of a magnifying glass. There was no sign of any fungus.

Finally he was satisfied. 'I know I'm right. That's not a

green monkey. That's not *Cercopithecus viridens*. I'll stake my scientific reputation on it.'

'You've staked more than that,' Stephanie said. 'You just staked your life.'

They climbed back up the hill together. Stephanie was puffing with the exertion – she wasn't as fit as she thought – but still she was able to express her perplexity, her utter bewilderment.

'How can this baby monkey be a grey-green monkey and all the others green monkeys? How can they be part of the same tribe and still be a different species?'

'They can't,' Ngenzi spoke quietly. 'That's just not scientifically possible.'

'Did they kill the wrong monkeys then? But how? I don't understand. I just don't understand.'

'I don't either,' the tall gentle Tutsi replied. 'But we'll find out.'

CHAPTER ELEVEN

COLONEL ALBERT MUGAMBU was pleased by the way it had all gone. He was more than pleased; he was delighted.

The two specially constructed crates had been safely loaded into the cargo compartment of the plane. Now, conscious of a job well done, he sat curtained off from his men like a sultan in his splendour, a glass of Tuborg Export beer in one hand and his ever-present fly-swat in the other. From time to time he looked out of the window and by the light of the full moon saw the thick equatorial jungle unroll beneath the wingtips.

He took another pull at his glass of beer as the plane, showing no lights, began to drop down towards a deserted airfield once used by the West Germans for a 'secret' rocket project. (The Germans had pulled out, largely as a result of political pressures, after the 'secret' became known, but the installations remained. The jungle had begun to encroach on the perimeter; nevertheless, the runways were perfectly serviceable.) Mugambu burped contentedly. Yes, he reflected, he had more than fulfilled his task. Men like that pompous American, Lowell Kaplan, might think of him as a drunken oaf. How wrong they were! Half a dozen of the darts used in the operation in the crater had been tipped not with curare but with a highly potent tranquillizing drug. Two of these darts had been used to good effect. The still-alive bodies of two green monkeys, instead of being burned with the rest, had been secretly removed from the crater area – it was easy enough to find a moment when the attention of the WHO team was engaged elsewhere – and had been placed in crates that formed part of Mugambu's personal baggage.

Mugambu had every confidence in those crates. He had personally taken delivery of them from his contact in Kinshasha. He had inspected the life-support system, the air-filtration system, the recycling system and so forth. He was personally quite convinced that there was no danger that any virus could escape from the animals while they were contained within the crates. But to make doubly sure he had insisted that his hand-picked team retain their masks and pressure suits at all times when handling the load.

The airstrip rose suddenly to meet them out of the forest. Then they were down. The Zaire Air Force DC8 taxied bumpily to the side and waited. Mugambu remained on board. There was nothing to tempt him out of the plane – the forest which loomed on all sides had a distinctly unfriendly appearance. And besides, the arrangement was that his cargo would remain on board until the other party arrived.

Sweating, now that they were on the ground, and smelling of beer, Mugambu went to stand by the open door of the plane. He lit a cigarette and the tip of it glowed in the night. He could feel the tension mounting inside him. What if the American didn't come? Should he fly on to Kinshasha? But then what would he do with the animals? How would he dispose of them? What if somebody else came and not the American? He fingered the belt of his service pistol nervously.

He saw the big transport plane almost as soon as he heard it. It was a long-range Lockheed Hercules. He guessed that it had probably flown down from one of the U.S. bases in Southern Sudan. Trust the Americans, Mugambu thought. They never did things by halves. The big plane landed, rolled down to the end of the tarmac, then turned and came back until it was parked next to the DC8. A side door opened and a man stood there, outlined in the light which came from the interior of the plane. He had a torch in his hand with which he flashed a recognition signal. Mugambu responded. The first man went back inside.

Seconds later, the cargo doors on the Hercules opened and two jeeps drove onto the runway. Mugambu could see that the personnel in the jeeps wore protective clothing.

'All right,' he told his men. 'Get on with it.'

The Congolese soldiers let the stairs down and Mugambu descended to supervise the transfer.

When it was finished, the tall balding American, who had first signalled with the torch and who had clearly been in charge on the American side, came over to him.

'I guess that's it, Albert. We'll be taking off now.'

He passed over a bulging brown briefcase. 'I'm sorry it's so heavy. We thought you'd prefer small denomination bills.'

'You're sure they're genuine?'

The tall American gave a short laugh. 'I don't pay in counterfeit money!'

A minute later, the engines on the Hercules were started for take-off. The big plane lumbered off into the night sky. The DC8 followed a few minutes later.

On the flight back to Kinshasha, Colonel Mugambu sat with the bulging brown briefcase on his lap. Once he opened it to check on the contents. He had never seen so much money in his life. His men would have to have some of it, but the bulk he would keep for himself. He considered it a proper reward for being the right man in the right place at the right time.

*

They found the boat where they had left it, moored at the water's edge on the Zairian side of Lake Tanganyika. They began the crossing as soon as it was dark. Four hours later, Stephanie Verusio was back in her old room at the Source du Nil Hotel in Bujumbura. She lay on her bed trying to sleep. But sleep would not come. She was too exhausted to sleep.

In some ways the mental exhaustion was worse than the physical. Her mind kept on going round and round the same set of facts and bumping up against the same inconsistencies.

Fact number one: there had been an outbreak of virus disease in Marburg in Germany in 1967. The episode was not widely reported but it happened.

Fact number two: monkeys were suspected as a cause of the disease. The link had not been investigated at the time because of the desire on the part of the West German authorities to cover-up a politically explosive event.

Fact number three: it subsequently appeared that a green monkey, coming from the Kugumba region of Eastern Zaire, had been implicated in the 1967 deaths.

Fact number four: a green monkey, also coming from the Kugumba region of Eastern Zaire, had been implicated in her sister's death earlier that year.

Fact number five: a tribe of monkeys existed or (she corrected herself) had once existed in the Kugumba region of Eastern Zaire at precisely the location indicated.

Fact number six: this tribe consisted not of the green monkeys but of grey-green monkeys.

Had the Marburg episode and her sister's death been caused by the grey-green monkey, not the green monkey? Had there been a mistake in classification? That was one possibility but she doubted it. In any case, the baby monkey which she had found in the crater had now been taken off to Ngenzi's laboratory in Bujumbura and tests would soon show if the animal was diseased.

If there had been no mistake in the classification of the

species, then there must have been some other mistake. Could it be that the Marburg deaths and her sister's death had indeed been caused by green monkey disease *with the green monkeys themselves coming from somewhere other than the Kugumba region of Eastern Zaire?* If this hypothesis was true, what accounted for the error of location? And how could such an error have been made twice? What did it all mean?

These thoughts went round and round in her head as she lay there. Finally, as the dawn was beginning to break on the mountains across the lake, she fell asleep.

Several hours later she woke with a start. The sun was streaming in through the window and the telephone was ringing.

She immediately recognized the deep kindly tones of Michel Ngenzi.

'How are you, Stephanie? Recovered?'

'Recovering, thanks.' She shook herself awake.

'We just had the first results of the tests at the laboratory. That monkey is not diseased. It's as healthy as a newborn baby. I just thought you would like to know.'

'Phew!' Stephanie could not honestly say that Ngenzi's news helped to clarify the situation. But she felt deeply relieved that Ngenzi and the others who had risked their lives bringing the animal back were not in jeopardy.

'What are you going to do with it now you've finished the tests?' Somehow, Stephanie minded a great deal about what happened to the animal.

'I'm going to keep it,' Ngenzi said. 'It can run around

with the donkey and the peacocks.'

Stephanie went to Ngenzi's house that afternoon. They sat together on the veranda. Stephanie cradled the little monkey in her arms, happy to see it safe. But Ngenzi seemed ill at ease. He nodded in the direction of his two Hutu servants who were, as usual, down at the bottom of the garden slashing away with their pangas at ever-threatening weeds.

'There seems to be trouble brewing among the Hutus. I don't like the smell of it. Those two are loyal to me; I'm sure of that. But they're under pressure. Someone is trying to stir the Hutus up.'

He changed the subject.

'What are you planning to do now, Stephanie?'

Ngenzi's question gave her a chance to formulate an idea which had been hovering at the back of her mind since she had woken up that morning. It was really nothing more than a wild hunch, inspired by a few moments of conversation with Kodjo, the 'monkey man'.

'Michel, could I ask you a great favour?'

'Go ahead.'

'I wanted to know if I could go with Kodjo to his village. Can you spare him? He's really anxious for me to come. I think he wants to show me his family. He says they'll make a 'mwemba' for me!'

Ngenzi laughed. 'Of course you can go. You must go. You can have my car and my driver for a few days. Charles will be glad to take you.'

For a fraction of a second Stephanie wondered how sure Ngenzi was of Charles. She remembered the exchange she had seen him have outside the hotel with Victor Mtaza and his subsequent denial of it. But the offer seemed too good to be questioned.

She flung her arms round Ngenzi's neck. 'That's marvellous.'

Two days later, seated in style in the back of Professor Ngenzi's car, Stephanie set off up country. Charles, Professor Ngenzi's chauffeur, took the wheel. Kodjo, whom Stephanie continued to think of as the 'monkey man', sat up in front beside him.

Stephanie had been invited to stay by a German couple, friends of Michel Ngenzi.

'You have to meet Peter and Helga Lustig,' Ngenzi had said. 'They're delightful. And they know as much about Burundi as I do myself. He's been out here fifteen years with one international assistance project or another. He started with tea, I believe. But now he's moved on to coffee. He's done very well. Burundi coffee is some of the best in the world. He works hard. They both do. But they play hard too. You'll see the place they've built up there. They've taken one of the old colonial houses and transformed it.'

When she arrived at the Lustigs', Stephanie immediately understood what Ngenzi meant. They had driven in a north-easterly direction from Bujumbura. In early afternoon, climbing all the time, they had left the main road – if such it could be called – for a dirt track which curled up towards the treeline. Two miles later they turned into the drive of the Lustig estate.

Her hosts came out to greet her, and they stood for a while talking on the terrace.

'How is Michel? He is a marvellous man, isn't he?' Helga Lustig had fair close-cropped hair and a warm enthusiastic voice. She managed to make it plain that it was as much pleasure for her to receive visitors, as it was for them to be received in her magnificent home.

Stephanie agreed wholeheartedly with Helga's verdict on Michel Ngenzi.

'He's almost like a second father to me,' she said simply. They spent some time on the terrace admiring the view.

Peter Lustig, a dapper fifty-year-old who clearly believed that style was the essence of life, pointed out the geography.

'What you're looking at straight ahead is the Nile-Zaire ridge. It's one of the great watersheds of Africa. Rain which falls one side of the ridge ends up in the Nile; rain which falls on the other side ends up in Zaire – in the Congo River.'

He saw that Stephanie was looking at a towering crest in the middle of the ridge almost opposite the house.

'That's Mount Lwungi,' Peter Lustig explained. 'It's one of the highest summits in the Nile-Zaire ridge, with the finest stand of primeval rain-forest in the whole country. It's also the site of an *ibigabiro*.'

'What's an *ibigabiro*?' Stephanie asked.

'A royal burial ground. Sacred to the ancient kings.'

'Oh, yes, I heard a bit about that already.' Stephanie recalled the conversation she had had with Kodjo a few days earlier.

If the distant view was spectacular, so too was the nearer. The lawns in front of the house stretched for two full acres; there was a tennis court and swimming pool, and a paddock for the horses which were Helga Lustig's pride and joy.

'If you marry a man who decides to make his life in the bush, you may as well make the most of it,' she exclaimed. 'I've got my horses; I've got my garden. This is a wonderful climate for growing flowers. It's high; it's moist. There's a freshness in the air.'

Stephanie nodded. 'I'm beginning to love it.'

'And I've got my stereo too,' Helga Lustig continued. 'I don't know where we would be without the tapes.'

They went inside. Charles and Kodjo departed with the car into the nearby village of Bugamba.

'We won't see them again till the morning,' Peter Lustig said. 'This is Kodjo's home village, isn't it? There will be a lot of beer drunk tonight.'

They had dinner, just the three of them, rather solemnly in the dining-room. Seeing that both of the Lustigs had changed for dinner, Stephanie had done the same. Afterwards, Helga dismissed the servants. They had coffee outside. Darkness had long since fallen and they felt rather than saw the looming mountains across the valley.

'What would you prefer?' Helga Lustig asked. 'Mozart, Schubert, Beethoven? We have everything. As long as I have my tapes, I can live anywhere.'

Soon the evening was full of sounds. Stephanie leaned back in her chair and took it all in. A week earlier she had been marching through the jungle a couple of hundred miles to the east, sweating and uncomfortable. Tonight, she was bathed and clean; had had an agreeable dinner with two charming people; and now she was listening to the finest offerings of that great flowering which was German music in the nineteenth century.

'How long are you visiting Burundi?' Helga Lustig asked.

'I can't really say for sure. I'm looking for something but I haven't found it yet.'

For the next hour, with occasional interruptions while Helga Lustig refilled the coffee cups or changed the background music, Stephanie told them the story of the last month of her life. She began with the tale which Lowell Kaplan himself had told her about the outbreak of disease in Marburg in 1967. She continued with her sister's death and with her own decision to come to Africa. Finally, she came to the events of the last few days: the trek into Zaire and the slaughter at the crater.

The Lustigs, as she had known they would be, were horrified.

'What a pointless massacre!' Helga exclaimed. 'Even if those monkeys had been carrying the virus, they had no right to kill them. What harm were they doing to anyone up there in the crater?'

What astonished the Lustigs most of all was the fact that, even though they were Germans, they had never heard about the Marburg affair.

'Fancy that!' exclaimed Helga. 'Of course, 1967 was after we left. Peter and I were already married by then and we were on our first assignment – in South West Africa. Right out in the bush about three hundred miles from Windhoek. It's not surprising that we never heard. And then when we did go back to Germany on home leave in 1971, well, I suppose by then everyone had forgotten.'

'I don't think many people knew about the outbreak anyway,' said Stephanie. 'The German authorities kept very quiet about it.'

'I'm surprised the old woman didn't mention it, though.' Peter Lustig pulled reflectively on his pipe. 'She must have been in Marburg about then. I gather she came here some time towards the end of the 'sixties.'

It was one of those moments when Stephanie knew, intuitively, that something important had just been said. For the last several days she had, mentally, been trying to fit the pieces of the jigsaw together. But she hadn't managed to do so. Either the pieces weren't all there; or else she wasn't looking at them the right way up. Now, suddenly, she realized that the casual reference to an old woman who had lived in Marburg at the end of the 'sixties could be the clue she was looking for.

'What old woman?' she asked sharply. 'Does she live in Burundi now? Near here?'

'She does indeed,' Peter Lustig replied. 'The locals call her Kagomba, which is the Kirundi word for wild cat. She must be getting on for seventy now. She's some kind of recluse. She's been living alone up on the peak there' – he waved a hand across the valley in the direction of the mountains – 'for God knows how many years. From time to time, she comes down to the village for supplies. But for the most part she's self-sufficient.'

'And she's from Marburg?'

'That's what she said. I've talked to her a couple of times. But she didn't stop long. She scuttled back into the forest. I imagine her German's getting pretty rusty by now. At least Helga and I have each other to talk to.'

'Oh, I talk to my horses in German too!' Helga said.

They all laughed.

That night Stephanie lay awake trying to fit this new piece into the jigsaw. Could the old woman conceivably be the person whom Stephanie thought she might be? If so, what was she doing here in Burundi?

The next day, Kodjo and Charles came for her early, to take her on the long-promised visit to Kodjo's village.

Kodjo was apologetic. 'We not make 'mwemba' this morning, miss. Today is market-day. We make 'mwemba' later.'

'Anytime you say, Kodjo.' Stephanie didn't at all mind missing a hard day's drinking. She didn't have much of a head for local beer.

On the way down, Stephanie asked Kodjo if he knew about the old woman.

Kodjo laughed. 'You mean Kagomba, the wild cat. Yes, we see her from time to time. Two or three times a year we see her at the market. Then she disappears into the forest again.'

'What does she do?'

He rolled his eyes as if to indicate that this was not his concern.

'Have you seen where she lives?'

Again Kodjo rolled his eyes.

'She inhabits the *ibigabiro*, the sacred grove. We are not supposed to go there but I sometimes do. That's where the tambourine is hidden.'

'Tambourine?'

'In my country when the mwami – the king – dies, we do not say 'yapfuye', which means: 'the king is dead'. We say, 'yatanze', which means: 'he has given up the tambourine'. The tambourine is the symbol of royal authority. It is buried with the mwami. The wood for the tambourine comes from the *ibigabiro* on the summit of Lwungi. That's where the monkeys are too. My friends the monkeys,' Kodjo added with an air of proprietorial pride.

Again, Stephanie had a feeling of things at last clicking into place.

When they reached the outskirts of the village, Stephanie saw that it was indeed market day, a typical African scene. Fruit and vegetables were spread out on the ground; colourful print dresses were hung up for sale; fish had been brought up from the lake and were being cooked over a wood fire; small boys offered boxes of matches and chewing-gum.

Stephanie got out of the car.

'Wait for me here, would you please? I'm just going to wander around.'

Charles and Kodjo were quite happy to sit in the car waiting for her. They had seen a thousand village markets if they had seen one. A boy brought them Coca-cola, and they drank it, while Stephanie drifted off.

At the far end of the market, out of sight of the car, was a stall which sold odds and ends, such as radio batteries. It was well frequented – the transistor radio had penetrated into the interior of Burundi as into much of the rest of Africa. Attracted by the small crowd, Stephanie wandered over and found herself standing next to a small wizened old woman, who held out a fistful of coins, asking to be served. Stephanie looked at her once quickly, casually, and turned away.

But there was something about the old woman which brought her back for a second look. She appeared to be talking the native dialect; her skin was deep brown; yet Stephanie knew at once that at some point in the past, perhaps the long-forgotten past, the woman had been a European.

Her transaction completed, the woman turned away

from the stall. Stephanie knew that unless she spoke now, she might lose her opportunity. The little old woman would quickly be swallowed up in the crowd.

By an effort of will, she dredged up her school German. 'Frau Matthofer? I was hoping that I would find you here.'

The old woman started as though she had been struck.

CHAPTER TWELVE

IRVING WOODNUTT SAT at his desk on the eighteenth floor of the Pharmacorp building, overlooking the Golden Triangle in downtown Pittsburgh. He felt vaguely dissatisfied. On the surface, everything had gone right for him. Under his leadership, Pharmacorp had grown into one of the largest drug and pharmaceutical corporations in the land, ceding place only to giants like Mercx and American Cynamid. He himself held a commanding position among the heads of the large corporations, not just in Pittsburgh, but across the nation. He had power. He had influence. He could pick up the phone and be put through to the President. Or at least to one of the top Presidential assistants. That kind of thing counted. At the golf club, people would point him out – a large, thickset man, almost florid and running to fat.

'That's Irving Woodnutt,' they would say. 'He's President of Pharmacorp.' And they would stop and stare for a moment as Woodnutt drove off down the fairway before heaving himself into the electric golf-cart to follow the ball around the course.

Irving Woodnutt's vague dissatisfaction with life had, therefore, nothing to do with Pharmacorp Inc.'s performance among the ranks of *Fortune*'s first one hundred American companies. It had nothing to do with Pittsburgh as a place to live. The air pollution which had once been such a feature of the city was a thing of the past. The waters of the two great rivers, the Allegheny and the Monongahela, which flowed together at the point of the Golden Triangle, were cleaner than they had ever been. The fact that great corporations such as Westinghouse and Pharmacorp had chosen Pittsburgh as their national and international headquarters had brought to the city lustre and prestige and the civic amenities had improved accordingly. The city's orchestra was world-renowned; its libraries extensive; its suburbs on a par with, if not better than, those to be found in the large cities of other eastern states. No, if Irving Woodnutt wore the beginning of a frown on his broad tanned face, it was because – at the ripe age of fifty-three – he was looking for a new challenge in life.

Such as politics. Out of the window, as he mused, he saw a string of barges being towed down the river. They were carrying coal to the great new power plants which, over the vociferous objections of the environmentalists, had been constructed downstream. Either coal or nuclear, the environmentalists had been told. Ultimately, he thought, as the last of the barges disappeared from his line of vision, everything's political. If you're not in politics, you're nowhere. For the moment Woodnutt had concluded that in spite of the appearances to the contrary he himself was still nowhere.

Realistically, Woodnutt knew that at his time of life, if he was going to make the jump into politics, he would have to go for Senator. It was that or nothing. The House of Representatives didn't interest him. You did that for starters. But he wasn't looking for starters. He was looking for the main dish. To be elected to the Senate he needed support; not just support from the party in the state: support from the party at the national level.

It was therefore a particularly happy coincidence that, just as Woodnutt had reached this point in his reflections, the telephone should ring.

Woodnutt noticed the light flashing, but left his secretary to take the call.

'It's Mr Peabody from Washington; Mr George Peabody, Mr Woodnutt. Do you wish to take the call?' The voice of his secretary came through on the intercom.

'Don't be naive, Louise,' Woodnutt spoke sharply. 'Of course I wish to take the call.'

As he reached for the telephone, Woodnutt reflected that anyone who was interested in running for the Senate and didn't wish to take a call from the Hon. George Peabody must be out of his mind. For George Peabody was a wily Quaker who, after an immensely varied career which (amongst other things) included a stint as director of the CIA, now looked after the national fortunes of the Democratic Party. Without a fair wind from Peabody, there was no way a Woodnutt candidacy for one of the two Pennsylvania seats in the Senate could stand any chance of success.

'Irving, how are you?' The cracked tones identified the man as surely as a red marker.

'Fine, George. Just fine.'

'That's great, Irving. Just great.' Peabody came straight to the point.

'Irving, is there any chance of your getting down to Washington within the next day or so? There are one or two things I and some friends of mine would like to discuss if you had a moment. It could be important. I know you're thinking about that Senate seat, Irving, if you follow me.'

Irving Woodnutt followed him only too clearly. 'Just name the time. I'll be there.'

Two days later, the President of Pharmacorp Inc. caught the morning flight from Pittsburgh into Washington's National Airport. There was a limousine waiting for him, an anonymous black car. On the driver's door the words 'U.S. Government – Federal Service agency' were printed in small gold letters.

Woodnutt had assumed that he would be meeting Peabody downtown – probably at the headquarters of the Democratic National Committee. However, instead of crossing Memorial Bridge into the city, the driver turned off the freeway at the Arlington exit. Five minutes later the car pulled into the underground garage of the Arlington Sheraton.

They took the elevator up to the top floor of the hotel from the garage, without passing through the lobby.

'Why the secrecy?' Woodnutt asked. The driver was noncommittal.

Peabody was already waiting for him. He was a tall man, nearer seventy than sixty, with bushy eyebrows and a firm handshake. There was another younger man with him.

'Hi, Irving. Good of you to come.' He introduced the other man. 'You know Dick Sandford, don't you? My successor at the Agency.'

Woodnutt gave a start of surprise. When on the telephone Peabody had mentioned some 'friends', he assumed that Peabody was referring to some political cronies. He had not imagined for one minute that he would be meeting the present director of the CIA.

He shook hands with the thin dark-haired bespectacled man whom Peabody presented to him. He knew Dick Sandford by repute as one of the toughest operators in Washington; but they had never met.

While Sandford and Woodnutt were introducing themselves to each other, George Peabody was looking around the room as though sizing it up.

It was a penthouse suite and the large windows provided a superlative view of downtown Washington. Across the Potomac, the Lincoln Memorial gleamed white in the sun. The planes roared in low to land at the airport. Nearer at hand, the traffic curled off the Arlington Expressway bound for the Pentagon or for Alexandria.

'Don't worry about the room, George.' Dick Sandford had noted Peabody's interest in his surroundings. 'The Arlington Sheraton is one of our safe houses. We use this place often.'

He turned apologetically to Woodnutt. 'You must forgive the cloak and dagger,' he said. 'When George and I have finished telling you what we want to tell you, you'll understand why we can't afford to have any official log of this meeting.'

The three men sat down. There was coffee in a flask and they helped themselves to it. For a few moments they made polite conversation. Then Peabody looked at his watch. He turned to Sandford. 'Dick, I think the best thing would be if you led off on this one. I have to run along in any case. But that doesn't matter. After all, I'm just the intermediary. You needed to get to Irving here and Irving happens to be an old friend of mine whose political career I'm following with interest.' Peabody leaned over and punched Woodnutt's shoulder to make quite sure that the President of Pharmacorp didn't miss the point. Then, as Sandford began to speak, he slipped away.

Sandford launched straight into the substance of the matter. 'You probably know,' he said, removing his spectacles and polishing them as he spoke, 'that the Strategic Arms Limitation Agreement between this country and the Soviet Union doesn't cover chemical and bacteriological warfare. SALT is, as its name implies, limited to strategic arms.'

Woodnutt nodded. 'I know.'

'One of the consequences of this situation is that the United States as a whole, and clandestine agencies like the CIA in particular, have been devoting many more resources than in the past to CW and BW. This is more or less inevitable. The system is geared up for a certain amount of military spending. If you stop the money flowing down one channel, it merely flows down another.' Again Woodnutt nodded. This was the kind of reasoning he followed easily. It wasn't so different in industry. Once the budget was approved, the pressure to spend was there. And if it didn't go on one thing, it would go on something else.

'Frankly,' Sandford continued, 'CW and BW have become one of the Agency's priorities. Of course, the United States is party to various general conventions which are meant to limit the use of chemical and biological weapons. Pious platitudes from the United Nations. The usual rubbish. The language is so vague you can drive a coach and horses through each subordinate clause. In any case, most of the international conventions which are meant to limit CW and BW are still couched in terms more relevant to the First World War and German mustard gas drifting over the Allies' trenches.'

'You mean the CB/BW parameters have changed?'

'You bet they have. For some time one of our main priorities in the CW/BW field has been to examine the potential of exotic viruses.'

'Potential for what?'

'Potential for influencing the balance of power or terror.' Sandford warmed to his subject. 'Imagine,' he said, 'that the United States and the United States only is in possession of a lethal exotic virus which the whole world believes has been eliminated once and for all because the vector for this lethal exotic virus has itself been eliminated. Imagine what the United States might be able to do with that virus, under certain circumstances!'

While Woodnutt listened fascinated, Sandford explained what he meant. Twenty minutes later the Director of the CIA was nearing his conclusion.

'Only the firm – the CIA – knows about this,' he said. 'It's an Agency concept. The Secretary for Health and Human Services – HHS – has no idea. The National Institute of Health – NIH – has no idea. Nor does the Center for Disease Control at Atlanta, Georgia, or any of the people there. Lowell Kaplan, whose reports initiated this whole thing, is completely unaware of what we are doing. Frankly, I don't think we could ever expect HHS or NIH or CDC to approve our action. Those institutions are run by medical men and medical men are guided by medical criteria and priorities. Do you follow?'

'Perfectly.'

'But the mandate of the Agency, of the CIA, is different. We have to look at the interest of the United States as a whole. We cannot afford to take a narrow sectoral view. And it is our best judgement,' he spoke with deliberate emphasis at this point so that Woodnutt should not fail to catch his meaning, 'that the United States cannot afford to let this opportunity slip.'

'What exactly do you mean?'

Sandford took him through the logic of the thing, step

by step. 'Look at it this way,' he said. 'As far as the outside world is concerned, the WHO-sponsored operation has been successful. The green monkeys have been eliminated and the threat of Marburg disease has been eliminated with them. As we know, the newspapers have carried the story. José Rodriguez, that fat Brazilian who runs the World Health Organization, has had his picture on the front page of the *New York Times*. Up here on the Hill, Congress has shown its pleasure by increasing the appropriations both for WHO and HHS. Congressmen like this kind of thing much better than Medicare, you know. It's effective; it's dramatic and above all it's cheap.'

'Well?' Woodnutt still didn't quite see what Sandford was driving at.

Sandford took his time. He lit a cigarette before continuing, and offered the packet to Woodnutt, who declined.

'I said,' Sandford repeated, 'that the outside world thinks we have made a clean sweep of the green monkeys. In fact that isn't quite true. There were two survivors of that particular massacre and both of them' – he leaned forward and prodded the air dramatically with his forefinger – 'are now in the care and control of the Central Intelligence Agency of the United States.'

Woodnutt gasped with astonishment. But before he could say anything, Sandford had gone on to describe the circumstances under which two green monkeys had been returned to the United States. Without specifying the precise nature of the inducements offered to Colonel Albert

Mugambu by the CIA's local director and without mentioning the secret airbase in the Congo where the transfer of the animals had taken place, Sandford was nevertheless able to embellish his story with a wealth of convincing detail.

Intrigued though he was by the daring and sheer inventiveness of the CIA's approach, Woodnutt believed he saw a fatal flaw in the whole concept.

'Surely you can't take a bunch of viruses and send them marching off like soldiers in a fore-ordained direction? Diseases spread in the most unpredictable way. Pharmacorp has been in this business a long time. We try to forecast the course of disease because that way we can have our products at the right place, at the right time. But we're often wrong, I can tell you. In my view, you can't take a BW agent like the Marburg virus, or whatever it's called, and direct it at the Soviet Union without repercussions on the United States. The thing's just not feasible. It would get back to us somehow and the population of the United States would have no effective protection, any more than the Soviets.'

'Who said the United States would have no protection?' Sandford asked the question quietly, but with great force.

'Well, what protection against the Marburg virus is there?' Woodnutt sounded petulant. 'Nobody's mentioned any protection so far, except isolation and serum. And as we all know, that's a very limited strategy indeed. I wouldn't risk anything on that. And the Russians would know that.'

'But my dear Irving,' – for the first time Sandford sounded patronizing – 'I was not suggesting that we should go in this without protection. If the Marburg virus is to take its place in our national arsenal as a credible deterrent, or – under the worst case assumption – as an actual and usable weapon of war, it is precisely because the United States will have an effective protection against that virus and will, if necessary, be known to have such a protection.'

'But surely, there is no protection available on a mass basis?'

An element of sarcasm had now crept into Sandford's tone of voice.

'Do I hear right? Do I hear the President of Pharmacorp suggesting there is no remedy against this Marburg virus? Is that the kind of positive thinking Pharmacorp's shareholders have come to expect from the head of America's fastest growing pharmaceutical corporation? Today, for the first time, we have the real live vector to work with. We have two live green monkeys, steaming hot from the tropical jungles of Zaire. Those monkeys contain the Marburg virus in their blood. I'm not an expert but, as I understand it, that virus can be isolated; it can be attenuated; and it can then be mass-produced as a vaccine for the American population.'

Sandford stood up, carried away by the excitement of his own irresistible vision. 'That changes the picture, doesn't it? If we have the virus *and* we have the vaccine... And the bloody Russians don't have a goddamned thing?'

Suddenly, Woodnutt saw the whole thing clearly. 'You want Pharmacorp to find a vaccine?'

Sandford, who was still pacing the room, turned in mid-stride. 'Oh, more than that. Much more than that. There's a lot in this for Pharmacorp, you know. I'm not just talking about discovering the vaccine. Your people can do that all right. You've got six Nobel Prize winners on your research staff. I know you've got the technical capability.' Sandford dropped his voice. He was kicking a bit more into the pool. 'I'm talking about a multi-million dollar operation. When you find that vaccine, you're going to put it into mass-production.'

'Twenty million units?'

'Twenty million? No! Two hundred million units and more! I want to see every man, woman and child in the United States protected against Marburg virus. I want us to be a wholly-protected population. It's not enough to have the occasional fall-out shelter here and there. I want total protection.'

Irving Woodnutt was silent for a long time as he reviewed what Sandford had said. He could not help focusing on the limitless possibilities which a scheme of this nature offered for himself and Pharmacorp. Two hundred million units at a minimum. At, say, $10 a throw? $20?

'Wholly underwritten, I suppose?' he asked. 'We wouldn't be manufacturing on spec.'

'No, of course not. The U.S. Government would guarantee to purchase the whole amount.'

Woodnutt thought he saw another flaw in the plan. 'I thought the U.S. Government as such wasn't overtly party to this. How are you going to get 200 million doses of anti-Marburg vaccine into the American population without going public?'

Dick Sandford smiled at him. A warm, frank, friendly smile which told the President of Pharmacorp in no uncertain terms to mind his own business.

'Let's take one step at a time shall we? I'll look after my problems. You look after yours.'

One last thought occurred to Woodnutt as they rose to leave. 'These monkeys, then. Where are they? If we're to start working on the vaccine straight away, we had better get them over to our laboratories in Pittsburgh as soon as possible.'

Sandford smiled yet again. An even warmer, franker, friendlier smile than before.

'Didn't I tell you! We flew the monkeys straight to Pittsburgh. We're holding them for you now at the airport there. They're still on the plane, awaiting collection.'

Irving Woodnutt felt slightly ruffled.

'You kinda took me for granted there, didn't you!' Sandford laid an encouraging hand on the other man's arm.

'Aw, come on. Peabody's an old hand. He doesn't make mistakes. At least, not that kind of mistake.'

*

Mrs Irving Woodnutt, alias Gloria Nimmo, came to the airport to meet her husband at the end of his long but interesting day. Normally, his driver would have picked him up to take him home. But, when he called from Washington, Gloria had insisted. 'No, darling. Let me do it. I haven't seen enough of you lately. I'd like to meet you.'

He hadn't said much on the way back from the airport. He needed to unwind. His arm rested lightly on the back of her seat as she drove skilfully in the evening traffic. Once he put up a finger and brushed her lightly on the cheek. She turned to him, for a moment taking her eyes off the road.

'You'll tell me about it, won't you? Your day in Washington seems to have done you good.'

She was pleased for him at that moment. She knew how desperately keen he was on politics and how frustrated he had been lately because that particular ball didn't seem to start rolling. At last something had happened. Or so it appeared. And if she was pleased for him she was also pleased for herself. In the long run she was more interested in her role as Mrs Irving Woodnutt than she was in being Gloria Nimmo. The movie-going public was notoriously fickle. And her looks wouldn't last for ever. She stole a glance at herself in the driving mirror.

He noticed. 'You look pretty good yourself. We ought to get together some time, what do you say?'

She gave an imitation girlish squeal. 'Darling, I can't wait.'

Over dinner, he took her through the events of the day step by step.

When he had finished, she asked simply: 'Are you going

to do it?'

He pushed back his chair and stood up from the table. 'Let's go outside.'

They went out onto the balcony. It was a warm balmy night. Woodnutt put his arm round his wife's waist. He noticed, as he did so, the slight thickening that had occurred over the last two years. 'Watch that, my girl!' he thought to himself. In the movie-business, an expanding waistline could spell the beginning of the end.

'Darling,' he pointed out across the lawn, 'do you see those lights in the distance?'

She followed the direction of his gaze. 'I see them.'

'Do you know the house the lights come from?'

'Of course I do. It's Fallingwater, isn't it?'

He turned back to her. 'Yes, that's Fallingwater out there. Back in 1935 Frank Lloyd Wright built the house for Edgar J. Kaufmann right here in this Pittsburgh suburb. I was down at the Golf Club the other day and an old boy who remembered the house being built told me how it all began. Apparently, Lloyd Wright was a blustering cantankerous fellow. He used to give the shopgirls hell if they didn't let him have a discount. But he knew his onions as far as architecture was concerned...'

He could see her eyes shining as he spoke.

'How marvellous! How thrilling!' She saw her own home with new eyes. 'It makes this place seem very dull, doesn't it, when you think of Fallingwater.'

He had made his point. He led her back inside.

'Gloria,' he said quietly, 'you asked me what I was going to do. And I tell you: I'm still thinking.'

He looked at her handsome face across the room. 'If we go ahead with this idea; if I and Pharmacorp play ball, this time next year you'll be able to pick your own site anywhere in the United States. You'll be able to choose the best architect and walk over the ground with him. Anything that Frank Lloyd Wright did with Fallingwater, you and your man will be able to do better.'

He walked over to her and took her hand. 'Honey, this is the big time. A deal like this could put Pharmacorp at the top of the league. We'd be past Mercx and American Cynamid and the others so fast they wouldn't even know it. In personal terms, given the stake I have – we both have – in the company, we'd be up in the multimillionaire class. And in political terms, you can be sure that George Peabody will be as good as his word. Anything that man *can* deliver, he will deliver. The rest is up to me.' He laughed. 'After all, the candidate has to do some work too.'

She was proud of him. Immensely proud of him. He was going to make it. She was sure of that. He was tough enough to play with the big boys. She stood on tip-toe and kissed him full on the lips.

'What's holding you up?'

He looked her in the eyes. 'You approve?'

'Of course, I approve.'

For a second he held her at arm's length. Then he clasped

her to him. Hungrily. His heavy florid face thrust into hers, searching greedily for her mouth. It was as though he had waited a long time for this moment.

CHAPTER THIRTEEN

THE TALL DISTINGUISHED gentleman who was Chairman of the Senate SubCommittee on Health and Scientific Research rapped on his desk in Room 1202 of the Dirksen Senate Office Building. The gathering subsided into silence. Photographers who had been popping away with flashbulbs before the session withdrew. The witnesses who had come into Washington for the day shuffled their papers and prepared themselves for interrogation.

Senator Matthews availed himself of the customary privilege of an opening statement:

'Today,' he began, 'the SubCommittee on Health and Scientific Research convenes to discuss the Administration's proposed program for immunization against influenza. It is not sufficient to have a vaccine that will protect those who receive it from illness. We must be confident that we can get that vaccine to people in the right time and place, at an acceptable cost and without creating exorbitant and unpredictable legal difficulties.'

The Senator raised his head from his prepared text to look directly at the row of witnesses who sat across the room from him, each one marked by an appropriate name-card.

'We will want to know, therefore, from the witnesses here today exactly how this new program will work. We will want to know how much vaccine we can actually get to the American public. We will want to know how each of the necessary participants – the Federal Government, the state and local health agencies, the vaccine manufacturers, the public health professionals, the insurance companies – regard the program. Above all, we will want to look at the size of the program itself. The Administration proposes an immunization program that is focused on, indeed I might almost say limited to, critical groups such as the elderly, the chronically ill and children.'

Once more he looked up from his text, this time for effect. 'But is a program of this nature really an adequate response to the challenge of the day? We will hear evidence this morning of the progress which has been made in recent months and weeks by the new flu virus which first originated in Japan known' – he looked down at his notes to make sure he had the name right – 'as A-Fukushima. We shall be told whether and to what extent this new virus threatens the health of the population of the United States. And we shall have the opportunity to discuss and to decide upon the necessary steps to be taken.

'Ladies and Gentlemen. The SubCommittee recognizes its first witness this morning, Dr Frank Kimble, the Deputy Assistant Secretary for Health at the Department of Health and Human Services. Dr Kimble, would you care to address the SubCommittee?'

Dr Kimble, a short wiry-looking man with close-cropped hair, was an impressive performer. Over the years he had had considerable experience with Congressional committees. He knew how to appeal to the vanity of the men and women before whom he was called to testify, to make them feel that it was their voice and their voice alone which counted in the counsels of state. At the same time, he knew how to cajole and to bully. In spite of the fact that the committees were on the whole well-served from the staff point of view, including the research side, Kimble knew that he disposed of immensely greater resources. He could call on facts and figures to support his case which the committee members barely knew existed. Statistics could be dredged up in the depths of his Department which, as far as the committee was concerned, were irrefutable because they had no access to the raw material on which those statistics were based. Kimble was a master at playing the numbers game. He knew that a good number, like a good photograph, says more than a thousand words.

That was how he began his testimony that morning. With numbers.

'You've raised some questions, Mr Chairman, about the extent of the Administration's flu immunization program for the upcoming flu season. Let me say straight away that it is a by no means negligible effort that we are proposing. Secretary Marshall's Conference of January this year' – he was referring here to the Secretary of State for Health and Human Services – 'recommended provision of Federal support for influenza immunizations for high-risk individuals. After extensive consultation with the Association of State and Territorial Health Officers, a proposal was developed and announced on February 23 by Secretary Marshall. On March 23, the President submitted a supplemental budget request to Congress which included $15 million for this year, of which $10.9 million was to be used as project grant funds for state and local health departments. This level of funding would provide 8-9 million doses of influenza vaccine to high-risk individuals who would not otherwise have received it through private means. This level of activity was based on reports from states as to their expectations of ability to provide Federally supported vaccine...'

'With respect, Mr Kimble,' Senator Matthews interrupted his first witness with a somewhat acid comment, 'surely the size of the program should not be determined by the ability of the states to use Federal money. If the states don't believe they can get the vaccine to where it's needed, surely they must improve their administrative performance? And in any case, you yourself have admitted that the Administration's proposal was developed in February this year. But this was prior to the outbreak in Asia of A-Fukushima' – this time he had no trouble with the name. 'Are you telling the Committee that the Administration's thinking has not been modified by the appearance of this new flu virus in Asia and the prospect that A-Fukushima will reach the continental United States by the next flu season? Did the President's supplemental budget request for this fiscal year reflect this fact?'

'No, sir, it did not. Our proposal was based on an evaluation of the states' capacity to deliver.'

'Not on the medical requirement itself? Not on the need to protect human life and health in absolute terms?' The Senator was thrusting deeply now. The television lights had been turned on to register the brief moment of drama, and the cameras had begun to roll. Matthews was making the most of his opportunity.

Frank Kimble sighed. How he hated politicians! They were all as dishonest as each other.

'Chairman,' he said quietly, trying to repair as much of the damage as he could. 'This Administration is cost-conscious. I am sure Congress, including this Committee, would not have it otherwise. In my view, there is no such thing as an absolute requirement to protect human health. The risks must always be measured against the potential benefits. If today the Administration were to recommend to the Congress a substantially enlarged flu immunization program as a result of A-Fukushima, and if the states were to make a maximum effort to deliver that program and if, after all that, there was no outbreak of A-Fukushima in the United States this year, I might find myself accused before this Committee of squandering public funds and resources which could have been better devoted to other programs, including of course medical programs designed to save human life.'

Kimble had been looking at the other members of the SubCommittee as he spoke. While some of them, like the

Chairman himself, still looked sceptical, he saw from the occasional approving nod that he was not entirely without support.

The discussion continued for some time along these lines. Other Senators intervened and Kimble replied to their questions. Eventually Matthews brought matters to a head.

'Gentlemen, we can go on like this for some time but I think there's a risk that our deliberations could become purely theoretical. I believe that what we need at this stage is an up-to-the-minute presentation of the A-Fukushima threat. We are not in February or March any longer. We are in mid-summer and this Congress is about to go into recess. If we are going to act or react as far as A-Fukushima is concerned, we have to do so now. If we don't it may be too late. I propose that we call our next witness, Dr Leslie Cheek, Director of the Center for Disease Control in Atlanta, Georgia. Agreed?'

There was a nod of approval from the other members of the SubCommittee.

'Dr Cheek,' Chairman Matthews continued, 'what we would like from you today is your latest evaluation of the threat posed by A-Fukushima or any other flu virus for that matter to the health of the people of this country. And when I say latest, I mean latest. Preferably this morning's news. If not, this morning, then at least last night's.' He smiled encouragingly at the next witness.

'You may go ahead, Dr Cheek.'

As he began to speak, Leslie Cheek was clearly uncomfortable. He was a thin, worried-looking man with a scraggy neck that sat awkwardly on a pair of narrow shoulders. He had a nasty feeling that this neck was at that precise moment near, if not on, the chopping block. He had before him the recommendations of the meeting which had been held a few weeks earlier in Atlanta, under the chairmanship of his Deputy, Dr Lowell Kaplan, head of the Center's Epidemiology Division. He had carefully studied the conclusions of that meeting. (The record showed that Kaplan had been called away in the middle on urgent business – the Marburg affair as Dr Cheek recalled – and that after his departure the chair had been taken by James McKinney of Virology.) At the time he had agreed with the conclusions of the meeting, when they had been passed up to him. Essentially his experts had advised him that even though there was some evidence that A-Fukushima represented an antigenic shift, rather than a drift, it was not thought to represent a substantial risk. The meeting had not recommended any modification in the existing flu vaccine nor any major expansion in that season's proposed flu immunization program.

Dr Cheek understood, of course, the reason which lay behind this expert caution. Everyone at the Atlanta Center for Disease Control remembered only too clearly the so-called 'swine flu fiasco' of a few years back when a major immunization program had been launched after some Army recruits in training at Fort Dix, New Jersey, went down with an unknown respiratory ailment, subsequently identified as swine flu, which hadn't been seen in the United States since the late 1920s. And when one of these recruits died the Atlanta people had shown their concern by recommending a massive program of vaccination. As it happened, the swine flu epidemic never materialized. Instead, the Federal Government which, in a totally unprecedented way had assumed liability, was left with a host of negligence and malpractice suits to settle. Some of these were purely frivolous – one claim, alleging not only paralysis but loss of appetite and sleep, sought $900 million. But others had better foundation. The fact was that in a small but measurable number of vaccinees the so-called Guillain-Barré syndrome occurred, with occasionally fatal results.

Leslie Cheek was very well aware that, only that morning, the Deputy Assistant Secretary for Health at HHS had taken a pretty clear line in favour of restricting the immunization program to something fairly modest and limited. That line had, at least to some extent, been based on the conclusions of the meeting chaired by Kaplan and McKinney. If he, Cheek, were now to change that position he would have to have – taking it all together – a very convincing motive indeed.

And yet, in spite of it all, he felt uncomfortable. There were still another three or four months to go before the flu season proper began in the United States. A flu virus could travel a long way and do a lot of damage in that time. It was no good waiting until October or November to see if or how the danger developed. If the manufacturers were going to produce the vaccine in massive quantities, they had to have ample advance warning. As a public health man, he felt it made sense to err on the side of caution. He hadn't been at the CDC at the time of the swine flu affair, so he hadn't been among those who cried wolf and got egg on their faces. He didn't feel constrained in the same way.

But there was one overriding reason why Dr Leslie Cheek decided, as he took the floor that morning, to depart from his prepared text. That reason had to do with a call he had received earlier that morning.

He had been about to leave for the Hill when the telephone had rung in his room at the Madison Hotel.

'Leslie? This is Tom Stevens.'

It was a voice from the past but none the less familiar. When Leslie Cheek had been with the National Institutes of Health before he went down to Atlanta, he and Stevens had been members of the same country club in Chevy Chase. They had often played tennis together and taken their drinks by the pool later. Cheek knew that Tom Stevens was 'in government' somewhere but he had never found out exactly what the other man did. Tom had always been rather vague about it.

'Tom. Good to hear you! How did you know I was in town?'

'Oh, word gets around, you know.' The upper-class drawl of the Princeton man was pronounced.

Stevens came to the point.

'I know you're going down to the Hill in a minute or two. Senator Matthews' Office put out a list of the witnesses they'll be hearing from this morning and it came across my desk last night. There's something I want to talk to you about before you testify. Do you think I could stop by in a few moments and give you a lift? It's on my way.'

Leslie Cheek had been delighted to accept the offer. The two men had ridden down Pennsylvania Avenue together in Tom Stevens' car and, as they drove, Stevens had explained his problem.

'Look, Leslie,' he said. 'This is strictly personal. Between us. I called you because I know you.'

They swung past the Executive Office Building and then the White House loomed up to the right, resplendent in the morning sun.

Stevens nodded in the direction of the historic building. 'Believe me, Leslie, this is on the level. There are people in there who know I'm talking to you this morning. I don't say the Man himself knows. He doesn't need to know. Not yet. But there are guys on his staff, my kind of guys, who know and who approve. John Shearer is one of them. Do you follow me?'

Dr Leslie Cheek followed him. He had heard of John Shearer, the young man from California who served in effect as the President's Chief of Staff. He nodded and waited for what was to come next.

But Tom Stevens had not been particularly forthcoming. He had simply said, as they were passing the new wing of the Smithsonian: 'I can't tell you the background. Not now. I may never be able to tell you the background. I just want you to know that there are very powerful reasons indeed for going ahead with a large-scale flu immunization program this fall. The Administration made a mistake in recommending the modest effort it did. But it's not practical politics, for any number of reasons, to go in now with a new proposal. The HHS people will scream. But, frankly, if Senator Matthews' SubCommittee came out with some fairly radical upgrading, we wouldn't mind in the least.'

Leslie Cheek looked at his friend, as he drove. 'Why don't you get to Matthews?'

A smile circled round the edge of Tom Stevens' lips. 'Oh, we have. Believe me, we have.' Taking his eyes off the road for a moment, he looked Leslie Cheek straight in the eye.

'Don't get me wrong, Leslie. I'm not asking you to violate your personal or professional conscience. I'm simply saying that if you have any doubts about the Administration's proposal, then for heaven's sake don't keep them to yourself. Of course, if it doesn't work, we'll simply have to come at it some other way. If necessary, we can work on HHS to reformulate. But it would be neater, much neater if this thing came from the Committee – on its own initiative as it were. We feel the Administration needs to keep a certain distance on this one.'

It was delicately put. Leslie Cheek appreciated the tact that had informed the other man's presentation. No one should ever ask a scientist to lie. But under certain circumstances it is quite permissible to ask a scientist to change the emphasis here and there.

'Tom,' he said as he got out of the car in front of the

Dirksen Building, 'I don't really understand what you're getting at. And I don't suppose that I'm meant to understand, but I hear what you say and I'll think about it.'

'Thanks.' The enigmatic Mr Stevens had waved him goodbye. Cheek had watched the big black Pontiac pull out into the morning stream of traffic. Then he had mounted the steps to the Committee Room.

Well, he said to himself as Senator Matthews called upon him to speak, he had thought about what Tom Stevens had said, and it made sense. The old boy net was just as valid a way of communicating instructions in government as memoranda which followed the correct hierarchical channels, up and down, with copies to A, B and C and blind copies to X, Y and Z so that they could know what A, B and C knew without A, B and C knowing that they knew. Cheek had absolutely no doubt that, in the nicest possible way, he had been told what to do that morning. Whether he did it or not depended entirely on him.

'Chairman,' he began. 'Gentlemen. Thank you for giving me the opportunity to appear before your SubCommittee this morning. I certainly appreciate the importance of the discussion you have just had and will be glad to answer your questions.'

Chairman Matthews came directly to the point.

'In your view, Dr Cheek, does the Administration's proposed flu immunization program correspond to the needs *as you now perceive them*? I stress those last words deliberately. We need to consider the situation today; not as it was last

January or February or March.'

Dr Leslie Cheek spent a full fifteen minutes giving his reply to that question. It was a masterly piece of evidence. He reviewed the motivations behind the Administration's original proposal; he reviewed the status of A-Fukushima; he went into the question of the states' capacity to carry out a major vaccination program with full Federal funding; he expressed his belief that much more was possible if only the resources could match the will and the will could match the resources.

And his conclusion, when he came to it, was a brilliant reordering of the evidence. He didn't actually contradict or disavow his own people at CDC. What he did was to leave the strong, almost indelible impression on the members of the Committee that there was a real case for a rethink and that he and his people were in no way opposed to such a rethink.

'The CDC is in no sense doctrinaire, Mr Chairman,' he had affirmed. 'We are not, in principle, for massive pro-grams of immunization. We are not, in principle, against such programs. We are in favour of doing what is right and necessary to protect American lives and American health. If it is the considered opinion of this Committee that the new situation calls for a new program, you may count on our fullest cooperation. Thank you.'

There had been a round of applause as he sat down. Clearly he had gauged the mood of the Committee accu-rately.

The full report of the Senate SubCommittee on Health and Research was published at noon the following day. Staffers had worked overnight and the Printing Office had done a rush job.

'Dammit,' Senator Matthews had protested, 'if they can do it for the Congressional Record and print up overnight God-knows-how-many pages of the nonsense my colleagues sometimes talk on the floor, they can do it for us.'

And he had got his way.

The wire services ran the story immediately. AP and UPI both gave it prominence: 'SENATE SUBCOMMITTEE RECOMMENDS MAJOR FLU IMMUNIZATION PROGRAM JAPANESE VIRUS A THREAT' was AP's lead; while UPI, whose Washington man was a good friend of one of Senator Matthews' legislative aides, injected a more personal note: 'SENATOR MATTHEWS (D: CA) CALLS FOR NEW EXPANDED FLU PROGRAM AGAINST JAP MENACE.'

'I'd stress the Jap thing, if I were you,' the legislative aide had advised. 'That's the way to put the point across to the American public. They'll think of Pearl Harbor. Hell, we could be in a Pearl Harbor situation.'

The UPI man had looked sceptical. 'Come off it, Jimmy. You can kid the public but don't try to kid me. That Japanese line is a phoney. Matthews has his own reasons for wanting to push this thing. Isn't that right?'

'You're fishing, Bud. You're fishing,' the aide had said. 'But I'm not biting.'

Susan Wainwright was waiting for Lowell Kaplan in his

office when he returned from lunch in the CDC's cafeteria. In some undefinable way she felt that Kaplan had changed since his visit to Europe and Africa. He seemed to be under some internal pressure. Once or twice she had tried to draw him out, but his responses had been gruff so she had let it ride. She knew that Kaplan had suffered considerable anguish over the fate of the monkeys. But she wondered whether there might not be something else which could account for his tense and irritable frame of mind. When she had asked him how his encounter with Stephanie Verusio had gone, Kaplan had been positively brusque in his reply. And that for him was most unusual.

Susan Wainwright had now to deal with a particular problem in addition to this general concern for Kaplan's well-being. She showed him the reports from Washington as they had come off the tape that lunch-time. (The CDC was following the deliberations of the Senate SubCommittee attentively since the Center would inevitably be heavily involved in any flu immunization program.) Kaplan read the accounts with astonishment.

'Jesus!' he exclaimed. 'Are they out of their minds?'

'That's not all. Read it through to the end. Apparently Dr Cheek testified in favour. Or at least made noises to that effect.'

When he saw what Leslie Cheek had said in Washington, Kaplan almost hit the roof. With the print-out still in his hand, he stormed through into his superior's office.

'Did you read this?' he thrust the wire service report into

the Director's hand. (Cheek had caught the last plane from Washington to Atlanta the previous evening, while the Committee's report was still being printed.)

The other man glanced at the print-out in a strangely off-hand way and tossed it on the desk.

'Yeah, I had a feeling that's the way the Committee would come out. When a politician thinks there are some votes around, health is an absolute, whatever the cost-benefit boys may say.'

'How about your testimony?' Kaplan found it hard to keep an accusing note out of his voice.

'My testimony?' Cheek sounded wholly innocent.

'You spoke in favour apparently?'

'I didn't speak in favour. I said the position was open.'

'It says in the report that you supported a new major flu program.'

Cheek was beginning to be irritated. 'Lowell, when you're up there on the Hill, you're not operating in a wholly scientific environment. It's a political environment. Things aren't black and white. They're grey. Different shades of grey.'

He had turned to his papers and Kaplan realized that the conversation was at an end. Inwardly fuming, he had gone back in his office and expressed his annoyance to his assistant.

'I don't know what's got into Leslie Cheek, Susan. We're about to be saddled with a new flu program – they're talking of 200 million doses – would you believe it – and he's not going to fight it.'

He sat down heavily at his desk. Something was going on which he didn't understand. The CDC's position on the flu immunization program was clear. Cheek knew what that position was. He'd had the summary of the meeting, and he'd also had the detailed transcript which Kaplan had insisted on having made.

'Why did Leslie fluff it, Susan? That's what I don't understand.'

Susan Wainwright tried to calm him down. 'Ultimately, I suppose, it's Dr Cheek's decision, Lowell.'

'I suppose it is.' With an effort of will, Kaplan dismissed the matter from his mind. 'It sure beats the hell out of me, though. Anyone would have thought we all had enough work on our plates at the moment.'

★

'Come in, Ed. Sit down.'

Irving Woodnutt addressed Pharmacorp's Vice President for Research and Development in the friendliest manner.

'Have a cigar?'

'No thanks, Irving. Not before lunch.'

Woodnutt lit himself a large Havana. (Thank God the U.S. had more or less patched things up with Castro, he thought – at least you could get a decent cigar again.)

'Ed, we've got a job to do.' Woodnutt spoke through a cloud of enveloping smoke. '*You've* got a job to do.' He came straight to the point. 'Assume you and your people were starting from scratch, Ed. Assume you've got a new live virus to work with. Assume that funds and facilities are no object and that you can devote maximum resources to the job. How long would you need to develop a vaccine? Could you do it in, say,' he paused, 'three weeks, a month?'

Ed Werner, a balding fifty year old with a pale wrinkled face and narrow, ambitious eyes, looked at the President of Pharmacorp Inc. with something approaching amazement.

'Hell, Irving, it took Jonas Salk five years to come up with a polio vaccine!'

'Salk and Sabin were working in the dark, Ed. You know that. They had to identify the virus in the first place; they had to find a medium; they had to test.'

'Wouldn't *we* have to do all those things? And even when you do, there's no guarantee it'll work.'

Woodnutt laid his smouldering cigar in an ashtray. He leaned forward and pressed the tips of his pudgy fingers together expressively.

'This could be an emergency, Ed. We might have to take some shortcuts.'

Two hours later, when Ed Werner left Woodnutt's office on the eighteenth floor of the Pharmacorp Building in downtown Pittsburgh, he was a shaken man. Woodnutt had refused to listen to any arguments; he had brooked no objections.

'Go after it. That's my final instruction.' The President of Pharmacorp had been emphatic and he had hinted that if Werner succeeded in his task, then he would be the logical candidate to follow Woodnutt himself in the number one spot in the event that Woodnutt moved on to, say, the Senate.

'Believe me, Ed. You'll have my support. I can carry the Board. As a matter of fact, if you've found the Marburg vaccine and we've pumped that vaccine into two hundred million Americans, it won't be a question of carrying the Board. They'll be falling all over themselves to have you.'

Ed Werner had, frankly, been staggered by the scope of the project.

'But, Irving,' he had protested, 'how the hell can you vaccinate two hundred million Americans, when as far as the outside world is concerned – and, from what you tell me, that includes the American health establishment – the Marburg virus doesn't even exist any longer?'

Woodnutt had looked at him with condescension.

'Don't you read the papers, Ed. Didn't you see that under congressional pressure, particularly from Senator Matthews' Sub-Committee, HHS just reversed itself on the flu immunization program.'

'You mean... ?'

'Yeah, that's precisely what I mean. They've handed Pharmacorp the contract to make the flu vaccine. We're batching the eggs right now, as you know, and production will start this week. You come up with the Marburg vaccine and we'll work it into a multipurpose unit. For $9 a unit, we give protection against flu, especially this new strain of

A-Fukushima which has them so worried. That's the cover. But Pharmacorp Inc. gets another $11 a unit for *building anti-Marburg protection into the dose at the same time.*'

Ed Werner had said very little more for the rest of the interview. But in the elevator going back to his office, he muttered under his breath.

'The man's mad. Stark staring mad. It just can't be done.'

When he got back to his desk he sat there for a long time, thinking. He buzzed his secretary and told her that he was not to be disturbed. He had to make a decision. A difficult decision. As a scientist who had spent his life in R and D activities of various kinds he knew that what Woodnutt was proposing was next to impossible. You simply didn't discover a new vaccine and put it into mass production from one month to the next. But as an ambitious businessman, who wanted to be President of Pharmacorp Inc. more than he wanted anything, he realized he had to give it a try.

He buzzed his secretary.

'I want Philip Mason of our Virology Unit to meet me downstairs in the lobby in ten minutes.'

Mason was already waiting for Werner by the time the latter reached the lobby. He was a young man, with reddish hair and a developed sense of humour. Werner had brought him into Pharmacorp some months earlier as his special protégé and had made him Head of the Virology Unit.

'Where are we going, Ed?' Phil Mason asked. 'I was counting on an evening at home.'

'I'm sorry, Phil. Something has come up and it's urgent. We're going out to the labs and we may be back late.'

The rays of the sun were slanting into the summer mists that swirled over the Monongahela river and the last lab technician had gone home from Pharmacorp's research laboratories, located some twenty miles west of Pittsburgh, by the time Ed Werner and Philip Mason were finally ready to start work.

The two monkeys, whom they had christened Sam and Griselda, were in isolation within Pharmacorp. Werner and Mason donned their pressure suits and masks before entering Pharmacorp's own 'Hot Lab', a completely separate unit inside the research compound. Once inside, they released an anaesthetic gas into the airtight cages where the monkeys were kept. Only when Sam and Griselda were unconscious did they proceed with their work.

They began with the electron microscope. That was the obvious way to start. Werner and Mason took it in turns with the giant machine, whose invention had so dramatically revolutionized the science and practice of molecular biology.

Earlier that day, when he had been talking to Woodnutt, Werner had indicated that it would be useful if he could contact the CDC direct in Atlanta to discuss the results of their own EM examinations. But Woodnutt had emphatically vetoed the idea.

'Forget it,' he had said. 'As far as CDC is concerned, Marburg no longer exists. However innocent sounding you make your enquiry, it will seem odd to them. We don't want to excite suspicion.' Instead Woodnutt had passed over to Werner the data sheets which had been constructed by the CDC at the time of the Marburg outbreak in the United States.

As they settled down to work, Werner read out some of the details.

'I've got Lowell Kaplan's original report on Diane Verusio here, Philip. She was the first person to die, you remember. It was when he looked at the sample from Verusio that Kaplan made the Marburg identification. He says,' he consulted the notes, 'that the morphology of the Marburg virus is unusual and that we should be looking for pleomorphic filaments of exceptional length. Straight rods, horseshoes, hooks, loops, b's – we may also find dilation or branching in one of the poles.'

Mason had his eyes to the instrument.

'Frankly, Ed, I don't see anything of the kind at the moment. I see a healthy cellular structure pretty much the same as a thousand other samples I've looked at.'

Ed Werner was puzzled. 'That's odd. Try increasing the magnification.'

'I'm running at X 300,000 at the moment. If we can't see a virus of 'exceptional length' as you put it at that power, what the hell can we see?'

'Try, anyway.'

Philip Mason tried at the higher powers but the result was still negative.

'I'm damned if I can see anything. You try, Ed.'

Pharmacorp's Vice President for Research and Development took over the EM. He stared steadily for three minutes.

When he came up for air, he shook his head. 'You're right, Phil. There's nothing there. Absolutely nothing.'

They went through all the samples one by one, checking and double-checking. It took them most of the night. Round about four in the morning, they broke for coffee.

'Phew, it's great to get out of those damn pressure suits,' said Philip Mason. He turned to the older man.

'Well? What do we do? It looks as though Woodnutt's been taken for a ride, doesn't it? Those monkeys are clean. They sure as hell haven't got any Marburg virus.'

Ed Werner rubbed his eyes and poured himself a cup of coffee. 'Dammit,' he sounded rueful. 'I was quite excited back there when Woodnutt was talking to me in his office. Of course, what he was suggesting was mad; you can't find a virus, attenuate it and develop a vaccine in the time it takes you to drive from Chicago to San Francisco. But he got me to the point where I was really prepared to have a go.'

Mason smiled. 'I'll let you break the news to Woodnutt, Ed. That's one of the privileges of seniority. I don't know how he'll take it.'

Ed Werner shuddered. 'Nor do I. But I don't think it's going to be a pretty sight. I could tell from the way he spoke that he has a lot riding on this. But what the hell can we do?' He spread his hands. 'We can't make a vaccine, if we don't have the virus to work with.'

In the event, Ed Werner misjudged his man. Bleary-eyed

from lack of sleep, he had confronted the President of Pharmacorp shortly after nine the following morning. When he had finished his report, Woodnutt had for a few moments paced up and down his office deep in thought.

Then his heavy face had broken into a broad but sinister smile. 'Ed, I think you and Phil Mason have done a great job. In fact, I'd say our task is now a whole lot easier than it was twenty-four hours ago. It takes the time-pressure off for one thing.'

Werner was amazed. 'What do you mean?'

Woodnutt sat down at his desk again and patiently explained. 'Look at the logic of the thing. Originally the BW experts needed an anti-Marburg vaccine because they thought they had the Marburg vector in the form of two captured monkeys. You don't use or threaten to use a lethal virus against an enemy unless your own population is massively protected. But now it turns out that the two surviving monkeys are clean. In other words we know that the Marburg virus was finally and completely eliminated in the Zaire massacre. Right?'

'Right.'

'That means,' Woodnutt continued, 'that *we don't need a vaccine because there's no threat of disease.* But Pharmacorp can still play ball. If the CIA thinks it has a virus on its hands and it wants a vaccine, we'll give 'em one. It can't do any harm and, who knows, it might even do some good. We all know that immunization programs have spillover effects. People come and see a doctor who normally wouldn't go near one.

'So,' Woodnutt concluded, gleefully rubbing his hands, 'we can put in any goddamn thing we like into that flu vaccine, short of arsenic and cyanide. And we can tell Washington that Pharmacorp has made a multi-purpose unit as requested. And the whole two hundred million unit program can blast ahead and nobody, repeat nobody, will be any the wiser. Do you follow?'

It took a moment or two for the full beauty of the scheme to become apparent to Ed Werner. But when understanding finally came to him, he broke into a great guffaw of laughter. He rocked in his chair and had to wipe the tears from his eyes.

'Oh, boy!' he exclaimed. 'That's a beaut! That's a real beaut.'

They spent the next hour working out the details. They had to have a realistic timetable. They couldn't put the mythical vaccine into production so fast that suspicions would be aroused. On the other hand, they had to produce a schedule proving that Pharmacorp was willing and able to work under pressure.

As he was preparing to leave, Werner thought of one final thing.

'Now that we've *ostensibly* isolated the virus and developed the vaccine, we can't afford to let those monkeys stay around here any longer. You and I know that they're not dangerous. So does Phil Mason. But nobody else does. The normal thing for a responsible scientist to do with a dangerous vector, once he's finished with it, is to destroy it. Particularly since in this case we don't want anyone taking a second look at the monkeys and discovering they are clean after all.'

Woodnutt nodded sagely, his mind already somewhere else. 'You have a point there, Ed. You'd better deal with that.'

Later that day Ed Werner and Phil Mason made a second visit to Pharmacorp's laboratories outside Pittsburgh.

The two men stood in front of the cage.

'Hell, Ed,' said the younger man, 'I hate seeing those little animals die.'

'So do I, Phil. I really do. But we have no choice.' He went over to the airtight cage.

'Goodbye Sam,' he whispered. 'Goodbye Griselda. Some fool who didn't know what he was doing brought you from the jungle. This isn't the place for you anyway. It's better like this.'

Ed Werner pressed the lever and the lethal gas hissed into the airtight cage.

As they turned to go, Werner gripped Mason's arm just above the elbow.

'I'll tell you something, Phil, I'd prefer to be with those monkeys in there than standing in our shoes if Woodnutt's scheme misfires. We're in this thing up to our necks, you know.'

He drew a hand expressively across his throat.

CHAPTER FOURTEEN

AFTER STEPHANIE HAD SPOKEN to her, the old woman remained for a few seconds rooted to the spot. She blinked hard twice; and then, clutching her radio batteries in her hand, she scuttled off into the crowd. A few seconds later Stephanie had lost sight of her.

For at least half-an-hour she paced through the market trying to find the strange figure once again. But it was a hopeless task. The old woman seemed to have burrowed into some hole like a crab. A little brown crab, moving side-wise to avoid capture.

In the evening, Stephanie told her hosts about the strange event.

'I'm sure I'm right. I could absolutely swear to it. When I said the name 'Frau Matthofer' she jumped as though she had received an electric shock. I could tell it meant something to her.'

'Why don't you ask Kodjo?' Peter Lustig suggested. 'He comes from the village, doesn't he? Maybe he knows something or could find out.'

Stephanie agreed that that was a good idea. 'We already talked a bit about the old woman. Kodjo told me she lives on the summit opposite. But maybe he can be even more helpful.'

Kodjo was summoned and entered beaming. He was enjoying the prestige which his association with a beautiful American girl and a large fast car had brought him in the village.

'Yes, I saw the old woman this morning at the market. I saw you talk to her, miss. She caused me a lot of trouble this morning, that old woman did. All the village people, they come up to me and say, 'Kodjo where is the monkey?' They know I'm Kodjo the monkey-man. They know I'm the only one who dares go up to the *ibigaribo* on the summit of Mount Lwungi where the monkeys live. So that's why they come to me. But I didn't take any monkey, miss, from the *ibigaribo*. You know that. I was with you and Ngenzi-bwana over the lake.'

'Kodjo, you had better explain. What monkeys are you talking about?'

'The monkeys who live with the old woman up on the mountain. She was furious this morning when she came to the market. She said maybe some bad man had come up to the *ibigaribo* and had taken a monkey. The man would die, she said. The spirits would get him,' Kodjo explained.

'The taboo?'

'Yes, the taboo. But still the old woman told the people in the market she wanted to find the monkey.' Kodjo shrugged his shoulders. 'My guess is nobody took the monkey off the mountain. But maybe it came down to the village and then some trapper caught it and passed it on already. I think the old woman came too late.'

Stephanie had a sudden flash of intuition. At last she was beginning to understand.

'Helga? Peter?' she addressed her hosts urgently. 'You've both of you lived here a long time. Tell me: do you remember if there was always an *ibigaribo* at the top of Mount Lwungi? Think back carefully,' she pleaded. 'Was there a sacred grove there before, say, fifteen or twenty years ago? Kodjo, you try to remember too. When you were a child, was there an *ibigaribo* there? Was there a taboo?'

Kodjo, who replied first, seemed sure. 'Yes, of course, there was a taboo. My mother would never let me go up to the mountain top.'

'Why not?'

Kodjo thought about that. 'She said we would become ill,' he replied finally. 'Sometimes people who went up to the mountain became ill and died.'

'But did she speak of an *ibigaribo*? Was it a place where royal ancestors are buried? Or was it just the sickness which made people avoid the mountain top?'

Kodjo looked puzzled. 'I think it was the sickness,' he replied slowly. 'I think the story of the royal ancestors came later. That was another reason not to go up to the mountain top. But it wasn't the main reason.'

Stephanie shot a quick look in the direction of the Lustigs. 'What do you think?' she asked.

Helga Lustig looked faintly bewildered. She felt that she was getting out of her depth. But Peter Lustig had been following closely the thrust of Stephanie Verusio's questions.

'Maybe this will help.' He stood up and walked over to a bookcase and, after a bit of searching, took out what he was looking for. 'I've got a book here which describes the royal burial grounds in Burundi. It gives some maps as well. We can check to see whether the peak opposite was mentioned. Of course, if it isn't mentioned, that won't prove anything. But at least it will be an indication.'

'When was the book written?' Stephanie asked.

Peter Lustig consulted the volume which he held in his hand.

'At the end of the 1950s. The author was a Belgian priest. He belonged to a missionary society which was active in Ruanda and Burundi known as 'Les Pères Blancs', the White Fathers. His hobby was a study of the royal burial grounds and the rituals associated with the passing of the tambourine from one king to another.'

He flipped through the volume and pulled out a map. Spreading it out on a table in front of them, Lustig continued: 'Bugamba is certainly in one of the main areas for burial grounds according to Père Leclerc. Look,' he pointed to the map, 'you've got a site here at Bugarama and another here at M'teshi.'

They studied the map for a time.

'But nothing actually at Bugamba?' Stephanie asked. 'Not as far as I can see.'

'What does it say in the text?'

It took Peter Lustig a few minutes to locate the relevant section of the Belgian priest's itinerary, since the index was somewhat deficient. Finally, he found what he was looking for. He glanced over the page.

'This may be what we're looking for. I'll read it out.'

With evident interest, Peter Lustig provided a rough and ready translation from the ornate French in which Père Leclerc had recorded the results of his researches.

'One region,' he began, 'in which I found indications of a taboo' – it's the same word in French as it is in English – 'was near the village of Bugamba. This village which is itself some twenty-eight kilometres from Bugarama lies at the foot of one of the great summits in the Nile-Zaire ridge, known as Lwungi. I spoke at some length to the villagers, who told me of their dread of approaching this summit. On the whole, they said, very few people indeed had been up there and those that did were supposed to have been visited subsequently with a dangerous sickness so that death was often the result.'

Peter Lustig looked up from his reading.

'Now we come to the fascinating part,' he said. 'Père Leclerc goes on to say, and I quote '*Toutefois*... however, I was not convinced from my enquiries that the existence of this taboo which did indeed appear to be genuine was also associated with an *ibigaribo* on the summit of Lwungi. From my own researches, brief as they were, I could find no record of royal burials in this particular part of the Nile-Zaire ridge. Nor did I have the time to visit the summit myself. Even if I had had the time, I doubt whether I should have been able to find a willing guide in the village of Bugamba.'

Peter Lustig closed the book.

'Well?' He looked round at the others. 'What do we make of that?'

Kodjo, who was still with them, obviously made very little of it.

He had fallen asleep in a corner of the room.

From the others, there was a long silence. A silence which Stephanie at last broke with a determined emphatic statement.

'I'm going up there. There's something going on up there and I want to find out what it is.' She spread her hands and ticked off the key points, just as she had the day she and Ngenzi returned to Bujumbura from Zaire.

'Number One – we have the original Marburg incident apparently caused by a green monkey coming from Zaire.

'Number Two – we have my sister's death and a subsequent outbreak of Marburg disease in the United States whose cause seems to be some contact my sister had with a green monkey, coming from the same part of Zaire.

'Number Three – a WHO team sets off to eliminate the green monkey tribe in Zaire but Ngenzi and I believe that in fact they eliminated a tribe of grey-green monkeys, not green monkeys; and that these grey-green monkeys are not in fact the vector for the Marburg virus.

'Number Four – we learn that a woman from Marburg whom I believe to be Frau Matthofer, the Professor in charge of the clinic in Marburg at the time of the first outbreak, came to Burundi shortly after that outbreak and has been living as a recluse up there in the mountains surrounded by a tribe of monkeys.

'Number Five – we believe that the taboo which surrounds the mountain crest where Frau Matthofer and the monkeys live is associated not with the presence of a royal burial ground but with the fact that those who visit the summit are supposed to contract some strange sickness.

'Number Six – in so far as the taboo is associated with the supposed presence on the summit of an *ibigaribo*, the indications are that this story might have been put around at a later date and might have been designed deliberately to reinforce the idea in the local people's minds that Lwungi was a dangerous place. Do you follow me so far? Peter? Helga?'

'Are you suggesting,' Peter Lustig asked, 'that the monkeys on the top of Mount Lwungi might be the ones which carry this so-called Marburg virus?'

'Yes. That is precisely what I am suggesting,' Stephanie replied. 'I'm suggesting that somehow the references we have to a tribe of green monkeys living in Zaire were wrong. I'm suggesting that the real green monkeys may be right here in Burundi, living with Frau Matthofer on the top of Mount Lwungi.'

Peter Lustig rose to his feet and walked to the window. The outline of the mountains opposite were still dimly visible as night fell.

He turned back to Stephanie. 'Wake Kodjo up,' he said.
'What for?'
'He's seen the monkeys on Lwungi, hasn't he? He must

know what colour they are.'

Roused from his torpor, Kodjo was only too happy to reply to their questions.

'You say what colour are the monkeys on Lwungi, miss?' He put his head on one side and thought about the problem.

Finally he said: 'The monkeys on Lwungi, Miss Stephanie, are the colour of the grass which springs up around the dry waterhole after the first rain of the season.'

'Are they *green* monkeys, Kodjo?'

'Oh yes, miss,' Kodjo burst out laughing. 'That's the word. Green.'

'Goodness!' Stephanie was exhilarated. 'Why didn't you say so before.'

'You never asked me.' Kodjo rolled about with laughter. Stephanie made up her mind.

'I'm going up the mountain. Will you come with me, Kodjo? You're not afraid of the taboo? Or of the sickness?'

'No, miss, I'm not afraid. The sickness will not touch Kodjo. I know the monkeys. When do we leave, miss?'

'Tomorrow morning, Kodjo. Can we do that?'

'Any time you say. I'm ready. I show you the way up the mountain.'

When Stephanie Verusio went to bed that night, she tossed and turned, thinking about the monkeys and about the old woman. Once she found herself wondering what had happened to Lowell Kaplan. Did the man know that the massacre in Zaire had been pointless? What would he say if he *did* know? What glib excuse would he come up with? She went to sleep at last, her mind still on Kaplan and her thoughts a strange mixture of anger and longing.

They left at dawn. The mists still swirled across the opposing peaks and only as they climbed did the enveloping wreaths of cloud thin out. The forest itself was breathtaking in its splendour. This was no secondary growth. It was the pristine jungle, its glorious canopy spread out against the roots of the sky.

Kodjo was Stephanie's sole companion. The Lustigs had wished to come with her, but she had dissuaded them.

'Let me go only with him,' she had said. 'I think it's better. Four of us will inevitably make more noise than two. In any case, if these are the monkeys which harbour the virus, you will need protection to go near them. I am protected by serum and Kodjo has probably developed some natural immunity from living close to the monkeys. But you two should stay behind.'

Reluctantly the Lustigs had agreed.

Even two made enough noise, thought Stephanie, as they pressed on upwards. Branches snapped underfoot however warily they trod. Birds started overhead and small animals darted across the path, veering crazily into the bush as soon as they caught sight of the intruders.

It took them the best part of two hours to cover the first thousand feet. The going was rough and in places the path had almost disappeared. More than once Kodjo had to slash away with his panga at a tangle of creeper and tendril.

They pushed on regardless. If the old woman could come down from the mountain to the village, they could go up from the village to the mountain.

'Her camp is the other side of the summit, on the Ruanda side,' Kodjo told her. 'I saw it once before when I came up here.'

They were moving along the contour of the hill now, about five hundred feet below the summit. Stephanie took out the field-glasses, but the foliage was impenetrable. The danger was that, without forewarning, they would simply stumble on the old woman unawares with unpredictable consequences.

Kodjo realized the problem. 'If we climb to the very top,' he said, 'we can look down into the jungle. We may be able to see the camp from above where we cannot see it through the trees.'

By noon, with the sun vertically above them (for they were almost on the Equator), they had reached their objective. The view from the summit of Mount Lwungi was breathtaking. North, south, east and west – the hills and forests rolled away. From the vantage-point which they enjoyed, they could – virtually – see the whole of Burundi. For a moment Stephanie wondered whether, after all, Lwungi was not the site of some ancient burial ground. If I were the King of Burundi, she thought, I wouldn't mind being buried here with my whole kingdom in view.

After she had let the field-glasses range for a while over the horizon, she turned to the scene nearer at hand.

It was extraordinary how the forest canopy, which from a distance seemed to be a solid wall of green beneath them, was transformed by the magnification of the glasses into a shimmering variegated expanse where individual trees could be distinguished, and branches on those trees and even the animals moving on the branches.

Suddenly she clasped Kodjo's arm. 'Look, down there!' she cried. 'Monkeys! I think they're green monkeys too. In that clump of trees by the outcrop of rock. Here,' she handed him the glasses.

It took Kodjo a few seconds to find the target. 'Yes,' he said at last. 'You are right. Those are the monkeys. The old woman will not be far away.'

They spotted the clearing almost immediately.

'Good God!' Stephanie exclaimed, having retrieved the glasses from her companion. 'There's a whole complex hidden in the trees down there.'

This time Kodjo needed no mechanical assistance. Once Stephanie had pointed it out, he could distinguish with his naked eye a series of huts which had been built around the perimeter of a clearing in the forest. Nor did he need any help in distinguishing the old woman as she came out of one of the huts. The crablike shuffle which Stephanie had noted in the course of their one brief encounter at the village market had disappeared. The old woman strode purposefully across the open circle.

'There she is, Kodjo! There's the old woman. Do you see her?'

'I see her, miss. And I see the other men too.'

'What do you mean?'

But before Kodjo had time to answer, Stephanie saw for herself what he meant.

For two people had followed Frau Matthofer out into the clearing. One was a white man, about forty years old. Stephanie had a clear view of his face through the glasses and she knew she had never seen him before. The other was black, tall and handsome. She gave a start of surprise as she recognized Victor Mtaza.

'Look, Kodjo! That's Victor Mtaza. What's he doing here?'

Kodjo just had time to observe them through the field-glasses before the old woman and her two visitors disappeared into a hut at the other side of the clearing.

'Yes.' He lowered the glasses. 'You are right. That's Victor Mtaza. I don't know what he is doing here, miss, but I'm sure he's up to no good. Victor Mtaza is bad music, miss. Very bad music.'

'We can find out, Kodjo.'

'You want me to go down?'

'No. I'll go myself. You wait for me here.'

'Are you sure? It will be dangerous.'

'Yes, I'm sure.' As she spoke, Stephanie realized that she had never felt surer of anything in her whole life.

★

Seen from near at hand, the huts formed a distinct pattern around the circle of the clearing. As Stephanie crept closer, she realized that the one on the far side was clearly the place where Frau Matthofer lived. A line of washing was hung out alongside and the assorted garments, most of them very much the worse for wear, flapped limply in the breeze. There was a porch of sorts, and a faded deck-chair had been placed so as to catch the late afternoon sun. The hut had a chimney and Stephanie could visualize the old woman lighting a fire against the chill of the evening.

She crawled past the hut and round the edge of the clearing, taking care to stay under the cover of the trees.

The second hut was placed opposite the first. Its windows were barred with tough bamboo and there was a block of wood on the door which could be dropped down into position from the outside. Panting from the exertion, Stephanie raised herself on tiptoe to peer through the window of the second hut.

As she poked her head above the sill she was greeted by a sudden quick chattering. She had time to glimpse a line of monkeys in cages set around the wall before ducking out of sight once again. She crouched where she was, as she heard voices. Frau Matthofer and her visitors had obviously heard the disturbance and had come out to see what it was.

She heard the door of the hut open and the old woman talking to the animals.

'Was passiert, meine Liebchen? What is the matter, my pets?' she crooned in German. 'What's got into you? Did something frighten you?'

Stephanie sensed rather than saw the old woman come over to the window and look out into the forest. She kept low to the ground, held her breath and hoped for the best.

Inside the hut, the old woman was joined by first one, then both her visitors.

'Qu'est-ce qu'il y a? What is it, Irma?'

The old woman replied this time in French: 'I don't know, Louis. Something seems to have frightened them.'

'Perhaps it was a chimpanzee. Monkeys are always frightened of chimpanzees.'

'Perhaps.'

Stephanie could hear only fragments of the conversation which took place within the hut. What she could understand of it alarmed her deeply.

She recognized at one point the deep booming voice of Victor Mtaza.

'Two weeks from now, Irma, and it's all finished anyway. Your job will be over. Louis here will organize the last shipments – the normal route.'

'Brussels?'

'Yes, through Brussels.'

When she heard Brussels mentioned, bells rang in Stephanie's mind. She remembered that Kaplan had spoken of a man called Louis – Louis Vincennes – the son of Count Philippe Vincennes. He had said that Louis had been away in Africa at the time of his visit to Belgium. Could it be the same man?

Before she had time to pursue this line of thought, she heard the old woman intervene.

'And after Brussels? Will there be any further transshipments? My monkeys hate long journeys, you know.'

Stephanie heard the reassuring tones of the man called Louis. 'Don't worry. After Brussels, they'll fly straight to Moscow. Plenty of food and water for all of them, I promise you.'

'Ah!' Frau Matthofer sounded deeply relieved.

Before Stephanie had time to digest what she had just heard, the old woman spoke again.

'What will happen to the monkeys who are left behind? I don't want them to be harmed. They are my children, you know. I love them.' There was a beseeching, almost terrified, note in her voice.

'Don't worry, Irma,' Stephanie heard Victor reply. 'No harm will come to the animals that are left. They will live in the forest just as they have always done.'

Stephanie could tell from the intonation in Victor Mtaza's voice that the man was lying but somehow Frau Matthofer missed it.

'Good,' the old woman's gratitude was unmistakable. 'I could not bear it if they were harmed. Gentlemen,' suddenly she became brisk and businesslike, 'can I offer you some lunch? It is modest fare I am afraid, but I was able to visit the village the other day – at my age I find the climb tough going – and I have acquired some fresh fruit. Here I am surrounded by so much greenery,' Stephanie could imagine the old woman spreading her hands, 'and yet fresh fruit is a luxury. Oh yes, and I got some new batteries for my radio so I will be able to hear the signal about the next shipment. Stay here, gentlemen. I'll call you when lunch is ready.'

The old woman left the hut and the two men followed her out.

But instead of crossing the clearing after her, they stayed where they were – talking.

'Poor Irma,' Victor Mtaza said. 'She doesn't know yet. She mustn't know.'

'Know what?'

There was a hint of impatience in Mtaza's reply.

'About the monkeys of course, Louis. They're doomed. All of them are doomed. Once you have got your last plane-load out of Bujumbura, those that are left have to be destroyed. Utterly and completely. Down to the last one.'

For five minutes Stephanie lay there in the undergrowth digesting what she had heard. What did the reference to Moscow mean? Why were the green monkeys being shipped out from Burundi to Russia? Why did Victor Mtaza say that in two weeks the operation would be finished? What operation? The only thing Stephanie realized with absolute clarity was that she could no longer handle this one on her own. There were forces at play far beyond her poor power to comprehend. But the problem was: whom to ask to help? Who were friends? Who were enemies? Or were the enemies, like Lowell Kaplan, really friends? Deep down, she wished she could be friends with Kaplan. Whatever their differences, she found herself missing him.

From the hut across the clearing came the murmur of meal-time conversation. Stephanie judged it safe to proceed. But before she left, she wanted to visit the third hut, the hut to which Frau Matthofer had first taken her visitors.

Once more she crawled through the undergrowth at the edge of the clearing. Once more she poked her head above the sill. This time the windows were not barred. There was a plain sheet of glass and that was all.

Stephanie peered through the glass. It took some time for her eyes to become accustomed to the gloom. When at last she was able to see clearly, she gave a gasp of astonishment. For the walls of the hut were lined with shelves from floor to roof. And on every shelf vials of liquid stood six deep. She strained her eyes to see what was written on each vial. And then suddenly illumination dawned. For each tube was marked with the date of its completion, and below the date appeared the words, written in Frau Matthofer's unmistakably Gothic handwriting: 'MARBURG VIRUS – ANTISERUM FROM GREEN MONKEY'!

'Oh God!' Stephanie suddenly saw it all. How much time did she have? She shut her eyes and prayed that she would have enough time. Then she slipped back into the forest.

CHAPTER FIFTEEN

HARRY BOLBECK had been at the Bronx Zoo for over six months. He was enjoying himself enormously. He sometimes felt that dropping out of school to take a job with the animals had been the best thing he had ever done. Animals weren't like teachers. They didn't pressure you and muck you around all the time. They didn't mind if you showed up late, unless it was your turn on the feeding run in which case they minded a great deal – but that was understandable. Frankly, Harry Bolbeck preferred animals to human beings. He particularly liked the monkeys with whom he had been working for the last two weeks.

The monkey-house was next to the Sea Lions and opposite the Carnivores. Each morning he took the Lexington Avenue express to East Tremont Avenue and walked the few hundred yards north to the Boston Road entrance of the zoo. He would show his pass at the turnstile and then enjoy, for the next fifteen minutes, the magical walk through the woods, past the elephants and buffalos, then down the hill to Wolf Wood and up again to the monkey-house where he would check in with the Head Keeper before getting on with his work.

The monkeys fascinated him. The Bronx Zoo had all sorts. They had two six hundred pound gorillas – the equivalent of three football full-backs rolled into one; they had chimpanzees and orangutans. They had gibbons, the most skilled brachiators among the apes (Bolbeck had learned that a brachiator was an animal which used its arms to swing through the trees). They had langurs from India and colobus monkeys from Africa. They had a proboscis monkey from the island of Borneo which was the only place in the whole wide world where the 'nosiest of the simians' as the proboscis monkey was sometimes called, still survived. Bolbeck's job was to look after them all; to feed them and water them. And to love and cherish them as well. He had learned early on that monkeys and apes of whatever kind responded wonderfully to affection. The monkey-house at the Bronx Zoo was not a spectacularly sympathetic place. Those who had designed and built it had done their best to maintain the fiction that a small tropical sanctuary existed somewhere between the seals and the lions. But they had not wholly succeeded. The cages were large and airy; they were filled with trees and branches to swing on. There were rocks to scramble over and forest pools to drink from. But, in the last resort – whatever the pretence –the animals were in a prison. And they knew it.

That was why the instinctive sympathy which Bolbeck brought to his work was so important. He was, on the surface, an unattractive youth. He had long dark hair which was certainly not as clean as it should have been; a straggling unkempt beard and a tendency to acne. But the animals loved him notwithstanding. He seemed to be able to talk to them in a language which they could understand. Monkeys gibbered. And Harry Bolbeck had learned to gibber back.

One Friday morning in the late summer, Harry Bolbeck realized as he walked through the woods of the Zoo on his way to work that he was in a particularly good mood. One reason for the good mood was the approach of the weekend. He and his friend, Steve Mulliner, took it in turns to have the weekend off and this time it was his turn. Another, perhaps more important, reason was the sheer enjoyment that Bolbeck was deriving from trying to communicate with a new batch of monkeys – guenons of various sorts – which had arrived at the zoo earlier in the week. Bolbeck probably liked the guenons more than any other kind of monkey. He liked the variety – they came with all kinds of colours, spots and stripes. He liked the clear markings, white bibs, white nose blobs, white tiaras. He liked the athleticism of the species, though of course the limits of the monkey cage acted as a severe restraint on the kind of aerial dynamics at which they were so adept. Above all he liked the guenons' sense of humour. It was marvellous to see the little animals play tricks on each other and then roar with laughter, rocking back on their haunches, when the trick succeeded. The previous day he had seen one of the new arrivals, a guenon with an odd bright green fur, peel back the skin of a banana and eat the fruit. Then it had picked up a stick of approximately the same dimensions as the fruit it had just eaten and had pushed the banana skin around it so that it seemed, on casual inspection, as though the fruit remained untouched. Bolbeck had seen the little green monkey take up the fake banana and offer it to one of the others. Then, when the deceit had been discovered and the empty banana skin had been thrown angrily to the floor, he had witnessed an eruption of mirth such as he had never seen before.

Where on earth had the little green monkey learned that trick? he wondered, as he changed his clothes in the staff-room of the monkey-house. His colleague, Steve Mulliner, had arrived for work ahead of him and was already changing.

'Hey, Steve, do you know what I saw in the guenon cage yesterday?'

'No, what?'

Steve Mulliner, like Bolbeck himself, worked with the animals of the Bronx Zoo for love not for money and he had been fascinated by the tale of the bananas.

'Man, isn't that something!' he had exclaimed. 'I'd love to see that. Do you think he would do that again?'

'We can try.'

Later that morning, at a time when there were very few visitors to the monkey-house, Bolbeck and Mulliner went into the guenon cage with a bunch of bananas.

'That's the one.' Bolbeck pointed to the green monkey as it sat in the crotch of a tree-trunk some distance from its fellows. 'Here.' He held up a banana.

The rest of the new arrivals fled chattering and suspicious as he raised his arm. It would take them some time to get used to the rewards as well as the drawbacks of captivity. But the little green monkey showed an exactly contrary reaction. With a single continuous movement he leapt off his perch, seized the banana and returned to the tree where he sat and eagerly stripped away the peel to get at the fruit inside.

'Look!' Bolbeck drew Mulliner's attention to the process of consumption. 'See how carefully he's folding back the skin.'

They watched fascinated as the monkey finished off the banana; laid the skin in the fork of the tree; then skittered off in search of a piece of wood of the right size and consistency. When he had found what he was looking for, the animal retrieved the skin and repeated on an unsuspecting colleague the trick he had already played the previous day.

'He chose a different fall-guy today,' Bolbeck commented. 'Yesterday, he tried it on a Diana monkey. Today, he's going after the Patas.'

'Shit!' Mulliner shook his head in disbelief as the small charade unfolded.

This time when the Patas monkey discovered the trick, it did not merely content itself with hurling the empty skin to the floor. It launched a full scale attack on the perpetrator of the deception and the green monkey was forced to retire to the very top of the cage and swing from the roof with its long prehensile tail.

'See. He's laughing! He's really laughing!'

Steve Mulliner, regarding the scene for himself, could not disagree with his friend's observation.

'I've never seen anything like it,' he said. 'What kind of monkey is it anyway? Where did it come from?'

'It came in on the last African consignment. They've put it down as a grass monkey of some kind, but they haven't got around yet to the precise classification. Our labelling people are running a bit behind.'

Steve Mulliner regarded the little animal with interest. The fun and games finished, it had once more regained its customary perch in the fork of the tree.

'That animal has been in contact with human beings before, Harry,' Mulliner said. 'I don't think he invented that trick himself. I think he learned it somewhere.'

'Could be.' Bolbeck sounded unconvinced. 'But I don't see why he couldn't have worked it out for himself.'

They both stood there in the monkey cage for the next few minutes watching the animals. Outside a small knot of people watched them, as though expecting something to happen.

Bolbeck picked up the discarded banana skin from off the floor. 'Let's play the same trick on the monkey and see how it reacts.' He stuffed the skin with a piece of stick and then, to increase the verisimilitude, bound up the peel with a piece of clear adhesive tape.

'Give me that bunch of bananas, Steve.'

Bolbeck began tossing bananas to the various monkeys

in the cage. The animals ate them avidly. When it was the green monkey's turn, he held out the fake banana.

'Here, come and get it! Have a sip of your own medicine.'

The little monkey bounced off his perch and took the banana in his paw. Then he paused as though he was about to spring back to the tree but had just thought better of it.

'He knows there's something wrong, even without opening it.' Bolbeck could not suppress his astonishment.

Suddenly the monkey hurled the banana straight at his keeper's face, forcing Bolbeck to duck so that the missile passed harmlessly over his shoulder. Then, without warning, it leapt onto his shoulder and bit him hard in the lobe of his left ear.

'Goddammit!' Bolbeck shouted in pain. 'The little bugger's bitten me.' He put his hand to his ear and felt the blood.

CHAPTER SIXTEEN

THE SECOND OUTBREAK of Marburg disease, occurring by unlucky coincidence like the first in New York, threw the authorities into a state of alarm bordering upon panic.

The problem was mathematical. The initial case, the index case, was poor Harry Bolbeck, whose monkey-bitten ear was the immediate source of infection. He in turn transmitted the disease to five persons before being hospitalized in Columbia-Presbyterian Hospital's maximum isolation ward. Those five persons – and they included his work-mate, Steve Mulliner, and Mulliner's girlfriend, Judy Cox – were themselves traced and isolated but not before two of the five had infected respectively eight and nine other people. So the ripples spread in ever-widening circles. By the morning of the twelfth day six deaths had already occurred (Bolbeck had been the first to go, followed closely by Mulliner and Cox); all isolation units throughout the United States were already full and the limited supplies of serum were nearing the point of exhaustion. It only needed a few more cases for the dam to burst and for the flood to become truly unstoppable.

The President's reaction, once he was informed of the crisis, was immediate:

'Why in God's name don't we have a vaccine? You people' – he was addressing an emergency meeting of Federal and state health officials – 'have a vaccine for polio and flu and whooping cough and even the goddam common cold. So why haven't you got a vaccine for Marburg if it's the deadliest disease known to man.'

After the meeting, John Shearer, the hard-hitting aide from California who had been White House link-man in the CIA's secret plan to develop an anti-Marburg vaccine, had stayed behind in the Oval Office.

'Actually, sir,' he had addressed the President with an unusual degree of deference, 'we do have a vaccine. Pharmacorp have it in the final stage of development. We've been working closely with Irving Woodnutt, who's the head of Pharmacorp.'

The President nodded. 'I know Woodnutt. A real shit if ever there was one. He thinks he's going to run for Senate on my coat-tails, but I tell you he won't make it to first base.'

'I don't disagree with your evaluation,' Shearer interrupted diplomatically. 'But the fact is, under Woodnutt's pressure, Pharmacorp have enough vaccine available now for trial tests and, after that, we can undertake a crash campaign of preventive inoculation. We can inoculate 200 million Americans if we have to. Pharmacorp have built it into a multi-purpose flu shot.'

'Why didn't you say so at the meeting?' The President had been thunderstruck.

'Circumstances, sir,' Shearer had replied diplomatically.

He had gone on to explain the background. It had taken a long time because he had had to deal with the first outbreak of Marburg and with all subsequent events so that the President could have a clear picture.

'Jesus,' the President exclaimed when he had finished. 'Those people always try to be too clever, don't they?' He was referring of course to the CIA. 'Why couldn't they just go along with the WHO scheme? Why take the risk of bringing the monkeys back?'

'But it wasn't Sam and Griselda,' Shearer protested.

'Who are Sam and Griselda?' the President asked impatiently. 'Were, not are. Sam and Griselda are dead.' Shearer explained the circumstances and added: 'Those two never infected anybody. Not as far as we know. Bolbeck caught the disease from a monkey in the Bronx Zoo. That monkey is dead now. Incinerated.'

'What happened? I thought you said the WHO operation was wholly successful.'

Shearer shook his head. 'We don't know what happened. It's a mystery. I guess they just didn't get all of them.'

They turned back to the subject of the vaccination program. 'How soon can you get it going? From what they told us today, we are dealing with a geometrical progression, aren't we?'

'We are.' Shearer agreed. 'If we don't stop the outbreak within the next few days, we shan't be talking about hundreds or even thousands of dead Americans. We shall be talking about hundreds of thousands.'

For a moment the President put his head in his hands. Then he looked up. 'For Christ's sake, get on with it,' he said. 'For once it looks as though the CIA didn't goof. You may have taken a risk in bringing the monkeys back but by God you've got a vaccine now, just when we need it. You can get the Press and the Television in here and show me rolling up my shirt sleeve and being jabbed.'

He smiled. 'That will make good copy, won't it? That will reassure the nation!'

Shearer sensed the lightening of the President's mood.

'I'm told the buttock is the preferred location, sir. Could you stoop to that?'

'I'll stoop to anything, John, if I have to.' The President laughed. As an afterthought, he added: 'Once I've had the jab, I'm going to visit one of the internment centres. We don't want panic to spread. If the American public realized that I've had the anti-Marburg vaccination and that I have complete confidence in it, that will have an immensely calming effect.'

'I don't think you ought to take unnecessary risks.' Shearer sounded worried. 'Pharmacorp assure us that the vaccination will be effective. But I'm not sure the President of the United States should be right in the firing-line.'

'Let me be the judge of that.'

★

Ed Werner was sweating with anxiety.

'What if the President himself is vaccinated and then visits an internment centre where he's in contact with the virus?'

An almost manic look came into Woodnutt's eyes as he faced his colleague across his desk.

'Ed.' He had obviously made up his mind. 'We're going to bluff this one out. If the vaccine doesn't work, they'll discover it soon enough. But that could just be scientific error; nothing criminal. Marburg's an unknown disease. So we say nothing. Agreed? Pharmacorp is in this up to the hilt. We have two hundred million units in the pipeline and I'm not going to stand up and say that we knew all along there would be no anti-Marburg protection. Did the car-men ever say that the Pinto's gas-tank would explode in a rear-end collision?'

Ed Werner made one last feeble protest.

'What about the President? Shouldn't he be warned at least?' Woodnutt looked at him witheringly.

'Werner, you've got to get your priorities straight. There are a lot of people ready, willing and able to be President of the United States. If one man goes, another man will step up. But Pharmacorp is another matter. One hint of the truth and this corporation is finished. I repeat what I said. We tough this one out. I want all the vaccine production schedules tightened. I want a crash program to get the multi-purpose doses ready. Is that clear?'

Ed Werner left the room, shaking his head. Sometimes

he wondered whether Woodnutt didn't carry ruthlessness too far.

If Ed Werner had been privy to the conversation Irving Woodnutt had the following morning, he would have been more than confirmed in this view. For the head of Pharmacorp was sitting with his wife in the breakfast room of their lavish mansion outside Pittsburgh. (Gloria Nimmo was already dreaming of her very own equivalent of Fallingwater in which an even more sumptuous breakfast room would feature.) They were both of them reading the papers; both of them transfixed by the accounts of the new outbreak of the Marburg virus in the New York area.

'Gloria, you've got to do it.' Woodnutt sounded completely emphatic. 'The President's going to have a shot and is going up there to visit an internment centre. You've got to go too. Dammit, Pharmacorp makes the bloody vaccine. We've got one hundred million units in production already and another batch on the way. But the public has to believe in it. They have to be persuaded that a vaccination is the only chance of stopping America going under.'

'Why me? Why not the President just by himself?' Gloria Nimmo tossed back her glorious blonde hair. She looked worried.

'Because you're my wife. Because Pharmacorp makes the stuff and I'm head of Pharmacorp.'

'You mean because you're running for the Senate and it will do you a lot of good to have pictures of Mrs Irving Woodnutt, alias Gloria Nimmo, standing shoulder to shoulder with the President on his mercy mission.'

'As long as you don't get closer than that. You know his reputation with women!'

Gloria Nimmo laughed. 'Okay. I'll do it. I guess it's all part of the job. When do I report for work?'

'The President is going up to New York in the course of tomorrow. You can join him there. The visit to the centre is planned for first thing the next day.'

They sat together in silence for a few more minutes. Then Woodnutt, who was still reading the paper, exclaimed suddenly.

'Good God! Do you see that?'

'What?'

'European countries have banned all international flights originating in the United States.' He read out the item. 'In view of the present outbreak of Marburg disease in the United States – an outbreak which has already claimed over three hundred lives – and in order to guard against the possible spread of the disease through international travel, European members of IATA late yesterday acted unilaterally to prevent any US-originating flight from landing at a European airport. The ban will only be lifted when U.S. authorities can demonstrate that effective control measures have been taken to prevent the further spread of the virus.'

Woodnutt's wife whistled, 'It's Fortress America all over again, isn't it?'

'That's the way it looks.'

The head of Pharmacorp buried his face once again in the newspaper. If he felt sorry for his wife, he did not show it. By going up to New York to visit an internment centre alongside the President of the United States she would not only be demonstrating an unshakable belief in the efficiency of the vaccine, she would also be providing him and Pharmacorp with the most convincing alibi imaginable. How could anyone suggest, let alone prove, that Pharmacorp had knowingly and for motives of pure commercial gain produced a dud vaccine when the wife of the head of the corporation was willing to be vaccinated and to be exposed to the risk of infection?

A few moments later, Woodnutt thrust the paper aside and rose from the breakfast table.

He looked at his watch. 'I mustn't be late,' he said. 'I'm flying to Washington this morning to be present when the President receives his vaccination.'

'Why don't I get mine done at the same time?'

Woodnutt looked at his wife. There was no way of telling her that the vaccination was useless and she would be wasting her time.

'Come along then,' he said.

*

Lowell Kaplan was in the Hot Lab at the Atlanta Center for Disease Control. He was kitted out in the standard uniform – perspex face-mask, airtight suit, gloves – and he was working alone, hooked onto the airline with his own umbilical cord. The rules might call for the 'buddy system', i.e. never less than two people working together; but for once in his life Kaplan didn't give a fuck about the rules. He didn't trust anyone any longer. How could he? It just didn't make sense to trust anyone when suddenly, out of the blue, Leslie Cheek, his director at the CDC, could announce that yes, after all, there was a vaccine against Marburg and that a major inoculation program was under way with the President himself first in line.

Kaplan had exploded.

'What the hell's going on?' he had shouted at the thin scraggy man who sheltered anonymously behind thick horn-rimmed spectacles. 'I just don't understand. I don't care whether it's combined with the Fukushima-flu shot or not. That's all tactics. What I'd like to know is how did Pharmacorp make the vaccine in the first place? Where did they get the live virus from?'

When Leslie Cheek had explained about Sam and Griselda, Kaplan had been almost beside himself with indignation.

'The fools! The stupid unbelievable fools,' he cried, referring to the CIA. 'Can't they grow up? Can't they forget their Cold War tricks for just one minute? They were jeopardizing the health of the whole United States bringing those monkeys back here. The whole point of the WHO operation, and God knows it was a pretty gruesome business, was to achieve a total elimination of the virus, not to take risks by bringing live monkeys home, even if they were to be held under lab conditions.'

Cheek had attempted to soothe Kaplan down. 'At least it means, now that the outbreak has happened, we've got a vaccine ready and waiting. That's an almost unbelievable piece of good luck.'

Kaplan had remained outraged and sceptical. 'I'm going to take a damn good look at that vaccine.'

'Oh come on, Lowell.' The Director of the CDC had sounded irritated. 'Two hundred million Americans are lining up for doses. You're not trying to tell me that you actually doubt whether the vaccine works. Jesus, people just don't make that kind of mistake!'

Lowell Kaplan had left the room with a sombre, determined expression on his face. Late that afternoon, after a supply of the vaccine had been flown down urgently at his request from the Pharmacorp laboratory in Pittsburgh, he had begun his investigation.

After two hours of steady uninterrupted work, he put a call through to Ed Werner, chief virologist at the Pharmacorp Laboratories, tracking him down at his home.

'Ed, that material you sent me is a typical flu vaccine. You've got Brazil, Texas and now Fukushima protection built in. But as far as I can tell, there's no new viral material in it. What the hell are you people playing at?'

At the other end of the line the voice sounded smooth and unflustered.

'Let me just check on this, Lowell. There must have been some mistake our end.'

Half an hour later, Ed Werner rang back. Kaplan was

still in the lab, waiting with increasing impatience.

'Sorry, Lowell. There *was* a mistake our end. We sent you the wrong sample – you got the medium without the message, as it were.'

'This is no time for jokes, Ed,' Kaplan snapped. 'I've just wasted two hours looking at that stuff.'

Ed Werner sounded contrite. 'I really do apologize. It turns out that my assistant, Philip Mason, already realized that there had been some mix-up. He couldn't find me since I'd already left the office for the day. So he caught a flight earlier this afternoon with a new load. He ought to be with you any minute.'

They talked for some moments longer. By the time they had finished Kaplan felt slightly mollified. It seemed, after all, to be a genuine mistake.

He had barely put the phone down when he had a message over the intercom from Susan Wainwright. Susan was monitoring Kaplan's investigation from the work-area outside the Hot Lab. He could see her now across the glass barrier.

'Philip Mason has just come in from Pittsburgh with some new samples of the vaccine.'

'Tell him to scrub up, get suited and come on in.'

'Shall I stay on till you've finished?'

'No, don't worry, Susan. You go on home. I'll close the lab down.'

'Thanks. Don't work too late.'

Susan Wainwright stayed long enough to show Mason

the layout of the place – showers, changing area and so forth. When she had left, the two men worked alone together.

Philip Mason – it was the first time Kaplan had met the young man – sounded deeply apologetic.

'I just can't understand how the mix-up happened, Dr Kaplan.'

'You've checked on the batches which have already gone out, have you? Remember, the President himself has just been vaccinated and he's due to visit an internment centre tomorrow morning.'

Mason smiled behind his perspex face-mask. The convex material produced a slight distortion. Kaplan couldn't help thinking that Mason's smile had a sinister quality.

They set up the electron microscope. Kaplan thought the other man seemed nervous. But it was only a passing impression and he put it out of his mind as he became engrossed in his work.

It took him about ten minutes to adjust the delicate instrument so as to achieve maximum efficiency. When finally he was ready, he realized with a mixture of annoyance and amazement that the new samples which Mason had brought with him from Pittsburgh were no more relevant than the last.

'Hey, Mason – who are you trying to fool? This is still ordinary flu vaccine you're showing me here. There's no Marburg morphology.'

He looked up from the eyepiece of the electron microscope to see that the Hot Lab was empty. Completely empty. Mason had disappeared.

He glanced at the airline and saw that the pipe which a few moments before had been clipped onto Mason's airsuit was now swinging free as though it had only recently been relinquished.

Above the airline his eye caught sight of a flashing red notice. 'RESERVE AIR ONLY ONE MINUTE SUPPLY RE-MAINING.'

'Hell and damnation!' Kaplan swore out loud. Mason must have left the Hot Lab and turned off the external air supply. He strode over to the inside door of the airlock. It was locked. His eye fell on the telephone and he picked it up. But the line was dead. Mason had thought of that too. Above the airline the red plaque flashed again. THIRTY SECONDS RESERVE AIR SUPPLY LEFT ALL PERSONNEL SHOULD EVACUATE LAB AREA IMMEDIATELY.

Kaplan switched on his individual air supply. Every pressure suit used in the Hot Lab was equipped with its own airbottle. It was meant to cover the short period where a researcher, on entering or leaving the lab, had to unclip himself from the airline. He was standing there, still attached by the umbilical cord, when the red plaque signalled starkly NO AIR ENTERING LAB.

Reluctantly, Kaplan pulled out the plug. The plastic pipe hung free. For a few seconds he lost control. He strode back over to the door and hammered on the metal panels of the airlock as though by brute force he could force them to open. He swore out loud. Then, suddenly, the sense of panic left him. He knew that within seconds he would be without oxygen. He would, as a consequence, be forced to breathe in the air of the laboratory itself. That meant he would be directly exposed to the pathogenic material present in the lab. As his oxygen gave out, Kaplan lay face down on the floor. Spores would tend to rise with the air caused by his own breathing. He should try to keep as near the ground as possible.

Kaplan found himself thinking about his children. He still hadn't taken Jimmy on that white-water vacation. He hoped it wasn't too late. And then he thought about Stephanie. He wished things had gone better between them. If he survived...

If he survived! In his heart, Kaplan knew that he had little or no chance of survival. He didn't know how long the residual air in the Hot Lab would last but it couldn't, he imagined, be more than an hour or two at the most. Because of the system of negative pressure under which the Hot Lab operated, the room in which he now was, was virtually airless. They tried to achieve a near-vacuum. When you were clipped to the airline, that obviously didn't matter. Once off the airline, anyone who stayed in the Hot Lab would quickly suffocate. As he lay there, Kaplan reflected that some people might regard quick suffocation as a preferable alternative to the lingering and painful death that could be induced by some of the pathogens present in the laboratory. He looked at his watch. It was midnight. The first technicians would not arrive at the lab until seven a.m. at the earliest. That meant he had to hold out for seven hours! He lay totally still. Every movement, even turning his head, would use up the air quicker. His breathing was so shallow as to be almost imperceptible.

★

Susan Wainwright lived some twenty-five miles outside Atlanta. It normally took her around three-quarters of an hour to get home. Sometimes more, sometimes less. It depended on the traffic.

She was about five minutes from her door when something odd struck her. It was to do with the appearance of the young man, Philip Mason, late that day.

She knew that Kaplan had been analysing the sample vaccine. She knew that he had spoken to Ed Werner in Pittsburgh. She listened in to all Kaplan's conversations and took notes on them. That was part of her job. She had heard Werner say that his assistant Philip Mason had 'caught a flight with a new load' of vaccine. But she knew for a fact that there *was no plane in the late afternoon from Pittsburgh to Atlanta.* She had been there the other day at some toxics conference and she had tried to catch a plane home for the evening, only to find that they had changed the schedule. Yet Werner had certainly implied that Mason had taken an ordinary commercial flight, not some executive jet.

She jammed her foot on the brake and steered the car

round in a U-turn.

She hit ninety m.p.h. on her way back to the Center for Disease Control. It was after midnight and fortunately the road was clear. Her mind raced like the engine. If Mason hadn't come down on the afternoon flight, because there was no afternoon flight, then he must have been in Atlanta all the time. He must have been staying nearby – at the Sheraton Emory across the street? And he had obviously been in communication with Werner. What did it mean?

She tried to puzzle it out as she drove. Something was wrong. Very wrong.

She pulled into the parking lot outside the Hot Lab and ran across to the building. The lights were still on. That meant that Kaplan would still be there, thank God!

She opened the door of the control room and looked across into the Hot Lab the other side of the glass wall.

The flashing red of the wall panel caught her attention immediately:

NO AIR ENTERING LAB.

The lab appeared to be empty. The airlines were hanging free, unconnected to any human body. She frowned. Kaplan and Mason must have finished their work and gone home. But why had the warning lights come on? Perhaps there was some electrical malfunction. She would have to report it in the morning.

As she turned to go, she noticed the figure on the floor. She recognized Kaplan immediately. The shock of steely grey hair was unmistakable. She saw that his eyes were closed. From where she stood, behind the glass partition, it was impossible to tell whether Kaplan was still breathing.

Susan Wainwright was a decisive woman trained to think quickly in emergencies. She realized at once what had happened. The air supply had been cut off. Kaplan had had to unclip. He had possibly been exposed to the pathogens present in the Hot Lab. And now he risked suffocation through the exhaustion of the air supply within the lab unless, indeed, he had already succumbed. She realized also that, dead or alive, Kaplan was now an extremely dangerous commodity. Her immediate instinct might have been to open the door and simply drag the man out. But she knew that wouldn't do. You had to respect the drill otherwise the whole thing would go up the spout.

She spoke into the intercom. 'Lowell, can you hear me?'

The voice came to him, it seemed, from a long way down. He had sunk through caverns where green beasts swam. Lights burned on coral walls and weird shapes formed and reformed in his imagination. He thought he heard Susan's voice booming round the vast empty spaces. But he knew that this was absurd. Susan had gone home. And, anyway, he was dead.

Susan repeated the question, louder and more urgently. 'Lowell, can you hear me? Am I coming through?'

This time he was sure that it was Susan's voice. He roused himself with a great effort of will, clawed his way back through the caverns of time towards a state resembling consciousness.

'I hear you, Susan.' Kaplan's voice was barely more than a hoarse whisper.

'I'm unlocking the doors and turning the air supply back on. Can you manage to clip yourself on to the line?'

Kaplan raised his head from the floor. He saw the flashing red light go out, to be replaced by the green signal which indicated that the air supply was back to normal. He tried to rise to his feet but he found he was unable to go beyond a kneeling position.

'I can't make it, Susan.' Kaplan fell back to the floor.

She wondered, then, whether to throw out the rule book. If Kaplan couldn't clip himself back on the line, there was no other way of getting air to him quickly enough to make a difference except by opening the airlock. If she put on a pressure suit herself and went in there to help, it would be too late.

She saw him rise to his knees again. Once erect, he swayed uncertainly. Then, slowly, painfully, he began to inch his way towards the dangling airlines. Twice the plastic pipe slipped from his grasp as he reached for it. The effort seemed to exhaust him. He bowed and almost fell.

Susan watched in agony. 'Go on, Lowell. You've almost made it,' she urged him.

For the third time, Kaplan grabbed at the pipe and at last he had it. With his remaining strength he plunged the nozzle into the clip-on socket and pulled up the face mask.

The relief was instantaneous. Kaplan could literally feel the oxygen flooding into his blood, pumping into his brain.

He could feel the clouds dispersing, the pain receding.

For a few moments he knelt, allowing himself the luxury of recuperation. When he spoke, his voice had regained much of its customary firmness and vigour.

'Thanks, Susan,' she heard him over the intercom. 'I'll never forget that.' He smiled at her across the partition. 'And now you had better come in here with an airbottle. Mine ran out some way back as you may have guessed. And I want to get out of here.'

Kaplan smiled. When she saw that smile, Susan knew her man was on the way home. Before leaving the Hot Lab, Kaplan underwent the full decontamination procedure. He also received a complete range of preventive inoculations with Susan herself acting as a calm and competent nurse.

'I'm going to suppose that you were exposed to most of the pathogens we've got in the Hot Lab and I'm going to pump you full of antidotes. That'll do for a start. Then I propose to call the emergency team into action. They'll have to take a look at you and decide what to do.'

Kaplan had shaken his head vehemently. 'You'll do no such thing. I don't want anything to come out about tonight's accident. I don't want to give anyone an excuse to put me into convenient quarantine for the next few weeks. I don't trust anybody. Not now. No, Susan,' he concluded. 'I'm alive. I'm free and I propose to stay that way.'

Later, when they were back in his office, Susan had asked him: 'Why did Mason try to kill you? He *was* trying to kill you, wasn't he?'

'Of course. He wanted to kill me because I discovered that Pharmacorp have produced a dud vaccine. There's no anti-Marburg protection in any of that stuff, Susan. Pharmacorp are pushing two hundred million units of ordinary flu vaccine onto the unsuspecting American public while maintaining that it's an effective way of dealing with the Marburg virus.'

Susan Wainwright went pale. 'Why should Pharmacorp do that? I simply don't understand.'

'I don't understand everything, Susan,' Kaplan replied slowly. 'But I'm beginning to have an idea.'

He pulled the telephone towards him. 'Who are you calling?' Susan asked.

'Ed Werner in Pittsburgh. Make sure you have the recorder on.' Susan switched on the taping device which Kaplan used to record all his important calls. They heard the ringing tone and then a sleepy voice came on the line. 'Hello? Who is it?'

'Is that Ed Werner? This is Lowell Kaplan speaking.'

'Lowell!...' the voice exploded at the other end of the line. 'I thought you were...'

'Dead?' Kaplan smiled grimly into the mouthpiece. 'No, I'm not dead, but I might well be.' His voice took on a hard, almost savage note. 'Listen, Ed. You're in trouble. Big trouble. They could be booking you for attempted murder. We have a tape of every one of your conversations with Mason, including this evening's.'

Ed Werner gave an audible gasp. Kaplan continued mercilessly. 'I can't promise anything, Ed. But you may be able to help yourself if you cooperate now.'

'How?'

Kaplan knew he had his man hooked.

'Just tell me *why* Pharmacorp produced a dud vaccine. Weren't you and your people able to attenuate the virus? Or couldn't you find a suitable medium to culture it in?'

'Jesus, Lowell.' Ed Werner spoke so softly that he was barely audible. 'Don't you understand? There *was* no virus. We didn't have anything to work with. They brought back two monkeys but *those monkeys were clean.*'

He began to whine: 'I told Woodnutt, right from the start, that the whole idea was mad.'

Kaplan didn't listen to the end. The police would pick up Werner and Mason later. And Woodnutt too if it came to that. He banged down the receiver.

'He says the monkeys were clean, Susan. You heard him. That means one of two things. Either not all the green monkeys carry the Marburg virus and those damn fools who run the CIA managed to come up with two specimens who didn't have an ounce of poison in their veins. Or...' Kaplan paused, working it out.

'Or what?' Susan Wainwright prompted him.

'Or *we killed the wrong monkeys.*' Kaplan clapped a hand to his forehead. 'Oh, my God!' he exclaimed. 'That SABENA man at Brussels. The one who gave me the details of cargo movements at Zaventem the day Diane Verusio was there. Tim Boswell told me they tried to trace him later – without success. Perhaps Delgrave was a phoney. Perhaps he was deliberately feeding me misleading information.'

Susan looked sceptical. 'I don't understand. I thought Delgrave's information about the provenance of the green monkeys exactly confirmed the information you had in Marburg. Even the map references were the same.'

Kaplan banged the desk. 'My God, how blind I've been! You're right, Susan. If Delgrave is a phoney, then those old records in Marburg castle were phoney too.'

'You mean, there never was any outbreak of disease in Marburg in 1967?'

'Oh no, the disease happened all right. That's a historical fact.'

'Then, you mean it wasn't transmitted by green monkeys in spite of the fact that some people, somewhere, for reasons of their own, seem to be trying to prove that it was.'

'No,' Kaplan replied slowly. 'The disease was transmitted by green monkeys. I'm sure of that. But it wasn't transmitted by the monkeys in Zaire, by the monkeys we massacred. I'm sure now that the whole Zaire business was a deliberate red herring designed to divert our attention from the fact that somewhere in Africa the real green monkeys exist – I mean the monkeys which really were, and are, the source of the Marburg virus.'

He sat there at his desk, trying desperately to make sense of nonsense. He wished his mind was clearer. His brain, thanks to events earlier that evening, seemed quite literally to be suffering from a lack of oxygen. At last, he made up his mind. He looked at her across the desk.

'Susan?'

'Yes, Lowell.'

'I'm going to go to Germany.'

'Now?'

'Yes, now.'

'How will you go? There are no planes.'

'The military are still flying. I'll talk to the commander of the USAF base at Atlanta. He'll understand. He's a friend of mine. Anyway, this is an emergency.'

'What do I do?'

'Warn the President. Get hold of the White House. Tell them that the vaccine is a dud. Tell them we don't have any anti-Marburg vaccine, that they can forget about the whole inoculation program. Get the police onto Mason and Werner.'

'Do you really have tapes of Werner's conversations with Mason?'

'No, that was just bluff. To draw him out. But we have one tape,' Kaplan pointed to the recording device attached to the telephone. 'That ought to be enough to start with.'

Another thought struck him. 'Make sure they pick up Woodnutt too. He had to know about this.'

Kaplan shook his head as he contemplated the enormity of Woodnutt's offence. 'That man must be unbelievable! You know, his own wife would have been visiting the internment centre with the President – today, just a few hours from now!' A hard expression crossed his face. 'Make sure they really nail Woodnutt, won't you. And put McKinney in the picture. Tell him everything. Don't talk to Cheek. I don't trust Cheek with this one.'

'What if people ask where you are?'

'Stall 'em. For twenty-four hours at least. You'll hear from me before then.'

'And if I don't?'

'You will.'

Susan looked at him with concern. She couldn't help wondering whether the strain of recent days might not have taken its toll on Kaplan's mental stability.

He put his hand on top of hers. He was suddenly calm and confident. 'Susan, there are more ways than one of fighting an epidemic. There are plenty of people here who will do what needs to be done. Personally, I don't believe we have a snowball's chance in hell of containing this thing without new weapons at our disposal. We have fifty thousand suspected contacts in isolation at the moment. And each contact may himself or herself have infected twenty or thirty people. We can't bring them all in. It just isn't feasible. The dam is about to burst, Susan.'

'You think if you fly off to Germany, you'll find some new element which will change the equation?'

'I don't know. Surely it's worth a try. If the course of the disease follows the normal cyclical pattern, we've got six days before the next outbreak. If I use up one or two of them and come up with some kind of answer, with the 'new weapon' I said we need, then surely the time is well spent.'

Susan rose to her feet. 'I won't argue any more. You know what you're doing, Lowell. You always do. Come on. You'd better get through to the USAF base commander if you want a ride to Frankfurt tonight.'

He looked at her fondly.

'Stay by the phone, won't you? You're my link with reality.'

He kissed her on the cheek, a fraternal kiss. They had worked together a long time.

'And thank you again for coming back tonight. I wasn't enjoying myself much down there.'

She put a finger to her lips. 'Shh! You've got to get moving.'

Thirty seconds later, Lowell Kaplan was talking himself into a free ride to Germany.

CHAPTER SEVENTEEN

From the outside the towering Landgraf Schloss, which dominated the town of Marburg, appeared just the same as it had when Kaplan had seen it, in the company of Paula Schmidtt, a few weeks earlier. The sun hit the steep roof of the castle and threw the black shadows of the battlements across the cobbled courtyard. A knot of tourists had gathered on the surrounding parapet and was gazing down across the roofs of the old town to the river. Half a dozen pigeons hopped towards the knot hoping for handouts. Things might seem the same, Kaplan reflected, but the reality was otherwise. A veritable torrent of water had flowed down the Lahn since his first visit. Walking across the yard towards the arched entrance, he seemed to have experienced more action in the last fifty days than in the five years at the Center for Disease Control in Atlanta, Georgia – and no one had ever suggested that his work there lacked interest and variety!

He noted, as he entered the castle, that the old boy who had been on duty on the previous occasion had disappeared. Well, there was nothing unusual in that! The man might have been replaced – or else, it might be his day off in which case Kaplan reckoned he might encounter him later in one of the taverns of the town. There was a pale-faced, unpleasant-looking young German on duty, instead, who looked as though he was a university student earning extra money by doing a part-time job at the castle.

'I was here a few weeks ago,' Kaplan began. 'Fräulein Paula Schmidtt who, as you must know, is Head of Medical Records at Marburg Clinic, came with me. We were looking for some old files in the basement. Fräulein Schmidtt told me,' Kaplan lied, 'that it would be in order if I came back by myself to check on one or two things.'

'Oh! Fräulein Schmidtt told you to come back, did she?' The pale-faced young German showed signs of interest. 'But Fräulein Schmidtt has left the service of the University, don't you know that?'

Kaplan felt his anger flare. There would be time later to investigate the disappearance of Paula Schmidtt. For the present, he had only one concern. He leaned forward menacingly.

'Look, young man, am I going to see those records or not?' A sudden thought struck him. 'Better still, are *you* going to show me those records or not?' The last thing Kaplan wanted was to find himself locked in the dungeon of Marburg castle by an officious jailer.

The student appeared to sense the note of authority in Kaplan's voice. He removed some keys from his pocket. 'This way,' he said. Kaplan remembered the route perfectly – the jinking staircase, the mediaeval armour, the instruments of torture strategically displayed so as to discourage the faint-hearted. His guide opened the door to the storage area and turned on the light at the same time.

'No one's been down here for a long time,' he said. 'Not since Fräulein Schmidtt disappeared.'

For a moment Kaplan half-expected to see the corpse of Paula Schmidtt among the débris of junk and rotting paper. Someone had shot her father, because he had talked too much. Maybe Paula had suffered the same fate. But, then, he saw that the room was empty. Wherever Paula Schmidtt was, it wasn't here.

Keeping an eye on the German, Kaplan went immediately to the filing cabinet which had contained the crucial records in the form of the dog-eared, floppy covered book. What he hoped to find, he wasn't sure. Some evidence of forgery, he supposed – or, if he was very lucky, some indication of the true as opposed to fictitious origin of the green monkey which had infected the ill-fated Peter Ringelmann.

He pulled open the bottom drawer and went through the contents. He was sure it *was* the bottom drawer. But he could find nothing. No book of the right size and shape; nor any indication, in the form of a marker or message, that someone had removed the book which had once been there.

Working feverishly now, he went through the other drawers of the cabinet. Still he found nothing. He shut them again and looked around the room. Had he and Paula Schmidtt left the book out? No, he was certain it had been replaced. Paula Schmidtt, he recalled, had been very punctilious on that point.

He turned to the student and pressed twenty dollars into his hand.

'I'm sorry,' he said; 'I've been wasting your time.'

The young German pocketed the money. 'Fuck all you Americans,' he said.

Kaplan took a taxi to the Schmidtt residence. He didn't go all the way to the door. Instead he asked the driver to let him off at the corner of the street.

For a few minutes he observed the house from a distance. The front lawn, which had been so well-kept at the time of his earlier visit, now seemed distinctly untidy. The grass looked as though it hadn't been cut in weeks and weeds were sprouting up through the gravel of the driveway. The house itself had a heavily-shuttered look. All the windows were closed. The letter-box was stuffed full with mail and periodicals.

Kaplan was about to turn away when he thought he saw a curtain move in an upstairs room. Maybe there was someone there after all. He walked up the drive and rang the bell. There was no reply. Kaplan stood back and looked up at the front of the house. This time he was quite sure he saw the curtain move. He rang the bell again.

'Hello,' he shouted. 'Is anyone at home? It's me, Lowell Kaplan.'

He heard the shuffling behind the door and the noise of the chain being fastened. Then, with the chain in place, Heidi Schmidtt opened the door an inch or two.

Kaplan could barely see her through the crack but he could hear her clearly enough.

'Why don't you go away? Haven't you caused enough harm as it is?'

'Heidi, I have to talk to you. It's important. I can help you.'

'No one can help me now.'

'Do let me in!'

Reluctantly Heidi Schmidtt opened the door to admit him. Kaplan stepped across the threshold and was immediately shocked by what he saw. The inside of the house was in total disorder. Papers were piled on the floor; the furniture was all awry; dirt had visibly accumulated in the corners of the hallway and on the carpets. But what struck Kaplan even more was the change in Heidi herself. The last time he had seen her she had been a house-proud wife and mother, neat in both manner and dress. Now her appearance was totally dishevelled; her hair, which before had been carefully pulled back from her forehead, straggled around her face; there were dark shadows under her eyes.

'Why did you come back?' she hissed at him. 'I don't want to see you. Go away!'

Kaplan pushed his way into the sitting-room, forcing her to follow him.

'Where is Paula?' he asked roughly. 'I have to know.'

Suddenly, Heidi Schmidtt broke down. She sat on an undusted chair and the tears streamed down her cheeks.

'Mein Gott! First they kill Franz. Now Paula! I am sure

they have done something to Paula.' She sobbed uncontrollably. 'There is nothing for me now. I live for nothing.'

Kaplan walked across the room to stand next to her. He laid his hand gently on her heaving shoulders.

'Who killed Franz, Heidi? What do you mean by *they*? I have to know. It's important.'

Heidi Schmidtt looked up at Kaplan. The hatred, the hostility, seemed to fall away. She seemed to sense that Kaplan was, after all, a friend; and that her enemies were elsewhere. She blew her nose, rearranged her hair and sat upright on the seat.

'Can you really help me, Lowell?'

'Of course I can, Heidi.' He took her hand and held it. 'Good God, I've known you for almost twenty years.'

Heidi Schmidtt looked round the room nervously.

'I hope it's safe to talk. Franz died because he talked too much to you that evening. I'm sure of that.'

Kaplan reassured her. 'We'll look after you. You can count on that.'

She seemed to believe him. For a moment she paused as though wondering how to begin. When finally the words began to pour from her, it was almost as though she was engaged in an extended piece of self-justification, an *apologia* for her own and others' conduct.

'You have to understand what life was like here in Germany in the sixties,' she said. 'It was rough. It was tough. There weren't a great many luxuries. Franz and I had been used to a certain level of comfort during our time in the

States. It was a shock to come back to Europe to discover that things were very different.'

She seemed to be appealing to him. 'You do understand, don't you, that Franz and I were never out and out communists? We were sympathizers. But with Paula, it was different. She had lived in the States in her early teens except for the time, back in '61 when we sent her to Germany for the summer and she heard President Kennedy speak at the Berlin Wall. Then in 1966 we came back to Marburg. It was the height of the radical student movement. Rudi Dutschke was the hero of the younger generation. The Baader-Meinhof gang was beginning to form. Paula drifted towards radicalism, towards communism, and there was nothing Franz and I could do to stop her. Irma's influence was very important.'

'Do you mean Irma Matthofer?'

'Yes.'

'You say she was a Communist?'

'More than that. I say Frau Doktor Professor Matthofer was an agent of the KGB throughout her time in Marburg and that, to a greater or lesser extent, Franz and I, with our daughter Paula, were her colleagues or accomplices. The story Franz told you last time you were here was only partly true. There *was* a student duel; the infection *was* spread through the blood. There *was* a political scandal which was subsequently hushed up. But Franz told you that the Chancellor himself had been in Marburg that night. That wasn't true and he knew it. He only told you that to throw you off the scent. The real reason for the cover-up was to prevent any further enquiries into the origin of the disease, for those enquiries might have uncovered what Irma Matthofer was really playing at all along.'

Kaplan nodded. 'We knew the Chancellor wasn't present that night. We checked up on that.'

Heidi Schmidtt shook her head. 'Poor Franz. He was always making mistakes. He wasn't much good at the cloak-and-dagger side of his work.'

The German woman seemed to have brightened considerably during the course of the conversation and now seemed set to indulge in fond reminiscences about her late husband.

Kaplan knew that he couldn't afford to let her relax. He had to get at the truth now or he would never get at it.

'And what *was* Irma Matthofer playing at all along?'

Heidi Schmidtt turned to him and said matter-of-factly: 'The cholera research programme which Franz told you about was real enough. But more than cholera research was involved. Irma Matthofer was also engaged in secret work on dangerous viruses. The health authorities didn't know about this of course. When they sacked Irma after the Ringelmann affair and closed down the cholera programme, they were simply forcing Irma to go elsewhere.'

'So, where did she disappear to?' Kaplan sensed instinctively that he was coming close to some vital piece of information. So much seemed to turn on Irma Matthofer's whereabouts.

'She went after the monkeys.'

'The green monkeys? She knew where to go?'

'Of course. Irma Matthofer always kept careful records of the provenance of animals used in her research. She was looking for a lethal virus all along and when Ringelmann and the others died, she knew she had found it.'

For Kaplan, the moment of truth had come. 'So where exactly did the real green monkeys come from? Where did Frau Matthofer go? Where is she now?'

Without warning, the woman in front of him burst into tears. 'Help me, Lowell,' she said. 'I can't stay here. I'm finished. Help me start a new life. Let me come to the States and begin again.'

'Of course I'll help you.' Kaplan's voice was gentle. 'But first you have to help me. I have to know where Frau Matthofer went. I have to track her down. It's the last chance we have. We have only days left. Perhaps only hours. If we can find the green monkeys, we may be able to get enough serum from them to stem the outbreak of Marburg disease in the United States. If we don't stem it, then the United States will go under and believe me, Heidi, the rest of the world will not be immune. So tell me what you know, and I'll help you. If there's any life left worth leading in the United States, you can count on me to get you there.'

There was no mistaking the look of gratitude in the woman's eyes.

She stood up and went to a desk which stood to one side of the room. She opened a drawer and took out three picture postcards.

She turned back to him, holding them up in her hand.

'You realize of course that Paula faked the entry in the log-book?'

'I know. I've been back to the castle to find the book. I wanted to have another look at it. It's not there.'

'Paula took it. It wasn't safe to leave it. Anyone who examined it closely would have smelt a rat. Paula did what she was told. Somebody over there' – her hand gestured vaguely in the direction east of the Iron Curtain – 'knew about the tribe of monkeys living in Eastern Zaire and about their remarkable similarity with the green monkeys. They told Paula how to alter the records and the precise entry to make. But Paula never knew what the real provenance of the monkeys was. That was Frau Matthofer's secret. Right from the start she would never tell us where her source of supply was. All she would say was 'somewhere in Africa'. That at least was all we knew until these postcards arrived.'

'Can I see them?'

Kaplan examined the postcards one by one. 'When did you receive them?'

'The first one came about two years after Frau Matthofer disappeared. The second one came in the early 'seventies.'

'And the third?'

'The third came just a few months back. We were very surprised. We thought we had completely lost touch with the old woman and then out of the blue we hear from her again.'

'Is it her writing? You're sure of it?'

'Yes, I'm sure. I would know Frau Matthofer's writing anywhere.'

Kaplan tried to read the thin spidery script. It was hard to decipher. And the fact that the message was written in German didn't help either.

'What does she say? Take the last postcard, Heidi, and read out what it says.'

Heidi Schmidtt took the postcard back from him. 'It's nothing very dramatic. It just says 'Greetings from Frau Dr Irma Matthofer. I hope all the family is well and that Franz' research is progressing'.'

'What do the other two postcards say?'

'The same kind of thing.'

Kaplan turned the postcards over in his hand.

'All three posted in the same place. Bujumbura, Burundi. Have you been there, Heidi?'

'No. But I know where it is. We looked it up in the atlas when the first of the postcards arrived. We were curious to know where Frau Matthofer could have disappeared to.'

'Show me.'

Heidi Schmidtt fetched a large atlas from the shelf.

'I'm afraid it's a little bit out of date now,' she apologized. 'The names and the boundaries of the countries seem to change so fast in Africa.'

'It'll do.' Kaplan poured over the atlas. He found Burundi. And he found Bujumbura. He realized with some surprise that he had come very close to Frau Matthofer's retreat in the course of his own journey to Eastern Zaire. Only Lake Tanganyika and a few hundred miles of jungle had separated the 'false' monkeys from the 'true' ones.

He closed the book with a snap. 'So you know no more than that?'

Heidi Schmidtt shook her head. 'Isn't it enough?'

'I'm not sure yet. It may be.' He stood up to go.

'You won't forget your promise.' Heidi pleaded with him. 'I can't stay here now. Not after what they did to Franz. Not after what I told you.'

'Won't you mind leaving Paula?'

Heidi Schmidtt shrugged her shoulders. 'Paula has already gone. There is nothing to keep me here.'

Kaplan realized then that time was running out. If Paula had already gone over, it meant that the end-game had begun.

He looked at her with a sudden surge of pity. The poor woman's world had come crashing down. Her husband was dead and her daughter had defected.

'Don't worry, Heidi,' Kaplan told her. 'We'll get you out of here by this evening.'

This time, Kaplan flew from Cologne to Brussels. He couldn't afford any further delay. He knew he was taking a risk in going back to see the Count – alone. But he could see no other way. He still needed more information. Burundi was not a large country. Even so you had to know where to start looking. The postcards had a Bujumbura stamp but that meant nothing. Probably all international mail coming from Burundi had a Bujumbura stamp.

If Count Philippe Vincennes was surprised to receive a second visit from Lowell Kaplan, he gave no sign of it. He was, ostensibly at least, as courteous and as gracious as always.

He received Kaplan in the library.

'You will stay to dinner, won't you? A drink at least?' Kaplan declined both offers.

'Monsieur le Comte,' he began formally, using the other man's title even though once, in what now seemed the distant past, they had been on Christian name terms. 'I'm sure you know why I am here?'

The Count raised one eyebrow. 'Should I?'

'I think we should try not to waste each other's time.' Kaplan spoke calmly and without any trace of exaggeration. 'The last time I was here you tried to kill me. Why?'

For a moment the Count seemed flustered. He moved towards the tray of drinks which stood beside the bookshelf as though to indicate that even though his guest had refused, he himself was not averse. Then, having regained his poise, he turned back.

'Tried to kill you? My dear fellow, what ever makes you say that?'

Kaplan was not to be put off his stride by any sort of aristocratic *hauteur*.

'You knew I was on the track of the green monkeys. You thought your whole profitable trade in wildlife might be threatened and exposed if I probed too far.'

In the event, the Count Philippe Vincennes decided he did need a drink. But he still sought to maintain a calm exterior.

'I don't know what you're talking about.'

'I believe you do. Just look at this.'

Kaplan passed over a copy of the report he had found months earlier when he visited the New York apartment of Diane Verusio. 'This report,' he said, 'tells the whole story behind the illegal trade in wildlife. It points the finger fairly and squarely at Belgium, at Brussels and, by implication, at you and your associates like Willy van Broyck whom I had the pleasure of meeting last time I was here.' Kaplan smiled sarcastically.

The Count made as if to toss the report onto the fire that blazed behind him.

'Go ahead,' Kaplan said, 'the full dossier is already lodged with the appropriate authorities in half-a-dozen countries. They are simply waiting for the signal to begin prosecution.'

'And why don't you give the signal?'

Kaplan knew that the initiative had passed into his hands. 'Because, my dear Count, your illegal trade in endangered species concerns me only indirectly.'

'What does concern you?' The Count had retreated to an arm-chair in the corner of his library. He sat, lowering angrily at the intruder.

'I want to know precisely where the green monkeys have been coming from. How long have you been shipping them? From where? To whom?'

'And if I tell you what I know?' Philippe Vincennes spoke quietly, hopefully. Astute businessman that he was, he seemed to sense the possibility of compromise.

'If you tell me what I need to know, I may be able to persuade people not to act on this dossier. You are a revered man in Belgium and indeed internationally, Monsieur le Comte. The scandal would be great if the story came out. You would not, of course,' he added quickly, 'resume any of your previous activities where this trade is concerned. Nor will you inform your 'contacts' about my visit. We shall know about it if you do.'

The Count was silent for a few moments. 'Very well. I agree to your terms. I will tell you what I know.'

At last Kaplan himself sat down. They faced each other, warily, across the library. Kaplan looked at his watch. He hoped the old man would not take too long. Every minute counted.

But Count Philippe Vincennes was not to be hurried. He had had things his own way the whole of his very long life and he did not propose to change the pattern now.

He began almost casually. 'You know, I was severely reprimanded for my actions that day. They threatened to cancel the contract altogether. They said that I had acted on my own initiative, without orders, and that I could have caused the gravest confusion. Apparently, they had people all lined up to feed you the wrong information, and then suddenly I try to have you rubbed out on the road between here and

Brussels.'

The old man laughed – it was an almost obscene sound. 'Of course I apologized profusely. You see I was concerned with the whole of my trading operation and the threat which you and your people might pose to it.' He paused. 'You were not the first. I knew about the girl. About the dossier. I had no idea that she had been so persistent and so successful in obtaining information about our activities.'

'Did you have anything to do with her death?'

'No. Absolutely not.' The Count was quite emphatic. 'I heard about it, of course. I believe it was an accident.'

'So there *was* a sick monkey in the cargo shed at Brussels.'

'Yes. And it was destroyed. That was all true. As far as I understood it from what they told me later, the man you met at the airport lied only about the origin of the consignment. He told you it was Zaire, when of course it was Burundi.'

'Ah!' Kaplan uttered a sharp exclamation. Here was the confirmation he had been seeking.

'Where in Burundi?'

The old man took a long pull at his drink.

'I don't know, I'm afraid. My son Louis does most of the travelling nowadays. He could tell you. He has actually visited the site several times.'

'And where is Louis now? Can I speak to him?' Kaplan could barely conceal his impatience.

Count Philippe Vincennes shook his head: 'Louis is still

in Africa somewhere, but I'm not sure exactly where. He may even be in Burundi at this moment. He has not been in touch for a week.'

Kaplan walked over to the other man. He spoke in icy tones.

'If you are not telling me all you know, and I mean all, Monsieur le Comte, I shall personally see to it by one means or another that you are a broken man.'

'My dear Kaplan,' the Count gave a short laugh. 'There is no need to resort to such crude threats. I have told you that I don't know precisely where the monkeys come from in Burundi. But I do know the original colony numbered some five hundred. For the last six months, we have been shipping them out at the rate of twenty a month. So the total population of green monkeys which remains on site is probably something under four hundred at the present time.'

'Where have you been shipping them to?' Kaplan thought he knew the answer without having to ask the question but it was as well to have the reply in the Count's own words.

'To Moscow, of course. Where else?' The old man looked alarmed. 'Don't misunderstand me, Kaplan. I'm not a spy. I'm just a businessman. As long as people pay the bill, I'll provide the goods.'

'That's one of the problems.' Kaplan could not keep the scorn from his voice. 'There are too many people who think like you do, Count. And other people, innocent people, suffer for it.'

'Of course. I hope I have been of service.'

After he had left the Count, Kaplan stopped at a pay-phone on the motorway and put a collect call through to his office in Atlanta. Susan Wainwright sounded intensely relieved to hear him.

'Thank God you called, Lowell. I've been trying to reach you for the last two hours.'

'What's the problem?'

'A call came through for you from Burundi.'

'From Burundi?' Kaplan was amazed. 'Who was it?'

'Stephanie Verusio. She said she had to speak to you urgently. It was a matter of life or death.'

'How can I get hold of her?'

'She gave me a number where she can be reached for the next few hours. She said she'll stand by the phone.'

Three minutes later – for once the international connection worked perfectly – Lowell Kaplan was on the line to Bujumbura.

Stephanie had thought long and hard before finally deciding to call Lowell Kaplan. Any happy impressions she might have had of their time in Paris together had been obliterated by his participation in the Zaire massacre. She found it hard to reconcile the image of Kaplan – the epidemiologist, macabrely kitted out in pressure suit and helmet – with that of Kaplan, the man she had known and made love to – a few weeks earlier.

But when she returned to Bujumbura from her visit to

Mount Lwungi; when she reflected on what she had seen and heard at Frau Matthofer's camp, Stephanie realized that she could no longer continue to act on her own. She did not understand all that was going on; but she understood enough. It was not a question of saving a tribe of monkeys – important though that might be. The whole future of humanity – or at least of the Western world – could be at stake. If she turned to Kaplan now, it was because she knew that this was the quickest and surest way of getting the authorities to act. Whatever his faults – and Stephanie was convinced that they were many – Kaplan would know how to set the wheels in motion.

So she sat by the telephone in her room at the Source du Nil hotel, biting her nails. When the call came through, she picked up the instrument on the first ring.

In spite of the thousands of miles that separated them, the transmission was perfect.

'Is that Stephanie Verusio?'

'It is.'

'This is Lowell Kaplan speaking.'

'Lowell. Thank God you called. I've got something important to tell you. Very important.'

'Go ahead, Stephanie.'

Now that her moment had come, Stephanie could barely get the words out. Somehow, the accumulated tension of the last few days seemed to overwhelm her.

At last she managed to say what she had to say.

'I've found the green monkeys. The real green monkeys.' The bitterness in her voice was only too apparent. 'You and your team killed the wrong monkeys, Lowell. You know that, don't you?'

At the other end of the line Kaplan found himself blushing with shame.

'I know, Stephanie. I can't tell you how sorry I am. I'll have to talk to you about that later. We'll find the time.'

'Believe me, Lowell. You'll need time to explain. I hated you then. I really hated you.' Stephanie sounded only slightly mollified.

For the next seven minutes, Kaplan listened while Stephanie told him what she had seen and heard over the last few days in Burundi. From time to time, he nodded. It all made sense now. Every aspect of the plot was clear to him, with all its horrendous implications.

At last, when she had finished, he said to her: 'Stephanie, you've done a magnificent job. I don't know that we can ever thank you enough.'

'It's not over yet, is it?'

'No,' replied Lowell Kaplan. 'But it soon will be.'

He put down the phone. A few seconds later, he dialled again. A Washington number. When the number answered, Kaplan explained who he was.

'I want to talk to John Shearer, please, on a secure line.'

'Mr Shearer is in with the President right now.'

Kaplan mustered all his patience. 'Do me a favour, will you, and stop making difficulties. I want you to pass Shearer a message that we've found the green monkeys. He'll understand.'

Thirty seconds later Kaplan found himself speaking to the President of the United States himself. The genial friendly voice was unmistakable, even at a range of five thousand miles.

'Lowell Kaplan? I've heard a lot about you. What do you have to tell us?'

Kaplan spoke for five minutes. His recommendations were clear and precise. He represented the operation as a 'last chance' affair.

'If the serum is still there in bottles,' he told the President, 'we may be able to get hold of it. Or we may be able to come out with some 'clean' as opposed to infected monkeys and get serum that way. We have to try.'

The President agreed. 'You're right, Kaplan. We'll get this one moving. Be careful all of you, won't you? We don't want a repetition of that Iran fiasco.'

The President was referring to the time when the American team sent in to rescue the hostages had met with disaster in the Iranian desert.

'We'll be careful,' Kaplan replied.

Before the President hung up, he had a personal message for Kaplan. 'By the way,' the warmth in the President's voice was noticeable. 'I'm truly grateful to you for your warning about the Pharmacorp vaccine. But I went up there anyway. They pumped me full of serum – the last of the supply, I'm told. So I guess I'll survive. It would have caused a panic if I had pulled out at the last minute. That's why the vaccination programme is going ahead as planned. We can't cancel it now without creating all kinds of problems. What the hell' – amazingly the President was still able to find the situation funny – 'they're all going to get flu protection anyway. They may die of the Marburg virus, but they won't die of flu!'

★

Ever since the Iran hostage affair, the United States had kept a crack commando squad on permanent standby in Europe. They had learned the lesson the hard way. If you couldn't intervene within the first few hours, it was better not to intervene at all. Even so, the departure of the Hercules from the U.S. Air Force base at Wiesbaden in Germany less than eight hours after Kaplan's telephone conversation with the President had been a miracle of organization and logistics.

The plane droned on through the night. Yugoslavia, Greece, the Mediterranean. Kaplan could visualize the route in his mind's eye. When they were somewhere over the Sudan and still heading south, Colonel McSharry, the tough crew-cut commander of the Special Squad of Green Berets detailed for the mission (they were called McSharry's Raiders), asked him:

'What about the girl? Stephanie Verusio? Is she going to be on the ground?'

Kaplan shook his head. 'Negative. I told her she had

done a great job and to get the hell out of there. We have the coordinates now. We don't need her to pathfind.'

'I hope she does what she's told.'

It wasn't until they were over the Congo basin with the sun just beginning to poke over the starboard wingtip that they finally received clearance to land at Bujumbura airport.

The pilot came back to tell them the news.

'We had difficulty raising anyone down there. And when we did finally get hold of someone to ask, they didn't want to know. Jesus! We pump untold millions of dollars' worth of aid into these tinpot countries, good U.S. dollars. But just try asking them one tiny favour like permission to set down a C-52 transport in an emergency situation and suddenly they're all looking the other way.' He swore and went back to his cockpit.

'Why ask permission?' Kaplan asked McSharry. 'Why not just land anyway?'

McSharry smiled. 'It's more complex than you think, Kaplan. The other side probably knows we've got a C-52 in the air loaded with men and material. You can't keep a thing like that quiet. Someone will have seen it take off from Wiesbaden and they will have been following it all the way down. We ask for permission to land at Bujumbura and they automatically suppose, since we have made no intermediary stops, that the C-52 transport will arrive with the same load it had on leaving Germany. If there is a reception party planned for us, it will be at Bujumbura airport. At least, that's my guess.'

Kaplan was puzzled. 'But aren't we going to land there?'

'Oh, the aircraft is going to land there all right,' McSharry replied airily. 'But we are not. We're going to jump out right on top of the mountain. Right on top of those goddamn monkeys.'

'Me too?' Kaplan was more than anxious. He was positively alarmed.

'You too. I can't tell a male monkey from a female one. Let alone a 'clean' one from a 'dirty' one. As of now, you're part of McSharry's Raiders. Just don't get caught in the branches when you land. Some of those jungle trees are mighty high off the ground.'

Kaplan thought he saw a flaw in the plan.

'How do we get out of the jungle with the serum and the monkeys?'

'We're going to rendez-vous with new transport about thirty miles down the road to Kigali, just over the Rwanda frontier.'

Kaplan was incredulous. 'Is there an airstrip there?'

'No. No airstrip. Just a nice straight stretch of over-engineered road cutting through the jungle. I've looked at the specs, Kaplan. That road can take a plane large enough to get us all out.'

With that, McSharry fell fast asleep.

★

During his time as an army doctor Kaplan had undergone

parachute training. So the experience of swinging in the darkness of the night beneath a billowing canopy while the ground came up to meet his feet was not entirely new to him. What was new was the fact that in this case the ground was mountainous and clad with some of the densest growths of primeval jungle that existed anywhere in the world.

In all, forty of them made the drop and forty of them arrived. They landed, most of them, on cleared ground about half-way up the mountain. Over the years the fields had pushed further and further up the slope and the tree-line had receded towards the crest. Slash-and-burn cultivation had made deep inroads into the rich stands of forest. Under other circumstances, Kaplan might have regretted the waste of resources which this represented – and the erosion which resulted, over a brief season or two, in the earth being scoured wholesale from the denuded hillside. As it was, he was grateful to find his feet firmly planted on a scruffy patch of maize, when he landed, rather than on the topmost branches of the towering canopy.

It was twenty minutes before the whole party had assembled. The dawn, which they had seen in the east at twenty thousand feet, was now beginning to break down below.

McSharry studied the terrain and consulted briefly with Kaplan.

'It's time to move out,' he said. 'You can carry your face masks for the time being. When I give the word, put them on and connect up the air supply. That means we're in business.'

As they set off up the hill towards the summit, Kaplan wondered whether they had already been observed. Even though they had landed under cover of night, forty men dropping through the sky couldn't easily escape notice if anyone happened to be looking in their direction. The question was: was anyone looking?

The jungle as they began to penetrate it, heading for the summit, seemed preternaturally quiet. Almost sinister. Kaplan was waiting for the dawn chorus as black turned to grey. But there was silence. Nothing seemed to stir in the forest. Kaplan shivered. He felt the first twinge of fear.

*

When Stephanie Verusio put down the telephone after her conversation with Lowell Kaplan, the manager at the Source du Nil Hotel in Bujumbura, who had been listening in, immediately informed Victor Mtaza of the substance of what had been said. Ever since her arrival in Burundi (first noted and reported to Mtaza by the apparently sleepy immigration officer at Bujumbura airport) Victor Mtaza had, by one means or another, been keeping track of Stephanie's movements. Ngenzi's driver, Charles, had throughout been an invaluable source of information. So had the hotel staff in Bujumbura. Victor Mtaza had soon realized that Stephanie's concerns and his own were closely related.

When the boy arrived, panting, with the message about

Stephanie's talk with Kaplan, Victor Mtaza knew that his opportunity had come. For some time now, he had been looking for the spark that would ignite the dry tinder of revolution. That the Hutus were seething with suppressed anger after years of domination by the Tutsis was evident to anyone who had an ear to the talk of the beer-hut and market place. That this anger might one day explode into violence was, Victor Mtaza knew, highly probable if not certain. The problem was: how to control the anger, how to channel the violence so that it best served his ends. Mtaza believed that the affair of the green monkeys at last gave him the handle he was looking for.

It had not been too difficult for him to work out what was going on. For the last couple of years he had been Louis Vincennes' principal partner in the illegal export of Burundi wildlife. The fact that a member of the President's own family could participate in such activities was nothing new. What *was* new was the political aspect of the operation and its link with the big-power confrontation.

For the last several months Mtaza had realized that he was swimming in very murky water indeed. Together he and Vincennes had shipped out at least a hundred green monkeys from their sanctuary at the top of Mount Lwungi. The immediate destination had been Brussels but the ultimate destination was Moscow. Louis Vincennes had told him as much. In any case he was capable of putting two and two together. He knew that the monkeys on Lwungi carried a strange virus – anyone who lived in the area had heard legends to this effect, muddled up – of course – with stories about the *ibigaribo* and royal tombs. And he knew that one big power, namely the Soviet Union, was interested in obtaining this virus for its own ends.

He also knew that the old woman – Kagomba, the wild cat, as they called her – had been tapping the monkeys for serum. He and Louis Vincennes had been shipping out quantities of serum as well, although some of it still remained behind.

Victor Mtaza also knew that the Americans themselves were desperately searching for the source of the virus. They had gone off on the wrong track in Zaire. Now, it seemed, they had finally zeroed in on the target. Sooner or later, and Victor Mtaza suspected it would be sooner, the Americans would act. That would be his moment.

The Soviet Ambassador to Burundi, Leonid Kuznetsov, proud holder of the Star of Lenin, had been helpfulness itself. He had for some time now been a close observer of Victor Mtaza's activities. He had marked him down as the leader of the revolution, whenever it came. He had watched the mounting unrest among the Hutus and he had already made preparations to turn this unrest to the advantage of the Soviet Union. For months now a supply of Russian-made arms had been filtering into the country. All that was needed was the signal for the uprising to begin.

'Cher ami,' Leonid Kuznetsov had smiled unctuously. 'Of course, we will help you. That is what we are here for. We exist to encourage true revolutionary movements wherever they occur. That is our mission in life. You may count on us.'

Kuznetsov did not tell Mtaza that, through his own sources, he had learned the Americans were preparing to intervene. Count Philippe Vincennes had of course (notwithstanding his promise to the contrary) immediately reported on Kaplan's latest visit. Nor had the preparations at the USAF base at Wiesbaden gone undetected. This vigilance did not surprise Kuznetsov who had himself done a stint a few years earlier in Bonn. Some fifty thousand communist agents were, he knew, present in West Germany. Not all of them could have their eyes shut.

It took two long planning sessions before Mtaza and Kuznetsov were satisfied with their scheme. When they had finally finished, Kuznetsov rubbed his hands: 'The Americans will walk right into the trap we have laid. And they will regret it.' He refrained from adding that what pleased him specially was that not a drop of Russian blood would be spilled in the process. Ostensibly, there would be no Soviet involvement at all. It would be purely a case of native outrage at an insult offered to a sacred shrine or *ibigaribo*. The fact that Russian arms would be used in the subsequent uprising did not bother him in the least. Nowadays arms, particularly those of the smaller lighter variety, circulated everywhere. The presence of Russian-made arms was no proof of Soviet intervention.

Before they parted Mtaza asked the Soviet Ambassador a question which interested him greatly.

'There is a store of serum still in the camp. Do you plan to remove it before the Americans get here?'

Kuznetsov shook his head. 'No. There is no time for that now. Our transport links via Brussels are closed for the present and we have not made alternative plans. We don't need the serum ourselves, Victor. That is just a reserve supply which we have not yet evacuated.'

'But you don't want the Americans to have it either?'

'No, of course not.' Kuznetsov patted the other man reassuringly on the shoulder. 'The serum is the bait to lure them in, but there's no danger of it falling into the wrong hands. The Americans will find no solutions here. Six weeks from now, the Marburg virus will have brought that country to its knees. And our own plans in Africa and elsewhere will have come to fruition.'

Mtaza had one last question: 'And what about the old woman?'

Kuznetsov shook his head slowly and said with what appeared to be infinite sorrow: 'She has played her part, I am afraid.'

Mtaza nodded. He understood.

★

They had been climbing for the best part of an hour. McSharry held out his hand and the squad halted behind him. He pointed. About five hundred yards away and slightly below them they could see the clearing in the forest and the old woman's camp. Kaplan observed the position of the tree huts. It was all just as Stephanie had described.

As he watched, he saw the door of the right-hand hut open and the old woman come out. Then, to his amazement, a second figure emerged into the clearing, a figure whom he instantly recognized. It was Stephanie! What the hell was she doing here? Why hadn't she gone back home as he had requested? Kaplan was flabbergasted. He could not understand what was going on.

Before he could take any action, McSharry had beckoned the squad forward once more.

They were two hundred yards from the camp and closing fast when hell broke loose. The jungle burst into flame on all sides. The fire roared through the trees with the force of a whirlwind. Pillars of smoke burst through the canopy of the forest to be tinged red in the dawn light.

'Jesus!' shouted McSharry. 'What the hell is going on?' At that moment there broke out the weirdest and wildest ululations that any of them had ever heard or could have dreamed of.

What followed was confusion of the highest calibre. McSharry instantly ordered his men to make for their principal objective: the hut which, according to Stephanie, contained the stored serum. Firing from the hip as they ran, the Green Berets burst through into the clearing.

It was never clear to Kaplan who fired the shot that killed Frau Matthofer. As McSharry led his men towards the huts, a hail of bullets swept the clearing. Two of McSharry's men went down. As the Green Berets returned the fire, the old woman herself was hit. She spun round and collapsed at the edge of the clearing. Stephanie knelt beside her, holding her hand. She seemed to be trying to comfort her.

As he crouched at the edge of the clearing, uncertain of what to do next, Kaplan was suddenly aware of another noise, a high-pitched gibbering and shrieking. He realized that the green monkeys themselves had been caught in the conflagration. He looked up as the flames closed in on the camp and saw them leaping desperately from tree to tree.

The action seemed to swirl around him. But he himself seemed to be a still point in a turning world. Almost detachedly, he watched McSharry's men make for the hut which contained the serum. It's too late, you poor sods, he thought. Too late. Even if you find it, you'll never get it out.

As if on cue, the hut the men were heading for exploded with a bang. There was a great shower of glass and liquid which sprayed the trees of the forest.

'Hell,' Kaplan thought, 'we won't get any monkeys, and now we won't get any serum either. The game is over, gentlemen.'

He realized that McSharry was beckoning to him frantically. The Green Berets had grouped at the far side of the clearing where the flames were thinnest. They had slung the wounded men on field stretchers.

'Are you coming, Kaplan?' McSharry shouted. 'We're leaving now.'

'No. I have something to do here. Wait for me if you can

at the RV.'

Bent double, Kaplan ran back across the clearing to where Frau Matthofer lay. With McSharry's withdrawal the hail of fire had ceased in the immediate vicinity. It was clear from the sounds of gunfire in the middle distance that the action had moved elsewhere. Whoever it was had ambushed them in the clearing was now attempting to impede the Green Berets' departure. Kaplan had a minute of relative calm to examine the old woman. Propped up against a tree-root, she was still conscious but bleeding heavily from a wound in her side. Stephanie was trying, ineffectively, to bandage it.

Frau Matthofer groaned deeply as a wave of pain flooded through her. She lapsed into German.

'Ach! My monkeys. Do what you can for my monkeys.'

She closed her eyes so as not to see the engulfing flames; shut her ears so as not to hear the cries of the animals.

The blood had seeped through her clothes. Her face had gone very pale.

Kaplan looked at her. 'I think she's dead, Stephanie.'

Stephanie remained kneeling for a few moments beside the body in the jungle clearing. Her clothes were spattered with blood and her face was streaked with sweat and tears. When she rose to her feet, she said quietly: 'She may after all be a hero of our time.'

Then, without discussion, Stephanie took charge. 'Quick,' she said, 'come with me, I shall need help.'

She ran into the first hut, the hut from which Kaplan earlier that morning had seen her first emerge. Already the roof was smouldering and soon there would be flames.

They went inside. It was a primitive dwelling-place. A bed. A desk. Two chairs and a stove. Yet for fifteen years it had served as the home for one of nature's twisted geniuses.

'Get the files,' Stephanie called. 'They're on the shelf by the bed. I'll get the case.'

She stooped under the bed and pulled out a battered leather attaché-case. It was clearly of ancient vintage, having about it an air of solidity and craftsmanship. She grasped it firmly by the handle; stood up straight and looked around for the last time. Above her, the roof burst into flames.

'Let's go.'

As they emerged from the hut, they realized that they had left it to the last possible minute. Already the grass in the clearing had ignited and burning trees had begun to crash to the ground. They could barely see through the smoke.

Neither of them ever forgot their escape from the inferno. If Stephanie had not already been familiar with the path down from the summit of Mount Lwungi, they would never have made it, even three hundred yards. And if Kodjo, against express instructions, had not made for the crest to look for his beloved Miss Stephanie as soon as he saw, from the village below, the forest burst into flames, they would never have succeeded in negotiating the rest of the way through the crashing timber and blazing foliage.

They heard the 'monkey man' call as they fought their way out of the trap, with clothes smouldering and eyes half blinded with smoke.

'This way, Miss Stephanie, over here!'

They didn't go down to the village. Instead, after Kaplan had explained the situation, Kodjo guided them behind the base of the blazing mountain towards the rendez-vous which McSharry had fixed earlier.

'McSharry should still be there,' Kaplan explained. 'He'll wait as long as he can.'

In the event, Kaplan was right. McSharry and his men were at the rendez-vous point.

McSharry was battle-stained but obviously delighted to see Kaplan. 'Hell, I didn't think you were going to make it.' He looked enquiringly in Stephanie's direction.

'This is Stephanie Verusio,' Kaplan said, 'and this is Kodjo.' McSharry shook hands with both of them.

There were tears in Stephanie's eyes as she said goodbye to Kodjo.

'We'll meet again, Kodjo. Soon. I know we will. Give my best regards to Ngenzi-bwana.' Impulsively, she hugged the little man. Then he melted back into the jungle.

★

The plane came in low, skimming the trees. It touched down, bounced twice on the rough surface of the as yet uncompleted road, then, with a roar of reverse thrust engines, came to a halt in less than a hundred yards.

McSharry watched the landing with visible pride.

'That's the very latest development in STOL,' he told Kaplan. 'The U.S. Air Force used the basic concept of the Harrier jump-jet but expanded it to serve as a transport aircraft.'

Kaplan hardly heard what the other man was saying. It all seemed so irrelevant. He boarded the aircraft feeling exhausted, washed out. He hated to fail and yet, as he saw it, failure was the net result of the whole operation. What was more, the cost had not been negligible. Irma Matthofer had been killed and two of McSharry's men had been wounded. He had administered first aid to them on the ground before the plane arrived. The toll, Kaplan knew, would certainly have been higher but for the fact that McSharry had decided to pull out as soon as it became clear that the store of serum had been destroyed.

He sat next to Stephanie at the front of the plane. The pilot taxied and took off in even less distance than it had taken him to land. The turbo-jet seemed to rise almost vertically above the canopy of the forest. They saw the smoke still pouring from the summit of Mount Lwungi.

'The fire will burn itself out,' said Stephanie. 'It can't go below the treeline.'

Kaplan looked out of the window as the plane pulled away to the north.

'They were waiting for us. They knew. That was the problem.' He sighed, feeling deeply depressed. They were heading back to the States with no better idea of how to deal with the Marburg problem than they had when they left. And now their time had almost run out.

He turned in his seat to look at Stephanie directly.

'But how the hell did you get back in there? How did you get close to the old woman?'

Stephanie looked at him. They had, literally, been through the fire together. It was time to tell him the whole story.

'When I had finished talking with you on the phone,' she began, 'I couldn't make up my mind what to do. I knew you had told me to get away and I also knew that this was probably what I ought to do. But somehow I couldn't help thinking about Frau Matthofer. The few glimpses I had had of her fascinated me. Almost on the spur of the moment, I decided to go back in there. I wanted to see whether she would talk to me; I wanted to see whether I could get to know her. Above all, I wanted to find out what she was really up to. Somehow I had been involved in this whole business too long to be able to back out of it now just like that.'

'So that's what you did?'

'Yes, that's what I did. I left Bujumbura and went back to my German friends and told them my plan and they didn't try to dissuade me.'

'And then what?'

'I climbed back up the hill and found Frau Matthofer.'

'Just like that?'

'Just like that.'

Kaplan was silent for a few moments. He was amazed

by the girl's courage and intrepidness. When she went back up the mountain, she could have had no idea of what might happen to her there.

'Did you talk to her?'

'Yes I talked to her. I spent the whole of one night talking to her and much of the next day.' Stephanie warmed to her story. 'You know, once she had got over the surprise, I think she was glad to see another human face. Someone from her own background. Someone she could communicate with. I think those long years of solitude in the jungle had taken their toll. She was desperate for company.

'Of course she was nervous at first. Very nervous. Wanted to know who I was and what I was doing. I didn't say much. I told her the truth as far as I could. I said I had been visiting Burundi as a tourist, had been staying with some German friends nearby and that when I had learned that she was in the neighbourhood I had been fascinated by her story and had decided to visit her and say hello.'

'Did she swallow that?'

'I think she did. Above all, I tried to win her confidence and I succeeded. The first night we sat talking she poured out her life story. I think you know some of it.'

'Tell me anyway.'

'She told me that in the latter part of the 1960s she had been in charge of the toxicological unit of the medical school at Marburg University and that she had been doing research into cholera. She said that in 1967 there had been a scandal, that several of her students had become infected and had died as a result of a new disease more dangerous than any known to man. As a result of the scandal she had had to flee from Germany and had come to Africa.'

'Did she tell you what the disease was called?'

'She said that at the time she left Germany, no scientific name had been given to it. Later on, she said she learned it had been named the Marburg disease. She described her original programme of work at Marburg in purely scientific and toxicological terms.'

'That's probably what it was at the beginning. My guess is that Irma Matthofer didn't become a fully active Soviet agent until after the 1967 outbreak when the Russians realized the incredible potential in terms of biological warfare of the Marburg virus. They probably helped her flee Germany and certainly helped her continue her work in Burundi. Did she admit the link between those two phases of her life?'

'Yes, she did. She explained that she had come to Africa so as to be near her source of raw material, as it were. She told me an amazing story of how she had tracked down the tribe of green monkeys. She didn't at the beginning have much information to go on. She knew the green monkeys came from Burundi but she wasn't exactly sure where. So she worked through what she described as 'a Belgian company specializing in animal operations'.'

Kaplan nodded. 'That will have been Philippe Vincennes' network. And did she say that the same Belgian company helped her with the export of animals and serum once her operation was under way?'

'Not in so many words. But she implied it. She also said – I think this was on the following day when we were continuing her discussion – that her usefulness had come to an end. Apparently the operation was closing down; the last shipments had been made; they were in the cleaning-up phase.'

'What was to happen to her?'

'She didn't say. But I could sense that she felt very bitter. She had given fifteen or twenty years of her life to a particular cause. And then it seemed she was simply to be thrown on the scrap-heap.'

'Still without mentioning her basic affiliations?'

'No, still no word of that. I was left to understand that she worked for or with powers unseen.'

Kaplan once more lapsed into silence. There didn't seem to be anything more to say.

They sat there side by side. Throughout the conversation Stephanie had rested her hand on the old leather briefcase. She had not let it out of her sight since she had first taken possession of it back in the clearing in the jungle.

Glancing at the back of Stephanie's hand as she fingered the leather, Kaplan noted three short scratch marks.

'You've scratched yourself, I see.' He pointed to the marks.

'No, that's not a scratch!'

'What is it?'

'It's a vaccination mark! The first thing the old woman

did, once we got talking and she began to trust me, was to vaccinate me. Apparently, with this particular vaccination, the back of the hand is the best place.'

Kaplan was about to engage in a technical discussion of the merits or otherwise of the back of the hand as a place for vaccination as opposed to say, the upper arm or the buttock, when he suddenly understood the full implications of what he had just heard.

He jumped in his seat and was only restrained by the seat-belt which he had left fastened.

'Vaccination? Did you say 'vaccination'?' Stephanie smiled.

'I did.'

'But I don't understand... !' Kaplan began to splutter incoherently.

Stephanie put him out of his misery. She smiled a broad smile. 'We didn't fail, Lowell, we succeeded!'

She began to undo the fastenings on the leather briefcase. 'For the last five years,' she continued, 'Irma Matthofer was secretly working on a vaccine as the basic protection against the Marburg virus. A few months ago she found what she was looking for.'

She opened the case. Inside was a green baize tray with separate segments for storing phials and syringes and other items of medical equipment.

Stephanie picked up one of the phials. 'This is the vaccine, full strength.' She picked up a second phial. 'This is the vaccine, half-strength. Frau Matthofer told me that she gives a second half-strength vaccination three days after the first. It seems to give better protection.'

'You mean she has experimented already with the vaccine?'

'Oh yes, all the villagers from Bugambu who have been in contact with her or the green monkeys have been vaccinated.'

Kaplan whistled. 'And can we replicate it? Can we put it into commercial production? We're going to need millions of units of vaccine within a very few days. This has to be a crash programme if ever there was one.'

Stephanie Verusio picked up the notebooks. 'It's all in here,' she said. 'As long as you can read German, you can know the secret of the vaccine. And there's enough material in the briefcase for the first multiplications to be made.'

'What's the medium?'

'Frau Matthofer told me she used chicken embryos for multiplication purposes and that this was perfectly satisfactory. She kept chickens at the hut.'

Suddenly, Kaplan felt as though a great weight had been lifted off his shoulders. They were going to come through after all. Thanks to a half-crazed old woman living alone in the forest, they were going to come through.

But still he didn't understand it all.

'But why should she have told you all this, Stephanie? Why should she have given you the vaccine and told you its secrets? I realize you were a woman companion, a friendly voice. But if she was working for the Russians, why didn't she give the vaccine to the Russians? If she had done that, it would be game set and match to the Russians. They would not only have the virus itself as well as ample supplies of serum, they would have had the vaccine too.'

Stephanie Verusio took her time replying. 'I'm not sure I know the whole answer. As I explained, we never discussed Frau Matthofer's relationship with the Russians. My own guess is that a few years back Irma Matthofer began to be disillusioned with her political masters. She was a woman to whom professional achievement was of paramount importance. Her first disillusionment occurred when her early work in Marburg was not given the recognition which she thought it deserved. Indeed that may have been one of the principal reasons which inclined her to communism in the first place – a bitterness born of a sense of injustice. Then, during her Africa period, she saw it happening again. There's absolutely no doubt that her work with the green monkeys was of enormous scientific interest – after all, there she was living with a tribe of the animals on a day-by-day basis over an extended period of time. No one had done that before Jane Goodall and her chimpanzees. But I believe Matthofer was even closer to the monkeys and she certainly lived with them longer. I say nothing of the other aspect, the toxicological aspect. But in reality, at least until she discovered the vaccine, Matthofer showed remarkable courage in maintaining the kind of contact with the animals that she did. Maybe she was one of those rare persons who have a natural immunity.'

'But, surely, she must have realized that, in the circumstances, she could never achieve the scientific recognition that she sought. There was no way the Russians were going to publish, or let her publish, a paper on her work in the forest.'

'Agreed. But the old woman was really schizophrenic. She was more professional than political and she could never quite understand or accept that one sphere of her life could interfere with the other.'

Kaplan looked across Stephanie and out of the window. He saw that the plane was beginning to lose height. Down below, the edges of the Rift Valley began to stand out in bas-relief. Shortly they would be coming in over the game-park to land at Nairobi. And then the machine would take over. While there was still time, he wanted to get to the bottom of the mystery.

'All right, I understand all that. I think you are probably correct in what you say. But what did you promise her, Stephanie? You must have promised her something for her to tell you what she told you and for her to have shown you the vaccine and explained it all to you.'

Stephanie Verusio looked at him cannily. 'How do you know I promised her anything?'

'I just know.'

Stephanie sighed. 'You're right, Lowell. I did promise her something. In fact, I promised her two things. Somehow that old woman moved me. In her own way, she probably acted according to her lights.'

'What did you promise?' Kaplan repeated his question.

'First of all,' Stephanie replied, 'I promised her recognition. I told her I personally would guarantee that one day men would speak of the Matthofer vaccine and its cure against Marburg disease in the same way and with as much reverence as people talk of the Salk vaccine and its use against polio. You'll help me here, won't you? Even though the old woman's dead now, I owe this to her.'

Kaplan nodded. 'Of course, I'll help. I'll see Irma Matthofer's name is published in all the scientific journals. I'll get some rich man to endow a Chair in her honour.'

Stephanie smiled. 'That's what I told her. I said I had friends who could do these things and she believed it. The Russians would never have delivered anything of the kind, whatever promises they might have made. At bottom, she knew this.'

'Okay,' said Kaplan, 'so you promised her eternal fame. What else? You said there were two things.'

Stephanie looked out of the window. They were quite close to the airport now. She could see the animals in the game park below. 'Yes,' she spoke quietly, 'I did promise her something else. I told her of the conversation I heard that day when I was hiding outside the hut, and how Victor Mtaza had said that the green monkeys would be utterly destroyed once the operation was finished. I promised I would try to see that the monkeys were safe if anything happened to her. She knew she hadn't long to live anyway. She told me she was dying of cancer. That bullet was a blessing in disguise. Better that way, than a slow lingering death. You see,' Stephanie added simply, 'the old woman cared about the monkeys. Those green monkeys – so beautiful, so deadly. To her they were like children. That's why I promised to help.'

'Won't the fire have destroyed them?'

'Perhaps it will. Perhaps it won't. We may find that some have escaped the flames and are still living in the forest.'

'And you want to make sure that, if any have escaped, they are protected. In spite of the fact that they carry the virus?'

Stephanie turned to him. 'Oh, Lowell, sometimes you brilliant men can be so blind. The green monkeys have to be protected *because* they carry the virus, not in spite of it. That's where you and your WHO people were wrong, right at the beginning. You blundered into Zaire determined to eradicate the monkeys and you succeeded. Only you picked the wrong monkeys. Now you again say that the monkeys must be destroyed. But don't you see that the green monkeys are no longer a threat now that we have the vaccine? Any more than the mosquito is a threat now that we have quinine. But what would be disastrous, would be to deprive ourselves of the protection which the reservoir of living virus offers.'

Kaplan saw what she was driving at.

'You mean one day a new disease, like Marburg but not identical, might be discovered and our vaccine might prove ineffective. And that in this case we might need the living monkeys as a source of viral material with which to experiment for the production of a different, more effective vaccine.'

'Exactly. It may happen like that. Or it may not. What I'm saying is that all species, even apparently deadly species, should be allowed to survive.'

The wheels of the airplane hit the tarmac. Kaplan glanced out of the window and saw that there was quite a reception party on the tarmac of Nairobi airport. A large black limousine flew the Stars and Stripes – that was probably the U.S. Ambassador. There was a detachment of U.S. marines as well as local Kenyan troops. When they knew about the vaccine, he thought, they would rate a 21-gun salute.

'Stephanie,' he said. 'I'm not a romantic man. I'm a scientist and I know you think I'm rather a stupid scientist. But I just want to tell you that I appreciate what you've done. I appreciate the way you called me from Burundi when you saw how big this thing was. I'm glad that you trusted me in the end and I love you for it.'

'Oh, Lowell. What a silly formal speech.' She leaned across and kissed him on the mouth.

CHAPTER EIGHTEEN

ISAAC REUBEN SAT in the old, worn armchair in front of the fireplace in the living room of his brownstone house just on the edge of the Bowery, and smiled benignly at his visitors.

'So you're thinking of getting married, are you? Good luck to you!'

Stephanie smiled back at the old man who, for so many years, had been a family friend as much as a family doctor.

'We've both got your blood in our veins, Dr Reuben. That's a link, if nothing else is.'

'You two were pretty much on opposite tacks for a while there, weren't you?'

It was Kaplan's turn to speak. He was looking younger and fitter than he had for months. It was as though his life had suddenly turned a corner and was now headed in the right direction. 'That's my fault, not Stephanie's,' he said. 'I should never have gone along with that WHO scheme. It had a certain logic but it was morally wrong and aesthetically wrong. And I couldn't see it at the time.'

Stephanie leaned over and touched him lightly on the arm. 'Never mind, Lowell, there's more joy in heaven over the sinner that repents than over the ninety-nine who need no repentance.' They all laughed together.

Reuben poured drinks for the three of them.

'You know,' Kaplan said when they were seated, 'I don't think the Russians planned or intended the original outbreak of Marburg disease in New York. I'm convinced that Diane's death was a genuine accident. There's no question that she was investigating the illegal trade in wildlife; she had focused on Brussels as one of the main entrepôt stations. It's almost certain that she was poking around in the cargo shed at Zaventem when she was infected by a green monkey then in transit for the Soviet Union. She came back to New York and you know the rest of the story.'

Reuben saw the tears begin to glisten in Stephanie's eyes. The memory of her sister's death was still fresh. He moved the conversation ahead.

'But why did all the evidence indicate Zaire, rather than Burundi, as the provenance of the green monkeys?'

'That was quick thinking on the part of the KGB,' Kaplan explained. 'They saw that there had been an outbreak of Marburg disease in New York which miraculously we had been able to contain. They reasoned – correctly – that U.S. epidemiologists would be trying to track down the source of the disease, which might interfere with their own plans. They tried to forestall that. At the same time, they saw a golden opportunity to promote their own objectives.'

'How so?'

Kaplan sipped his drink and then placed it on the table beside his chair.

'Don't think I realized all this at once. I was pretty slow off the mark. But I did eventually understand that the reference to monkeys living in the Kugumba region of Eastern Zaire was entirely erroneous. It was fed to us, or more precisely to me' – here Kaplan coughed apologetically – 'by the Russians with the deliberate intention of misleading us.

'I should have realized of course – as I said to Heidi Schmidtt when I went to see her in Germany for the second time – that the business of finding that old record-book in the dungeon of Marburg castle was altogether too neat to be plausible. I should have suspected Paula of being an agent then. And I should have been suspicious when that little SABENA fellow – what was his name? Delgrave? – turned up with precisely the right information about the more recent shipment. And then when we were in the camp in Zaire, I should have smelt a rat when the trapper showed up and offered to take us straight to the valley where the monkeys supposedly were. I should have kept a closer eye on that Russian, Leontiev, who was Rodriguez' deputy at WHO. He was certainly in it up to his neck. But somehow my blood was up. The hunt was on. I was only seeing what I wanted to see and I didn't pay enough attention.

'I believe that from the Russian point of view it was a salvage operation,' Kaplan continued. 'Once we knew about the Marburg virus, their best plan was to try to trick us into believing that the disease had been totally eliminated so that we put the problem from our minds. Their original strategy was to ship a large number of green monkeys back to the

Soviet Union where they would have been held as a source both of the virus and of the serum. In addition the supplies of serum from immune monkeys which had been stock-piled over the years by Irma Matthofer were being trans-ferred to Russia. The Soviets would then have had a whole new weapon, more lethal than the nuclear bomb. And be-cause they possessed the supplies of serum they would, as it were, have had a kind of anti-ballistic missile system too. The Soviets could have decided when and where to deploy this weapon. It would certainly not have been done through one isolated contact, like Diane or like that zoo-keeper in the Bronx. They would probably have gone for a systemat-ic release of the virus in several major U.S. cities and our defences, which were virtually non-existent anyway, would have been overwhelmed. Of course, the release of the virus would never have been traceable to the Soviet Union. They would have blandly denied all knowledge of it, while offer-ing vodka and sympathy.'

'Go on. This is interesting.' For some reason, Reuben avoided looking Kaplan directly in the eye.

Kaplan needed no prompting. 'Alternatively,' he con-tinued, 'the Soviets might have had a different game-plan. Once they had the virus and the serum, they might have gone public and used them to improve their general bar-gaining position vis-à-vis the other great powers, namely the United States and China. If you know you can infect the other side without any danger of becoming infected your-self, and if you know that the other side knows this too, then you're in a very strong position indeed. Frankly, the Soviets would have been in a position to upset the balance of power, or terror, to a very considerable extent. In my view, not that I know a great deal about this – after all, I'm a scientist, not a politician – the Soviets could have exacted a very high price indeed.'

Stephanie interrupted Kaplan's speculations.

'But the United States could have had the virus too and the serum. The Russians hadn't shipped all the monkeys back to Russia. There were still some left in Burundi when we got there.'

Kaplan shook his head. 'No, we wouldn't have had the virus or the serum. You heard Mtaza talking to Louis Vincennes. The Soviet plan was always to eliminate completely the tribe of monkeys and any surplus serum. Our arrival on the scene merely served to accelerate the time-table.' He summarized the situation. 'The Russians have the virus and we have the vaccine. It works as the old woman said it would and we've pumped it into two hundred million Americans. As far as the Marburg disease is concerned, the United States is now a wholly protected population.'

'Shield and rapier, eh?'

'I suppose you could call it that.'

They lapsed into silence. Then Reuben asked: 'What about Vincennes?'

'Out of business,' Kaplan replied. 'Father and son together. The Belgian government at last had the guts to act on its own initiative without any prompting from the United States. Mind you, I would have done my bit. I'm quite sure Vincennes tipped off the Soviets about my second visit. So, as far as I'm concerned, all bets were off.'

Reuben seemed genuinely pleased that the Vincennes had got their come-uppance. 'That's good news.'

'There's more good news as well,' Stephanie added. 'We've learned that Victor Mtaza's revolution never worked. He only got a trickle of support. The idea was that there was to be this massive uprising against the government which had permitted the 'foreign devils' to desecrate the graves of the royal ancestors. But it fizzled out, even though it clearly had the backing of the Soviets. I guess potential revolutionaries don't feel strongly about royal graves! Anyway Victor Mtaza has fled to neighbouring Rwanda; his father has stepped down as President because of the unrest and our old friend, Michel Ngenzi, has succeeded.'

'That's wonderful!' Reuben had heard all about the gentle Tutsi professor. 'So that's where you're off now, is it? Back to Burundi?'

'Yes. Lowell and I are going on honeymoon there, actually.' Stephanie found that she was blushing. 'Ngenzi is arranging a special zoological expedition in cooperation with the World Wildlife Fund to the Mount Lwungi area. It appears that there may still be some green monkeys in what's left of the forest after the fire. If there are, we are going to find them. We're going to create a nature reserve for them, a national park where they can live in peace.'

Reuben had one last question. 'And what about the

green monkeys in the Soviet Union? What's going to happen to them?'

Stephanie looked at Kaplan. 'You tell him, Lowell.'

Kaplan smiled. 'There's good news there too. John Shearer and I talked yesterday about the green monkeys in the Soviet Union. Of course, the Soviets know the virus is no good to them now.'

'How so?'

'The population of the United States is already vaccinated against Marburg and we've taken care to ensure that the Soviets know that this is the case. The President has agreed to work through the World Health Organization and through U.S. aid programmes to ensure the worldwide dissemination of the vaccine. So the Russians know that they will be holding a virus which can be of danger only to themselves. For they have only the serum, in presumably limited quantities – and the President has determined that they shall not receive the vaccine unless...'

'Unless what?'

Kaplan concluded his sentence.

'Unless they ship back the green monkeys which they hold, every single one of them, to Burundi.'

'Lowell! Stephanie!' the old doctor rose to his feet. 'I want to hug you both.'

Isaac Reuben folded his arms around them in an all-enveloping embrace. Then he took their glasses and refilled them. When he was once again seated, he turned to his guests. He had a solemn, even portentous look on his face.

'There's something you both should know,' he said. He looked at Stephanie: 'You especially, Stephanie. It's about Diane, your sister.' He pulled a piece of paper from his pocket. 'We heard this morning that she is to be awarded posthumously the Congressional Medal of Honour. That's the highest peacetime award this nation can bestow. This letter is signed by the President himself.'

Stephanie read it first, with tears in her eyes. Then she passed it to Kaplan.

'I don't understand,' she said to Dr Reuben, 'why does the President write to you?'

'He thought I deserved to tell you the good news, I guess.' Reuben smiled. 'After all, Diane was my favourite pupil. I trained her. I probably taught her most of what she knew about exotic viruses.' Sadly, he shook his head. 'Your sister was a very brave woman, Stephanie. She knew the risks. But she would never let go.'

Stephanie still looked completely nonplussed, almost numb.

It was Kaplan who said: 'Dr Reuben, I'm as much in the dark as Stephanie is. I think you ought to explain.'

Dr Isaac Reuben examined the contents of his glass. 'You do understand, don't you?' he began quietly, 'that nothing of what I'm about to tell you now should go beyond this room.'

They nodded.

'Very well,' Reuben continued. 'I'll be as brief as I can.' He turned to Kaplan. 'A moment ago, Lowell, you gave a very fair summary of the Marburg affair. I was deliberately drawing you out to see how much you had understood. Frankly, you understood most of it. But there was one vital element which you left out. Diane Verusio was actually looking for those green monkeys at the time she got infected. She was a member of the CIA's top-secret BW – Bacteriological Warfare – unit specializing in virus diseases. I should know. I recruited her for the work in the first place.'

Stephanie asked: 'You mean you've been working for the government too all along?'

The old doctor smiled: 'If Lowell had looked me up in the register, he would have seen that my speciality was always tropical diseases and that there are a number of vague references to past government employment which of course were a cover for the real thing. And the general practitioner work in New York was at best a part-time occupation.'

Kaplan could not disguise his astonishment. He remembered so clearly the afternoon when he first visited Reuben's surgery in Greenwich Village. If anyone had looked the part of the benign family doctor, Reuben had, then.

'I still don't understand...' he began.

Reuben held up his hand. 'Let me finish. It's not so difficult. What you have to realize,' he said, 'is that the U.S. intelligence community has over the last few years become increasingly concerned by the growing Soviet interest in bacteriological warfare. It's logical enough, I suppose. Limit the arms race and the Russians naturally look for some other weapon. I was – and still am – in charge of the unit which tries to monitor Soviet efforts in this area. Diane was one of my top agents. I knew her first as a patient – what I told you about the Verusios and the Rabinowitzes arriving in New York together was all true. I recruited her when I realized that her work with wildlife and the trade in endangered species provided the ideal cover for the type of investigations we had to conduct. We wanted to know what diseases the Soviets were working with and where their source material was coming from.

'When Diane died – when you and I nearly died,' Reuben looked at Kaplan and both of them recalled that awful period – 'we knew that the Soviets were obviously in possession of some amazingly potent BW weapon. I think you were quite right, Lowell, to suppose that Diane's death was an accident. I'm sure it was. I agree with you that the Soviets would never have used their new weapon in such a random way. When I recovered from my illness, I and the other BW experts who worked with me in the unit faced the terrifying prospect that the Soviets might at any moment decide to deploy the weapon properly against the United States. We also knew,' Reuben paused to allow his words to sink in, 'that if the Soviets knew we knew they had the Marburg virus as a BW weapon, they might decide to use it immediately in a preemptive strike and the United States would of course have had no defence. And that, my dear Lowell, was where you came in with your splendid freelance activities.'

Reuben looked affectionately at the other man. Kaplan responded with a wan smile. He was not sure he liked the term 'freelance activities'.

'You see,' Reuben continued, 'your investigations in Marburg and Brussels, in Geneva and Zaire gave us a heaven-sent opportunity to convince the Russians of our own ignorance. We were playing for time and it worked.'

'I'm not sure I understand.' Kaplan still sounded offended.

Reuben looked at him in surprise. 'But surely you see that by participating in the Zaire expedition, by accepting the WHO philosophy of 'eliminate the vector', we were indicating our total lack of suspicion of Soviet intentions.'

'You mean you knew what the Russians were up to and never told me.' This time, Kaplan sounded positively indignant.

'Of course, we had our suspicions. We had Diane's death in the first place. Then we had Boswell's report from Brussels about how a non-existent Delgrave fed you with information. There was the fact that the Chancellor never visited Marburg at the time of the original outbreak. And there was Paula Schmidtt. We knew she was a Communist agent. And we rather suspected Franz and Heidi Schmidtt were as well.'

'Even Heidi?'

Reuben nodded. 'Yes. She disappeared soon after you spoke to her the second time. She had served her purpose.'

'Which was?'

'To make sure that in the end we knew about the true green monkeys and intervened. The object there of course was to create a political incident in Africa and further embarrass the U.S. That was overkill, if you like. Something the Russians threw in for good measure.'

Kaplan went completely red. 'You mean I was taken in by Heidi Schmidtt and by the others all the way along the line, and you knew about it all the time?'

Stephanie joined in the chorus of indignation.

'And you always knew the monkeys in Zaire were clean? You allowed that pointless massacre to happen?'

Reuben deflected their anger. 'It wasn't pointless. I'm sorry about it. As sorry as you are. But there was no other way we could convince the Russians we had swallowed the bait. Leontiev had to see you there, Lowell. What's more he had to see that you really believed in what you were doing. And you, Stephanie,' he turned to her, 'there was no way I could stop you doing what you wanted to do. When you called me from Paris and explained that you wanted some serum I realized what you had in mind. But if I had told you the truth then the whole operation would have been at risk. So we had to let you go ahead.'

Kaplan was beginning to understand the full dimensions of the thing.

'And the CIA bit? You knew about that too?'

'Of course we did. We set it all up. We had to ask ourselves: what would the Russians expect the U.S. to do in these circumstances? And then we had to do it. Now, obviously, in a situation where a vector is about to be totally eliminated the Russians would expect a self-respecting intelligence service on the other side to try to grab an animal or two. So that's exactly what we did. Then, Dick Sandford who runs the CIA got hold of Irving Woodnutt, head of Pharmacorp. Of course, we made sure the Russians knew what we were doing. That 'safe house' in the Arlington Sheraton where George Peabody and Dick Sandford met with Woodnutt was blown, only the Russians didn't know we knew it was blown.'

'Did Woodnutt know the monkeys were clean?'

'Only when he and his people found out in the laboratory.'

'And then you let them go ahead with their massive immunization programme knowing all the time that they must have been using a dud vaccine? Do you realize I almost got killed investigating that stuff?' Kaplan recalled with a shudder his experiences in the Hot Lab.

Reuben rebuked him gently. 'These things have a momentum of their own, Lowell, you know.'

Kaplan shook his head in disbelief.

'And what do you propose to do about Woodnutt and Werner. And Mason.' Kaplan uttered the last name with particular savagery.

'Don't worry,' Reuben replied. 'We've already gone after them. We won't even let them out on bail.'

Again, Kaplan shook his head, wondering at the madness of it all.

'You push them to make a vaccine when you know they can't and then you hit them when they pretend they can.'

'We like to know who our friends are.'

Kaplan pondered the events of the last few weeks.

'I suppose the Soviets were watching our efforts to control the second outbreak of Marburg disease. Presumably, once they were ready, they would have stoked the flames by the judicious release of Marburg as a BW agent if it looked as though the fire was dying down.'

'Exactly.' Reuben agreed with Kaplan. 'Frankly, if Stephanie hadn't been up there with Frau Matthofer; if she hadn't learned the secret of the vaccine, we would none of us be here today.'

The thought sobered them. It had been a close call. As close as any in U.S. history.

Reuben refilled their glasses. The moment of solemnity had passed. They had lived to fight another day. The doctor smiled at his guests.

'May I make a last suggestion before you leave? Talk to Ngenzi when you get to Burundi. Tell him about Diane's Congressional Medal. He'll be thrilled. He was very close to the Verusio parents.'

Stephanie nodded. 'We just heard from Ngenzi this morning. I told you about the national park we're going to set up. He says he's going to name it after my sister: The Diane Verusio National Park!'

She seemed to savour the phrase as she spoke it.

'That's wonderful,' said Isaac Reuben, 'just wonderful.'

POSTSCRIPT

ON MARCH 18, 1980, a United States State Department spokesman said the administration had received 'disturbing indications' that a large number of people in Sverdlovsk in the U.S.S.R. might have been contaminated in April 1979 by a 'lethal biological agent.' The spokesman said that U.S. officials had raised the matter at sessions called to discuss international compliance with the 1975 convention banning the development, production or stockpiling of biological agents or toxins.

Moscow quickly informed Washington that an outbreak of anthrax had occurred in Sverdlovsk, a city of 1.2 million people, but that the disease had been caused by improper handling of meat.

The State Department said the possibility of a natural outbreak of the disease had been ruled out. On March 20, 1980, a high-ranking intelligence aide said the new information left 'no doubt that the Soviets aren't telling the truth.' In particular, the official said intelligence reports showed that many residents of Sverdlovsk had contracted pulmonary anthrax, a form of the disease that affects the lungs after the anthrax organisms are inhaled. The official maintained that if the outbreak had been caused by bad meat, the residents would have contracted gastric anthrax which attacks the digestive system.

Other officials said that when the outbreak was discovered, Soviet authorities sealed off a large tract of land around a military installation outside Sverdlovsk. According to the officials, the first casualties from the disease were soldiers camped nearby.

However, the majority of casualties, according to the reports received by the administration, occurred at a ceramics factory downwind from the military site, and at residential areas near the installation.

Officials said the form of anthrax spread by the accident apparently was highly virulent, and that medical personnel and laboratory technicians had been brought in from Moscow to monitor the outbreak. Enormous amounts of antibiotics were distributed among the residents and an anthrax vaccine was said to have been widely administered.

U.S. officials said that Soviet authorities evidently had launched a major effort to cover up the incident and that as a result it was difficult to estimate how many people had died from the disease. 'It's pretty certain, however, that at least hundreds of people died,' one official asserted.

In the Autumn of 1983, after the so-called 'Marburg affair,' the U.S. intelligence community, on the President's specific instructions, reviewed the whole question of Soviet use of chemical and bacteriological agents. In the course of this review a startling new evaluation emerged of the Sverdlovsk incident. The report suggested that the biological agent in question was not anthrax but the Marburg virus. Furthermore it seemed possible, and even likely, that the deaths which had occurred had been caused not accidentally, but *deliberately*. The theory propounded in that very restricted section of the U.S. intelligence community which had access to the relevant information was that the Soviets had been engaged in a trial-run, a 'mock-epidemic' designed to test the ability of their own serum-based control systems. The report went on to suggest that the Soviets were on the whole quite satisfied with their ability to deal with an outbreak of Marburg virus should this occur in the Soviet Union, and that 'several hundred deaths' was regarded as being quite an acceptable price to pay for the possession of what the report called 'the ultimate biological weapon.'

As a result of Sverdlovsk, so the theory ran, the Soviets knew they had a weapon which worked. They also knew that they could control any 'backfire' effects, in the event that the virus, through some mischance, impacted the releasing as well as the target country.

The report came to the conclusion that the Soviet Union was, as a result of these tests, ready to contemplate the use of the ultimate biological weapon, namely the Marburg virus, within a relatively short time horizon and that their plans had probably been forestalled by the early accidental outbreak of disease in the United States and the consequential events.

Also by Stanley Johnson

FICTION

Gold Drain

Panther Jones for President

The Urbane Guerrilla

Tunnel

The Commissioner

The Doomsday Deposit

Dragon River

Kompromat

The Warming

MEMOIR

Stanley I Presume

Stanley I Resume

NON-FICTION

The Politics of the Environment

The Earth Summit:the United Nations Conference on
Environment and Development

The Green Revolution

World Population and the United Nations

Survival: Saving Endangered Migratory Species

The Politics of Population

The Environmental Policy of the European Union

Antarctica: The Last Great Wilderness

Where the wild things were

The Population Problem

World Population: Turning The Tide

Life Without Birth: A Journey Through the Third World
in Search of the Population Explosion

UNEP: the first forty years